OKSA POLLOCK

tainted BONDS

OKSA POLLOCK
tainted BONDS

ANNE PLICHOTA
CENDRINE WOLF

Translated by Sue Rose

PUSHKIN
CHILDREN'S

Pushkin Children's Books
71–75 Shelton Street
London WC2H 9JQ

Translation © Sue Rose 2016
Oksa Pollock: Tainted Bonds first published in French as
Oksa Pollock: Les Liens Maudits by XO Editions in 2012

Original text © XO Editions, 2012. All Rights Reserved
First published by Pushkin Children's Books in 2016

'Summer's Gone'
Words and Music by Brian Molko, Steven Hewitt & Stefan Olsdal
© BMG FM Music Limited, a BMG Chrysalis company

'Never Let Me Down Again'
Words and Music by Martin Gore © 1987
Reproduced by permission of EMI Music Publishing Ltd, London W1F 9LD

0 0 1

ISBN 978 1 782690 80 1

Set in 12 on 16 Arno Pro by Tetragon, London

Printed and bound by CPI Group (UK) Ltd, Croydon, CR0 4YY

www.pushkinpress.com

For Zoe, always,
and for the people we hold dear to our hearts.

PART ONE
CONQUEST

1

A DATE WITH DESTINY

DEEP IN THE SEVENTH BASEMENT OF THE GLASS COLUMN, the door was blazing with the mesmerizing intensity of molten metal. Oksa squinted, dazzled by the blinding light spilling out from around the door frame and through the keyhole. It was time to enter the Cloak Chamber at last. Images of the past flooded her mind, reminding her of everything she'd gone through, from the moment she'd discovered her remarkable gifts in her London home to her arrival in Edefia. These memories merely served to strengthen her resolve, though. She took a deep breath and turned round to look at the semicircle of people watching her—her father and the Runaways in the middle, flanked by Ocious and the Felons, who were glowering at her. Everyone was there. Everyone except the four people whose absence had left an aching void in her heart: her mother, Gus—who was so much more than a friend—Dragomira, her late gran, and enigmatic Tugdual, with whom she was so deeply in love.

Oksa screwed up her eyes to hide her violent emotions and protect her gaze from the intense glare radiated by the door. Endlessly reflected and magnified by the multifaceted precious stones lining the walls, the light was growing brighter with every second. The disagreeable stroboscopic effect created by the aerobatics of the Death's Head Chiropterans and Vigilians high above the Runaways' heads was also becoming unbearable. Oksa looked up in disgust at those revolting tiny bats and winged caterpillars, sorely tempted to put an end to the torture by cremating them all with a Fireballistico.

"At last!" whispered Ocious, raising his hand and clicking his fingers to halt the frenetic comings and goings of his airborne escorts.

The imperious old man took a few steps towards Oksa. Pavel Pollock stiffened but Abakum—the wise Fairyman—caught his eye and made a pacifying gesture.

"I've waited so long for this moment," exulted Ocious. "But since you arrived, my dear Oksa, those long, hard years have ceased to matter. The Cloak Chamber has reappeared and you will enter it as our new designated Gracious. There you will be enthroned, making it possible for me—for *us*—to accomplish our mission."

"Your mission? You're such a megalomaniac!" protested Oksa, clenching her fists. "Anyway, you know very well I'm not here for you, I'm here to save the two worlds! You've got nothing to do with it. Nothing at all."

The Felon gave an evil smile.

"Poor child," he said. "You're so naive!"

"You fancy yourself as the ruler of Edefia," continued Oksa furiously, "but you're just an ageing psychopath without a future. You've been nothing but a curse on the inhabitants of this magnificent land, which is dying because of you, and you still think you're stronger than anyone. You're pathetic! Can't you feel some remorse for once? There's still time to show you're a man, not a monster."

"Oksa," implored Pavel, "be quiet!"

Beside herself with anger, Oksa was pulling at the hem of her blue tee-shirt hard enough to rip it.

"I don't give a damn for your impertinent opinion," sneered Ocious. "Don't forget I'm the one with the power of life and death over your family and friends until you come out again."

Ocious waved a hand and the guards in leather armour posted around the vast circular hall closed ranks around the Runaways. Then, with a speed that took everyone by surprise, he launched himself at Pavel and caught him in a firm neck hold. Drawing himself up to his full height, he glared evilly at Oksa.

"Now, you'll do me the great pleasure of entering that Chamber, restoring the equilibrium and coming out again to open the Portal for me. Do you understand, girlie?"

Before Oksa could reply she was suddenly distracted by a movement in the highest part of the seventh basement's vaulted ceiling, which was lined with blue gems. A gorgeous bird with wings of fire flew among the Chiropterans and Vigilians, which scattered to let it pass. It circled above their heads with silent grace before landing at Oksa's feet. The heart-stopping solemnity of this moment caused both Felons and Runaways to hold their breath.

"My Phoenix!" murmured Oksa.

The sublime creature bowed, then stretched out its foot and opened its talons to reveal a key decorated with an eight-pointed star—the emblem of Edefia, which had changed Oksa's life when it had appeared around her belly button. The key fell to the ground, raising plumes of fine sparkling dust, then the Phoenix uttered a throaty caw and took off again, disappearing into the lofty dome.

"My Young Gracious is henceforth in possession of the final component," declared a small chubby creature, hurrying over to pick up the key and offer it to Oksa.

"Thank you, my Lunatrix," replied Oksa, holding out her hand. The key was surprisingly heavy and so cold to the touch that she almost dropped it. A few yards away, the door to the Chamber grew larger with a roaring noise caused by the intense heat. Oksa trembled.

"The flames of hell…" she said, with a grimace.

She felt a hand on her shoulder.

"No, sweetheart," whispered Abakum in her ear. "Your date with destiny."

Turning to meet the Fairyman's eyes, Oksa gave him a faint smile. Feeling powerful and actually *being* powerful were two different things.

"Will you at least let me give my daughter some moral support?" growled Pavel, struggling to free himself from Ocious's grip.

"If you must," sighed the elderly Felon. He released Pavel, but kept his Granok-Shooter trained on him.

Looking distraught, Pavel walked over to Oksa and held her so tightly she could feel his heart racing.

"Everything will be fine, Dad," she said quietly, as if trying to reassure herself.

Then, emptying her mind of all thoughts and refusing to look at anyone, she walked towards the Chamber, which was brimming with light.

2

MEETING IN THE CHAMBER

A s soon as Oksa put the key in the lock, she found herself transported to the other side of the dazzling surface. The door swung shut with a deafening crash that sounded like a thunderclap, then disappeared, merging with the wall. The alarmed shouts of the spectators were instantly cut off, as if Oksa had passed into another dimension.

"Hey! What's going on?"

Her body had just risen above the ground as if weightless and was now suspended in mid-air. She felt as light as a feather. Her chestnut hair was floating limply around her head as she pulled her arms through the air in a gentle breaststroke to move away from the door.

"Wow…" she murmured.

She couldn't help pirouetting. Although Vertiflying gave her an intense feeling of power, this new experience was incredible. She'd always dreamt of trying out zero gravity one day, like an astronaut, but who'd have thought she'd get the chance here, in Edefia, the invisible land, once lost and now found? She looked around carefully. The Chamber was too bright for her to make out its shape or size. She blinked, awed and intrigued. She was no longer afraid—this place and its astonishing lack of gravity had a calming, almost hypnotic effect, even though she'd never felt more alert. She was intensely aware of everything—her living bracelet, the Curbita-Flatulo, undulating steadily to regulate her unruly emotions, the pulse of blood as it coursed through her veins, as well as the uncanny silence of the Chamber.

※

Was the radiance dimming or was she slowly becoming more used to it? Whatever the case, Oksa was relieved that the brightness was growing more tolerable. Without any bearings to guide her, she moved forward with a few cautious breaststrokes, thinking about her gran. Dragomira had promised they'd see each other again on the day she was enthroned in the Cloak Chamber—and now that red-letter day in the life of a Young Gracious was here.

"Baba? Are you there?" she ventured hoarsely. Floating in the air, unsure whether she was horizontal or vertical, she wrapped her arms around herself for reassurance. It was slowly becoming apparent that the room was a vast, perfectly round igloo, supported by pearly-white columns. Oksa gazed about, her attention caught by a phenomenon occurring behind her. The walls had lost their cloudy appearance and were now crystal-clear, like a mirror without the silvering. Oksa could see everyone in the seventh basement. Her father was sitting on the ground, his elbows on his knees and his head in his hands. He was struggling to cope with this separation, which was, as far as he was concerned, the last straw after so many tough ordeals. Oksa "swam" over to the wall and put her hand on one of the blocks of crystal.

"Dad…" she murmured.

"He can't see or hear you, Dushka," said a voice close to her.

"Baba!" exclaimed Oksa, turning round, her eyes shining. "You came!"

The halo of light in front of her was hazier than the one she'd encountered in the cave of the Singing Spring a few hours earlier, but there was no room for doubt: the crown of plaits around her head, the regal silhouette and the low, soothing voice—Dragomira had kept her

14

promise. Oksa floated towards her and wailed with disappointment as she passed through the golden shadow that was now her beloved gran. Dragomira was there, but she was dead. Oksa was pained by this cruel reminder. What she could see before her was her gran's soul, an extension of her life, a manifestation from the eternal realm to which she now belonged. It was heartbreaking and, at the same time, so comforting... The shadow bore down on her, enveloping her in warmth. Oksa tried to smother a sob.

"I'm so glad you're here with me," she said, dashing her tears away with her hand. "I didn't want to be on my own in this place."

"Did you doubt me?" asked Dragomira.

"No!" replied Oksa firmly.

"Why are you crying, then?"

Oksa looked away, then turned back to the golden shadow.

"I miss you so much, Baba..."

The words stuck in her throat.

"I miss you too, Dushka. But this is no time for weakness, otherwise everything we've worked towards, everything we've gone through, will have been for nothing. Tell me exactly how you're feeling."

"I still don't understand all kinds of things," conceded Oksa. "One thing I do know, though, is that I'd like to take down that creep Ocious so I don't have to worry about what he might do at any moment to the people I love. He may be old, but he's strong. And very dangerous."

"He isn't that old!" chuckled Dragomira.

"Are you kidding, Baba? He must be at least a hundred!"

"Which is the prime of life in Edefia... and don't forget that he probably has some Nontemporentas in his possession."

"Pearls of Longevity? That's true," admitted Oksa. "I'm not afraid of him, you know. If he wasn't blackmailing me so shamelessly by threatening Dad and the Runaways, I wouldn't hesitate to face him, or his sons."

15

"I don't doubt it for a second, Dushka. Still, even if you can fight him, be on your guard. And watch out for Orthon, in particular. He's even worse than his father now."

Frowning, Oksa said nothing for a moment, then asked without preamble:

"Do you think I'll be able to leave Edefia again?"

The golden shadow dimmed appreciably. Until now, this subject had brought to mind the image of a mortally wounded Malorane, followed by that of Dragomira disappearing from the top of a dune. The cost of opening the Portal had always been the life of a Gracious, as stipulated by the Secret-Never-To-Be-Told. No one knew whether this was still the case now that the Secret had been destroyed. Did the Graciouses have to sacrifice their lives for others to pass through to the Outside? And, quite apart from the issue of opening Edefia's Portal, there was another burning question: would Oksa and the Runaways ever be reunited with the Spurned—the family and friends not permitted to enter Edefia? Breathlessly Oksa waited to hear Dragomira's answers, until she realized her gran wasn't intending to say anything. She sighed, then raised her head.

"What must I do, Baba?"

"Come here…"

Oksa allowed herself to be guided to the centre of the immense Chamber.

"Would you hand me the pendant you were given by the Corpusleoxes?" asked Dragomira.

Oksa slipped the strange gem over her head and took out her Granok-Shooter to summon a Reticulata. She examined it closely with the jellyfish-like magnifying glass, then handed the pendant to her gran; the miniature Earth was buffeted by hurricanes as seas ate into the coastline like a giant ravenous monster. The small ball vibrated in her palm and the ground in the Chamber began to shake: convulsed with pain, the world was continually being beset by new torments.

16

"Is this really the Earth?" asked Oksa.

"What you see is only a representation, of course, but it faithfully mirrors every occurrence as it happens," replied Dragomira.

Oksa glanced apprehensively at England and her face fell. She handed the pendant nervously to Dragomira.

"Mum and Gus are in danger, Baba," she whispered. "We have to act quickly!"

Oksa watched as the sphere floating in front of her rose to eye level and swelled to nearly twelve feet in diameter. Then it began revolving on its own axis, revealing the Earth's surface, badly ravaged by the disasters that had befallen it over the past few weeks.

"How terrible!" exclaimed the Young Gracious, alarmed by the extent of the damage, which was now clearly visible.

When the sphere had completed a full turn, the seas and lands became transparent, revealing what lay beneath, and Oksa could clearly make out the Earth's structure. The seabed, bristling with peaks and troughs, appeared before her. Oksa watched in amazement as the tectonic plates shifted and separated and magma formed in the depths of volcanoes.

"Look! The Mariana Trench!" exclaimed Oksa, staring at a huge gash at the bottom of the Pacific.

She found she could see into the dense, yet transparent, bowels of the Earth all the way to its core. Suddenly, the sphere shrank until it was half as small again and the planets of the universe appeared before her, from massive Jupiter to tiny Pluto. Finally, the majestic sun took up its position and everything began moving around it in a perfectly choreographed dance. Oksa looked around for the golden shadow of her gran.

"This is incredible, Baba!"

Her hair was tenderly ruffled by way of an answer. Oksa tried to catch hold of whatever had done it, but remained empty-handed. She frowned and her eyes misted over with inconsolable sadness. She groaned, lips trembling. Immediately, she felt Dragomira embracing her and tipping her chin up: she couldn't afford to become disheartened. She wiped away the tears and gently propelled herself forward by moving her arms through the air and kicking her feet, unable to tear her eyes away from the revolving planets as they followed their precise and complex path around the sun.

Suddenly a beam brighter than all the others shot from the fiery ball of the sun. Oksa waited for the Earth to complete a full turn and realized that the beam was widening to a cone of light which illuminated a small section of the Gobi Desert.

"That's Edefia, that's where we are, isn't it, Baba?"

"Yes," replied the shadow. "But watch what happens next."

Like a laser, the beam of light continued its journey *below* the surface of the Earth, burrowing into its depths to reach the core—which Oksa was sure she could see palpitating.

"But I've always thought that the centre of the Earth was inert!" she stammered. "Isn't it supposed to be made of iron? At least, I'm pretty sure that's what I was taught at school."

"Don't forget that everything comprising our world is alive," corrected Dragomira. "Listen, sweetheart…"

Doing as she was told, Oksa soon heard a weak, irregular beat that sounded like a sick heart.

"Let me guess, Baba—we've got to mend the Earth's core, haven't we? Like engineers? Or surgeons?"

Dragomira paused for a moment, then announced in a voice full of emotion:

"It would be more accurate to say that we're going to save the Heart of the Two Worlds, Dushka. Like Graciouses."

3

CARDIAC MASSAGE

S INCE OKSA HAD COME BACK FROM THE SINGING SPRING,
Orthon McGraw had done his utmost to dictate when Oksa entered
the Chamber. Two violent attempts to force her hand had been thwarted,
first by the ever vigilant Runaways and then by his father, Ocious, who
had authoritatively stepped in.

"Last time I looked, I was still the ruler of Edefia!" he'd declared to his son.

Orthon had swallowed his hurt pride as best he could, but no one
was in any doubt that the Felon's bitter resentment might prompt him to
commit all manner of atrocities—the most unforgivable of which would
be to harm Oksa in order to prevent her from accomplishing her rescue
mission. No one knew how far he would go and there was always the
chance he might commit a kamikaze attack. Orthon was a loose cannon,
a constant danger. If his father pushed him too far, would he destroy
everything to prove he was the stronger?

They had been living in a state of anxiety for so long that when a score
of Ageless Ones passed through the walls of the Chamber, Oksa's first
reaction was to arm herself with her Granok-Shooter, her magical blowpipe.

"Don't worry, Dushka," said Dragomira, enveloping her. "You're in
no danger here."

"It's time for your enthronement," said an Ageless Fairy, her hair
undulating like seaweed at the bottom of the sea.

Like her companions, she had a hazy silhouette and an incredibly soothing presence. The Ageless Ones approached Oksa holding out a long piece of deep-red cloth.

"Your Cloak, Young Gracious," she said. "We began embroidering it the day you were born."

"But how did you know it would be me?"

"We knew," replied the Fairy.

She unfolded the garment and Oksa examined the beautiful embroidery with a cry of admiration.

"The thread was made from the feathers of your phoenix," explained the Fairy. "Then each strand was dyed with decoctions made from plants or stones and embroidered onto a piece of fabric prepared by our most skilled weavers."

"It's magnificent," whispered Oksa, staring at the patterns. "I'm sure there isn't anything comparable on Earth. Not even the emperors in China had something like this!"

The bottom of the Cloak depicted the huge, intertwined roots of a tree, then uneven soil, and grass dotted with thousands of flowers, each one unique and sublime. Above this vegetation flew bees, birds, dragonflies and other winged creatures. Higher up, at waist level, the abundant foliage of the tree spread out in myriad shades of green. Then the red background darkened to an almost black night sky dotted with stars, planets and the sun with its magical beam falling to Earth. The Ageless Ones turned the Cloak to reveal the eight-pointed star, the emblem of Edefia. Oksa instinctively rested her hand on her stomach. She knew that the mark, which had designated her as the next Gracious, was still around her belly button. She could feel its comforting warmth.

"Take it, Young Gracious. This is your Cloak."

Oksa looked at Dragomira. Her gran was no ordinary woman. She'd agreed to give up her mortal life to open the Portal to Edefia, so that her loved ones and the two worlds would have a chance of survival.

However, her sacrifice meant that she'd never complete her training as a Gracious—she'd never enjoy the privilege of wearing her Cloak, of facing the future with her people, or of watching her successor grow up.

"I have a different destiny ahead of me, Dushka," came the much-loved voice.

"So the Lunatrix was right," murmured Oksa, a lump in her throat.

The Gracious's small steward hadn't wanted to tell Oksa everything he knew when she had questioned him, but the Young Gracious now realized that her hunch had been correct: Dragomira would be the Infinite Entity, the supreme Ageless One who embodied the equilibrium of the two worlds once their heart was saved.

"It's a huge honour for me to be able to help those I love," said Dragomira.

"It's so much more than that, Baba!" exclaimed Oksa. "You'll embody a new future for humanity! Everything will depend on you, do you realize how incredible that is?"

Dragomira's silhouette became more solid and Oksa could have sworn she saw her gran smile. A wave of affection washed over her, filling her with what she felt was unshakeable resolve. She floated towards the Ageless Fairy who was holding out the Cloak and let her drape it around her shoulders. Its colour was such a dark red that it looked almost black and its fabric was soft as velvet and light as silk. What was more, each fibre seemed to radiate power, a supernatural energy that galvanized Oksa like an electric shock. In amazement, she saw her whole life flash past her eyes, from her earliest moments of blissful innocence to her most painful ordeals, separations, betrayals and regrets. The last image of Marie Pollock, her mother, left behind on the cold sand of the desert, made her whimper. She saw again in quick succession her last memories of Gus and Tugdual, her lifelong attachment to the former and her irresistible attraction to the latter, their kisses, and her uncertainties. Then dark clouds crackling with flashes of lightning descended over the sphere hovering a few yards from her, and a terrible earth tremor shook the Glass Column to its foundations.

"Tell me what to do!" begged Oksa, her eyes fixed on the rising waters around Great Britain.

Without further ado, the Ageless Ones encircled her and led her to the darkened sphere. They rolled up the sleeve of the Cloak and the longer one of her tee-shirt, then took her hand and plunged it into the middle of the Atlantic Ocean. Oksa felt her arm plunge through the icy water, then pass easily through the Earth's crust. For a second she was afraid she might be burnt by the incandescent lava, which was bubbling fiercely, but her hand, guided by the fairies, sank as smoothly into the depths of the Earth as if it were… crème fraîche! Finally, with her arm buried up to the shoulder, she reached the core. The crucial moment had come.

"But what am I supposed to do?" wailed Oksa. "I'm going to ruin everything! Help me!"

"Take it in your hand, Young Gracious!" whispered an Ageless Fairy. "Take the Heart of the Two Worlds in your hand and bring it back to life!"

Oksa obeyed, determined not to allow panic to get the better of her and destroy their last hopes. She seized the core which was palpitating weakly and, instinctively, began to massage it.

Its spongy, elastic texture made Oksa think of raw flesh, which was disconcerting. Concentrating hard, she attempted to transfer to it the tremendous power she felt inside her, while continuing to exert a steady, rhythmic pressure. The waves of the ocean lapped around her shoulder, harmless on this reduced scale but lethal for anyone who was in the sea. As for the black clouds, Oksa saw them pass in front of her face. She tried blowing them away, but soon realized she was powerless to affect their course: the clouds were free as air. One of them, bristling with lightning, grazed her neck.

"Ouch!" she said, putting her free hand over the spot which had just been struck by a tiny bolt of lightning.

"Concentrate, Oksa!" rang out Dragomira's voice.

Flushing, the Young Gracious continued her resuscitation attempt. The Cloak poured its incredible energy into her muscles and nerves, while Oksa transferred strength and hope to the sick heart. The hours passed, and she was aching all over. Dragomira and the Ageless Ones floated by her side, powerless to do anything but give moral support and boost her spirits, which were sapped by exhaustion. Oksa had by now realized that the success of this massive rescue operation depended on her alone, and the anxiety this caused her soon became harder to bear than the physical exertion.

❋

The Earth steadily continued turning. The continents and oceans rolled past in slow succession and Oksa was alternately subjected to the heat of the deserts, the humidity of the tropics and the biting cold of the poles. The drastic changes in temperature made her shiver or perspire relentlessly, testing her body to the extreme. Vast Siberia passed before her eyes and she had a sudden thought. Part of her origins was down there, beneath the snow. A permanent part, as eternal as the mountains forming a wall through the centre of Europe. France brushed her cheek, then England appeared. Oksa followed the course of the swollen Thames. With her whole body tirelessly at work, she became aware that a piece of her was slipping away.

"Mum! Gus!" she cried.

4

Beyond a Shadow
of a Doubt

WITH THE SLEEVES OF HIS TRACKSUIT TOP ROLLED UP
to the elbows, Gus Bellanger was doing his best to stick down
the floor tiles that had lifted in the floods. Suddenly he raised his head,
automatically pushing back a strand of black hair which fell over his face.
A few seconds later, Marie Pollock gave a cry. Gus looked at her, amazed.

"It's not... possible..." he muttered.

He stood motionless in the middle of what had once been the Pollocks'
living room, his dark blue eyes wide. Then, coming back to his senses,
he slowly shook his head. Virginia Fortensky—Cameron's wife and
Leomido's daughter-in-law—hurried over, abandoning the dishes she'd
been drying in the adjoining kitchen.

"What's going on?"

Gus ignored the question and crouched down in front of Marie.

"You felt it too, didn't you?" he asked softly.

Clutching at the armrests of her wheelchair, Marie nodded, too choked
to utter the slightest word.

"Oksa? Are you there?" called Gus, reeling with excitement. "Oksa!"

The Spurned, who were now living in the Pollocks' London house in
Bigtoe Square, came running when they heard his cries. Gus was in the

middle of the room, gazing into space, clearly searching for something which he couldn't see.

Marie, who was just as agitated, was looking around wildly too.

"What's up with you both?" asked Kukka Knut.

Naftali and Brune's granddaughter stared at them, intrigued. Gus collapsed into a rickety armchair. He remained silent for a moment before he could reply:

"Oksa was here."

"What?" chorused the Spurned in surprise.

"Oksa was here," repeated Gus, brushing back a long strand of hair.

"But Gus, you know that's impossible!" said Kukka, going over to him.

She put her hand on his shoulder, her husky-dog blue eyes staring at him in disbelief. Gus violently shrugged her off, as if burnt by her touch.

"Don't look at me like that!" he yelled. "I don't need your pity!"

"But Gus," protested Kukka, going white. "It's not *pity*!"

Gus jumped up from his chair and went over to stare out of the window, his hands stuffed in the pockets of his tatty jeans. The deserted square was covered in mud and looked thoroughly depressing. There was the sound of sirens: the Thames was about to burst its banks again. But for those inside the house, that was the least of their worries.

"Gus is right," added Marie finally. "Oksa was here. I felt it too."

Andrew, the minister, rubbed his face, looking more sad than confused.

"You think we've gone mad, don't you?" asked Marie bitterly. "But I swear it wasn't a figment of our imagination. I don't know how Oksa did it, but she was here! I recognized her scent, I felt her presence, her hair against my cheek. She... she hugged me."

She hung her head and slumped down, weary and overwhelmed. Since the Spurned had returned to London, her condition had steadily deteriorated and the poison secreted by the soap made by Orthon McGraw continued to ravage her body. Despite the conviction in her words, she was more unsure than she'd ever admit. Was she losing her marbles? Perhaps she wanted Oksa to be there so badly that she'd *believed* she could sense her as surely as if she were right beside her. But no, she knew deep down that her mind wasn't playing tricks and that she wasn't hallucinating. Anyway, Gus had felt the same thing—but how could she get the others to accept the inconceivable?

"Maybe Oksa managed to Dreamfly," suggested Virginia in a well-meaning attempt to help her friend. "If so, that would mean she's become a Gracious and she's okay."

"From what I know, only the mind travels during Dreamflights," objected Andrew. "They don't allow for any physical manifestation."

The solemn silence grew and their expressions became graver. What if that apparition meant that Oksa and the Runaways were in danger in Edefia? What if it was some kind of... final farewell? Marie closed her eyes and moaned. Everything was spiralling out of control.

"We have to go upstairs!" Gus said suddenly, turning to face the Spurned. "The water's rising again."

His sharp words roused them from their gloomy thoughts. This was the fifth flood warning since their return to London. The last one had been worse than the one before, but the water had only reached the ground floor owing to the raised structure of the house. In the days afterwards, it had taken all the courage the Spurned could muster to restore a semblance of normality to the rooms damaged by the high water levels. Despite the shortage of running water, electricity and almost all essential survival aids, their hard work had paid off: the basement was uninhabitable, but the kitchen and living room were back in use. This time, however, the flooding appeared to be more serious and looked as if it might destroy everything. In the din of the army helicopters criss-crossing the sky while blaring words of warning through powerful megaphones and the continual wailing of the sirens, Gus and Andrew took hold of Marie's wheelchair and went up to the third floor.

❈

Dragomira's old apartment had been spared by the storms and floods, but not by the looters, who'd gleefully carried off everything that had made these cosy, unconventional rooms so appealing. The thieves had stripped the apartment of its countless paintings, console tables, curtains and rugs, leaving only the crimson sofas and the double-bass case, which were too bulky to be easily removed. The shelving unit which had housed hundreds of phials—some containing extremely rare ingredients—had been reduced to a pile of wood and glass.

Panting, Gus and Andrew carefully set down the wheelchair and went over to the windows. The square was gradually disappearing under brown water filled with an indescribable jumble of debris and refuse.

"If the worst comes to the worst, we still have Dragomira's private workroom," said Gus.

Fortunately, the looters hadn't managed to get into the room hidden under the eaves. After all, no one would have thought there was a secret passage behind the double-bass case. As a result, the workroom had remained undamaged, apart from a few broken windows and some tiles dislodged by the raging winds. The main reason the house was still standing, though, was its proximity to the other buildings in the terrace. Built adjacent to each other, they'd provided their neighbours with shelter, so damage was minimal. "A good principle to follow if we're going to withstand the hard blows life deals us," Marie had remarked gravely. Andrew, who was good with his hands, had managed to repair the holes, so the Spurned were able to save the invaluable stocks of food collected by Dragomira for her creatures—a treasure trove consisting mainly of cereals and preserves which enabled the Spurned to be self-sufficient and live in relative safety. Things weren't that simple, though. Despite the widespread presence of amphibious police vehicles in the city, there was the continual threat of looting. Urban guerrilla warfare raged in the streets and danger lurked everywhere, transforming the country into what was essentially a military state. Initial feelings of solidarity had begun to give way to selfish individualism, despite some qualms on the part of the majority. Then the power cuts had started, the shelves of the grocery shops had gradually emptied, and people had panicked, thinking that their kindness might backfire on them. The core principles of life were forgotten and the law of the fittest had taken hold. It was proving to be an unstoppable process with few exceptions. Severe shortages caused even the strongest wills to waver, and a small canister of gas or a jar of jam became an object of abject greed.

The Spurned had discovered this to their cost when they'd helped the Pollocks' neighbours, the Simmonses. Glad to share what they had, they'd decided to give a few packets of pasta and rice to this charming retired couple, who seemed to have stepped straight out of handbook on good breeding and etiquette. Two days later, the Simmonses had turned up again at the front door, much more demanding and much less friendly. Andrew had tactfully made the point that it was necessary to use foodstuffs sparingly: in two days the Simmonses had eaten enough to feed all seven people in their group for a week. Mr Simmons had lost his temper and had tried to force his way in, waving a collector's pistol which, in other circumstances, would have been a completely disproportionate, even ridiculous reaction. Gus had seen red and, without further ado, had put his karate classes to good use, ejecting Mr Simmons with a judo throw which had surprised their rude neighbour as much as the Spurned. Since that unfortunate incident, the Spurned had remained on their guard, disillusioned and very wary.

The sirens were still wailing, assailing their ears and straining their nerves to breaking point.

"I won't be able to stand this for long," whined Kukka Knut, sliding down the wall to a sitting position. "I've had it up to here."

Pulling her ecru sweater over her knees, she buried her head in her lap. Sympathetically, Gus left the window from where he was watching the Thames flow over the pavements and roads and went over to sit next to Kukka. In these troubled times, the authorities were dealing with the most urgent situations first and the weather agencies had been instructed not to make any more pointless forecasts. Things didn't look good: since their return to London, the Spurned hadn't seen a single day without rain. There hadn't been a ray of sunshine or a scrap of blue sky. Just cold grey water, which got in everywhere and left its dirty calling card on everything it touched. And in Bigtoe Square, morale, like the weather, was at an all-time low.

"We're cold, we're using candles to see, we can't wash properly and soon we'll have nothing left to eat either!" added Kukka, her head in her hands.

A greasy strand of blond hair escaped from her untidy bun. Gus reached out to tuck it back into place then, at the last minute, thought better of it.

"It won't last for ever," he murmured. "It can't last for ever."

Kukka looked at him out of the corner of her eye.

"I didn't expect such unbridled optimism from you!"

Gus immediately stood up.

"It's always a pleasure to try and help a friend," he grumbled, gazing at her forlornly.

"If you really want to help, then help me find my parents!" snapped Kukka.

Disheartened, Gus turned on his heels.

"Don't be such a spoilt brat," he growled, heading over to Marie.

Kukka blushed.

"Don't forget that Gus's parents are also in Edefia," Virginia remarked reproachfully to Kukka. "We *all* have loved ones there, we're *all* unhappy, you're not the only one, Kukka, far from it! Please don't make things worse by taking your bad mood out on us!"

Kukka stifled a swear word in Finnish—her mother tongue—and sat sullenly in her corner. Gazing into space, Marie took Gus's hand. The hope kindled by Oksa's fleeting presence had now been replaced by deep despair. The water lapping at the top step outside the house was about to flood into the hall. The current situation left a lot to be desired and the future wasn't looking bright for the Spurned.

5

FINAL FORMALITIES

THE VISIT BY OKSA'S IDENTEGO TO BIGTOE SQUARE HAD left her with very mixed feelings. She hadn't had time to learn how to control this singular new power, which allowed her unconscious mind to act for her in such a physical yet intangible way. Even though she understood how her Identego worked and how it could be used, she hadn't yet mastered it. But perhaps it wasn't a case of telling it what to do... there was no way of knowing. Apart from her and the first Gracious of Edefia, no one had ever had this power before. The only thing Oksa knew for sure was that it had again been triggered by panic—a blinding panic that had swept over her when she'd seen the Thames burst its banks. It had only taken a few seconds for her Identego to be hugging her mother. A rift in time had opened up and had plunged them both into some kind of disembodied reality in which they'd shared feelings of amazement, excitement and confusion. Gus had then appeared. She'd rushed over to hug him and her affection for him had overwhelmed her. Instinctively, she'd lightly kissed his lips, leaving Gus motionless with surprise. She'd have liked the visit to last for hours and yet, despite being brief, those embraces had done her the world of good. She'd felt everything as intensely as if her body had actually experienced it, the softness of her mother's skin, the lemony fragrance of Gus's hair, even the smell of damp pervading the house.

Then it had been time to return. The silence in the Cloak Chamber had been broken by a long wail of despair. This new power was magical, but far from perfect. It would take time to come to terms with the frustration caused by her Identego's inability to interact with the physical world. A long time.

❋

The task of massaging the Heart of the Two Worlds took many long, hard days, which left Oksa pale and trembling with exhaustion. Dragomira and the Ageless Ones did everything they could to support her colossal effort. Oksa had never had to give so much of herself. Despite being a Gracious, she was still human—the terrible cramps she suffered in her arms and hands were a painful reminder of that. Her work was made all the harder by the disasters befalling the sphere, which didn't leave her unscathed. As the days went by, Oksa was increasingly hard hit by the storms and volcanoes. Her body was wracked with pain, which she endured in dazed silence as red welts caused by splashes of lava streaked her skin and her lips became chapped by the wind and arid deserts. From time to time she allowed Dragomira to take her aside for a brief respite. She'd curl up with her Cloak wrapped around her and fall asleep immediately, her prostrate body floating weightlessly in the middle of the Chamber. Her only food was a strange drink prepared by her gran. Oksa was aware that her stomach was empty, but it didn't bother her because the drink was so refreshing.

"You haven't lost your touch, Baba!" she exclaimed cheerfully, sucking in bubbles of the potion floating around her.

Then she would get back to work, massaging the Heart of the Two Worlds with renewed energy and determination.

❋

Ten days and ten nights after Oksa had entered the Cloak Chamber, the Heart at last began beating more steadily and more strongly. Completely drained, Oksa carefully stepped back and gazed at the sphere and the planets spinning in perfect synchronization.

"Well, that's a good job done," she said softly, her hands on her hips.

The Ageless Ones and Dragomira clustered around her, brighter than ever.

"You've accomplished your mission, Young Gracious," said the tallest Fairy. "The Heart of the Two Worlds is still weak, but it's out of danger!"

"Does that mean… there won't be any more disasters?" asked Oksa.

The light around the tall Fairy dimmed.

"It means that the death of our two worlds has been avoided," she replied.

"The Earth will still be hit by disasters," continued Dragomira. "That's inevitable. But what you've just done, Dushka, is nothing short of a miracle. A true miracle!"

Suddenly there was a deafening rumble. The Chamber walls shook and there was a shower of dust from the ceiling. Oksa gave a wail of despair.

"It didn't work! You're wrong, all of you, I failed!"

The Ageless Ones immediately enveloped her.

"Rest easy, Young Gracious: you did succeed! What you're hearing is the sound of your Sovereign Hourglass moving into position. The Hourglass determines how long you'll be a Gracious."

Oksa struggled to understand what they meant.

"The Hourglass has just turned over, allowing the first grains of your reign to trickle through," continued an Ageless Fairy.

"So… will I reign for a long time?" she couldn't help asking.

The Ageless Ones began laughing among themselves, and their merriment was so contagious that she found herself grinning too.

"Okay, I understand!" she continued. "It's no big deal, I agree. But I have to admit I'd like to know all the same."

"Like the universe and all its components, the length of a reign is a living entity," explained the tallest Fairy. "It depends on the power of the ruling Gracious and the harmony she generates. It isn't something that is predetermined or controllable. It will only come to an end if harmony has been disrupted or when it's time to hand over to a New Gracious."

Oksa considered this information for a moment.

"Or when the Pledge has been broken, as with Malorane," she said eventually. "If the Gracious breaks the laws governing her reign, then everything grinds to a halt."

The Fairies seemed to nod.

"A reign that is a living entity," continued Oksa. "You certainly do things differently here! So where is this Hourglass? I'd like to see it."

"It's in there," replied the tall Ageless One, leading Oksa towards a door concealed in the blocks of crystal forming the walls.

The room adjoining the Chamber was completely bare. It was dimly lit, which made it seem stuffy, but peaceful, an impression heightened by its circular shape, reminiscent of a big top in a circus. Oksa floated inside, looking for the legendary Hourglass.

"I can't see it," she said.

The empty room had no corners and no nooks or crannies to search, just four smooth columns in the middle. The complete absence of anything piqued Oksa's curiosity further. She was hovering a few inches above the ground, scrutinizing the empty space, when the Ageless Ones stopped her.

"Look, Young Gracious! The Hourglass is there!"

The tall Fairy positioned herself just in front of Oksa, illuminating a small section of the tiled floor on which the Sovereign Hourglass was standing.

"But it's tiny!" exclaimed Oksa.

Twisting her body to keep her balance, she screwed up her eyes to study the ground, then finally took out her Granok-Shooter.

"Ah, much better!" she said, summoning a Reticulata.

33

The jellyfish-magnifying glass showed every detail of the microscopic object. At first glance, the Hourglass looked very ordinary in design with its dark wood frame and delicate metal screws. However, what the Fairy had called the "grains of the reign" were an incredible sight, dark and luminescent at the same time. Two grains had already trickled through—and Oksa was surprised to realize she felt put out. The Hourglass had only just turned over!

"It's flowing so fast," she grumbled, putting away her Granok-Shooter.

"It's time to complete your enthronement, Young Gracious," said the tall Fairy. "Then your reign can begin."

These words set Oksa's pulse racing: the future seemed even more complicated than everything she'd just achieved. In here, she was safe at least...

"Come!" said the Fairy, escorting her back into the Chamber. Dragomira had almost entirely regained her physical appearance; only the contours of her body looked hazy. She held out her hands to Oksa, who rushed over to her, upset by her Baba's sad smile. They hugged in an emotional silence, making the most of these brief minutes, before Dragomira whispered something in her ear. Oksa drew back slightly, kicking her feet gently, her eyes wide.

"That is the new Gracious Pledge," announced the tall Fairy. "Have you understood exactly what it means, Young Gracious?"

"Yes..."

"And do you understand the constraints it involves, as well as the consequences?"

"Yes..." replied Oksa, looking deathly pale.

"We'd like you to repeat what Dragomira just said to you, please. This will be the first and last time that the Pledge is said aloud."

Oksa obeyed. Although she'd only heard it once, the Pledge seemed to be engraved for ever on her memory. Suddenly she felt a kind of twitching in the region of her stomach. The feeling intensified until there was no doubt that *something* was happening under her tee-shirt! Panic-stricken by the movements which were now stretching the garment out of shape, she moaned.

"What now?"

Terrifying images raced through her mind, as she pictured all kinds of awful things, from an alien inhabiting her body to a grotesque mutation. Perhaps certain physical changes were part of becoming a Gracious! They could have warned her. Then she realized that *the thing* was trying to escape from under her tee-shirt. Carefully and apprehensively, she gripped the hem and lifted up the fabric, her heart pounding fit to burst. What she saw was a jaw-dropping phenomenon: the eight-pointed star, which had been encircling the skin around her belly button, was now a tangible object. Free of any restraints, the star floated away from Oksa's body and hovered in front of her for a few seconds before shooting with unreal speed towards the miniature solar system still rotating in the main Chamber.

"It's joined the other stars! That's insane!" gasped Oksa, awed and rather relieved. "Part of me is part of the universe now."

The Ageless Ones began shining as brightly as these myriad stars.

"Now you really are the New Gracious of Edefia!" they rejoiced.

Oksa frowned and ran her hand through her hair.

"The New Gracious of Edefia," she repeated, her eyes clouding over. "So… what happens now?"

"You'll go back to your father and our friends," replied Dragomira, "and help them to defeat Ocious and his cronies. There are hard times ahead—your enemies will hound you relentlessly, but you're strong and the people are on your side. Never forget that."

"What about you, Baba?" asked Oksa in a choked voice.

Dragomira looked away.

"Me? I'll stay here. I have a mission to accomplish, remember."

"You're the Infinite Entity, you're going to preserve the equilibrium of the two worlds," sobbed Oksa. "And I'll never see you again."

"Who knows what the future holds?" said Dragomira. "Who knows?"

As if symbolizing this new phase in Oksa's life, the Cloak gently slipped from her shoulders and fell to the ground. She suddenly felt exhausted.

"You must leave the Chamber, Young Gracious," the tall Fairy reminded Oksa, pushing her towards the far end of the room.

"Hey! This isn't the way!" she objected, realizing she was being taken towards the opposite side of the Chamber to the one she'd entered through ten days earlier.

"It's too dangerous to exit via the seventh basement. Ocious and his supporters are patiently waiting there for you."

Oksa shivered. The enemies of the Runaways were still after her.

"You'll be safe through here," said the Fairy.

A new opening appeared in the curved wall, leading into a dark, seemingly endless corridor.

"A secret passage? Brilliant!" exclaimed Oksa. "Where does it go?"

"It'll take you far away from here, to a distant place where no one will be able to harm you," replied the Fairy. "Don't worry though, you won't be alone for long, someone you trust is waiting for you."

"Who?" asked Oksa.

"You have nothing to fear."

Their answers were becoming increasingly terse and Oksa realized that the Ageless Fairies weren't going to say anything more. Before her, the corridor stretched away into darkness. She turned round. Dragomira's outline had already faded.

"Goodbye, Baba."

"Goodbye, Dushka," murmured the voice she loved so much. Oksa wiped her face with the back of her hand, took a deep breath and stepped into the corridor that would take her to meet her destiny.

6

En Route for the Borders of Edefia

T HE WALK ALONG THE CORRIDOR WAS LONG AND HARD.
Oksa wasn't enjoying her return to gravity one little bit—after
days of weightlessness, she felt as though she weighed a ton. The ground
was uneven and covered with rubble, which made her progress slow and
unsteady, there was very little light and the air was clogged with dust.
Oksa was also battling a heavy weariness that had descended on her like
setting concrete and was making every move difficult—even blinking
took effort. She twisted her ankle for the umpteenth time and cursed. As
if echoing her bad mood, her stomach gave a terrible growl: the Young
Gracious was starving. After what felt like miles, the ceiling of the corridor
became much lower, forcing her to bend down.

"That's all I need," she grumbled. "If this continues, I'll have to crawl
out of here."

Her thoughts turned to Ocious, the fierce old man who'd ruled Edefia
for decades, as well as his supporters and his two rival sons, Andreas, who
was his favourite, and Orthon, the black sheep. If any of them managed
to get their hands on her, it would spell the end of everything. All those
sacrifices, all those separations and all that suffering would have been
for nothing.

"You won't catch me!" she declared. "Ever!"

She pressed on as best she could, bent double, her back aching and her feet on fire. Her Curbita-Flatulo was undulating constantly around her wrist, attempting to ease her mood by applying pressure in different places, but it looked in a bad way too. Its tongue was hanging out of the side of its mouth and its tiny eyes were almost closed. As if to highlight its sorry state, some explosive noises from its nether regions reached Oksa's ears and she paused for a second, before reacting.

"Oh, Curbita, I'm such an ungrateful so-and-so!" she exclaimed, immediately rummaging in the little bag she wore across her shoulder. "You've been such a help all this time and I completely forgot to feed you. I'm so sorry! Hang on, I'll put that right immediately."

She hastily opened the Caskinette containing her Capacitors and food for the Curbita-Flatulo. "One granule a day, no more and certainly no less," Abakum had instructed. The small bear-bracelet devoured the granule which Oksa held out on her fingertip and its eyes opened slightly, misty with gratitude. Oksa stroked its downy head and continued on her way, impatient to reach the end of this interminable escape route.

※

She was starting to think she'd die a premature death in this corridor when she spotted a small patch of light in the distance. It grew bigger and bigger as she approached until she could clearly see it was the way out. About time! Despite her exhaustion, which made every step a test of strength, Oksa broke into a joyful run. The corridor filled with daylight and a trickle of fresh air reached her lungs. How good it felt to breathe properly! She sprinted the last few yards to the exit, abandoning all caution, then stopped dead, holding her breath, as a figure crossed her field of vision.

"Is that you, my Lunatrix?" she asked cautiously. The squat figure appeared again in front of the exit to the secret passage.

"The domestic staff of my Young Gracious provides the contribution of an affirmative answer," answered the little creature nasally.

"How glad I am to see you!" exclaimed Oksa happily, rushing out of the secret passage to hug him tightly.

The Lunatrix's chubby face turned the colour of ripe aubergine. He looked her up and down with a troubled expression, but Oksa was too relieved to see him to pay much attention to his confusion.

"What are you doing here?" she asked, her eyes shining. "Who told you I'd be coming out on this side? And how are the Runaways? Dad? Abakum? And Zoe? Are they okay?"

The Lunatrix stepped back, looking scared. His long arms twitched at the sides of his plump body.

"The volume of questionings achieves an abundance that creates a disturbance in the mind of your domestic staff, because your domestic staff made the gift of a promise which takes priority over all speaking. The enquiring of my Young Gracious will benefit from the provision of an answer after a secondary delay, when the communication stuffed with importance has been transmitted."

Oksa's face darkened.

"I understand. What have you been told to tell me?"

"Danger experiences strong survival and my Young Gracious must be directed towards a shelter of great safety to achieve the evasion of the hated, malevolent Felons."

Oksa couldn't help looking around. A barren, dusty, undulating landscape stretched as far as the eye could see, like a grey desert. The capital of Edefia, Thousandeye City, as well as any sign of life, seemed a million miles away.

"Have you any idea where I should go?"

"A single place affords the assurance of the complete protection of my Young Gracious: the borders of Edefia, where the Isle of the Fairies has its location."

"Really!" exclaimed Oksa enthusiastically. "I'm going to the Isle of the Fairies, am I?"

The Lunatrix nodded vigorously.

"A former Gracious will proceed to the accompaniment and the guidance of my Young Gracious and her domestic staff."

"Baba?" asked Oksa hopefully.

"The Much-Loved-Old-Gracious now possesses a mission in the intestines of the Earth in the Cloak Chamber."

Despite the sadness occasioned by this reminder, Oksa held back a smile.

"You mean... 'in the bowels of the Earth', don't you?" she pointed out politely.

"Your correction encounters exactitude," admitted the Lunatrix, gazing at her with boundless admiration in his large blue eyes.

"Hello, Oksa," said a woman's voice, which seemed to come out of nowhere.

Alarmed, Oksa immediately adopted an attacking position, right leg out in front, her arm extended. Although ethereal, the figure who appeared before her was much more clearly visible than Dragomira had been. This woman was beautiful and slender, with remarkably long hair and a melancholy face. She bore a striking resemblance to Dragomira and Oksa recognized her immediately.

"You're Malorane!" she exclaimed, resuming her normal stance.

The woman approached confidently and calmly.

"Yes, I'm Malorane, your great-gran. Despite the unusual circumstances, I'm honoured to meet you."

"My Antecedent Gracious," greeted the Lunatrix.

"My Lunatrix," murmured Malorane, stroking the head of the creature who'd once served her.

Oksa gazed at her, lost for words. How could she have imagined that she might one day come face to face with the woman responsible for

40

everything? The consequences of her secret relationship with Ocious had led to the clandestine birth of the twins Orthon and Reminiscens, the Beloved Detachment inflicted on the latter, the Great Chaos... This woman had been the cause of so many tragedies and, what was worse, as Oksa knew, none of it had been intentional. Malorane had been exploited and her trusting, naive nature had been deceived. How could she be blamed for that? Especially as she'd been the first person affected by her own mistakes, losing her loved ones, her Gracious powers and ultimately her life. Oksa stared at the former Gracious in awe, dying to ask hundreds of questions. However, this was hardly the time—other things were more important.

"We need to hurry!" whispered Malorane, her eyes sweeping the plain. "Ocious and his cronies will soon realize that things aren't going as planned. We need to get you to safety, and fast!"

For a second, Malorane's perfect face revealed all the frightened bitterness in her heart, which pained Oksa. Malorane gazed at her in concern.

"Can you Vertifly?"

"Of course I can!"

"I mean... aren't you too tired to Vertifly?" pressed Malorane.

"I'll be fine," replied Oksa, thinking she must look awful if her greatgran was that worried.

"Let's go then!"

Malorane picked up the Lunatrix, whose complexion immediately turned translucent, and soared into the dark sky, as magnificent as a shooting star, followed immediately by Oksa. The first few seconds were flawless, but Oksa soon understood Malorane's question. She was completely exhausted. Panicked by the energy it took to Vertifly, she wobbled. A black hole in her stomach seemed to be swallowing up her last—and very meagre—reserves of strength.

"This is no time for weakness, Oksa-san!"

That's what Gus would say to her if he were there. And so would her father.

"Dad, where are you?" she groaned.

A few miles behind, the Glass Column stood out against the horizon. Clouds formed dark, shifting shadows around the Gracious's residence: Death's Head Chiropterans, the Felons' lethal weapon. Oksa shivered at the memory of their vicious red eyes and razor-sharp teeth. Pavel and the Runaways must still be in the seventh basement, waiting for her to emerge from the Chamber, solidly flanked by Ocious and his henchmen. Oksa suddenly felt incredibly lonely. All her loved ones were a long way away. And she was here, in this louring sky, with a woman who was no longer alive… Dazed and depressed, she reeled in the air, losing altitude.

"Keep going, Oksa!" encouraged Malorane.

Instinctively, Oksa rummaged in her bag. It was now or never to use her provisions. She swallowed an Excelsior Capacitor with a grimace—it had such a foul, earthy taste… The effects were immediate: her sight cleared, her muscles flexed and the strength she thought she'd lost flooded into her body. Malorane turned round and the two Graciouses exchanged looks, the former anxious and the latter fierce: Oksa felt like her old self again! They couldn't get to the Isle of the Fairies soon enough.

7

A WAR OF NERVES

*I*N THE MEANTIME...
While rising waters had been wreaking havoc in London, Edefia
had been dying of drought. As a result, the sudden cloudburst created
widespread euphoria throughout the land. Not a drop of rain had fallen in
five years! Five long years during which Edefia, once a land of plenty, had
dwindled to a barren desert. Five terrible years during which the people
had huddled in their homes, sapped by poverty and tyranny. As soon as
the first few drops exploded on the dusty ground, the inhabitants rushed
out into the open, cautiously at first, hardly able to believe this miracle.
The soil, which was too dry to absorb the rain, gave off a damp, warm
smell that everyone thought they'd forgotten. Then the heavens opened
and a torrential downpour soaked the land and the people. Everyone was
laughing, singing and dancing, drunk on relief and hope.

❈

Although loud, the noise of pouring rain and general rejoicing didn't
reach the seventh basement. The Runaways and Felons had been shut
inside the lofty hall lined with precious stones for many days and nights.
Precisely twelve days and eleven nights, in fact, during which time the
two clans had been waging a bitter war of nerves. Despite the stifling

atmosphere and mutual provocations, the sworn enemies had stayed put. Even if it meant sleeping on the floor, eating sparingly and making do with rudimentary bathing facilities. Only the zealous creatures made endless trips back and forth to fetch basic provisions—which they did enthusiastically—providing their masters with blankets and food. The mood was tense and the Runaways and Felons kept their eyes firmly fixed on the door into the Chamber or on their enemies. They were all incredibly jumpy, so when a young guard burst into the hall yelling at the top of his voice, both clans sprang to their feet in astonishment.

"Master..." he stuttered, bowing to Ocious. "It's raining! It's raining!"

Ocious glanced at the high domed ceiling and the door to the Chamber, then stared icily at the Runaways. His face twisted in anger when Abakum returned his gaze with a faint smile. Two days earlier, the Lunatrix had asked to go back to the Gracious's rooms, arguing that his absence might have an adverse effect on the health of the other creatures.

"The Young Gracious is about to reach the ending of her salvage mission," he'd whispered to Abakum. "Her reunion with the exterior of the Cloak Chamber experiences imminence."

Contrary to all expectations, Ocious had agreed to let the small steward leave the seventh basement under the guard of two conscientious Vigilians. And all the Fairyman's hopes since the Lunatrix's sly departure were now being realized: Oksa had successfully restored equilibrium and had probably already left the Chamber! The news travelled fast, spreading like wildfire among the Runaways. There was mounting excitement as their hearts filled with joy and their tired eyes sparkled.

"She did it!" they whispered. "She's saved us!"

"Shut up!" yelled Ocious.

Everyone flinched. Pale and tense, the elderly leader of the Felons kneaded his temples.

"Surely you haven't lost control of the situation, Ocious," said Abakum.

"It looks like you might be fighting a losing battle, doesn't it?" asked Brune Knut, her countless bracelets tinkling.

The tall Scandinavian's eyes were shining with defiant joy.

"Oksa isn't in the Chamber any more," added Naftali. "She's managed to get one over you."

This wasn't the first time that the Runaways had tried to unsettle the Felon by coming up with various plausible theories, but Ocious had been much too stubborn and uncompromising to listen. He'd scornfully dismissed any suggestion that Oksa might escape because, according to the Gracious Archives stored for centuries in the Memory, there was only one way in and out of the Chamber. And he hadn't taken his eyes off that door since Oksa had entered. However, it not only looked as though things weren't going as the elderly Docent had planned, but also that the Runaways had suspected this might happen from the start. They'd done all they could to keep him in the seventh basement, giving Oksa time to escape. Ocious was fuming with rage. He should have acted as soon as the light had dimmed around the door, two days ago. That had been a sign, there was no doubt about it! He looked daggers at Abakum.

"You knew!" he thundered.

The two men glared at each other for a moment without saying a word, neither of them willing to look away first.

"Do you realize what you've done?" continued Ocious.

"Yes," replied Abakum gravely. "I've allowed Oksa, our New Gracious, to escape from your clutches and from probable death! Do you think we hadn't realized that you wouldn't hesitate to sacrifice her in order to achieve your ambitions?"

Renowned for his self-control, Ocious was very hard to read. Temperamentally more like a reptile than a big cat, his unpredictability made him all the more frightening. He might not betray any emotion for hours, then he'd suddenly launch into a fatal attack without the slightest warning. Even people who'd known him for decades could be fooled by his outward calm. So when he leapt at Pavel instead of turning on Abakum, everyone cried out in surprise. Watched by the members of their clans, both men toppled to the ground and rolled around in the sparkling dust.

"You're making a grave mistake, Ocious!" growled Pavel hoarsely, punching him repeatedly in the ribs.

As Chiropterans and Vigilians positioned themselves in serried ranks above the Runaways, Ocious realized he'd just made another bad decision: somewhat predictably, the Ink Dragon emerged from the tattoo on Pavel's back and wrapped its bronze wings around the two enemies, immediately putting a stop to their furious volley of blows. With little room for manoeuvre in the vast underground hall, the dragon furiously whipped its head back and forth in the air, breathing fire. The tongue of flame incinerated about a hundred flying monsters, and the sickening smell of burning flesh filled the hall. Everyone froze. Few people would be foolish enough not to treat Pavel and his dragon with respect; only Orthon was bold enough to attack. A Granok shot towards the dragon's mouth, only to be reduced to a tiny harmless ball of fire. The creature released its prisoner and resumed its ink form. Despite his aches and pains, Pavel struggled to his feet and watched Ocious stiffly walk over to rejoin his cronies. He'd made his point.

"This isn't over," threatened the elderly ruler, straightening his clothes.

Orthon stepped forward to help him and no one failed to notice Ocious's dismissive gesture or hear his cutting rebuke, sharp as the blade of a sword.

"Don't you ever fire a Granok in my direction again," he hissed, jabbing his index finger at his son. "Do you hear me?"

Orthon's face remained impassive. Only his grey eyes clouded, becoming dark as a stormy sky.

"How humiliating!" gasped Brune, her hand over her mouth.

Ocious stood there imperiously, stiff as a poker, his hands behind his back. He gazed at the Runaways in disgust, barely concealing his bitter resentment.

"You're all irresponsible!" he thundered.

Then, with his head held high, he concluded:

"Take them away! Lock them in their rooms and make sure they're well guarded!"

Assisted by ominously buzzing Vigilians, some thirty guards in leather armour surrounded the Runaways; Abakum, Pavel, Brune, Naftali, Pierre and Jeanne Bellanger went quietly, feeling both demoralized by imprisonment and hardship, yet cheered by their newfound certainty—emotions as contradictory as the rain outside, which was drowning Edefia to bring it back to life.

8

ACTION STATIONS

"WE NEED TO SEND MEN INTO ALL THE TERRITORIES TO question everyone and search every house, every nook and cranny, every mountain cave, every hole in the ground! That girl has to be somewhere!"

Looking out of the window of the apartment he'd claimed for himself on the top floor of the Glass Column, Ocious turned his back on his sons and allies. They didn't need to see his face, though—they could appreciate how angry he was from the set of his tense shoulders under his dark grey linen shirt.

"We'll find her, Father!" soothed Andreas, his voice hypnotic. "Edefia isn't that big…"

Orthon couldn't help sighing. Either his half-brother was blinded by optimism or he was just trying to avoid angering their father.

"How many men did you say we have?" he asked, an edge of mockery to his voice, thinking of Edefia's 75,000 square miles.

Andreas glared challengingly at his half-brother.

"I didn't," he replied, refusing to let Orthon rile him.

As if he would let himself be upset by such crude baiting. His lips curled slightly in satisfaction as he gazed again at the assembled men and women, who looked drawn with fatigue after the past few days. A woman with red hair and a grim expression turned to the Felons who'd returned from exile on the Outside.

"There are few towns left," she explained. "When our land was made barren by drought, people rallied together, forming new communities to help each other: it was simply a matter of survival. Besides Thousandeye City, there are now five towns, spread across Green Mantle, the territory of the Sylvabuls, and the Peak Ridge Mountains, which belong to the Firmhands."

"We have to be strategic," continued Andreas. "We need to take people by surprise so that no one sheltering the Young Gracious stands a chance."

Ocious finally turned round, rubbing his bald head absent-mindedly. He nodded silently before asking:

"What do our informers say?"

A stout man with a bushy beard and hard eyes began speaking.

"Our spies have closed the net they cast a few months ago. This major initiative has allowed us to flush out the agitator who was wreaking havoc in Thousandeye City."

Ocious straightened in his seat and his eyes brightened.

"Who is it?"

"Achilles, Arvo's son."

The Felons exclaimed in shock as Ocious stifled a curse. Orthon, one of the few who didn't understand the implications of this revelation, remained stony-faced.

"Arvo?" exclaimed Agafon, the former Memorarian who'd returned to Edefia. "Wasn't he the Servant for Irrigation in Malorane's High Enclave?"

"You have an excellent memory," replied Andreas. "Arvo rallied to our cause a few months before the Great Chaos. When my father appointed his High Enclave, Arvo was named Servant for Farming, because he was a brilliant agronomist—the best there was. He was the one who created new varieties of fruit and vegetables that could adapt to our land's decline, buying us a little more time before our world ground to a halt. Although he remained on our side for years, he became increasingly hostile to our notion of order and the way we ruled Edefia, until his views proved incompatible with ours."

"He contaminated his whole circle with his revolutionary ideas!" thundered Ocious, banging his fist on the table. "I've put my trust in men and women who've had no qualms about betraying me."

They all looked down, except Orthon and Andreas.

"Where is that traitor, Achilles?" continued Ocious.

"We neutralized him," replied the bearded man tersely.

"What about Arvo?"

"Arvo is being kept under close surveillance by our men."

"Good work!" congratulated Ocious. "I'll deal with his case later. What's the state of play in the rest of the territory?"

"Peace has been restored in Leafhold, the capital of Green Mantle. Sending in our most enthusiastic supporters seems to have quelled all traces of rebellion. It doesn't look like the protesters were particularly ambitious, so to speak. The inhabitants have gone to ground like rats and are just happy to survive."

"That's all we want them to do!" said Ocious.

Edefia's ruler looked both furious and scornful. No trace remained of the doubt that had shadowed his eyes a moment earlier and his expression was once more full of authority.

"What do you suggest?" he asked, addressing Andreas.

"I think we should form six commando units and launch simultaneous initiatives in each of the towns," he replied, revelling in his father's utter confidence in him. "There aren't that many places to hide and the people know they'd lose more by opposing you than they'd gain. They still fear you, Father. We'll soon flush out that..."

Andreas cast around to find the right words.

"... little pest!" he concluded finally.

With narrowed eyes, Ocious gave a savage bark of laughter that didn't bode well for the Runaways.

9

AN ISLAND IN DECLINE

T HE ISLE OF THE FAIRIES WAS NOTHING LIKE OKSA HAD imagined. When she'd thought about it, she'd pictured a timeless, placeless island whose incomparably lush landscapes were more beautiful than anything Earth could offer. But what she discovered now with her Lunatrix and Malorane was more like a faded earthly paradise than the fabled Garden of Eden. She could see that the place had once been magical, but its magnificence had been dimmed by years of hardship. Backing onto a white stone cliff polished smooth by what had once been a waterfall, the territory was not extensive, little more than a village dotted with stunted trees raising twisted branches to the sky. The stream running through its centre must once have been a fast-flowing river, but it now resembled a dwindling silver thread. There were a few sparse plants lining its banks, which gladdened Oksa, who hadn't seen any greenery for weeks.

Oksa's whole body crumpled when she landed, overcome by exhaustion. She knelt on the short, parched grass as her Lunatrix waddled hurriedly over to her.

"My Young Gracious makes demonstration of a muscular slackening and the heart of her domestic staff is riddled with anxiety!"

"Oh, my Lunatrix," sighed Oksa, her face drawn. "It's not just my muscles…"

She slumped even further.

"I must look dreadful," she said, looking at her scratched hands and grubby, tattered clothes.

"My Young Gracious is indeed covered by atrocities and filth," confirmed the Lunatrix, "but her heart is not."

Oksa gazed at him, blinking rapidly.

"You're adorable," she murmured softly.

Malorane also approached, floating above the parched ground.

"You have nothing to fear here. You'll be able to rest for a while, sweetheart."

Oksa looked up.

"But—" she began wildly.

"No 'buts'," interrupted Malorane. "You won't be fit for anything if you don't regain your strength. Come with me!"

Malorane's hands skimmed over her, but she was too ethereal to lift her up. It was the Lunatrix who applied himself to the task with considerable enthusiasm. Displaying unexpected strength, he grabbed Oksa's forearms and pulled on them to help her to her feet. His small podgy hands were so soft that Oksa would have liked to shrink to a fraction of her size and curl up inside them. Softness and human warmth were what she missed more than anything in the world. But that would have to wait... At her side, the Lunatrix diligently provided unfaltering support, refusing to let any obstacle prevent him from carrying out his mission.

"My Young Gracious must make use of her domestic staff as a cane," he urged, hunching his back.

His broad smile and assiduous expression were irresistible: Oksa had to obey and the odd pair followed Malorane along the stream.

"You'll be comfortable in there," said the former Gracious, pointing to a small mahogany gazebo overlooking the stream. Oksa obediently let herself be guided towards the building, her body heavy with weariness.

Filmy hangings fluttered between columns carved with delicate plant motifs, and when Oksa discovered what was behind them, she sighed with relief.

"Fantastic!"

Her main problem was to decide whether to eat or sleep first. These basic human needs exasperated her but, despite being a Gracious, she couldn't think of anything else. Her stomach gave a loud growl, which reached the Lunatrix's ears.

"The feeding of my Young Gracious makes a petition for urgency," he said in a panic, pulling Oksa towards the low table laden with dishes. "Starvation experiences imminence, feast yourself!"

Oksa didn't need to be told twice. She sat cross-legged on a large squashy cushion and greedily examined the buffet prepared for her: rolled pancakes oozing pieces of brightly coloured vegetables, slices of grilled fish marinated in aromatic herbs, a host of tiny cheeses topped with crushed walnuts and hazelnuts, slices of caramelized fruit and a slab of deliciously creamy butter. Oksa picked up a steaming bread roll and cut it in half with obvious pleasure.

"Come and eat with me, my Lunatrix!"

The small creature flushed pink.

"Ooohhh... my Young Gracious affords her domestic staff a colossal honour with the gift of this proposal!"

"You're hungry too, aren't you?" asked Oksa, her mouth glistening with butter.

The Lunatrix nodded as he stuffed a huge slice of still-steaming bread into his mouth.

"Your domestic staff was suffering from an encounter with food scarcity," he admitted.

Oksa couldn't help laughing. Above the railing of the gazebo, Malorane sighed.

"How wonderful it is to have both of you here."

"My Antecedent Gracious possesses verity in her mouth," remarked the Lunatrix.

"Well I have this delicious cheese in my mouth!" chuckled Oksa, devouring a savoury morsel.

Malorane and a few Ageless Ones dressed in long ethereal robes were watching them from a distance and Oksa was sure she saw them smile. She grinned back, drowsy with tiredness and relief. The Antecedent Gracious—as the Lunatrix called her—floated nearer.

"Thank you!" said Oksa. "I'd have starved to death if I'd had to wait another hour."

Malorane nodded and her long, abundant hair cascaded over her shoulders like a silken veil.

"We're all very glad to have you with us and to be able to help our people. But, first things first, you're in need of some attention. You're…"

"…in a bit of a state?" interrupted Oksa.

She could only see her badly scratched arms, but she was pretty sure that her face and neck hadn't escaped the disasters befalling the planet. Her skin was dehydrated and tight, and the feel of her tee-shirt rubbing against her shoulders was becoming increasingly uncomfortable.

"Am I disfigured?" she asked, seeing the Lunatrix's concern.

"The physiognomy of my Young Gracious has successfully preserved its appearance, but her skin has encountered several injuries. The evidence of burning is evinced by stripes of fire on the tender epidermis and the violence of the storms has produced the imprint of wounds packed with hideousness."

"Great," sighed Oksa. "So what you're saying is that I look like Frankenstein's monster."

Malorane intervened. Honesty is not always the best policy.

"It isn't as bad as you think," she said reassuringly. "There won't be a mark on you in a few hours. It's up to you now, Lunatrix!"

From his dungarees, the little creature took a case which Oksa knew was bound to contain all manner of dreaded creepy-crawlies like those foul seamstress spiders. She wasn't about to forget how the Spinollias had efficiently—and completely painlessly—repaired the cuts covering her body after her encounter with Orthon McGraw in the lab at St Proximus. The Spinollias were still insects, though, and Oksa loathed and detested them, whatever they were!

"My Young Gracious should proceed with the adoption of a horizontal position," suggested the Lunatrix.

Oksa obeyed, too exhausted to argue. However, when the Lunatrix picked up one of the spiders with his stubby fingers, and its delicate legs immediately set to work, she couldn't hide her revulsion. She closed her eyes, just in time to avoid seeing the small handfuls of Dermi-Cleaners which her small steward was placing on her neck and cheeks. The tiny orange worms began their work, sucking conscientiously at her wounds. In a few hours, her injuries would be a distant memory.

The weather was mild on the Isle of the Fairies. The stream babbled and a light breeze ruffled the hangings. Everything was so quiet and peaceful. Oksa's heart soon began beating more slowly in time with her undulating Curbita-Flatulo, as a delicious feeling of languor spread through her body. She fell asleep on the enormous cushions, feeling pleasantly full and completely worn out.

⁂

Was she dreaming or could she hear rain? She lay still, remembering the moments before she'd sunk into this wonderful sleep. It sounded as if there was some kind of commotion going on and she could make out unfamiliar voices coming from all directions.

"Oh dear," she murmured.

She decided to open her eyes and found herself face to face with the Lunatrix, who was staring joyfully at her. Suddenly he began yelling:

"My Young Gracious has performed a reunion with consciousness! Awakening is apparent! Awakening is apparent!"

Immediately, some Ageless Ones, led by Malorane, entered the gazebo. Others floated around the small structure. Oksa sat up, her eyes wide, as she became aware of the loud din outside.

"Is it raining?" she asked. "Is it really raining?"

"Yes, sweetheart!" replied Malorane. "You performed this miracle. You and my beloved Dragomira have given Edefia a new lease of life!"

Oksa's mind was overtaken by an avalanche of thoughts.

"That's... brilliant!" she said, a little lost for words.

She ran her hand through her tousled hair.

"How do I look?" she asked, examining her arms.

"During the dozing, the Dermi-Cleaners have performed digestion of the badness that was making holes in the skin of my Young Gracious," replied the Lunatrix, "and the Spinollias have accomplished an epidermal embroidery stuffed with triumph."

"Thank goodness," sighed Oksa. "Have I been asleep for long?"

"The slumber of my Young Gracious suffered from a long deficiency," explained the Lunatrix. "Her repose experienced tenacity for two days and two nights."

"What? That's terrible!" cried Oksa.

Her eyes filled with tears. The Runaways were in Ocious's clutches and she'd wasted two whole days and nights—sleeping! She leapt out of bed, which made her head reel. Shaking with anger at herself, she grabbed the railing and wiped her damp cheeks with the back of her sleeve. The faces of her loved ones paraded past in her mind's eye.

"Has anyone got any news about my father?"

Something stirred in the small bag she wore over her shoulder.

"My Tumble-Bawler!"

She helped the little conical creature haul itself out of the bag.

"Young Gracious, your wish is my command! What can I do for you?"

She whispered a few words in its ear and the Tumble-Bawler took off like a large, pot-bellied bumble-bee, heading south.

"Come back quickly," she murmured.

Although Oksa was weighed down by guilt, she had to admit that she no longer felt tired. Surrounded by Malorane and a few Ageless Ones, she carefully descended the steps of the gazebo. Standing in the rain was surprisingly pleasurable. In a few seconds she was drenched, but the downpour was so warm and soothing she didn't care. She lifted her face up to the cloudy sky, letting the torrential rain wash away the filth and dust, leaving her refreshed. She took off her shoes and trousers, then her tracksuit top, until she was in nothing but her tee-shirt. The wet earth under her feet felt wonderful and the makeshift shower was sheer bliss. She was tempted to roll around in the mud, which was as smooth as cream, but made do with plunging her hands into it instead. Standing up again, her hands stretched out in front of her, her face lifted to the overcast sky, she watched the rain wash her skin spotlessly clean.

Suddenly she became aware of an animal odour. In amazement, she noticed about ten odd creatures digging rivulets to channel the water soaking into the ground.

"Attendants! Amazing!" she exclaimed, screwing up her eyes to see more clearly.

Malorane shot her a surprised look. Replying to her unspoken question, Oksa explained.

"Baba told me about them," she said, pulling at the hem of her tee-shirt. "She'd have loved to see them for real," she added sadly.

"Oh, but she has!" explained Malorane. "And I can tell you they both thoroughly enjoyed the experience!"

The Attendants stopped working and came nearer. They pawed the muddy ground with their hooves, then bent their forelegs in deference, the long upright antlers on their human heads brushing against Oksa's feet as they bowed. The rain bounced off their warm brown hide, which was steaming slightly, making them look even more unreal. Oksa stared at them in thrilled admiration: submitting to the spell that would turn them into half-men, half-stags in order to live with the Ageless Ones, now that was single-mindedness of the highest order!

"Thank you for saving our Land, Young Gracious!" declared the oldest-looking Attendant with a pointed beard and huge antlers.

Then they immediately galloped back to their work.

"Er… my pleasure," stammered Oksa.

Instinctively she looked up at the sky, desperate to see the Tumble-Bawler on its way back. She wouldn't be able to do anything until she had news of her loved ones. Malorane came up to her, alert to Oksa's every mood. She hovered nearby, without a word. Even the Lunatrix was at a loss for something comforting to say. Oksa sat on one of the steps of the gazebo and chewed a nail—a bad habit that hadn't disappeared, despite the speeded-up ageing process. Then, unable to turn her mind to anything else, she waited, hunched with her tee-shirt pulled over her knees.

🔅

At long last, the small winged informer reappeared; Oksa was in agonies. She jumped up with a yell. The creature landed in her palm, dripping with rain.

"The Young Gracious's Tumble-Bawler reporting!"

"Tell me what you know, please!"

"My Young Gracious, I flew as fast as I could and was able to reach Thousandeye City seventy miles away in thirty-seven minutes—going by Outside measurements. I found many squadrons of Vigilians keeping guard around the Glass Column, so I had to be wily. I entered by crawling along the foundations—those vile flying caterpillars thought I was a harmless Coleopteran and I was able to get inside."

Despite hanging on the creature's every word, Oksa's involuntary gesture of impatience was clear enough and the Tumble-Bawler got straight to the point.

"I reached the penultimate floor, my Young Gracious, where the Runaways are housed. You must be informed that your father, Abakum and Zoe are no longer in the Column."

"What?" panicked Oksa.

Her heart missed a beat, and she immediately assumed the worst: Ocious had taken revenge for her escape by killing the people she loved most in the world. She gave a heart-rending wail. Terrible images filled her head as the Tumble-Bawler hovered in front of her face, humming like an engine.

"Don't alarm yourself, my Young Gracious! I don't know how they did it, but I'm sure that all three of them managed to escape."

10

THE HUNT FOR
THE GRACIOUS

E DEFIA'S INHABITANTS HAD ENDURED A GREAT DEAL OF
hardship over the past few years. By the time the Great Chaos had
come to an end, Gracious Malorane was dead and a handful of Edefians
had disappeared through the Portal: the future Gracious Dragomira,
her brother Leomido, the Fairyman, Orthon and a few high-ranking
officials. Most people believed they were dead, vaporized as they'd passed
through the Portal, and these happenings, completely unprecedented in
the history of Edefia, had violently traumatized the population. Nothing
had been the same since, and there were many who missed the good old
days when nothing was known about the Outside. It was now common
knowledge that they'd been kept in blissful ignorance for centuries by
the Graciouses and, after the initial shock and astonishment, everyone
understood why. There was no big mystery—it was simply crucial to
Edefia's safety and equilibrium.

However, for nearly sixty years they'd all been paying dearly for the
disclosure of the Secret-Never-To-Be-Told. Pride, self-interest and a
hunger for power… After watching Malorane's Dreamflights and seeing
these character traits in the Outsiders, the people of Edefia understood
to their cost that they had the same flaws as people whom they'd feared

at first, then come to know as a result of Malorane's revelations. "Because there is in mankind, on the Inside as on the Outside, both good and evil", the Secret had stated. It had been a rude awakening.

Little happened in the first few decades after the Great Chaos, with the exception that Ocious and his supporters seized power, despite having caused Malorane's fall and this terrible mess in the first place. The people of Edefia were in shock and did nothing to prevent them. The few protesters, who gained little support and were unaccustomed to opposing anyone, eventually gave up and became resigned to their fate. Things quickly went from bad to worse. In just a few weeks the sky became overcast with a layer of thick, dry clouds pressing down like a lead weight. The temperature and the light began to drop rapidly, water was starting to grow scarce, adversely affecting crops, causing desertification and bringing adversity. Ocious tried to halt the inexorable process that was bringing Edefia closer to destruction with every passing day. Assisted by the leading experts, he set up a system designed to conserve and use resources differently. Hundreds of square miles of farmland were abandoned to concentrate irrigation on smaller areas, wells were dug ever deeper to bring up water, now more valuable than the diamonds and sapphires from Peak Ridge, and the tribes joined forces to share resources and work together, since the people were exhausted from coping with shortages. However, hope was in shorter supply than strength and the bare essentials. Edefia's golden age was at an end and no one was fooled by Ocious's impassioned speeches: what had been lost would never be found again.

❋

Only a minority still believed in the future. Unlike the population, Ocious and his supporters were convinced that the Edefians who'd disappeared through the Portal had survived. However, they did have first-hand information which lent credence to this theory.

Along with Malorane's confidences, they had access to all kinds of information stored secretly in the Gracious Archives since the dawn of time. And it was in the Memorary, on the top floor of the Glass Column, which had been partly destroyed during the Great Chaos, that Ocious realized not only the far-reaching implications of the Secret, but also the infinite possibilities open to him if he managed to pass through the Portal. So he remained convinced over the years that he'd be able to leave Edefia one day and reign supreme over billions of human beings on the Outside. And like his ancestor, Temistocles, he put a great deal of energy into trying to work out how to pass through the invisible frontier.

For many years, he was a firm but fair ruler, an absolute monarch who prided himself on making the right decisions for the good of his people. However, his personal beliefs ended up taking priority over his sense of duty, and reason lost out to impatience and ambition. Convinced that the answer was to manufacture an ultra-powerful Werewall elixir, he made the heinous decision to place the people of Edefia at the mercy of the vile Diaphans. Enormous quantities of elixir were made, causing hundreds of people to lose the chance of experiencing romantic love for ever.

Edefia had just entered the worst period of its history: the Years of Tar, named after the nauseating substance that flowed from the melted nostrils of the Diaphans. At the same time as Dragomira was settling in Paris with Abakum and Pavel, the Diaphans in Edefia were dying from overdoses of romantic feelings, without providing Ocious with what he'd wanted. And for the first time the people on the Inside dared to rebel against their ruler's selfish barbarism and megalomania.

Although no one died, the repression was terrible. Intimidation, imprisonment in barren territories, excessive rationing—Ocious was unscrupulous and stopped only at murder, since the sacredness of human life was an immutable principle in Edefia. Industrial quantities of Werewall elixir were distributed to anyone prepared to enter the army of a sinister ruler who seemed unassailable. Terrified by the way things were turning out, many citizens accepted, swelling the ranks of the Werewalls and making Edefia, once such a harmonious land, into a martial state. As for Ocious, the more frustrated he felt at being trapped inside Edefia, the tougher he became.

In this way, the vast majority of the population lost the riches of their land, the comfort of love and any hope for a bright future.

※

When Ocious gave the order, his commando units descended on Edefia's six towns like a biblical plague. The cowed Insiders had been thunderstruck by the return of the Runaways and the arrival of the New Gracious, which had galvanized them into action. The news had spread like wildfire and the people had raised their heads again, keeping a weather eye open for the inevitable changes that their new Gracious would bring.

A few days later the rain had begun to fall. This was a clear sign. A very clear sign. And unexpected in more ways than one. Relief was followed by a period of waiting. Something was bound to happen, but nobody could have predicted what.

※

Escorted by swarms of irascible Vigilians and Chiropterans with razor-sharp teeth, Ocious's squadrons invaded the subdued cities in the middle of the night, forcing their way into homes. The soldiers threw inhabitants out of their beds, firing one question at them:

"Where's the Young Gracious?"

Faced with incredulous silence, the soldiers raised their voices.

"If you know where the Young Gracious is or you have any other information about her, then you'd better tell us now!"

"Or what?" asked the boldest.

The Vigilians answered by brushing the cheeks of these brave citizens with their extremely irritating cilia, making them howl with pain. Then, because no one would say anything after that, the soldiers searched the houses from top to bottom. From the humblest house in the trees of Green Mantle to the smallest cave in the Peak Ridge Mountains they ransacked homes, tossing out the contents of chests and cupboards, lifting mattresses, shattering objects and breaking their owners' spirits. A few furious citizens rebelled and tried to stand in their way, but the flying escorts proved even more formidable than the human commando units.

※

From the top of the Glass Column, Ocious was keeping a close watch on the operation carried out in Thousandeye City. At that very moment his two sons were conducting the biggest investigation ever seen in Edefia's principal city since the Confiscation of Granok-Shooters a few years earlier. That had been a brilliant, if poorly rewarded, operation, remembered the elderly Docent, waving his hand in the air as if to dismiss the less than glorious memory.

"Why do they persist in fighting me?" he sighed, watching as people gathered outside their houses, guarded fiercely by his soldiers.

His two sons were down there, in the streets turned to mud by rain that had been falling non-stop for days. Orthon and Andreas. Andreas and Orthon. They obviously hated each other. What about him? Did he love them? He snorted and turned his attention to a fire which was taking hold in the distance, in the suburbs of Thousandeye City.

※

"Why are you doing this?" a girl was yelling at Andreas.

Two soldiers were holding her firmly, one by her long hair, the other by her arms.

"Your father and grandfather are troublemakers," replied Andreas, standing in front of her to intimidate her with his height. "Troublemakers and renegades," he added. "They've betrayed Edefia."

His strangely calm, almost bewitching voice was in complete contrast to his harsh words and his eyes, black as his cropped hair. Andreas was no ordinary individual. Radiating an impression of dangerous, elegant refinement, he was a man of few, clear-cut and economical, gestures, and his intellect was formidable. He turned to look at the dismayed crowd, favouring some with his inscrutable gaze and others his perfect profile. The girl was struggling in front of him. The soldiers tightened their grip, tearing the sleeve of their captive's dress.

"My father and grandfather aren't renegades!" she spat. "They love Edefia more than you and your dictator of a father!"

Everybody thought Andreas would slap her, but they were wrong. He merely gazed at her long and hard, then snapped his fingers. Immediately several soldiers entered the girl's house and went on the rampage: everything was tossed out of the windows and a wrinkled old man was dragged outside.

"Leave him alone, you thugs!" cried the girl, struggling even harder.

"Get up, Arvo!" ordered Andreas. "Don't add to the shame Achilles has already brought upon your family."

"My father has done nothing wrong!" continued the girl, despite the swarm of Vigilians buzzing near her face. "It isn't a crime to say what you think!"

Andreas smiled and fixed her with eyes as black as night.

"Of course it isn't a crime," he sneered triumphantly. "But it is to sow the seeds of discord in such troubled times."

"Where is he?" asked old Arvo, covered in mud.

"He's somewhere where no one else can hear his lies," replied Andreas.

"You have no right!" protested the girl.

This time Andreas's tense face assumed a threatening expression. He stepped forward until he was just a few inches from the defiant girl and jabbed his finger at her forehead, right between her eyes.

"You're wrong, young Lucy: I have every right."

Then he spun round, grabbed a torch and set the house on fire as the terrified crowd looked on.

❈

A few yards behind him, Orthon was watching with a superior look on his face. Was that how his *wonderful, oh so talented* half-brother got his way? He was just a smooth talker at the head of a band of mercenaries who liked to throw their weight around. Shoving old men, terrorizing kids, burning houses—what a ridiculous show of strength! He, Orthon, the elder son, had more guts and more style. He took out his Granok-Shooter and whispered in Arvo's direction. The old man collapsed lifeless in a puddle, his eyes staring. As shocked as all the other witnesses, the guards released Lucy, who rushed over to her grandfather. Ignoring her tears and the horrified silence of the crowd, Orthon gave Andreas a long, challenging stare, then stalked off in the pouring rain. This war was now being fought on another level.

❈

The six towns were methodically and savagely sacked. The stakes were high and the message was clear, as the last few surviving principles collapsed like a house of cards. State authority and threats were obviously no longer effective, so reckless brutality took over, destroying everything in its path.

However Leafhold—the biggest city in the territory of Green

Mantle—put up unexpected resistance. Its layout was the first obstacle facing even the most enthusiastic of Ocious's soldiers: the houses were built at different heights in the trees and linked by zip-lines or monkey bridges, which made the task of Ocious's commando units even more difficult. But it wasn't just the stepped terrain that was problematic: a band of rebels were also causing no end of trouble. Led by a masked man with a Granok-Shooter, the Sylvabuls rebelled against this shameless use of force. As Ocious's men went from house to house as best they could, silhouettes appeared along the trunks of the giant trees. Agile as squirrels and cunning as foxes, they set all kinds of traps and snares, each more inventive than the last, which wreaked havoc in the soldiers' ranks. The victories they won were small, but they had great symbolic significance, despite the danger they involved. The soldiers, who suffered more from injured pride than actual flesh wounds, proved totally without scruple, and it was in indomitable Leafhold that the crackdown was most violent.

All to no avail, however, since no one talked and they found nothing.

11

Surrounded!

From the start, Ocious had guessed that the Isle of the Fairies would be the ideal hiding place for the Young Gracious. Agafon, the Memorarian, was quite adamant, though: nowhere in the Gracious Archives was there any mention of a human visiting this territory. No one could enter, except for Attendants and Graciouses, living or dead. Like the invisible Mantle around Edefia, the Isle was protected by an imperceptible barrier that acted as a deterrent—it would forcefully repel anyone who came near it. There was no way in without the co-operation of the Ageless Ones, and Ocious was well aware that they were no fans of his. Since that idealist, Malorane, had died, not one of the Fairies had put in an appearance. And yet, as Orthon had confirmed, they were still very active. They'd appeared several times to the Runaways on the Outside, and they'd no doubt taken Oksa in hand as soon as she'd entered the damned Cloak Chamber.

The search of the six towns of Edefia had proved one thing to the population: Ocious was still in charge of the country. However, the elderly ruler was far from being satisfied by this outcome. So, since he couldn't get into the Isle of the Fairies, he ordered the island to be surrounded by two squadrons: a highly trained air squadron led by Andreas and a land squadron led by himself and Orthon. Given that the Young Gracious was probably already there, she wouldn't be able to leave without being spotted. Then they'd see who had the upper hand.

❃

Everyone inside the Isle of the Fairies knew they were surrounded. Unseen, Oksa could watch the movements of the patrols escorted by horrible swarms of Vigilians and Chiropterans. She could even see Ocious, Andreas, Orthon and his son Gregor; rigged out in leather armour, they looked ready for anything. Oksa's heart swelled with resentment.

"They don't give up easily," she said with a grimace.

"You have no idea!" said Malorane.

Ever watchful and anxious, the former Gracious joined Oksa near the invisible shield and glared at Ocious, the man who'd caused her downfall. Usually iridescent white in hue, Malorane grew as dark as a storm cloud, streaked with black and purple. A reflection of her bitter hatred, Oksa thought.

She hadn't forgotten the terrible images she'd seen through Dragomira's Camereye: almost sixty years earlier, beside the wide-open Portal, Ocious and Malorane had mercilessly confronted each other. With blood dripping from her head, the deposed Gracious had leapt desperately into the air and dropped like a stone on her mortal enemy. She'd died that day and had become an Ageless Fairy, while Ocious had survived.

Suddenly, as if aware he was being watched, Ocious turned to look in their direction, staring straight at the two Graciouses. Oksa couldn't help crying out, while Malorane remained perfectly still, glaring at him with unrelenting defiance. Ocious drew nearer, his eyes narrowed, and time seemed to stand still. He knew they were there, a few inches from him, yet just out of reach. That explained the rage on his face. Then his expression changed and he gave a savage smile, which made Oksa shiver from head to toe. He came right up to the frontier and took another step forward.

Oksa realized that, instead of being ejected like the other soldiers, he was sinking into the invisible barrier. She couldn't help wailing in horror.

"Don't worry, sweetheart," said Malorane.

"I'm not worried," whispered Oksa. "But he is the strongest of the Werewalls and descended from Temistocles—he might be able to get in!"

"Neither he nor anyone else can," said Malorane. "This place is for the Graciouses and their guests, no one else is welcome here. Trust me, Oksa."

Several Ageless Ones surrounded her with their gentle halo of light. Confirming the former Gracious's reassuring words, Oksa watched Ocious back away, without losing his defiant expression.

"What are we going to do?" asked Oksa.

She could see herself being trapped on this island for months, since Ocious was determined enough to keep up the siege for a long time. A very long time. Tears pricked her eyes. She was stuck in a bubble that was turning into a gilded cage, while her loved ones were still fighting. There was so much to do!

"You're a Gracious now," replied Malorane.

"Well, I don't feel as though that's any kind of advantage!" broke in Oksa angrily, kicking the muddy ground.

"You're a Gracious," repeated Malorane. "That gives you certain unique powers."

"I can't… I can't fight *that*!" said Oksa, pointing at the squadrons of soldiers and the swarms of insects.

"No, you're right, you can't fight. Not without risking your life, and that's out of the question. But you can escape."

Oksa ran her hands through her hair and groaned:

"How?"

"Have you an idea what might help you do that?"

Frowning with worry and concentration, Oksa muttered to herself for a few seconds before hunching her shoulders in despair.

"Apart from becoming invisible, I don't see…"

When she said this, Malorane's hazy silhouette regained its pearly white hue and a tremor ran through the Ageless Ones. The Lunatrix approached, his large blue eyes shining with exultation.

"My Young Gracious has just achieved the placement of her finger on the solution," he said.

Oksa looked from the Ageless Ones to the small happy creature.

"You mean I can become invisible?" she exclaimed in astonishment. "Is that... because I'm now a Werewall?"

The Lunatrix shook his head.

"My Young Gracious does not express the proper reason," he said. "But her domestic staff will proceed to the availability of vital clues. Has my Young Gracious made the conservation of the memory of her visit to the silo belonging to the much-loved Fairyman?"

Oksa rubbed her face.

"Um, yes... there were all kinds of things in there! Let me think: Centaury, Nobilis, Pulsatilla, magic herbs, Monkshood, Sleepy Nightshade..."

"Neither the plants nor the herbs will afford the gift of invisibility to my Young Gracious," broke in the Lunatrix.

"So what will?" she asked, startled.

She might be older now and a fully fledged Gracious, but some things didn't change, unfortunately: she still found herself blinded by panic. The image of Gus flashed into her mind. In this type of situation, he was the one who always came up with the answer. He had the memory of an elephant! But Gus wasn't there.

"Come on, Oksa, use your brain!" she muttered encouragingly to herself.

She forced herself to breathe calmly and thought back to Abakum's house, the former grain silo, the hothouse inhabited by incredible plants, the Ptitchkins fooling around... Her face lit up and she suddenly cried out:

"The Invisibuls! That's what it is, isn't it?"

71

The Ageless Ones lit up with renewed brilliance, while the Lunatrix clapped with captivating ineptitude. Oksa was delighted—she'd known the answer all along and had worked it out for herself. The Invisibuls weren't just flying tadpoles able to form a moving picture to welcome her, they were also skilled chameleons which could use their mimetic power to make her invisible. Oksa remembered now: when she'd asked Abakum if she could try, he'd replied somewhat mysteriously, "In due course, yes, you can." Well, it was now or never, wasn't it?

"Unfortunately, we only have enough Invisibuls for you and your Lunatrix," declared Malorane. "None of us can go with you, sweetheart. Even if we aren't flesh and blood, Ocious will spot us, which will endanger your escape."

"Don't worry, I'll manage!" exclaimed Oksa.

She broke off, her eyes darkening.

"But—what should I do? Where should I go?"

"Would you give us your Tumble-Bawler?" said Malorane, holding out her hand.

Oksa obeyed and, while an Ageless Fairy quietly gave the small creature the necessary directions for the Young Gracious's route, Malorane said in a fierce whisper:

"Your supporters are waiting for you, my dear Oksa. Go safely."

12

A NARROW ESCAPE

WHEN THE INVISIBULS COVERED HER BODY, OKSA thought she'd scream in disgust. The tiny creatures weren't insects, but being plastered in sticky tadpoles wasn't high on Oksa's list of favourite pastimes.

"Oh… I'm not sure I can bear this," she mumbled, trying not to open her mouth too wide.

Fortunately, her Lunatrix was clinging to her, which was some comfort. In a few seconds, both of them were coated with the creatures and had disappeared from view. Aware of the huge advantage this new power gave her, Oksa took a deep breath, emptied her mind in an attempt to forget the thick layer of Invisibuls crawling over her, and shot into the air above the island.

The Ageless Ones accompanied her to the invisible frontier, infusing her with courage and determination. Although Oksa didn't lack these qualities, the thought of being surrounded by her worst enemies, despite being invisible, was more daunting than she'd have imagined.

As if sensing her presence, Ocious lifted his hand and roared, bringing half the land patrols into the air. What had he seen? A movement in the protective field around the island? A gap in Oksa's covering? He examined the cloudy sky with narrowed eyes. He knew she was there. When she was just a couple of feet away from him, Oksa met his suspicious eyes, which almost threw her off-balance. It was so odd to see without being seen!

"Everyone to me, now!" commanded Ocious.

The squadrons raced towards their leader. In an instant, a hundred men at least formed a wall around him. Oksa was furious with herself. Instead of grimacing at how sticky the Invisibuls were, why hadn't she asked the important questions like would her body lose its density? Could she be hit by Granoks? Could they capture her? Aware of her fears—especially her pounding heart—the Lunatrix tightened his arms around her.

"My Young Gracious should make the acquisition of one piece of information," he said to Oksa, who could feel panic taking hold.

"I'm listening," she whispered.

"The Invisibuls procure an encounter with transparency full of completeness. My Young Gracious can exhibit the conviction of not being seen or heard or felt or touched. A single inconvenience nevertheless experiences survival: the gestures of my Young Gracious have no power to implement consequences."

"What?" exclaimed Oksa, feeling a sudden surge of confidence. "You mean I'm immaterial? Like a ghost?"

"The affirmation is complete, my Young Gracious."

That was all it took for Oksa to make up her mind. Gathering speed, she hurled herself at the human wall in front of her.

"Let me pass, you lousy bastards!" she screamed at the top of her voice.

There was a slight feeling of resistance as she passed through the bodies of several soldiers, but nothing that could stop her. The men also seemed to sense some kind of movement, but couldn't work out what had caused it. Some of them looked at each other sceptically, while others looked round, trying to locate the source of this strange sensation.

When Ocious attempted to fire a Knock-Bong, the blow felt to Oksa like a puff of wind: under the layer of Invisibuls, her hair was ruffled and a gentle breeze skimmed over her skin.

Oksa gloated, dizzy with excitement. Then she suddenly came face to face with Orthon, her age-old enemy, and her jubilation instantly turned to a towering rage. The Felon was standing motionless in mid-air, on the lookout. Oksa hovered just in front of him in a stationary Vertiflight and glared into his aluminium-grey eyes.

"I hate you!" she yelled, protected by the Invisibuls which deadened her every sound. "You're the worst scumbag in the two worlds! And I'm telling you now: you will pay dearly for everything you've done to everyone I love!"

Orthon might not have heard the words, but the Young Gracious's rage seemed able to penetrate any kind of defence, including the ultra-powerful layer of Invisibuls. Orthon suddenly shot out his arm and his hand connected with Oksa's shoulder. Petrified, she didn't dare move an inch. The Lunatrix clung to his mistress with all his might.

"My Young Gracious should proceed to an escape," he murmured. "Now."

Shaken out of her immobility, Oksa took off in a flash, soaring above the clouds in record time. Leomido—her beloved teacher—would have been proud of her: Ocious, Orthon and their damned squadrons could look for her all they liked, they'd never find her!

❋

As usual, the Tumble-Bawler proved to be an exceptional guide. Covered with a fistful of magic tadpoles, it led Oksa through the sky with frequent words of encouragement. Still trembling from her aerial encounter, Oksa was very grateful for its support. She had to admit that it was hard to brave such dangers on her own.

"My Young Gracious will never make the encounter with loneliness," said the Lunatrix suddenly, wrapping his long arms around Oksa's neck. "Her life will always experience unfolding in the company of her creatures."

Oksa slowed down.

"You're so kind, my Lunatrix," she said eventually. "And I know you're right!"

Touched by his words, she kept following the Tumble-Bawler, which was panting as it flew. Beneath them Edefia was now a dismal, endless wasteland, a muddy desert crossed by rivers in spate after the continual rain of the past few days. From time to time soldiers flew past without seeing them and, every time, Oksa felt stronger. More resilient. Steadfast in the face of adversity. She'd regained so much more than her energy after her restorative stay with the Ageless Ones.

"Where are we, Tumble?" she asked.

"Tumble-Bawler of the Young Gracious reporting!" said the creature, continuing to flap its wings. "We're forty miles from our destination, heading south. Given that we're Vertiflying at an average speed of sixty miles an hour, we can expect to arrive in forty-one minutes."

"Are we travelling that quickly?" asked Oksa in surprise.

"That was an average, my Young Gracious. You're capable of flying much faster. For example, you hit your maximum speed fifty-seven minutes ago, when you came face to face with Ocious's soldiers. Your escape then permitted you to reach a speed of eighty-two miles per hour."

Oksa whistled.

"Not bad at all!"

Fired by this information, she performed a fearless pirouette in mid-air, which made the Lunatrix chuckle with pleasure.

"What about our destination?" she went on. "Can you tell me where we're going?"

The Tumble-Bawler turned to hover in front of her, beating its wings rapidly, its small round eyes wide.

"We're heading for a place that was once the most splendid city in Green Mantle, my Young Gracious. The native city of your great-grandfather Waldo and the Fairyman: Leafhold."

"I thought so!" exclaimed Oksa eagerly.

Twilight was gradually darkening the horizon. A magnificent, freakish oasis of greenery, bristling with giant trees, appeared in the middle of the muddy waste. Oksa felt capable of anything. She was finally going to see the legendary city, the birthplace of the Sylvabuls and of part of herself, and instinctively she knew that this new phase would play a decisive role in her destiny.

13

ENCOUNTER IN
THE DARKNESS

L EAFHOLD WAS SURROUNDED BY A WIDE STRIP OF WITHER-
ing vegetation. Trees with bare, twisted branches were dying
between the desert which was encroaching on the forest and the giant
trees which seemed to owe their survival to that sacrifice. Still covered
by Invisibuls, Oksa Vertiflew until she was about a hundred yards from
the first colossal trees, then dived towards a sand dune, where she hid
and watched, the soft, warm body of the Lunatrix still clinging to her.

In the foreground, it was impossible to ignore the soldiers in leather
armour patrolling the perimeter of the tree city, both in the air and on
the ground. Oksa hesitated: which camp did these men belong to? Were
they Felons in Ocious's pay or inhabitants of Leafhold anxious to protect
their own?

"My Young Gracious should encounter the necessity to examine
supreme precaution," whispered the Lunatrix, banishing her doubts.
"The soldierly density assumes dependency on the orders of Ocious,
the hated Docent."

Instinctively, and despite her invisibility, Oksa pressed even flatter
against the damp sand and continued to watch. The extraordinary oasis
of green foliage could have been plucked from the fertile mind of an

imaginative, megalomaniac botanist and had a distinctly surreal quality. Between the trees, some of which were so huge that their tops couldn't be seen for clouds, an impossibly intricate network of bridges, walkways and aerial corridors linked the houses built among the branches. With darkness descending on the forest city, hundreds of tiny lights sparkled brightly among the branches from inside the houses, while a moving beam appeared on every platform.

Apart from the soldiers, who were keeping the city under constant surveillance, Oksa couldn't see any signs of life. And yet, she could sense intense activity going on in the depths of the thick forest.

"There is some practical information my Young Gracious should know," said the Tumble-Bawler, landing on her shoulder.

"I'm listening," whispered Oksa, keen to find out more.

"Leafhold covers a circle which is four miles in diameter. It stands above one of the last groundwater tables in Edefia, which is the reason for the city's survival. Three hundred and forty-eight people and five hundred and twelve creatures currently live here, not to mention the two hundred and twenty soldiers in Ocious's patrols, twenty-three Long-Gulch and Firmhand refugees, four Runaways and eleven creatures who escaped from the Glass Column."

Oksa stared wide-eyed.

"Four Runaways? Did you say four?"

"That's right, my Young Gracious," confirmed the little messenger.

This revelation set Oksa's mind whirring.

"But you told me that only my father, Abakum and Zoe had managed to escape, didn't you? So who's the fourth?"

"I'm terribly sorry not to be able to answer that question," stammered the Tumble-Bawler.

"My Young Gracious should take delivery of a piece of information which will riddle her heart with happiness," added the Lunatrix.

Oksa looked at him hopefully.

"The Much-Loved Fairyman experiences the proceeding of a geographic approach."

Oksa immediately peered through the dense darkness. Apart from the twinkling lights in the trees, and the Polypharuses on the soldiers' helmets, she couldn't see a thing. Not a single thing.

"Abakum!" she whispered.

She searched the pitch-black night. Despite the cool air, a droplet of acid sweat trickled down her temple. What if Abakum didn't see her? She had a great desire to remove the layer of Invisibuls but her fear of being visible was even greater. As long as no one could see her, she had nothing to fear. So she continued to call to Abakum in a sustained whisper, then more loudly.

"Does my Young Gracious have the will to turn her eyes in the direction advocated by her domestic staff?" asked the Lunatrix suddenly.

"Whatever you want!" whispered Oksa, so worried she couldn't think straight. The little creature then pointed his chubby finger at… nothing. After just a few seconds, though, Oksa realized that this apparent nothingness was deceptive. No one else would have been able to make out a shadow approaching through the darkness over the dunes without the keen sight she and her Lunatrix possessed. It was the Fairyman. The Shadow Man. Barely detectable, like the negative of a photograph, the light grey shape glided over the sand as smoothly and silently as a snake.

"Abakum! I'm here!" Oksa couldn't help calling.

"I know, sweetheart, I know!" replied a voice she'd have recognized anywhere.

"You can hear me?" asked Oksa, suddenly worried that she'd become audible.

"Have you forgotten my animal side?" teased Abakum.

The shadow came closer and lightly caressed Oksa, who felt the movement of the air rather than his touch.

"I can't tell you how glad I am to see you, Abakum!"

The shadow rippled.

"Come with me and do exactly what I say. It's high time we were all back together again, don't you think?"

᛭

Oksa felt as if she were taking part in a slalom event on the way to Leafhold. They first had to weave their way between the scores of tents belonging to Ocious's squadrons, then bypass troops of suspicious, and highly mobile, soldiers and Vigilians. Matters were also complicated by the unexpected realization that the Invisibuls loathed the flying caterpillars at much as Oksa did. Every time one of those vile creatures came anywhere near them, Oksa felt sick—and the Invisibuls contracted, squeezing Oksa's body with a strength directly proportional to their disgust.

"I'm going to be suffocated to death," she grumbled. "How ridiculous is that?"

Sitting astride her shoulders, the Lunatrix puffed with all his might and waved his arms to chase away the caterpillars, but it didn't work. Her freedom of movement hampered by the physical compression of her body, Oksa kept walking as best she could without taking her eyes off Abakum's transparent shadow as he led her towards the massive forest.

"Try to avoid going through people!" instructed Abakum. "You might be immaterial, but they're battle-hardened and may sense your presence."

It wasn't too hard to dodge the soldiers, but the Vigilians were another matter. It was an awful ordeal for Oksa to feel hundreds of caterpillars passing through her body! Their wings were beating with a nauseating hissing noise and their tiny cilia grazed her like the wings of a poisonous butterfly. And she couldn't do anything to stop it; she couldn't even reduce those monstrosities to small piles of ash with a well-aimed Fireballistico, which was the fate they so richly deserved! Instead, she felt each of them pass through her, as well as having to put up with the involuntary contraction of the Invisibuls, which were having the most trying time of their magical lives. With her nerves stretched to breaking point, she ended up charging straight ahead, screaming and waving her arms, not caring that she looked like a madwoman.

⁂

When the barrier of soldiers and the belt of dead vegetation were finally behind them, it took her a few moments to convince herself that the worst was over. The Invisibuls relaxed, she took a deep breath and helped the Lunatrix clamber down from her back and onto the ground. Her heart swelled with affection as her small steward slipped his plump hand into hers.

"Victory wallows in completeness, my Young Gracious, and the mind of her domestic staff is swamped with relief."

Oksa laughed softly and heard Abakum echo her.

"We're right behind you, Abakum!" declared Oksa, head held high.

The shadow took a wide, clear path lined with Polypharuses. The illuminating tentacles of the octopuses lit up the trunks of the enormous trees, creating a strangely beautiful, if somewhat eerie, scene. Giant spiral staircases encircled the trees, leading up from their bases. Oksa craned her neck in awe. She could see the light spilling from Sylvabul homes, built on platforms fixed to the junction of several thick branches, as high as sixteen feet from the ground, or even higher.

"Wow!" murmured Oksa.

They continued walking for at least a mile and a half, occasionally passing groups of four or five soldiers.

"They're everywhere," grumbled Oksa, hating this dictatorial atmosphere.

The plants lining the path quivered, rustling their serrated leaves, which turned out not to be the effect of the breeze, as Oksa had thought.

"The vegetation performs the manifestation of salutations packed with esteem for my Young Gracious," explained the Lunatrix.

Oksa stopped dead.

"You mean these plants can see me?"

The Tumble-Bawler and the Lunatrix burst out laughing.

"My Young Gracious makes the expression of comical words! The plants do not discover objects with vision, but with *supra*-sensory clairvoyance!"

"Er... yes, of course, that's what I meant," said Oksa, correcting herself with an amused smile.

❋

Oksa didn't grow weary of gazing at the forest as they went deeper into it, wreathed in the silence of night, and she was convinced it would be an even more incredible sight in broad daylight.

"When I think that a short while ago I was living a normal life, going to school and rollerblading through the streets of London," she thought, her eyes moist. "And here I am covered in magic tadpoles, walking through a mind-boggling forest where even the plants are saying hello to me. You couldn't make it up if you tried."

The small group soon came to a tree far bigger than any of those Oksa had seen before. It looked like the trunk was at least 160 feet in diameter and its foliage disappeared from sight far above the clouds.

"We're here," announced Abakum.

He guided Oksa and her small companions towards the foot of the tree, which made the Young Gracious feel as though she were standing at the base of a skyscraper covered in bark. Looking carefully around, the Shadow Man resumed his physical appearance. The dim light couldn't hide his pinched face and drawn features, much to Oksa's concern. Feeling her eyes on him, Abakum turned his head to avoid her gaze, and took from his pocket a fluorescent green scarab beetle—the same one that had locked and unlocked the front door of his house on the Outside.

The living key burrowed beneath the bark of the tree and the dull clatter of countless bolts could be heard. An opening formed in the bark, just wide enough to allow everyone to file inside the giant tree, then closed again immediately.

14

SAFE AND SOUND

RATHER THAN CLIMBING THE STAIRS, WHICH SEEMED TO go on for ever, Abakum led Oksa towards a folding door in the inner wall of the trunk, which concealed a narrow staircase leading down through the roots of the tree into the bowels of the Earth.

"Abakum?" shouted Oksa, before going any farther. "Could... could you get these *things* off me?" she asked, motioning to the layer of Invisibuls still covering her.

The Fairyman looked at her in surprise, then grinned.

"They've done me a great service," continued Oksa, a little embarrassed. "And I swear I'll be grateful to them to the end of my days, and even longer, but I just can't bear it any more!"

The Lunatrix agreed, nodding vigorously, still clutching Oksa's hand.

"Take out your Granok-Shooter," instructed Abakum. Oksa rummaged around in the little bag she never let out of her sight and produced the magical blowpipe.

"Now, hold the end level with your heart and say these words:

> *By the power of the Granoks,*
> *Think outside the box*
> *And retract the Invisibuls*
> *Which make my form ethereal.*"

As soon as Oksa moved her Granok-Shooter towards her ribs while murmuring the spell, the millions of tadpoles concealing her from the sight of everyone—with one exception—were sucked back inside the meerschaum and amber blowpipe. She, the Lunatrix and the Tumble-Bawler were all relieved of their protective covering in a few seconds.

"Fantastic!" she exclaimed in wonder. "So what do I have to do if I want them back? I might need them again, you never know."

"I'm sure you will," said Abakum. "All you have to do is say 'summon' instead of 'retract'. But be careful! Remember that this power only belongs to the Gracious and you can only call on it when the need is great."

He gave her a sidelong look, with a slight smile.

"Don't even think of using it for fun!"

"As if I would!" said Oksa, feigning indignation. "Playing with tadpoles is hardly my idea of fun, even if the Invisibuls are wonderful."

The elderly man winked at her, happiness vying with sadness in his face.

"We're all human again now!" remarked Oksa, feeling herself. "I can't say that I'm sorry."

Eyes shining, she walked over to the Fairyman and snuggled up against him.

"Oh, Abakum," she whispered. "If you only knew…"

He put his arms around her—a simple gesture that provided all the warmth and comfort she'd been missing—and gazed down at her. Of course he knew. He was about to say something, then thought better of it and released Oksa. Turning his bowed back towards the staircase leading down into the depths of the giant tree, he took out his Granok-Shooter and summoned a Polypharus. The octopus slowly unfolded, as if underwater, then made itself comfortable in the crook of his shoulder, shedding its bright light over the wooden walls.

"Let's go," he murmured. "You're expected."

※

Oksa didn't know whether it was weight of tiredness or impatience, but the journey seemed to take for ever. Were they going to the very centre of the Earth? The steps, carved out of the soil, were irregular and obstructed by roots which hindered their progress. Oksa had to be careful not to fall flat on her face with every step she took. Still, the going wasn't anywhere near as hard for her as it was for the Lunatrix, who'd just fallen for the umpteenth time. Compassionately, Oksa eventually picked him up.

"Ooohhhh, my Young Gracious," wailed the little steward. "Your domestic staff is experiencing tumbles in perpetuity. His clumsiness covers his body with cuts and bruises and fills his heart with humiliation in gifting my Young Gracious with the obligation of raising the kilogrammic burden of her domestic staff afflicted with awkwardness, oooohhhh…"

"Don't worry, my Lunatrix," she said reassuringly, stroking his downy head. "I really don't mind."

"The goodwill of my Young Gracious encounters no limit," sighed the poor creature, snuggling against his young mistress.

They continued their descent in absorbed silence. From time to time, tunnels appeared on either side of the staircase, creating the impression of an extensive underground labyrinth. The living roots reared up as they continued down, barring some of the entrances as Oksa and Abakum reached them, which unsettled Oksa.

"Don't misunderstand their intentions," said Abakum. "They're only showing us the right way. It would be easy to get lost in this maze."

From time to time barely glimpsed shadows flitted past the end of corridors, which made Oksa jump. To her huge relief, the staircase eventually widened out into a huge room shaped like a fish tank lined with misshapen roots—and the first person she saw filled her with happiness.

"Dad!" she yelled, unceremoniously dropping her Lunatrix.

All her black thoughts and tiredness were forgotten. She ran to her father, threw her arms around his neck and burst into uncontrollable tears of relief, releasing days of pent-up tension.

"It's so wonderful to see you," murmured Pavel, hugging her with overwhelming emotion. "I was so afraid I'd lost you."

Oksa looked at him, laughing and crying, her cheeks glistening with tears. "We'll never be apart again, Dad, I swear it!"

"I promise too," he said breathlessly. "It was unbearable this time."

His face bore the traces of their recent ordeals. His cheeks were hollow and covered in stubble, there were dark bags under his blue-grey eyes, and it was impossible not to notice the countless silver threads in his ash-blond hair. Oksa buried her head in the crook of his shoulder to hide more tears and they clung together, oblivious to everyone else for a while, until Oksa gradually stopped sobbing.

"I saw Mum, you know," she announced out of the blue.

Pavel flinched. He gently extricated himself and stood back to see his daughter better. He wiped her filthy cheeks with the back of his index finger, tucked a strand of hair behind her ear, and Oksa could sense his devastating confusion and grief.

"I have a power," she explained softly. "A power that lets me leave my body and do things."

"The Identego!" broke in Abakum.

"Yes, that was what Baba called it," agreed Oksa. "I used it to see Mum. She's in London with the other Spurned, and she's fine," added Oksa, deciding not to mention the rising flood waters.

"Thank God," breathed Pavel.

"I even hugged her," continued Oksa. "And I think she *really* felt I was there. It was incredible, Dad."

"And... did you see Gus?" came a familiar voice.

"Zoe!"

Oksa rushed over to her second cousin—and best friend—and they hugged warmly.

Zoe looked awful. Her Venetian blond hair was tied back, accentuating her greyish complexion and the unfathomable grief in her huge brown eyes.

"Yes, I saw Gus," replied Oksa. "He's fine too. He's coping brilliantly, you know." _

Zoe smiled.

"What about you?" continued Oksa. "Are you okay? You're going to have to tell me all about your great escape!"

"Hold your horses, young lady!" said Pavel drily. "I think you've got quite a bit to tell us too. May I remind you that we know nothing about your time in the Cloak Chamber. Gracious or not, you're very much mistaken if you think you can keep your poor old dad and lowly friends in the dark!" .

Oksa couldn't help chuckling.

"Poor old dad and lowly friends indeed! You're the most powerful people in the two worlds."

"If only," groused Pavel.

"Well, you managed to escape, so there's your proof!" continued Oksa.

"That's true," admitted Pavel with a slight smile. "But before we start swapping stories about our heroic exploits, I'd like to introduce you to a few of the people who were instrumental in securing our freedom."

A few people stepped forward, but Oksa only had eyes for one. The Runaway whom, deep down, she'd hoped to see with the three other escapees.

"Hi there, Lil' Gracious…"

15

A Thrilling Reunion

OKSA COULDN'T MOVE OR SAY A WORD. SHE WAS ROOTED to the spot, her arms by her sides, the blood raging through her veins like a tempest.

Tugdual was standing three yards away, equally still, his hands stuffed in the pockets of his black trousers and his head slightly cocked to one side. His chilly eyes stared at her with a disturbingly neutral expression.

What was he thinking? What was he feeling? Had she ever known?

Then he gave that tiny familiar smile and she launched herself at him and began pummelling his chest.

"You, you!…" she roared.

Tugdual caught hold of her fists to stop her and folded her tightly in his arms, as Oksa furiously tried to struggle free. The sound of a violent storm could be heard distantly in the underground chamber, as a shower of earth fell to the ground.

"Calm down," whispered Tugdual. "Please." He tightened his arms around her as if to force her to obey and Oksa could feel his heart thumping against her. Her resistance crumbled as a wave of warmth washed over her.

"I missed you so much!" she growled. "I hate you!"

Tugdual laughed softly and, putting his hand on the back of her neck, he urged her to rest her head on his shoulder. She did so, then put her arms around his waist. Everyone tiptoed out, leaving them alone in this strange root-lined room.

Everyone but a slender silhouette, which stayed hidden in the shadows, watching them intently.

"How could you leave like that, without a backward glance or word?" asked Oksa softly, a lump in her throat.

"If I'd looked at you, I wouldn't have had the heart to go," replied Tugdual, a shadow passing over his face. "And if I'd stayed, Ocious would've given me to the Diaphan."

His eyes hardened and, trembling, he took Oksa's face between his hands.

"And I'd have lost you for ever."

He kissed her forehead gently, stroking her tangled hair.

"Oksa… Oksa," he sighed.

His lips brushed Oksa's.

"It was Zoe who saved me," he said softly. "She was the one who chose to sacrifice herself for you. For us. She was bluffing when she said all those horrible things about me and it worked. Orthon thought he might be taking a risk by giving me to the Diaphan: if I really hadn't been in love with you, the Diaphan wouldn't have been able to feed on my feelings and it would have ruined everything. You'd have become very sick and eventually died, and that would have made it impossible to leave Edefia."

Oksa took a step back to study him closely.

"Tell me the truth—did you know Zoe was bluffing?"

"No! She's good. Very, very good. I couldn't compete. She threw me completely. It was sheer torture believing she really thought that badly of me. I couldn't bear it. But she was so convincing, she had everyone fooled."

"I wasn't!" protested Oksa.

"You didn't *want* to believe it, that's different," corrected Tugdual.

Oksa didn't reply. She couldn't tell Tugdual about the nagging question that had tormented her since that awful day: had Zoe been in love with Gus or Tugdual before suffering Beloved Detachment? "But Zoe... you can't be sure about anything," Oksa had argued, trying to dissuade her from abandoning any chance of romantic love forever. "You don't know how things might turn out, you don't know... what your life will be like! There are other fish in the sea—Gus isn't the only one!"

"Gus? Who said anything about Gus?" Zoe had answered.

Oksa had felt like she'd been hit by a bombshell. Until now she'd always thought that Zoe was in love with Gus and that she was voluntarily sacrificing this love. Gus would never love her because he loved Oksa, so what was the point? That's what Zoe had said to Ocious and the Runaways. But perhaps she was just pulling the wool over their eyes? If Zoe had been in love with Tugdual, then letting him offer up his heart to the Diaphan would have dashed any hope that he might one day fall in love with her. Which changed a great many things. Oksa groaned, poisoned by her doubts. No longer about Tugdual, but about Zoe, her secretive cousin. She buried her face in the crook of Tugdual's shoulder, stroking his back. She loved him so much...

"So, apart from all that, are you okay?" asked Tugdual suddenly, his casual tone at odds with the present situation. "There's a rumour going round that you saved the Heart of the Two Worlds!"

"It's true, actually. I did that, and a couple of other things too," replied Oksa in the same tone.

"Well, you certainly took your time. Do you realize how long I've been waiting for you?"

"Oh, that's all down to the Fairies. We had such a blast in the Cloak Chamber! They were such fun, and then they invited me round to their place, but it was a real mess so I had to tidy up a bit. What about you?"

"Oh, nothing special, I moved around a bit, I met some cool people and we decided to go and rescue a few Runaways in Thousandeye City."

"That was you, was it?"

"I didn't think it was very good for their health to stay cooped up in the Glass Column all the time."

They burst out laughing, then stopped at the same time and gazed into each other's eyes.

"Even filthy, you're still a babe, you know," said Tugdual, stroking her dirty cheek.

"You smell like a wet dog but, hey, I'm quite fond of you all the same," she replied.

A little dimple appeared when she smiled. Tugdual wrapped his arms around her and they clung together. Oksa felt light-headed as their lips joined again, the way their hearts had done.

※

"Ahem, ahem…"

The Lunatrix was tactfully pulling on Oksa's tee-shirt. Oksa looked down, embarrassed.

"Does my Young Gracious experience the will to make a lending of attention?"

Some twenty people had appeared behind the small steward.

"Sorry, Dad!" murmured Oksa, running over to her father and giving him a smacking kiss on the cheek.

Pavel, who clearly didn't mind, glanced covertly at Tugdual.

"I can't believe we're all here, beneath this giant tree, it's unreal!" said Oksa, looking around.

"Miraculous, you mean," remarked her father. "And the only reason we're here today is because of our powerful allies. I wanted to introduce you, but Tugdual has been monopolizing your attention," he added with a smile.

Unfazed, Oksa replied: "I want to hear all about it!"

Pavel led her towards some huge, multicoloured cushions as thick and soft as quilts, arranged in a circle around the centre of the room. In the glow of torches protected by round, opaque glass shades, everyone followed them and sat down, their attention riveted on the Young Gracious.

Before satisfying her own curiosity, however, Oksa had to tell everyone in detail about her experiences, which were greeted by numerous cries of surprise and wonder.

Sitting hunched with elbows on knees, Tugdual was staring at her with an intensity that was both gratifying and unsettling. Beside him, Zoe was listening gravely with her legs folded to one side, and Oksa couldn't help noticing the immense sadness in her eyes, as well as her fierce intelligence. As for Pavel and Abakum, who became more and more engrossed with every word Oksa spoke, no one could fail to be aware of their heartfelt sorrow and relief when Oksa mentioned Dragomira, followed by her brief visit to the Spurned. Abakum's eyes welled with tears and he hunched over, as if trying to make himself smaller, while Pavel clenched his fists, looking ashen-faced and tense.

They were the only four people Oksa knew. From time to time, when her gaze came to rest on someone else, she was flustered by their intense expression of enthralled admiration—being the focus of attention really wasn't her thing. When she'd finished her story there was a respectful, contemplative silence, interrupted only by the snuffling of her Lunatrix. Oksa put her elbows on her knees and buried her face in her hands, feeling embarrassed.

"What an incredible story!" eventually said a girl with long chestnut hair.

This remark acted like a trigger—people began talking at once and waving their arms around enthusiastically. Everyone was having their say, cheeks flushed with excitement.

Unable to add anything further, Oksa watched these men and women talk about her, darting the occasional captivated glance in her direction. She raised her hand to her mouth, feeling the urge to bite her nails.

"You know the girl who just spoke?" asked Zoe suddenly, leaning towards Oksa.

Oksa nodded.

"You'll never guess who she is," continued Zoe mysteriously.

"You know I'm no good at guessing games!" protested Oksa, sitting up straighter. "Tell me."

"Well, her name's Lucy and she's a Getorix groomer."

Oksa's smile quickly became a roar of laughter.

"A Getorix groomer!" she spluttered. "That's so funny, I love it!"

Seeing her amusement, everyone stopped talking and Oksa again felt completely isolated.

"Um," she stammered. "Hello Lucy, I'm delighted to meet you."

She gnawed the inside of her cheek, worried she might have been tactless or, worse, rude to this girl, who seemed so nice. Lucy didn't look offended though: she came over with a broad grin and bowed, Oksa fidgeted restlessly.

"I take my hat off to you for working with those unruly creatures!" she said, throwing out the remark the way she might throw a lifebuoy into the sea.

"Thank you, Young Gracious," said Lucy. "Those little monsters certainly do give me the runaround!"

She looked reverently at Oksa.

"You probably won't remember, but I was there when you arrived in Thousandeye City. You were Vertiflying between Ocious's guards."

"I remember it clearly," broke in Oksa. "You were in the street, you waved to me."

"You saw me? Really?" exclaimed Lucy, in delight. "My grandfather was sure you were the New Gracious. And he was right!"

Her voice broke.

"Lucy's father is Achilles and her grandfather is Arvo, two of our staunchest allies," explained Abakum.

Lucy immediately buried her face in her hands. Abakum stood up and put his arms around her.

"Achilles and Arvo were friends and supporters of Ocious," he explained, helping Lucy sit down beside him. "They swapped sides and paid dearly for it, like all the men and women here today. Oksa, I'd like to introduce you to your most steadfast supporters, those who for nearly sixty years have been preparing for your return."

16

THE ESCAPE

A MAN WHO LOOKED STRONG, DESPITE HIS GREAT AGE, stepped forward to greet Oksa reverently. He was so elegant, with his hair tied back in an Asiatic-style bun and his immaculate grey kimono, that Oksa felt shabby in her torn jeans and dirty tee-shirt.

"My name is Edgar, my Young Gracious, and I was your great-grandfather Waldo's best friend. We knew each other when we were children and I was with him until he died. Welcome to the Monumental Tree. Please accept our protection."

Oksa didn't know what to do or say so she looked at Abakum for some guidance. The Fairyman began speaking:

"Long before the Great Chaos, Edgar had alerted Waldo about Ocious. But Waldo, like Malorane, was an idealist. He couldn't imagine anyone letting their dark side take control. A dark side which everyone has, I should add... Then disaster struck, claiming lives, dashing illusions and shaking certainties. The Edefians had always believed themselves to be good, peaceable citizens, but this turned out to be a huge mistake—none of us is a saint and the vast majority of people, devastated by this realization, simply kept their heads down in the hope of surviving. A brave few, on the other hand, held on to their pride and rolled up their sleeves to fight. Edgar and our friends were among those. During all those years and despite the decline ravaging Edefia day after day, they remained hopeful that a new day would dawn and they have worked tirelessly behind the scenes planning for the future. And that future, thanks to you, begins today."

Oksa studied the men and women gazing intently at her. They weren't all venerable elders, they weren't all forces of nature, but they had the same light in their eyes: an unyielding strength that could move mountains.

"Even before the first Velosos—our tiny long-legged messengers— had arrived to tell us you were in Thousandeye City, we knew you were expected," continued Edgar, speaking to Oksa. "At that time, Lucy was working in the Glass Column and everything she observed was reported back to us by Achilles and Arvo. Ocious's apartments on the top floor of the Column had been a hive of activity for several days, and our Docent's mounting tension made everyone suspect that something important was in the offing. It wasn't long before these suspicions were confirmed: the Young Gracious and the Runaways flew across Edefia's sky, and it was the most extraordinary thing I'd seen in the past six decades. From the top of this tree, I saw the Gargantuhen flanked by Ocious's guards. I saw our hated ruler leading you, and I saw Abakum, the Fairyman, whose integrity has never been questioned. I realized then that the strangers with him were going to reverse our disastrous destiny. The Velosos spread the news throughout the territory. There was no one in Edefia who didn't know that the New Gracious had arrived. Then we waited. For several weeks nothing happened. Dust continued to consume our land and hope began to fade. Many slipped back into defeatism, thinking that no one could save us from ruin. Others of us clung to hope. No—it was more than hope, it was a certainty. And yet we had no more news since, following her father's arrest, Lucy was no longer welcome at the Glass Column. Fortunately, fate brought us just the person we needed."

He gestured at Tugdual, who ducked his head, letting a strand of hair hide part of his face. He suddenly and unexpectedly fixed Oksa with an icy look which, to her annoyance, made her heart lurch. Sometimes ice could burn worse than fire, she should know that by now, but she still let herself be caught unawares.

"Where were you?" she asked quietly, but Tugdual had clammed up.

"Our Firmhand allies found him more dead than alive at the bottom of a canyon in the Peak Ridge Mountains," continued Edgar, when Tugdual didn't answer. "He'd been seriously injured by the Vigilians pursuing him. Our friends took him to one of the troglodyte dwellings we use as a secret base in that region. They tended to him, aided his recovery and then brought him to us. Tugdual gave us some invaluable information about what was happening in Thousandeye City and particularly in the Glass Column. This allowed us to plan a rescue operation to free the Runaways held captive on the penultimate floor. We were almost ready when, one day, the sun filtered through the thick cloud cover which has plagued us for so long. The sunshine was so beautiful and so strong! That was the sign we'd all been waiting for. It didn't last long because the heavens immediately opened and it started to rain. Can you imagine, Young Gracious, what the rain meant to us?"

Wide-eyed, Oksa shook her head.

"It was a miracle," continued Edgar. "A blessing for our poor dying land. And do you know what struck me most of all? It was my great-grandson's reaction. He'd just turned five and he'd never seen rain falling. That day, when everyone was overcome with joy, he was frightened and he started to scream with terror at the torrential water tumbling from the sky. That was when I thought to myself that we'd been very near the end."

The old man nodded several times, lost in his memories.

"What happened next?" asked Oksa, as gently as she could, given her impatience to know more.

"Ocious had already gone to great lengths to show everyone he was in charge," replied Edgar in a flat voice, "and we thought he'd reached the limits of what was tolerable. But he proved us wrong."

Edgar and his friends looked glum. A woman turned away, pale as death.

"What did he do?" urged Oksa after several long seconds.

"He went beyond the point of no return by attacking his people. Your disappearance made him furious. His overweening pride had been wounded and there's no worse injury for a man like him. He launched commando operations throughout the territory to find you, completely disregarding the last principles we'd managed to preserve despite our decline. Even the Great Confiscation of Granok-Shooters wasn't as violent as this."

"Ocious confiscated your Granok-Shooters?" cried Oksa, looking aghast.

"Yes, about ten years ago. Only his supporters and the members of his guard were allowed to keep theirs. It was a hard blow for us, because it was like losing part of ourselves."

"But what could he possibly do with them?" asked Oksa. "Granok-Shooters can only be used by the people they're made for, so what was the point?"

"Oh, he didn't want to do anything with them. It was just to deprive us of some of our power and strengthen his hold over us. He, at least, didn't endanger our lives."

"Ocious isn't the worst one!" suddenly cried Lucy angrily, then burst into tears.

A few people went pale and Abakum squeezed her shoulder sympathetically.

"His son is the lowest of the low! I hate him!" wailed Lucy with a loud sob.

Oksa looked enquiringly at her father.

"Orthon killed Lucy's grandfather right in front of her eyes," Pavel told her softly.

"Orthon?" Oksa couldn't help crying.

Everyone turned to look at her, including Lucy, her eyes full of tears.

"That's terrible," she gasped.

"Ocious and Andreas are hard-hearted, but Orthon seems far worse than them in many respects," explained Edgar.

"He's rotten to the core!" remarked Oksa. "I hate him too."

Everyone fell silent for a few seconds, lost in dark thoughts.

"There was no going back after that appalling act of violence," continued Edgar. "It was the last straw. We had to do something so, making the most of the confusion caused by the fighting, we paid Thousandeye City a visit by night. Tugdual had the most accurate knowledge of the Column and Ocious's security measures. Forewarned is forearmed, so our small group was able to make full use of all the information he generously gave us. The Vigilians weren't a problem: we had with us Edefia's leading entomologist and, when all's said and done, the Vigilians are just caterpillars."

"What did you do?" asked Oksa, shivering at the thought of those vile creatures.

"We have a secret recipe," said the old man. "Would you like to know what it is?"

Oksa nodded vigorously, bringing an amused smile to Edgar's face.

"There's a substance contained in the roots of the Majestics, the trees which produce Zestillia beans," he explained.

"Oh, yes, the beans that make food taste just how you want? I know."

"Well, it just so happens that eating this substance can severely disrupt spatial awareness. It doesn't alter gravity, just the way it's perceived."

"What do you mean?"

"Vigilians are greedy creatures," replied Edgar. "They wolfed down the pellets prepared by our friend. A few minutes later they were crawling on the ground, convinced they no longer had wings. They couldn't break free from the Earth's gravitational pull, which they believed was stronger than it is."

"So the Vigilians were crawling, were they?" cried Oksa. "I'd have loved to see that!"

She saw Tugdual give a slight smile.

"I have to confess it was very hard to resist the temptation to crush them underfoot," continued Edgar. "But we had a mission to fulfil. Tugdual and Lucy led us up to the penultimate floor. Lucy and our Sylvabul friends passed through the inner gangways, while those gifted with the power of Alpinismus followed Tugdual up the façade outside."

"The Spiderman technique!" exclaimed Oksa. "Brilliant!"

"Despite the prospect of facing Ocious's men, who were far more battle-hardened than us, it was exhilarating to do something for a change and to use our gifts," sighed Edgar with obvious pleasure.

"Could you tell what was going on from your apartments?" asked Oksa, turning to her father, Abakum and Zoe.

"Nothing happening in the Column escaped the notice of some of our ultra-sensitive creatures," said Pavel with an amused wink.

"We soon realized something was afoot from the reactions of our inquisitive Ptitchkins and the highly strung Squoracles," added Abakum. "When Ocious also realized he was being attacked on two fronts, he burst into my room with Orthon and Andreas to take me away."

Oksa gave a startled cry.

"Remember the corrosive effect of the spittle from one of our dear creatures?" asked Abakum.

The Young Gracious's eyes sparkled.

"Don't tell me they came in for a shower of Incompetent spit?"

"Let's just say that the damage caused created a useful diversion," replied Abakum mysteriously.

"Fantastic!"

"Everyone did their bit, you know. Ocious had made a big mistake not checking if we had Granok-Shooters. He probably assumed we couldn't make them on the Outside. So when Tugdual appeared at my side and we began to counter-attack by firing Putrefactios and Colocynthises, he knew things weren't going to be as easy as he'd thought."

"Did you manage to hit him?" whispered Oksa, captivated by this story.

"Tugdual hit Orthon."

"Nice work!"

"Don't forget Orthon is a powerful Werewall with an unusual metabolism," said Abakum. "Still, our surprise attack made life very difficult for Ocious and his sons. The Knuts and the Bellangers managed to get out of their apartment-cum-prison to help Reminiscens and Zoe, who'd been dragged away by Andreas and around fifteen men. Zoe managed to escape, but our dear Reminiscens is still in their clutches."

Abakum's face tensed almost imperceptibly. Oksa put her hand over his.

"We'll get her back soon, I know we will," she said softly. "She's Ocious's daughter, she won't come to any harm."

"Unfortunately, I'm not so sure, sweetheart. Still, I live in hope," he added, his lips trembling.

It broke Oksa's heart to see him looking so unhappy and ground down by worry. Abakum had devoted his whole life to others. He'd watched tirelessly over Dragomira and her family at the expense of any kind of love life of his own. Reminiscens had been his one true love. It was a love he'd never confessed and one which had been doomed for ever when the young Reminiscens had fallen madly in love with Leomido, and again when she'd suffered Beloved Detachment. Nonetheless, Abakum's feelings had remained unchanged. Despite sixty years of separation during which all hope had faded, the Fairyman still loved Reminiscens, and saving her from Impicturement had been one of the high points of his life, even though Leomido had given up his life there. Everyone knew and respected the depth of this unspoken love. Oksa squeezed his hand in compassion and support. Abakum gently shook his head, as if to banish unwelcome thoughts, then looked sadly at Oksa, and continued:

"It would have been best if we could all have escaped, but the battle was in full swing. So when your father and his Ink Dragon appeared, breaking windows and balconies, I grabbed the Incompetent and we jumped onto the dragon's back. 'Hurry!' your father yelled to everyone in the Column. Inside, our Runaway friends were battling with all their might: Naftali and our supporters were protecting Zoe from Orthon's attacks. Capitalizing on their animal instincts, the Firmhands were using their fingers as talons and their bodies as barriers, while the Sylvabuls, with their mastery of plants, attacked with nets and spray guns filled with highly toxic plant extracts. Then I caught sight of Tugdual, who was filling my Boximinus while Brune and the Bellangers provided cover. It was an absolute brainwave, as well as being very brave: the creatures are one of our main trump cards, and Ocious made his second big mistake by leaving them with us. Which is just as well…

"Tugdual threw the Boximinus to me through a broken window and disappeared into the raging battle. The dragon continued to breathe billows of fire at Ocious's guards, while being attacked by hundreds of Granoks. The situation was becoming untenable and we had to retreat. Any of our allies who couldn't Vertifly jumped onto the dragon's back, along with Zoe. Then Pierre appeared. 'Leave! Now!' he bellowed. Reluctantly the dragon took flight, immediately followed by a host of Vertifliers, not only our friends who'd been held prisoner and our Firmhand supporters, but also Ocious and his men. It was impossible to take action without running the risk of hitting one of our own."

"What happened to the Runaways?" asked Oksa tensely.

"Tugdual and a few of our companions did everything they could to set Brune and Jeanne free," replied Abakum, looking upset.

The old man fell silent. Oksa gripped his arm, holding her breath. Her eyes prickled as she searched the Fairyman's face for the answer to the question she couldn't bring herself to ask. Brune… Jeanne…

"Orthon was able to recapture them, despite our best efforts," continued Abakum at last. "Naftali managed to cling to the dragon for several miles, but fell when Ocious fired a paralysing Granok at him. He just plucked Naftali out of the air like a flower," he added bitterly.

"What about Helena? Little Till? And the Fortenskys?" asked Oksa.

"They were all recaptured."

Oksa could barely breathe.

"Are they still… alive?"

"According to our feathered informers, everyone's safe and sound. They are in very low spirits and some of them are injured, but their lives aren't in danger."

Despite Abakum's reassuring tone, Oksa looked sceptical.

"Could that change?" she asked.

She saw Tugdual stiffen. She gnawed her lower lip and clenched her fists. Curiosity killed the cat; contrary to all expectations, it was Tugdual who answered:

"Of course it could change. Ocious could decide to kill all of them at any moment."

"Ocious, or Orthon," added Abakum, gazing into the distance.

17

A Gentle Awakening

Although comfortable, Oksa's first night in Leafhold was unusual, to say the least. Sleeping in a hard-earth hollow between the roots of a giant tree was hardly run-of-the-mill, even by Oksa's standards, and she'd racked up an impressive list of bizarre experiences. Her hosts had showered her with kindness, giving her an area with a canopied bed surrounded by fine grey linen curtains and covered with a purple wool throw, a small chest of drawers topped with a basin and a tiny mirror, as well as some clothes laid out on a bench formed by one of the roots. She was too exhausted to wash, though. On the ceiling, a Polypharus cast a gentle light, creating restful movements reminiscent of those in an aquarium. Oksa collapsed onto the bed, fully dressed. All feelings of suffocation, claustrophobia and anxiety gradually ebbed away and sleep soon claimed her.

It was strange waking up somewhere like this. Being a few hundred yards below ground made it a little airless and, although she knew where she was, she had no idea of the time. Was it still dark or already light? Had she slept for two or twelve hours? One thing was certain: she felt perfectly rested. Somewhat reluctantly, she clambered out of her cosy bed and proceeded to scrutinize her appearance.

"Hmm… I've definitely looked better," she groused, inspecting parts of her face in the tiny mirror.

Since she'd undergone that accelerated ageing process, she hadn't had many opportunities to study her reflection or get used to it. Her face was so drawn, with purple bags under her slate-grey eyes, and her hair so tangled that she struggled to recognize herself. She ran her fingers over her cheeks, leaving streaks of black dust. Her jeans and tee-shirt were covered in glistening marks like snail slime, clearly showing where the Invisibuls had been.

"I look disgusting," she sighed.

Instinctively her thoughts turned to Tugdual. How did he manage to be so irresistible all the time? Whatever the circumstances, he remained ab-so-lu-te-ly flawless, as if he were untouchable. "It's like he's from another planet," thought Oksa, giggling at that incongruous thought. "He's just a bit more supernatural than everybody else here!"

"What's so funny, my Lil' Gracious?" asked a familiar voice behind her.

Oksa turned round and blushed when she saw Tugdual casually leaning against the earthen wall, his arms crossed and his eyes fixed on her. He was wearing that incomparable half-smile that made his cheekbones stand out and left his cheeks in shadow.

"Oh, I was thinking that I look awful compared to you!" she replied, incapable of saying anything else. "The grubby scullery maid and Prince Charming, you get the sort of thing?"

Tugdual approached with feline grace. He put his hands on her shoulders and landed a light kiss at the corner of her mouth.

"A grubby scullery maid, yeah right," he sighed, looking her up and down.

"Stop looking at me!" murmured Oksa nervously.

Rather than obeying, Tugdual picked up a cloth, dampened it in the water in the basin, then gently washed Oksa's face while she trembled with embarrassment.

"That smells nice," she whispered.

It didn't help that Tugdual was so close to her, which made her flush even redder. Why couldn't she learn to keep her mouth shut? Why did she keep saying such stupid things?

"It's essence of Nobilis," explained Tugdual. "If you like, I'll show you where they grow in their hundreds."

Oksa nodded. She remembered her first "encounter" with a Nobilis. She'd been in Abakum's secret silo and the plant had chuckled with pleasure, caressing her with its petals. Another bizarre experience. Meanwhile, Tugdual continued to clean her face, the bridge of her nose, her eyelids, and her fingers, while she was desperate for him to kiss her. But he didn't, signalling the end of this wash by gently stroking her cheek.

"Put those on now," he said, pointing to the clothes laid out on the root bench. "I'll wait for you next door."

He went out, closing the curtain that divided the room from the rest of the underground dwelling. With a great deal of difficulty, Oksa pulled off her jeans stained with pearly streaks and her dirty tee-shirt and put on a pair of trousers and a short khaki tunic fragrant with a clean, comforting smell that reminded her of their house in Bigtoe Square, her mother and normal life. Tears sprang to her eyes. No. It wasn't a good idea to dwell on the past. Not when it spoilt the present, anyway. She took a deep breath, held her head high and opened the curtain.

※

She hadn't seen them when she'd arrived, but the creatures and the "living" plants were also there beneath the tree. There were those she knew well—Incompetents, Squoracles, Getorixes, Ptitchkins, Polyglossipers and Goranovs, all belonging to the Runaways—and others she'd never seen before, particularly a kind of hedgehog with soft spines and a strange marmot-like animal with an electric blue pelt.

"Watch out! Watch out!" cried the Goranov. "The Young Gracious is among us!"

"That should make you happy, not upset, lettuce!" retorted the Getorix, tossing back its abundant hair. "If the Young Gracious is here, it's to save our skins."

Shivering violently, the Goranov uttered a long wail. Then, after one final convulsion, all its leaves collapsed down the length of its stem. The shock had overloaded its sensitive mind.

"I like it here, and there's nothing wrong with my skin," remarked the Incompetent languidly.

Oksa couldn't help it: she burst into contagious laughter, attracting the attention of all the men, women and creatures, who laughed too. Except for the Incompetent, which didn't know what was funny and was staring at her with a blissfully stupid expression on its face.

"I'm so happy to see it again!" she said, wiping her eyes.

She tried to regain a straight face before greeting everyone who was eating lunch, sitting cross-legged on big cushions before trays on three-legged stools. Her father and Abakum looked tired, but less worried. As for Zoe, although her smile didn't hide her sadness, Oksa appreciated it and smiled back with genuine warmth.

"The presence of my Young Gracious in this forest site meets with honour reinforced with unanimity on the part of all beings endowed with life," announced the Lunatrix from a work surface where he was cutting bread.

Beside him, the comical creature with soft spines was spinning round and busily hoovering up every falling crumb.

"Would my Young Gracious experience the desire to ingest a piece of bread and butter?" went on the Lunatrix. "And does she express the wish to proceed with quenching her thirst?"

"Yes, please," replied Oksa. "I have to admit I'm a bit hungry."

No sooner said than done: the Lunatrix rushed over, almost dropping the little tray he was carrying. It was Zoe who reacted first, rescuing the tray with a flick of her index finger.

"I keep forgetting I know how to do that," whispered Oksa, winking at her friend.

The piping-hot white bread went down a treat. She devoured five slices of bread and butter thinly spread with a delicious jam, whose taste she couldn't place. However, when she took a sip from the cup of steaming liquid brought by the Lunatrix, she couldn't help pulling a face.

"Boohoo, the face of my Young Gracious makes the demonstration of deep disgust," lamented the small steward. "Her domestic staff encounters failure stuffed with smarting pain, boohoohoo…"

He slumped against the wall, inconsolable.

"Poor thing!" exclaimed Zoe. "He forgot to tell you he'd added some Zestillia bean extract. You have to think how you want your drink to taste and the Zestillia will do your bidding."

Oksa smacked her forehead with the flat of her hand. Of course! She concentrated, sipped her drink again and smiled. The Lunatrix, watching his mistress's reactions closely, immediately raised his large head.

"The forgetfulness of that instruction will perpetuate remorse in the heart of your domestic staff until the end of his days," he sobbed.

"There's no harm done, my Lunatrix," cried Oksa, kneeling in front of him. "You're a miracle-worker!"

She hugged him and gave him a resounding kiss on the cheek. The Lunatrix turned as purple as an aubergine.

"What flavour did you choose?" asked Lucy.

"Black tea with citrus and spices," replied Oksa. "A Russian 'Dragomira-style' recipe."

Her eyes misted over. She buried her nose in her cup and drank the rest of the tea, despite the painful lump in her throat.

"Right, Lil' Gracious, now I'd like to show you something," said Tugdual. "Come on!"

18

A Private Chat
in Leafhold

O KSA WAS SURPRISED HOW EASY IT HAD BEEN TO GET HER father and Abakum to let her go out, even thought they'd hit her and Tugdual with an avalanche of advice first. The main reason for this unprecedented freedom was that Ocious's garrisons were billeted around Leafhold and they only maintained a presence within the city at strategic points such as exits, squares and shopping areas. Before moving aside, Pavel had given Oksa one last slightly worried look, then had glared threateningly at Tugdual—if anything happened to his daughter while she was in his care, Tugdual would have to face his wrath.

"After everything I've gone through, don't you think I'm capable of looking after myself? Don't be such a scaredy-cat!"

Pavel had been about to tousle her hair, but had thought better of it. His little Oksa was now the New Gracious.

When the two teenagers emerged after climbing countless steps, Oksa was finally able to breathe in the pure air of Leafhold. She'd glimpsed snatches of the tree city the night before, but hadn't had a chance to appreciate its scale and vitality.

The tree on which she and Tugdual were perched was at the centre of the vast forest. The lower branches of this magnificent sylvan giant were nearly seventy feet above the ground. An internal staircase carved in the trunk led up to a platform that provided a foundation for about ten homes. Tugdual grabbed Oksa's hand and pressed it against the bark.

"Hey! It's breathing!" she exclaimed.

She rested her cheek against the trunk to hear the tree's steady respiration.

"That's insane!" she cried, her eyes shining. Tugdual smiled and began leading her among the houses. It wasn't very bright, as the daylight was absorbed by the thick cloud cover and then by the many feet of foliage and branches which stopped it from penetrating to the ground. Lower down, the undergrowth had been cleared away but was still plunged in dark green, shifting shadows. When a patch of light finally filtered through, Oksa gave a cry of surprise at the hive of activity on the ground. Men and women were walking back and forth with wheeled baskets or tools, accompanied by various creatures. Their clothes boasted natural shades of brown, green, grey and russet and they were carrying a variety of unusually large products which aroused Oksa's admiration: potatoes as big as watermelons, olives the size of melons, and some enormous tubers she didn't recognize.

"Make no mistake, Lil' Gracious," Tugdual informed her. "Just because you see this quantity of food doesn't mean that people aren't going without. A lot of things are still in short supply and the soil has become much less fertile. It's as exhausted as the people."

They walked across the platform side by side, passing men and women who greeted them deferentially. Oksa peered inquisitively into windows and marvelled at the complex system of zip-lines and pulleys that allowed goods to be transported to every level. Drainpipes and gutters were fitted to trunks and roofs to channel drips of water into reservoirs at the foot of every dwelling or above the plants that grew over their walls, since every house was adorned with vertical crops that had taken root in the packed earth. "What a clever way to save water," thought Oksa. She noticed a wooden hoist with steel cables that seemed to extend much higher. She looked up: about fifty feet above, several platforms rested on the massive branches of the surrounding trees. Linked together by a number of movable bridges, these terraces formed a jaw-dropping multi-level labyrinth which Oksa wanted to visit, so she made her way towards the hoist.

"We don't need machines," said Tugdual. "Follow me."

He began climbing the trunk.

"Hey! I can't do that!" protested Oksa.

"Then do what you know how to do, Lil' Gracious," called Tugdual.

He seemed to be clinging to the tree bark by the sheer strength of his nails, which galvanized Oksa into action and she launched herself into an energetic Vertiflight.

"See what you can do if you want to," remarked Tugdual, continuing his ascent.

They passed several floors of inhabited platforms to reach the one at the top of the tree, Tugdual as nimbly as a monkey, Oksa as effortlessly as a starling. Oksa kept circling Tugdual clinging to the trunk, mocking him with pirouettes each more acrobatic than the last.

When they reached the top terrace they sat down beside each other, their feet dangling in space, and gazed at Leafhold, spread out in all its glory. Open-mouthed with wonder—she'd never seen anything more breathtaking—Oksa surveyed the landscape of giant trees stretching towards the horizon like a sea of green.

"Beautiful, isn't it?" said Tugdual softly.

"Out of this world," replied Oksa. "Just think of all those houses, and all the people living in them, among the branches. They're like green skyscrapers."

"They are, although unfortunately most of the houses are empty now," said Tugdual.

"Why?"

"From what Edgar told me, Leafhold had over three thousand inhabitants when Edefia was at the height of its splendour. Since the Great Chaos, the population has dwindled. What with the shortages, the Diaphans and the decline, people no longer had the heart to bring more children into the world. In fact, you'll see very few toddlers and even fewer babies. That's how a civilization fizzles out: people die without handing over the reins."

Beyond the green belt of the forest, the desert formed a shocking contrast. Despite its vast size, the tree city seemed to be clinging on for dear life in the midst of a vast, deadly wasteland that would wipe out every living thing given half a chance. This was apparent from the skeletons of trees around the city, their bare branches desperately twisted towards the survivors as if calling for help—or as if wanting them to share their fate. Oksa shivered. Tugdual put his arm around her shoulders and, instinctively, she leant her head against him. Relishing this time together, she reached for Tugdual's hand and their fingers entwined.

"Kiss me," she found herself demanding.

"Whatever you say, my Lil' Gracious."

Had she ever experienced anything so intense?

So right?

Tugdual was perfect for her. He softly began singing the chorus from 'Never Let Me Down Again' by Depeche Mode.

> *We're flying high*
> *We're watching the world pass us by*
> *Never want to come down*
> *Never want to put my feet back down*
> *On the ground.*

A flock of swiftly moving birds of a species neither of them recognized flew overhead. The birds suddenly dived into the foliage of the trees, then emerged cheeping loudly, which amused Oksa. However, when an enormous dragonfly flew near her, she tensed with disgust.

"It won't hurt you," said Tugdual reassuringly, tightening his arm around her.

"Yes, but look at the size of it! It's like an eagle!"

Tugdual burst out laughing.

"An eagle? A blackbird, at the very most. Look how pretty it is!"

He put out his arm and the dragonfly landed confidently on it. Its iridescent blue-green wings were beating very fast, making a tractor-like drone that contrasted with their delicate appearance. Oksa recoiled.

"Your relationship with insects doesn't seem to have improved," said Tugdual.

Oksa pulled a face.

"It won't. I'll never be able to bear those disgusting creatures!"

"They do have their uses though," teased Tugdual, letting the dragonfly fly away.

"Well, let them be useful as far away from me as possible."

Suddenly a group of youngsters flew past, clinging to flying boards similar to the ones Oksa had seen used by Ocious's guards when they'd come to "welcome" them to Edefia. They were literally surfing over the air to stretch a rope between two treetops.

"What are those things?" she asked, fascinated.

"Aeropellers," replied Tugdual. "They're made from a material that harnesses and stores solar energy."

"You're such a know-all!"

"Excuse me, but while the Young Gracious was busy having fun in the Cloak Chamber, I was gathering material and learning all kinds of interesting things. Contrary to appearances, I'm an inquisitive and open-minded person."

"Yeah, you're a real humanist, aren't you?" replied Oksa, her eyes sparkling.

They watched the sky surfers for a while. Oksa's sighs grew louder and more pitiful with the passing minutes. Tugdual glanced at her out of the corner of his eye and smiled.

"I know what you're thinking, but they're reserved for people who aren't lucky enough to be able to Vertifly."

"That's such a pity," sighed Oksa. "I'd have loved to have a go."

"There's too little solar energy to spare now but perhaps one day, when things get better…"

Tugdual fell silent, watching the comings and goings of the Sylvabuls farther down.

"Do you think things will get better?" asked Oksa, almost inaudibly.

Tugdual didn't answer for a few interminable seconds.

"Yes. Things are *already* better."

"Do you really think so?" asked Oksa, sounding unsure.

"You escaped Ocious and Orthon."

"Is that enough?"

"It's the only thing that counts. Everything else is secondary."

Oksa turned her head sharply to look at him.

"Do you realize what you're saying?" she asked, while he stared doggedly at the horizon.

"Do you realize what you represent?" he retorted.

Oksa didn't reply. Sometimes she felt that her role meant more to other people than it did to her, and this wasn't the first time that it had been pointed out. Ashamed, she nibbled a nail, watching Tugdual out of the corner of her eye.

"What happened in the Peak Ridge Mountains?" she asked, changing the subject abruptly.

Tugdual took a deep breath and stretched, cracking his knuckles.

"Only what Edgar told you," he said.

Oksa was seething. It wasn't what Tugdual said, but his deceptively casual tone that infuriated her.

"Edgar didn't say anything," she protested. "He just told us—"

"—what you needed to know," snapped Tugdual, interrupting her.

Oksa shifted away from him. Her cheeks were flushed and her eyes darkened.

"I'm just trying to work out… who you are," she growled.

"Don't you think I should work out who I am first before I can tell you?"

Oksa froze, despite her frustration, which was making it hard for her to catch her breath.

"Why don't you trust me?" she managed to say.

Tugdual sat perfectly still. Oksa wasn't even sure he'd heard the question. Then suddenly the floodgates opened, and he poured out his heart just as he'd done on the boat taking the Runaways to the island in the Sea of the Hebrides.

"What do you want me to tell you? That leaving you with Ocious hurt as badly as watching my father leave? That thinking I'd lost everything almost sent me out of my mind? That I didn't want to be saved when I lost myself in those mountains? The Vigilians almost killed me when I was perfectly capable of reducing them to a smoking pile of ashes. If you really want to know, I was so unhappy that I didn't care if I lived or died. I only let those people save me because they needed me. Can you understand that? I needed to be needed!"

Those last words were hammered out with all the force of his overwhelming despair and Oksa froze, holding her breath. It was only when her body told her she was about to suffocate that she gave a violent start, as if waking from a nightmare. And her confusion only grew when Tugdual took her face in his hands and kissed her even more fiercely after his intimate revelations.

"Being around you isn't for the faint-hearted," she murmured. Tugdual didn't have time to reply. Suddenly on the alert, he jumped up and examined the mass of greenery around them. He grabbed Oksa's hand.

"Let's go," he said. "Ocious's men aren't far away."

They both slipped from their high perch and plunged into the emptiness below.

19

PURSUIT THROUGH
THE FOREST

O KSA DROPPED LIKE A STONE.
   "Vertifly!" shouted Tugdual.

"I can't!" she yelled, frantically flapping her arms to no avail.

Immediately Tugdual flew over and grabbed her tightly from behind, halting the fall that would have killed her.

"Don't be silly!" he whispered. "Of course you can!"

Anxiously, his eyes scanned the area like a radar. He gradually relaxed his grip, giving Oksa time to shake off the paralysing panic. Just below, a troop of guards in leather armour was walking through the forest between the trees. Oksa needed no further prompting: her face tense with concentration, she took off and followed Tugdual for two miles to the borders of Leafhold, heading in the opposite direction to the patrol. The belt of dead vegetation, which was a stone's throw away, formed a hideous contrast with the lush abundance of the forest city. Tugdual guided Oksa to a dilapidated platform with four seemingly abandoned houses where they landed, out of breath.

"Whatever happens, don't take out your Granok-Shooter, okay?" warned Tugdual. "Only five of us here have one, so it wouldn't be hard for them to work out who we are."

He suddenly shoved her under the withered arbour of one of the houses and pressed himself against her, standing perfectly still behind the tattered dry stems and leaves. A few seconds later about twenty guards sped past. Tugdual put his hand over Oksa's mouth.

"They're searching for you."

Oksa's eyes widened with fear.

"What are we going to do?" she whispered.

Tugdual carefully looked around.

"We'll head back to the Monumental Tree. If you see one of Ocious's guards, try to act naturally, as though you live here. Don't go too quickly or you'll attract attention."

"But Sylvabuls can't Vertifly!" objected Oksa. "They'll notice us immediately."

"Although the Sylvabuls are in the majority here, a few Long-Gulches and Firmhands live here, and some of them have done for several generations. Vertifliers are a common sight, so there's nothing to be afraid of. In that respect, anyway."

He looked right and left, then up and down, and took Oksa's hand.

"The coast is clear. I'll go first and you can follow me."

"What if we're separated?" asked Oksa, her voice shaking.

"The Monumental Tree is straight ahead. At the worst, Vertifly high up. It's taller than all the other trees, so you can't miss it."

He took her face in his hands, gazed intently at her and dropped a kiss on her forehead.

"It'll be okay, Lil' Gracious."

They took off cautiously and disappeared into the forest.

❊

Everything went smoothly until they came face to face with a patrol that appeared without warning. The two Vertifliers stopped dead, like Oksa's heart when the guards surrounded them. Tugdual glanced steadily at her, urging her to stay calm and strong.

"State your identity!" ordered one of the men.

To Oksa's great surprise, Tugdual replied:

"Henning, son of Gunnar, Firmhand."

The guard consulted the crystal tablet in his hands. He looked perfectly happy with Tugdual's answer. Then he turned to Oksa:

"What about you?"

Acrid sweat trickled down the Young Gracious's temple.

"This is my cousin, Ingrid," said Tugdual.

The guard again examined his tablet, then eyed Oksa suspiciously. Few of them had been privileged enough to see the New Gracious in person and, despite Ocious's description, the girl before him looked just like any other girl of her age. Unless she had that famous distinguishing mark...

"Show us your belly button!" he demanded authoritatively.

Tugdual looked at Oksa and unwittingly his forehead furrowed. The alert guard reacted immediately.

"Is that a problem?"

The guards instinctively positioned themselves to take immediate action.

"No problem!" answered Oksa.

As Tugdual struggled to hide his concern, she raised the bottom of her tunic.

"Okay!" declared the guard, after staring at it for a few seconds.

Oksa's belly button looked completely ordinary. There was no trace of any star like the one Ocious had mentioned.

"Who's your father?"

Oksa stared at him, appearing much calmer than she actually felt. Around her wrist the Curbita-Flatulo was undulating with all its might to keep her from showing any weakness. However, the grey sky was becoming more overcast. If the situation worsened, the storm would break. There was no doubt about it.

"My father?" she asked.

The guards closed in.

"Don't mind her. It's not her fault," said Tugdual.

He pressed closer to Oksa, holding her arm firmly. It wouldn't take much for her to shoot into the air.

"She's a bit... you know..."

"A bit what?" pressed the guard.

"A bit simple," continued Tugdual confidingly. "Her father's Lars. We came looking for provisions in Leafhold."

The guard studied them long and hard with an unpleasant expression on his face. After a few moments, which felt like light years to Oksa, he moved back.

"Okay, you can go." he said. "Try not to wander around on your own."

Oksa almost asked him if he was worried they might meet the wrong kind of people, but Tugdual was already pulling her away.

"Let's get out of here," he murmured.

She obeyed.

⁂

"That was a narrow escape!" said Tugdual.

He glanced at her enquiringly.

"I didn't know about your star."

"The star marked me out as the future Gracious," explained Oksa. "When I was enthroned, it floated away. I knew it was safe to lift up my tunic. You had me fooled, though."

Tugdual had given her a masterclass in keeping cool and she was impressed.

"Well done!" she said softly, Vertiflying level with him. "How did you know all that?"

"It wasn't hard to know what they were bound to ask. I just made sure I had the answers off pat."

"Is there really an Ingrid? And a Henning?"

"Of course!" replied Tugdual. "In these circumstances, it's always a good idea to have an alias up your sleeve."

"Okay," nodded Oksa. "I'll try to remember that."

"Anyway, let's not get ahead of ourselves. It's possible I didn't convince them. I may only have delayed them by sowing the seeds of doubt."

They continued Vertiflying carefully side by side.

"I was afraid of that," exclaimed Tugdual suddenly, without even bothering to look back. "Don't turn round, they're following us."

"Oh, no," wailed Oksa, "why won't they leave us alone?"

They flew faster, zigzagging between trees and terraces, trying to act as naturally as possible, but the guards didn't seem to be deceived. They'd been joined by another patrol, so they were being pursued by a good fifty of them. Oksa and Tugdual began dodging in and out of the trees in earnest, rising and falling, turning suddenly to the right, forking sharply to the left. Despite their skill, though, they couldn't outdistance Ocious's men, who had the advantage of numbers.

"Stop!" cried a voice.

Far from obeying this order, Oksa tried even harder to stay beside Tugdual. During this time, scores of Leafhold's inhabitants had leapt to their defence and were doing their bit by blocking the Vertiflying guards' route using the most ingenious methods: casting nets, releasing helpful birds, catapulting wooden balls... Oksa was over the moon to see a guard hit head-on by a basket fired from a zip-line. One down! However, guards were flocking from all directions and the danger facing Oksa and Tugdual was growing greater with every second. So, when Tugdual pointed to a platform below, they swooped down without a moment's thought and, covered by a defensive Sylvabul front, they slipped beneath the terrace and clung to the wooden beams like spiders, hidden by a curtain of hanging vines.

"I'm going to fall," muttered Oksa, concentrating all her energy on her hands and feet.

Around the tree where the two friends were hiding, the battle raged. Sylvabuls riding on Aeropellers raised hell in the ranks of Ocious's guards, rocketing past like screaming hurricanes.

Suddenly a trapdoor opened above Oksa. An arm appeared and grabbed her tunic, pulling her out of her temporary shelter. Thinking her last hour had come, she shut her eyes, feeling heartbroken. Ocious had won.

"Come on, Young Gracious!" whispered someone, roughly man-handling her.

She opened her eyes and her face lit up: she was inside one of the houses on the platform and Edgar, the venerable Sylvabul, was facing her. She was so glad to see him that she could have flung her arms around his neck! The trapdoor banged open, then immediately shut again: Tugdual had just joined them.

"This way, quickly!" whispered Edgar.

He turned to face one of the walls covered in brown brick and, using his fingertip, traced the invisible contours of a square whose sides measured about three feet. In just a few seconds, this shape became a convenient opening. Edgar pushed down on Oksa's head, urging her to slip inside the hole. Mechanically Oksa climbed into what proved to be the trunk of a hollow tree. After Tugdual and Edgar had also entered, the old man closed the exit just as magically as he'd opened it.

Beyond the wall, the three of them clearly heard terrifying shouts, threats and the sound of the front door of the house being smashed down. Then, while Oksa, flanked by Edgar and Tugdual, hid inside the tree trunk, Ocious's grim-faced guards burst into the empty house.

20

AN OLD, MAIMED LION

O CIOUS EXPLODED SO ANGRILY THAT HIS ENTOURAGE thought he might have a heart attack. It was bad enough that the Young Gracious had escaped his clutches, but the fact that everyone in Edefia was talking about his failure incensed him even further. Especially as this setback brought with it bitter disappointment: the people of Edefia had never put up such strong opposition before. No one had ever dared to insult him like this and he was reeling from such a painful blow to his ego. He couldn't remember ever feeling older or wearier. Like a maimed lion, he was looking a good deal the worse for wear, but he was still trying to maintain a certain swagger. Everything had been going downhill since the Runaways had returned. It went without saying that the presence of a New Gracious did open up new horizons for them, just when they'd thought all hope was gone. She'd saved the Heart of the Two Worlds, the rain had returned and there was a good chance they'd be able to reopen the Portal… He would at last be able to fulfil his dearest dream: to see the Outside and make the most of his overwhelming superiority over the humans, none of whom, not even the strongest, could rival his vast abilities. However, in the meantime, the Last Hope was undermining the social order he'd spent his whole life establishing.

"You were right, Father," announced Andreas dully. "The Young Gracious was in Leafhold."

Orthon glanced scornfully at him. How low would his hated half-brother stoop to get into their father's good books?

"You all seem shocked by their reaction," he said, fixing his strange aluminium-coloured gaze on Ocious. "But this rebellion was not only predictable: it was inevitable."

He kept his eyes on his father.

"I know what you're thinking," he said softly. "You and I are the same, we know that strength is all that matters and that fine feelings have nothing to do with the acquisition of power. Your big mistake was to treat your people with restraint, and what happened in Leafhold only proves it."

Ocious was surrounded by about ten of his staunchest supporters. They all squirmed on their seats—the prodigal son was going too far. Everyone held their breath as the Docent glared at him with narrowed eyes.

"How dare you?" he growled through clenched teeth.

Orthon didn't look flustered. He smoothed back his hair with one hand, then continued:

"Instead of reprimanding me, you should face facts. You took too many precautions to avoid hurting these people. And the end result is that you've turned them into rebels who no longer respect your authority."

He paused for a second, before delivering his damning conclusion:

"The people of Edefia aren't afraid of you any more, Father."

A heavy silence ensued and everyone in the room looked down in dismay, lost for words. Everyone except for the Docent and his two sons. Orthon and Ocious were facing each other and Andreas was glowering at his half-brother with icy hatred.

"You have no idea of the difficulties we've endured for nearly sixty years," thundered Ocious. "I've done what I could to maintain order and preserve life in a slowly dying land. Do you think it's easy to uphold the law in these conditions? Do you think it's simple to survive when everything is collapsing around you?"

His lower lip was trembling when he added:

"Do you think it isn't painful coping with a nation's ingratitude?" Orthon interrupted with an insolent snort of laughter, shocking everyone. He sank into his armchair, placed his arms on the armrests and crossed his legs. Ocious paled with rage. His eyes flickered almost imperceptibly, but Orthon didn't miss a thing.

"Father, you might be able to fool everyone into believing you're acting for them and with them," Orthon said, motioning to Ocious's supporters. "But not me. Don't tell me you're convinced you've been magnanimous! You haven't, and the people aren't ungrateful, as you persist in saying: they've merely realized that you've been using them to satisfy your own personal ambitions for years. And you know it!"

"Your father is an extraordinary man!" protested a bearded man near Ocious. "Everything he's done has been for us, the people of Edefia."

Orthon sighed noisily.

"My words might be harsh, but I respect my father," he said. "I respect him and I understand him. And that's because, in many ways, we're very much alike."

"You're greatly mistaken, Orthon," snapped Andreas. "Father and you are complete opposites. Despite what you think and despite criticism by the people of Edefia, Father has always obeyed certain principles, while you have no scruples and accept no limits. You criticized him for being ambitious, but what ambition did you mean? That of wanting to leave Edefia? Few of us haven't at least once in our lives wanted to see the Outside. That of wanting power? For your information, our land has been in such a bad way for so many years that it's been more of a burden than a privilege."

With a sceptical stare, Orthon clapped slowly with a mocking smile.

"You'll reduce me to tears in a moment," he said.

Ocious raised his hand, his large palm outward.

"Enough of this bickering!" he bellowed.

Turning to Orthon, he said:

"Well, my son, if you're so clever, why don't you give us the benefit of your dazzling intellect and experience and prove to us that your methods are better than mine. If I've been going about things in the wrong way, then show me the right way. What do you have in mind?"

❃

It was after this fraught conversation that Ocious decided to listen to the fascinating theories put forward by the son he'd never really believed in. Speaking to an attentive audience, it took Orthon several hours to explain what he'd learnt after years of witnessing various political and ideological upheavals on the Outside. In particular, it had been his career with the CIA—the powerful American intelligence agency—that had given him an insider's insight into the mechanisms, challenges and strategies of men in power, whether they were committed democrats or power-hungry dictators. Ocious didn't interrupt. He listened enthralled, his mind working furiously, as Orthon revisited different times and places. Ocious's silent attention strengthened the Felon's credibility and earned him valuable brownie points. Occasionally Ocious frowned or gasped in surprise at his similarity to some of the Outside's most hated leaders. He was also amazed to learn so much from the son he'd always regarded as a loser.

After this speech, aware of his own limitations, Ocious put his trust in Orthon, which would have been an unthinkable concession a few days ago. Despite the general disapproval, Orthon seized the opportunity without a second glance at his hated half-brother and the honourable Werewalls who'd blindly followed Ocious for nearly six decades.

21

CRISIS MEETING

"I PROMISE WE WERE CAREFUL, DAD!"

Oksa blinked the tears away as she faced her father.

"I know, Oksa," Pavel said eventually. "That's not the problem."

She looked at him questioningly.

"Ocious knows you're here now," he continued. "And that's bad."

Everyone in front of her looked gloomy.

"We're ready to give our lives for our Young Gracious!" came one voice.

Other men and women echoed the words, while Oksa shuddered.

"Don't say that," she whispered, deathly pale.

"Ocious will do his utmost to get his hands on you," added Abakum. "And we'll do everything we can to stop him. Still, the balance of power may not be as much in his favour as he thinks."

"What do you mean?" asked Oksa.

"Men like Ocious have always underestimated their enemies. He may have been proved right often in the past, but things change. I think he was shocked to the core by the way our friends in Leafhold protected you because, despite his dictatorial approach, he's ill-equipped to deal with opposition. That's usually the Achilles heel of tyrants: their power is often based on the fear they inspire. People keep quiet, convinced they've no choice but to submit. Then, as soon as someone throws a spanner in the works, the tyrant panics."

Oksa looked dubious.

"Ocious still has the power to hurt you," she remarked. "He can do a lot of damage. Don't forget he has soldiers and weapons, as well as everyone's Granok-Shooters. How do you plan to counteract that? It seems to me that the balance of power is very one-sided: we're far more vulnerable than him."

Oksa was trembling.

"I have a horrible feeling that out-and-out war is coming and that frightens me a little," she whispered, unable to meet anyone's eyes.

Tugdual walked over to her and discreetly took her hand. Pavel gazed at her with an expression of deep sadness.

"More than a little," she continued quietly. "I'm terrified."

She gnawed her lip. She would have done better to keep quiet, but despite the ordeals she'd gone through and her adventurous nature, she'd never felt less like a Gracious. These people had waited so long, only to end up governed by a wimp. What a disappointment she must be to them!

"Oksa, sweetheart," said Abakum suddenly. "Believe in yourself. Believe in all of us."

Then, turning to the gathered throng, he added:

"My friends, we have some difficult times ahead, but I'm asking you to have faith. Even if you think everything is hopeless, remember we have secret allies."

He looked at them one by one, then announced mysteriously:

"Please don't think I'm abandoning you at such a time of great danger— instead cherish the belief that I'm preparing for the future."

With these words he turned into a hare. Oksa put a hand over her mouth to stifle a cry as he bounded up the staircase inside the Monumental Tree that led to the surface.

❖

A violent jolt shook the underground roots of the tree. Oksa glanced up in concern at the ceiling as small clumps of earth showered down. She was now alone with her father and Tugdual, a hundred feet below the surface, feeling angry and powerless. All the Edefians who'd welcomed her so warmly were putting themselves in danger for her and because of her—it was almost more than she could bear.

"Don't even think about it, Oksa," said her father sternly.

"But, Dad, we can't let them get themselves killed without lifting a finger to help!" she protested.

They were too deep to hear anything. The total silence was oppressive and it made the wait even worse. Unable to bear it any longer, Pavel suddenly jumped up.

"Don't leave this room!" he ordered, jabbing his finger at Oksa. "This is the only place you're safe, no one will look for you here."

Oksa gazed at him imploringly.

"No, Oksa."

Pavel turned to Tugdual.

"Tugdual, I'm counting on you."

Tugdual nodded silently, as Oksa stifled a cry of anger.

"I'm fed up with this!" she raged, as her father took the stairs four at a time. "No one trusts me!"

"You know very well it's got nothing to do with trust, Lil' Gracious."

Minutes passed, feeling like hours, then Oksa again voiced her disagreement.

"This is the first time I've hated being left alone with you," she grumbled, glaring at Tugdual.

Tugdual shrugged without replying, which exasperated Oksa even more.

"I can't believe you'd rather obey my father than make me happy."

"This isn't about making you happy, Oksa."

Tugdual only called her "Oksa" when he was deadly serious, and she didn't like it one bit.

"You're so annoying."

"These are tough times," he replied. "Why don't you stop acting like a child?"

Oksa gasped: Tugdual didn't seem to be joking. At all. She hunkered down on her cushion, her mind seething. Dismay was soon replaced by steely determination.

"May I get a glass of water, Mr Foreman?" she asked defiantly.

"Go ahead!" he replied, waving her on. Oksa got up and went over to the work surface where the kitchen utensils and drinking water were kept. Tugdual had his back to her: she'd be mad to pass up such a perfect opportunity. Unfortunately, the only way out was at the other end of the room. She couldn't get past Tugdual without him seeing her. What about through the wall? She rested her hand against the packed earth.

"You've not been a Werewall long enough," came Tugdual's voice. "It's not that easy, you know."

Oksa cursed. How had he guessed? You'd think he had eyes in the back of his head, or that he could read her mind. It was so annoying. She hadn't exhausted all possibilities, though. She opened her Caskinette—the small magic box filled with Capacitors—and swallowed an Excelsior to boost her mental performance. Then she sat back down opposite her stubborn friend, her face expressionless. She met Tugdual's eyes and stared at him unblinkingly.

"What are you doing?" he asked quietly. "Are you trying to hypnotize me? Or seduce me with your lovely eyes?"

Oksa concentrated very hard to remain impassive.

"It won't work, whatever you're trying to do," continued Tugdual. "I won't be swayed by any of your machinations."

She loved him so much and she really regretted what she was going to have to do to him. But she had no choice.

22

THE LEAFHOLD REVOLT

THE TWO FIREBALLISTICOS SPURTED SIMULTANEOUSLY from Oksa's right and left hands and flew straight at Tugdual, who had to throw himself on the floor to avoid them. The Young Gracious immediately made a dash for the staircase and began climbing quicker than she'd ever thought possible. It didn't take Tugdual long to react. He raced in pursuit, matching her impressive burst of speed, but she was determined not to lose her slight lead. She took the stairs four at a time, avoiding the roots, with her head down and her muscles flexed. But despite her best efforts, Tugdual was gaining on her—his feline side was a definite asset.

"Stop, Oksa!"

Oksa didn't bother to reply. She merely redoubled her efforts to outdistance her pursuer. However, a hand suddenly grabbed the bottom of her tunic.

"Enough now!" scolded Tugdual, yanking on the garment.

Oksa twisted violently to free herself. The fabric ripped, freeing her to continue her ascent, leaving Tugdual sprawled on the stairs.

When she reached what qualified as ground level in the Monumental Tree, she had to make a quick decision: should she exit now or continue climbing inside the trunk? With her hands on her thighs, she caught her breath and considered carefully. The entrance of the tree was a secret. If anyone saw her coming out, the Sylvabuls' only safe refuge would be discovered. She looked up at the second spiral staircase carved inside the trunk and continued her ascent. There were landings every sixty feet, providing access to a platform. Oksa decided to stop at the third level. The noise from outside wasn't as muffled as it had been when she'd been among the underground roots. Obviously, as Abakum had predicted, Ocious had attacked: shouts, explosions, the smell of burning—it didn't bode well. Oksa took a deep breath, grabbed her Granok-Shooter and pushed open the door built into the trunk.

She ventured a cautious look outside and clapped her hand over her mouth.

"Oh no…"she groaned.

Only the night before, the luxuriant undergrowth had been the epitome of order and abundance. It had taken Ocious and his henchmen only a few hours to lay waste to one of the few places in Edefia where a certain harmony still reigned.

Around the Monumental Tree, in the deepening twilight, a pitiless battle was being waged among the Parasols and Broad-Leaved Ball trees: Ocious's ruthless and destructive soldiers were pitting themselves against the inhabitants of Leafhold, who were driven by sheer force of desperation. Fire was proving ineffective—after the heavy rain of the past few days, the flames weren't burning for long—so the soldiers were firing explosive Granoks which Oksa had never seen before and which were causing widespread damage. They decimated everything: houses, platforms, trees, bridges, people. Ten Sylvabuls clinging to Aeropellers flew past the terrace which was Oksa's vantage point. Holding on to their flying boards with one hand and a long whip with the other, these courageous fighters swooped down on a group of soldiers preparing to attack a Majestic. Lifting their whips in the air, they brought them down with all their might on the vandals. Some of the soldiers crashed to the ground, others dropped their Granok-Shooters, which were immediately snatched up by a band of Vertifliers. There was another explosion to the left: a Feetinsky, an Edefian variety of banyan tree, had come under attack by the soldiers. If the tree had been endowed with speech, Oksa was sure it would have been screaming.

But she had no need to hear it to know how much it was suffering: its aerial roots were writhing in agony. They suddenly convulsed, reached for the sky, then froze and collapsed with a loud crash like an enormous green octopus. The Feetinsky was dead. Oksa was furious. She lay flat on the platform, wriggled to the edge and began aiming at any of Ocious's soldiers within reach of her Granok-Shooter.

> By the power of the Granoks,
> Think outside the box
> Arborescens, with your knots,
> Bind them on the spot.

"Do you want a hand?"

Oksa was concentrating so hard on her attack that she didn't even bother to look round.

"You took your time," she muttered, firing two Granoks.

"I'll have you know that I was attacked by a madwoman who did her best to kill me!" grumbled Tugdual.

Oksa dimpled as she gave a barely restrained smile.

"Well, since you survived, make yourself useful! Get to work!"

Tugdual took out his blowpipe and, hidden on their terrace, the two of them showered the soldiers with Granoks, wreaking havoc. The men dropped like flies, trussed up by sticky creepers.

The astounded inhabitants of Leafhold watched this rout. They circled the trees on their Aeropellers, then swooped down on fellow Edefians who were now their enemies, confiscating their Granok-Shooters.

After this, time seemed to stand still. No more soldiers appeared. It was quiet except for the cracking sound of platforms and houses in the last stages of collapse. A few Sylvabuls were circling the Monumental Tree, looking for their rescuers. Oksa noticed Lucy Vertiflying. When she spotted Oksa, she flew over.

"Thank you, Young Gracious!" she said, waving to her.

"Look out!" cried a man behind her. "The soldiers are coming back."

Some fifty men clad in armour and leather helmets suddenly materialized from the undergrowth strewn with debris. Blowing into their Granok-Shooters, they fired hundreds of explosive Granoks at the Monumental Tree. The hoist and several terraces exploded, showering the Sylvabuls with fragments of wood and metal. All the higher structures seemed to have been destroyed deliberately to trap the people below, many of whom had been injured, some fatally. Horrified, Oksa and Tugdual spared no effort, firing a continuous volley of Arborescens and Putrefactios, until one soldier pointed at them and made a beeline for their perch. Oksa recognized him immediately.

Whatever she did and wherever she went, from St Proximus College to the borders of Edefia, Orthon McGraw was always standing in her way. She gave a shout of rage. Tugdual tensely motioned to her to vacate their spot. They crawled round to the other side of the tree as fast and nimbly as large lizards, while Orthon tried to stop them by firing Arborescens after Arborescens at them. Pressed flat against the trunk, Oksa waited patiently, eager to cross swords with her sworn enemy. Suddenly, though, Tugdual pushed her against the bark and, to her great surprise, she felt herself sinking into the tree. Her protests were smothered as she found herself inside the trunk, with Tugdual at her side.

"Why did you do that?" she protested. "I could easily have beaten him!"

"Don't be so sure," replied Tugdual, dragging her up the stairs to the higher levels of the Monumental Tree.

"I thought my Werewall skills were too new to pass through material! Anyway, what was the point of doing that? Orthon can still get to us."

"No, he can't."

Oksa stopped dead. She was out of breath from talking and climbing the stairs at the same time, and furious. With Tugdual. With Orthon. With everyone.

"What do you mean, 'he can't?'"

"The Monumental Tree is a sensitive tree," said Tugdual, continuing to climb. "It's only receptive to certain types of people."

"What? Are you telling me that it can screen people?"

"Yes. At every entrance, it detects who can or cannot come in. It'll never let Orthon in."

"How is that possible?" continued Oksa, astounded.

"It just is. Now stop asking questions and get a move on!"

She said no more and continued to climb the interminable spiral staircase. They could hear that Leafhold was still under attack from the commotion that reached the heart of the tree. At every level, Tugdual poked his face through the bark, then came back inside, looking ever more serious.

"Hey!" cried Oksa. "What's going on out there?"

"Orthon has realized we're inside the tree. He's destroying all the platforms and the structures connecting the Monumental Tree with the other trees. He's trying to trap us, Oksa. He's trying to trap *you*."

Oksa rubbed her face.

"So why are we going up instead of down to the underground rooms?"

"The staircase on the second level collapsed just after I came through. We can't get to the basement from inside any more. Be careful now, because we're at the top."

Oksa's nerves were at breaking point and she was breathing raggedly. Tugdual tried to take her hand but, instead of letting him, she reached into the little bag she wore across her shoulder and grabbed her Granok-Shooter. Tugdual nodded, doing the same, then pushed open the trapdoor concealed in the ceiling. The strong arms of two soldiers immediately lifted him up and unceremoniously sent him sprawling onto the topmost platform, the one where they'd both spent such an enjoyable interlude a few hours earlier. Oksa had just enough time to see who was waiting for her before she disappeared under a thick layer of Invisibuls.

23

A Gracious Lesson

EVERYONE WAS THERE, LOOKING AT TUGDUAL: THE PRISON-
ers from the Glass Column chained to heavy rings in the platform,
the Felons accompanied by a hundred men in armour, as well as Ocious,
flanked by Orthon and Andreas. Pavel and his Ink Dragon were circling
above with Zoe perched on its back. Instinctively, Oksa hoisted herself
through the trapdoor and rolled onto the platform just as Orthon stormed
over. If she hadn't been protected by the Invisibuls, the Felon would have
swooped on her like an eagle catching its prey. He knelt down and leant
into the trapdoor above the spiral staircase, thundering:

"Where is she?"

Tugdual gave a faint smile as Orthon yanked him upright and seized
his face in his hands.

"Where is she?" he repeated, speaking very slowly and clearly. Tugdual
stared at him unblinkingly.

"What's your considered opinion?"

Orthon's cruel expression didn't slip.

"So you think you can play fast and loose with me, do you? What do
you say to this?"

Stalking back to the trapdoor, he brandished his open palm towards
the opening.

"Orthon!" thundered Ocious.

"Yes, Father?"

Ocious gave his son a stern look, tinged with reproach.

"Now now, Father," said Orthon, with a predatory smile. "I'm just making the best of a bad job!"

Saying that, he fired a Fireballistico inside the trunk of the Monumental Tree. Flames licked at the trapdoor as the roaring fire destroyed everything in its path.

The Column's prisoners screamed in horror and the dragon bellowed, sending an ominous red tongue of fire into the sky. Orthon smugly watched Tugdual.

"So, my young friend, are you still lacking an... opinion? Or do you intend to run away like you did a few weeks ago?"

Tugdual blanched. That was a low and hurtful blow. But the Felon didn't leave it there. He turned to the prisoners—the Knuts, Bellangers and Reminiscens.

"I wonder why you persevere with someone who keeps proving that he has divided loyalties. He seems somewhat half-hearted in his support for your cause."

He drew closer to Tugdual.

"Which side do you really belong to?" he whispered. "You don't seem to be sure."

Tugdual glared at him defiantly.

"You're wasting your time."

※

Oksa felt sick beneath her layer of Invisibuls. She watched the Felon swagger slowly over to the trapdoor and fire a flurry of Fireballisticos inside the tree trunk. The fast-spreading fire was intensified by the draughts created by the platforms. At every level, bursts of flame escaped from the shaft, mercilessly devouring what was left of the buildings and structures.

Oksa Vertiflew around the giant tree, saddened by this wanton destruction and worried for the creatures that had been deep beneath the roots when she'd left. She hoped the fire wouldn't reach that far. She was so tempted to cast off her layer of Invisibuls and take revenge on Orthon for his unforgivable crime against this innocent tree. She flew back to the treetop, brushing past her father and his Ink Dragon then, gazing at the securely surrounded captives, gave up the idea. She was convinced that any action on her part would lead to heavy losses, particularly as the soldiers had their Granok-Shooters trained on the Runaways.

"Right," said Orthon, rubbing his hands complacently. "Since our young friend stubbornly refuses to break his gallant silence, we'll have to get serious."

He descended on Helena, Tugdual's mother, and snatched little Till from her arms. Panic-stricken, Helena screamed:

"No! Leave my son alone!"

She tried to run to him, but her chain held her back and she fell heavily on the rough wooden floor. Open-mouthed in amazement, the little boy stared at the Felon.

"How about a swap, my young friend," continued Orthon, walking over to Tugdual.

Till was struggling, so the Felon tightened his grip enough to reduce him to silence. Helena wailed. Beside her, Naftali and Brune were in agonies: with their feet and hands bound, and guards behind them, they were powerless to do anything as Orthon lorded it over everyone, including Ocious and Andreas.

"I'm not your young friend!" declared Tugdual, struggling to break free from the iron grip of the soldiers holding him.

Orthon brought his face very close to Tugdual's face.

"No, you're not," he said, smiling evilly. "You're so much more than that."

His steely gaze rested on him for long seconds. No one spoke. The silence was broken only by the sound of Helena sobbing and the flames crackling in the branches of the Monumental Tree.

Oksa was perfectly placed to watch the scene. Orthon, Tugdual and Till were within easy reach, yet she couldn't do anything while invisible. She walked through the Felon several times in the vain hope of deflecting him from his evil plan—she had no doubt that he was planning something totally unspeakable. But she was as immaterial as a ghost, just as she'd been when she escaped from the Isle of the Fairies. Orthon finally continued:

"Let's discuss our swap, shall we? You might say it's mere child play," he added, stroking Till's curls.

He was the only one to laugh at his little joke.

"The life of this cute little toddler in exchange for the surrender of our beloved Young Gracious. I know she's here. She's probably listening to us right now. Aren't you, Oksa?" he added, looking up.

Naftali cursed and struggled like a bear held fast in a trap, causing Ocious's henchmen to tighten their grip. Orthon lowered his voice so that only Tugdual could hear him—and Oksa, although he didn't realize it.

"For that matter, one might almost believe you were bringing her to me. Is that what you intended, Tugdual? To hand her to me on a plate? How very generous, although I didn't expect anything less. Unfortunately, though, our Young Gracious was smarter than you."

Fazed, Oksa studied Tugdual. For a fraction of a second, a brief moment detached from reality, she was gnawed by doubt, unsure of the truth. The last few hours flashed past in her memory. Tugdual had led her into danger twice: was that just an unavoidable coincidence in these troubled times or a deliberate ploy?

"You're mad!" growled Tugdual, fists clenched. "And let me tell you something: Oksa will always be stronger than anyone. And do you know why? Because, unlike you, she isn't alone."

Seeing how tense her friend was, his eyes full of deep despair, she realized he was struggling not to show any weakness. An expression like that didn't lie. How could she have believed... she silently promised herself that she'd never again let doubt get the better of her. She knew full well that Orthon would stoop to any level. He still had his Granok-Shooter aimed at sweet, angelic little Till, who was paralysed by fear. Oksa made up her mind. There was no way she was surrendering. Out of the question! But she was definitely going to make Orthon pay for what he was doing. More determined than she'd ever been, she hid behind the tree trunk to remove her Invisibuls and then, bringing her Granok-Shooter to her mouth, she targeted the soldiers guarding the prisoners.

> By the power of the Granoks,
> Think outside the box
> This twisting gale of wind
> Will put you in a spin.

A shower of Tornaphyllons descended on the Felons. Oksa had opted for this particular Granok because it posed no danger to the Runaways, who were chained to the platform. A terrible twister developed, sweeping away everything and everyone in its path. Neither Ocious and his henchmen nor the soldiers could withstand the might of the tornado. The prisoners curled up and clung with all their strength to their chains, which Oksa prayed wouldn't break. Zoe, Pavel and the Ink Dragon didn't escape unscathed. They were swept a good three hundred yards away as the wind raised by the Tornaphyllons brushed past, although it wasn't strong enough to prevent them from coming swiftly back.

Before firing the Granok which would carry Orthon off, but which might also sweep Tugdual and Till away, Oksa emerged from her hiding place without the layer of Invisibuls. Orthon had his back to her. He'd been so amazed at the sight of his allies being blown away that he'd temporarily forgotten to watch his rear.

The Young Gracious knew she only had a few seconds to save Tugdual and his little brother. She met Tugdual's eyes over Orthon's shoulder and quickly pointed at Till and the sky before Orthon could suspect anything and turn round. Mustering her courage, she threw herself at the Felon screaming, firing a Knock-Bong at his back—an underhand but effective attack which took Orthon by surprise. Dropping Till, he was sent rolling along the floor and crashed into a huge branch, which dazed him. Tugdual grabbed the little boy and took off from the platform in a super-fast Vertiflight.

Surrounded by the chained Runaways, only Oksa and Orthon were left on the terrace, which was being consumed by the fire started by the Felon. Still befuddled by the Knock-Bong, Orthon struggled to his feet, his body aching and his senses dulled. Before being swept away by a mighty tornado, he just had time to dive to the floor to grab his precious Granok-Shooter, which had landed several yards away, and hear the Young Gracious he was so desperate to capture yell:

"You'll never get your hands on me! Do you hear me? Never!"

24

REPERCUSSIONS

LEAFHOLD WAS LANGUISHING IN A STATE OF COMPLETE apathy, like its inhabitants. This dark mood wasn't helped by the torrential rain that had started falling after the rout of the Felons, transforming the soot into a sticky mud that plastered every tree, house and path in the forest city. After the terrible attack, the survivors had gathered at the foot of the Monumental Tree, which had been reduced to a giant charred skeleton. Some were crying silently over the lifeless bodies of those who hadn't survived the conflict; others were staring into space and huddling close to each other, trying in vain to find some comfort. Ocious and the Felons had committed a despicable and unpardonable act and no one could quite believe that they'd crossed that line.

✻

Sitting on the ground, her arms around her knees, Oksa was recovering in a makeshift tent at the foot of the battered tree, surrounded by the freed Runaways and the creatures which had been saved in the nick of time before the underground passages collapsed.

"My Young Gracious makes exhibition of a dejection garnished with depth," murmured the ashen-faced Lunatrix. "Her mind experiences the colouring of great blackness."

"What I am is exhausted, filthy and at a loss…" she replied flatly.

"Exhaustion and filthiness can meet erasure owing to the generosity of rest and soap," replied the Lunatrix. "As for the lost heart, it experiences transient emptiness. The return to the triumphant path makes the assurance of great proximity."

Oksa gave him a tremulous smile. The Lunatrix knew just what to say to make her feel better. He rubbed his large downy head against her and nestled into the crook of her shoulder. Oksa stroked him gratefully. She met Tugdual's gaze and found herself avoiding his eyes before she could absorb what she saw there: the pain they all shared at the terrible price of their victory, as well as another more intimate, more private source of suffering. She was soon distracted, though, by the Getorix, feebly jumping in puddles, and by the Incompetent, standing nearby, looking tired but incurably serene. A Polyglossiper was striving hard to break the remaining chains around Naftali's and Reminiscens' ankles.

Leomido's Lunatrixes had taken up nursing and were treating the injuries of the wounded with healing ointments.

Everyone was silent, locked in grief, whether they were keeping busy or regaining their strength. When Oksa saw people gathering to bid a final farewell to the dead, she stood up. Some Croakettes hurried to hold the broad leaf of a Parasol tree above her head as an umbrella. Not wanting to be singled out for special treatment, Oksa signalled them to stop, but the Croakettes blithely ignored her. Oksa decided not to press the issue and slowly trudged over to the circle, accompanied by her Lunatrix.

⁂

Edgar, the venerable Sylvabul who'd been her great-grandfather's friend, was the first to be covered with damp soil.

"These people are dead because of me," murmured Oksa.

Her hair fell over her face as she looked down and frantically blinked away the tears.

"It is not my Young Gracious who confiscated the life of her supporters," whispered the Lunatrix. "It was the hated Felon, Orthon, and his warriors."

Pavel and Zoe came to stand beside her and the inhabitants of Leafhold let them pass, saluting them with great solemnity and respect. Suddenly a voice rose in the crowd:

"Long live our Young Gracious!"

People lifted their heads and stood straighter. Everybody was soon echoing this cry and cheers erupted from all sides, sounding unexpectedly loud given the sad circumstances.

Rooted to the spot by contradictory emotions, Oksa winced. How could she enjoy such enthusiastic acclamation when the dead were lying at her feet? She found her father's hand and squeezed it as hard as she could. The situation was unbearable.

She wanted to go back through the crowd and find some peace and quiet at the top of a tree or the bottom of a burrow—anywhere she wouldn't be seen. Anywhere no one expected anything of her. Anywhere she wouldn't pose a danger to anyone. She was shaking all over now, as well as soaking wet, dirty and terribly unhappy. The cheers of Leafhold's inhabitants reached her ears, but not her heart.

"If you give up now, you'll ruin their only chance of regaining the world they love," said Pavel softly, without looking at her. "Let them believe in you, Oksa."

The Young Gracious considered those words for a few seconds. Then, with a grateful nod to her father, she accepted one of the flower shoots being handed out by Lucy to anyone who wanted to honour the dead. She gazed at the delicate roots at the end of the damp stem, then plunged the shoot into the small mound of earth that formed Edgar's grave. The shoot immediately quivered, then began growing and swelling until a magnificent flower with creamy blue petals opened at the end of the stem. The plant bowed low, stroking the earth, and began to sing a gentle melody that sounded like a lullaby.

Oksa turned round in wonder and looked enquiringly at her father. Pavel merely smiled knowingly. He walked over to the gently swaying plant, followed by all the others gathered there, and a few minutes later all the graves were covered with sweet-smelling, melodious flowers. Pavel put his arm round Oksa's shoulders and everyone stood in complete silence. Words were unnecessary as the message was very clear—Oksa definitely belonged to this world.

※

The ceremony had only just finished when the Velosos, which were acting as sentinels, sounded an alarm: a creature was flying towards them from the city. Everyone looked up and scanned the rainy skies.

"Ah, it's our Young Gracious's Tumble-Bawler!" announced one of the Squoracles, swaddled in a mohair jumper. "We wouldn't say no to some good news about the weather. The hydrometric levels around here are disastrous."

Oksa gave a sigh of relief. Her little informer was back at last from the reconnoitring mission she'd given it at the end of the terrible battle.

"Come here quickly, Tumble! Tell me what you know."

The roly-poly creature landed on her filthy shoe. The Runaways gathered closer, accompanied by a few Sylvabuls, eager for information.

"Young Gracious's Tumble-Bawler reporting!" it said, puffing out its tiny chest.

"I'm listening."

With bulging eyes, the Tumble-Bawler shook itself and began:

"After being swept away from Leafhold by my Young Gracious's Tornaphyllons, Ocious and his allies intended to go back to the Glass

Column, but when they got to Thousandeye City they were prevented from doing so."

"What do you mean?" asked Oksa.

"Thousandeye City is now securely defended," replied the Tumble-Bawler.

They looked at each other in surprise and their breathing quickened. Some faces brightened with wild hope, while others darkened.

"Who is defending Thousandeye City?" asked Oksa, her voice shrill with apprehension. "Orthon? He's turned against his father, hasn't he?"

"I'm sorry to have to contradict my Young Gracious," replied the Tumble-Bawler.

Oksa's eyes widened.

"You're sorry to have to contradict me?" she exclaimed. "Please do, I'm *begging* you! We're desperate for you to contradict me!"

The Tumble-Bawler swayed from left to right, its long arms at its sides, then said in one breath:

"Neither Orthon nor any other Felon is in Thousandeye City. Ocious, his family and their supporters were forced to flee. They've taken refuge in their troglodytic stronghold in the Peak Ridge Mountains in western Edefia. The defence of Thousandeye City was assured by the Ageless Ones and their magical Attendants who have put a shield around and above the Glass Column. The exit is well-guarded and the Gracious's residence is protected."

Close to suffocating, the little creature took a gulp of air and its eyes rolled back in their sockets. It seemed about to explode.

"The Ageless Ones and the people are ready," it concluded. "They're waiting for you, my Young Gracious!"

25

OKSA'S ARMY

"THIS IS INSANE—IT'S LIKE WE'RE IN A FILM!"

Pavel smiled. Oksa was right, the scene looked exactly like something from a big-budget Hollywood production. Hundreds of men, women and children were Vertiflying through Edefia's turbulent sky behind the Ink Dragon, which was steadily beating its broad, resplendent wings.

They'd come from all over Edefia, from the borders of Green Mantle to the hinterlands of Peak Ridge, and more were swelling their ranks with every passing minute. Even the birds hadn't resisted the call, forming noisy, multicoloured flocks around the Vertifliers. Below, on the ground, a pack of Sylvabuls were running and leaping with the agility of wild cubs. The noise of their feet pounding over the soaked ground was accompanied by shouts of encouragement from the flightless creatures carried by the Gargantuhens, Leomido's giant hens. Unsurprisingly, the Getorixes were the most excitable, pretending to crack imaginary whips against the backs of the runners, although no one needed any encouragement: despite all the ordeals and the heavy losses, their hearts were full of hope and their eyes determined. Led by the New Gracious, the people of Edefia, galvanized by their sense of conviction and purpose, were regaining control of their lives.

The Runaways led the way, escorted by those with Aeropellers. Freed from their chains, they were now hell-bent on taking their revenge for weeks of captivity and frustration. Since they'd arrived in Edefia, most of them had seen nothing but the inside of their apartments in the Glass Column. As a result, when Orthon had come to take them to Leafhold, their relief had outweighed their fear of danger. The Bellangers and Fortenskys, Reminiscens and the Knuts had seen their status change from prisoner to hostage which, despite being more hazardous, had broadened their horizons. The risk had paid off, and the end result had surpassed all expectations: they were back together again and reunited with their Last Hope.

"Look, Tug!" shrieked little Till. "Look what I can do!"

The little boy performed several pirouettes in the air under the amused and watchful eye of his mother, Helena. His white-blond curls formed a halo around his beaming face—what a sweet little angel he was, Oksa thought, as her eyes rested affectionately on the toddler for a moment, then strayed towards Tugdual, whose smile for his little brother was full of love and suffering.

"Well done, Till!" he said, flying nearer. "Where did you learn to do that, my little champion?"

"Mum and Granddad showed me," said the apprentice Vertiflier. "I'm almost as good as you now!"

Tugdual withdrew into himself. Oksa tried to catch his attention then immediately regretted it: she knew there was no getting through to him when he looked like that. She clenched her fists with a vexed pout. What was the matter with him now? She looked round for him again, but he'd disappeared among the crowd of Vertifliers.

"You can be so annoying, Tugdual," she muttered. "Gus was much less complicated than you!"

She winced. Not only had she just compared the two of them—something she'd secretly forbidden herself to do—but, worse, she'd thought about Gus in the past tense. That was dreadful. Her nostrils pricked as tears filled her eyes. As if they sensed her dismay, Pierre and Jeanne appeared at her side.

"You okay, Oksa?"

"I was just thinking about Gus," she couldn't help replying and then gnawed her lip until she drew blood.

Pierre had lost so much weight that he looked as if he were melting away. His skin and hair had turned grey, his eyes, once so bright, were now dull with deep sadness. The man who'd once been called "the Viking" was a shadow of his former self. And, unintentionally, Oksa had just cruelly reminded him of the main reason for his suffering.

"We think about Gus too," said Jeanne as gently as usual. "Thank you so much for bringing us some news—it's such a relief to know he's well and safe in London."

"I miss him," said Oksa, in a strangled voice. "He'd have loved to see this!" she added, gazing at their surroundings.

Gus's mother took her hand and squeezed it warmly.

"I'm sure we'll be able to tell him all about it one day," she said suddenly.

Oksa almost replied, but stopped herself in time.

"Anyway, in the meantime, we have a battle to fight!" continued Jeanne, her brown eyes sparkling.

Although Oksa's account of her brief visit to the Outside had upset Pierre badly, Jeanne had been unspeakably happy to hear the news, which had transformed this frail, reserved woman into a warrior with an iron will. The contrast was disconcerting and not a little depressing.

"Thousandeye City in sight!" shouted someone. "We're almost there."

A loud murmur rose from the ground and filled the air. Everyone quickened their pace considerably, impatient to arrive. The creatures fidgeted on the Gargantuhens.

"Come on, chicks!" screeched the overexcited Getorixes, frantically brandishing their imaginary riding crops. "Much too slow! Faster, faster!"

The giant hens gave a long, raucous squawk. The Lunatrixes and Squoracles on their back, clinging to their feathers, screeched too, forming a noisy and dishevelled escort. Oksa squinted: the vertical Column stood out against the horizon. Around it, bluish-grey and mauve streaks filled the sky. The setting sun could be glimpsed behind thick clouds. Only that strange ray of sunlight managed to pass through and plunge deep into the heart of the Column. Oksa had to summon a Reticulata to make out the crystalline contours of the shield described by the Tumble-Bawler. It hung over Thousandeye City like a gigantic transparent cloud with a substantial yet hazy outline. Oddly enough, its presence filled Oksa with reassurance. She glanced at her father with his Ink Dragon and the enormous crowd following them, then flew as fast as she could towards the capital of Edefia.

26

BORDER CONTROL

F ROM HIS CLIFFTOP VANTAGE POINT NEAR THOUSANDEYE
City, Orthon watched as the sky darkened, not with threatening
clouds, but with a dense, triumphant throng. A huge dark stain was also
spreading over the ground like a lengthening shadow, accompanied by
a subdued commotion. The Felon clenched his fists. Damn that Oksa
Pollock! She'd won, and the whole nation was with her. Or nearly...
Orthon screwed up his face in a scornful grimace. A paltry thousand
subjects had respected the allegiance they'd sworn to Ocious. All the
others had gone over to the New Gracious's camp.

"Traitors and scum," he snarled.

Although it was virtually transparent, the cloud suspended over the city
also came in for close scrutiny from Orthon. A protective screen—how
ingenious. And annoying. That had to be one of Abakum's ideas. That
damned Fairyman was always putting a spoke in their wheels. One day, he,
Orthon, would kill him. That was a promise. However, in the meantime
the first Vertifliers and runners were nearing the city's boundary. So
when about fifty people flew overhead to join the ranks of the Gracious's
supporters, he soared with a predatory smile towards the man who was
bringing up the rear.

✳

With her hands on her hips, Oksa was inspecting the protective membrane over Thousandeye City. Like a thin layer of barely rippling water, it slightly distorted their view of the city. The enormous crowd with her seemed to have come to a tacit agreement that she should be first to enter, and everyone had stopped before what served as the city's boundary. Oksa held her breath and reached her hand out warily. She brushed the strange surface with her fingertips and looked at her father in puzzlement: nothing was happening. Pavel frowned anxiously. Suddenly, the transparent surface of the membrane quivered: two huge shapes were drawing closer. A shudder ran through the ranks. Some of the oldest citizens recognized them from when they'd been invited, many years ago, to visit the Singing Spring or had been peremptorily denied access. For everyone else, the Corpusleoxes were a legend that many people had dearly hoped was real. These splendid creatures with the body of a lion and the head of a woman advanced until they were almost touching the crystalline barrier, then bowed down before Oksa.

"Young Gracious, we're honoured to meet you again and to serve you," they chorused.

Their words rang out above the enormous crowd as if amplified.

"It's wonderful to see you again here," stammered Oksa. "Thank you for all you've done," she added, glancing at the protective membrane.

The Corpusleoxes shook their manes and straightened to their full, impressive height.

"We're not the only ones who have prepared for your arrival," they announced.

Behind them, the floating halo of the Ageless Ones was glowing softly. Then a much-loved silhouette appeared in the half-light.

"Abakum!" exclaimed Oksa.

Impulsively she rushed forward. The Corpusleoxes took a few steps back as a narrow opening formed in the membrane and Oksa was able to throw herself into the arms of the man she loved like a grandfather.

Dragomira's Watcher had always been a pillar of strength and comfort, and now he was hers.

"I didn't think you'd do anything by halves," she said, her face radiant.

Abakum put his hands on Oksa's shoulders and studied her, his eyes joyful at this auspicious reunion.

"This protective shield is known as the Aegis. It will give us some much-needed breathing space," he said with an expansive gesture.

"It's amazing! And did you see?" continued Oksa, pointing at the hundreds of people waiting on the other side of the membrane. "I didn't come alone!"

The old man's face darkened.

"We must remain on our guard, sweetheart. Your loyal supporters would lay down their lives for you. They've already proved that and will do again, I'm sure, because this isn't over. We've won a big victory, but Ocious and his followers aren't beaten yet. There are men and women in the pay of the Felons hiding among those with you today. We mustn't take any chances."

"How will we know who they are?"

Abakum smiled mysteriously.

"There's one foolproof method…"

"I know exactly who you mean!" interrupted Oksa, revitalized. Her great-uncle Leomido's words were engraved on her memory. "This little creature plays a very interesting role as a revealer of the truth, because it looks beyond appearances. In Edefia, the Squoracle was used as a lie detector."

"They're never wrong," confirmed Abakum.

Oksa peered outside and called:

"Squoracles? Where are you? Come here!"

Four tiny hens emerged from the crowd and entered easily through the membrane. Oksa couldn't help laughing inwardly at the sight of them trembling in the woollen sweaters that Abakum had knitted personally. They were even more vociferous than usual.

"Young Gracious," one of them twittered, true to form, "although the humidity is awful because of all this rain, you should know that we don't hold it against you, because the temperatures here are much easier to bear than those we had to endure in Great Britain or, worse, in Siberia, where we almost froze to death."

Oksa snorted with laughter.

"Thank you for bringing us back to our land, Young Gracious!" they chorused.

"We need your help, Squoracles," said Oksa, unsmiling again.

"Our loyalty and our gratitude know no bounds. We're at your service."

Oksa looked solemnly at the tiny hens.

"We need to screen everyone entering Thousandeye City to make sure that no Felon gets inside. Do you think you can do that?"

The Squoracles spluttered with excitement.

"That's what we do best, Young Gracious! There is no truth or lie, however deeply buried in the mind of man, that can escape our detection. To work, my friends!"

They positioned themselves in front of the only entrance, flanked by the Corpusleoxes, which made them look even tinier, and held their pointed beaks high.

"Everyone must be examined before they can enter the Aegis," said Abakum. "There could be Felons everywhere."

One by one the inhabitants of Edefia were assessed by the Squoracles, whose shrewd talents proved to be the best possible protection against anyone harbouring ill will. There was no need for people to state their identity or even speak at all. No one could hide anything: the tiny, cold-fearing hens sensed, understood and saw everything. Which was just as well since, as Abakum had feared, Oksa's supporters had been infiltrated by Felons trying to get into Thousandeye City, which sent the Squoracles into a black rage. These would-be interlopers were given good cause to regret their actions—they were tightly bound then forcefully expelled by droves of those excitable flying frogs, the Croakettes.

"There are plans of evil intent deep in your heart," squawked the Squoracles. "You're not one of us!"

It didn't take more than a few seconds, or occasionally a few minutes, to analyse an individual, which meant that people were allowed inside in dribs and drabs, although no one showed any tiredness or impatience. As though they were being poured through a very narrow funnel, the supporters gradually gathered behind Oksa and the Runaways, their faces glowing with exultation despite their ordeals. Oksa never tired of watching the men and women come in. Apart from the way they dressed, they looked just the same as Outsiders. And yet, there was something fascinating about the power they all possessed. Even the youngest child— Edgar's great-grandson, as it happened—had greater abilities than the strongest Outsider. Once they were allowed in by the Squoracles, they filed in front of Oksa and greeted her, offering their sincere thanks. The Young Gracious replied with a few kind words, a nod of the head or a smile. Occasionally she caught her father or Abakum watching her, their eyes bright with emotion.

"I'm proud of you, darling," said Pavel softly.

"We're going to pull it off, Dad, we're going to pull it off!" she replied, thinking much further ahead than the present moment.

❊

Night had fallen long ago when the last few stragglers appeared before the Squoracles. Many citizens had already been given a warm welcome by the Long-Gulches of the city, who still had houses and could offer them board and lodging. Oksa and the Runaways, though, had preferred to remain by the entrance to Thousandeye City until the end of the screening process. The Getorixes and Lunatrixes saw to their every comfort, providing their mistress and her entourage with ample food and drink.

"You bearing up, my Lil' Gracious?"

After keeping his distance, which had worried Oksa, Tugdual had finally approached the Aegis. His entry into Thousandeye City hadn't been straightforward—one of the Squoracles had hesitated. Its feathers quivering and its beak in the air, the tiny lie detector had experienced a few long moments of indecision, which had deeply concerned Abakum, Oksa and Zoe, who were watching.

"What's going on?" Oksa had asked softly, suddenly worried.

"Our little feathered friend is probably getting tired," the Fairyman had said, putting a firm arm round Tugdual's shoulders to lead him into the Aegis.

"Aching all over from the high levels of humidity and the drop in temperature, yes—but tired, no!" the Squoracle had squawked, before turning its attention to a new candidate who wanted to join the Young Gracious's supporters.

Tugdual had come over to sit near Oksa. Straddling the low seat with his long legs and resting his elbows on his thighs, he'd stared at her with icy vehemence. Oksa just nodded in answer to his question.

"You're doing really well, you know," he continued.

"Thank you," said Oksa. "I'm doing my best."

"It's working. They love you."

She greeted a man who bowed to her, then continued:

"This is insane, isn't it?"

Tugdual smiled and Oksa realized that she wanted to do something completely inappropriate, given the circumstances: she wanted to kiss him. Her eyes widened in surprise at such an incongruous thought.

"Patience," mouthed Tugdual.

Again he'd seen in her eyes what was running through her head.

"Please stop smiling," she whispered, her cheeks scarlet.

"What if I don't?"

"If you don't, I'll lock you up in the filthiest basement of the Glass Column and throw away the key."

"There aren't any filthy basements in the Column," retorted Tugdual, looking amused.

"Well, I'll have a really squalid one built just for you. You'll laugh on the other side of your face then, I promise you that!"

"Aren't you afraid that people will think you're an evil dictator if you do?"

"Actually, I don't care, because anything would be better than putting up with that smirk for a day longer than I have to."

Her eyes sparkled as she turned away, although not fast enough to hide her attractive dimples.

※

There were about fifty people left outside the city, a group of Firmhands who wanted to join the Young Gracious, when there was another hitch.

"I don't believe it!" Pavel suddenly roared, a few yards from the entrance.

Abakum was trying to calm him down, his hands resting on his friend's shoulders. Nearby, flanked by the Corpusleoxes, a blonde woman was waiting, her arms at her sides and her face careworn, accompanied by a scared young boy.

"Annikki," murmured Oksa. "Annikki and her son."

"We're quite adamant!" shrieked the Squoracles. "This woman's heart is honest, and it contains no evil intentions."

"But still," objected Pavel, white with anger. "She's Agafon's granddaughter, and he supports Ocious and Orthon."

He looked at the Runaways and the Gracious's supporters, who'd drawn nearer.

"If you don't trust us, then we'll resign, simple as that!" threatened the Squoracles indignantly, the feathers on their heads sticking up.

"You can't have forgotten already that she was involved in Marie's abduction," continued Pavel in a choked voice.

"Dad, Annikki is a nurse," gasped Oksa. "And you know full well that it was because of her that Mum survived on the Island of the Felons. They were very fond of each other."

She looked at her father with shining eyes.

"Annikki isn't like them," she added softly. "Her origins are more of a burden than a motivation and, like us, she's paid dearly for coming here: her husband is still on the Outside."

Pavel groaned at this reminder.

"Remember what Baba said," finished Oksa, "emotional affinities are more important than blood ties."

Her words finally persuaded her father. His shoulders sagged and he gave Annikki and her son a long, sorrowful look as they timidly crossed the boundary. Then he turned and walked away, his back bowed.

⁂

It was late into the night and everyone was growing tired. There were nine people waiting outside the protective membrane and Oksa had to admit that she couldn't wait to see the only entrance to Thousandeye City closed. However, when Tugdual stiffened in his seat she snapped alert. The expression on Tugdual's face was serious, almost savage.

"What's wrong?" she asked softly.

He didn't reply. Oksa followed his gaze, which was resting on one of the men in the group. The plump man, who had tangled, greying hair and gleaming eyes, was staring so fiercely at Tugdual that soon everyone was watching them to the exclusion of everything else. Abakum took a few steps forward, looking anxious, and the Squoracles squawked excitedly.

"Please get down to work," he told them, sounding troubled.

The four Squoracles approached the man, who didn't drop his gaze by one iota. He just puffed out his chest and clenched his fists. The creatures sniffed him, then peered at him with tiny eyes and recoiled:

"You're not who you're pretending to be. Whoever you are, you're not welcome here!"

Everyone who was still there gathered together.

"You're the worst person of all of us," shrieked the oldest Squoracle angrily. "Get out!"

Immediately, Pavel and Abakum threw themselves in front of Oksa, shielding her with their bodies. Oksa cried out in surprise, clapping her hand over her mouth. She felt as though all the blood had drained from her body.

"It's impossible," she stuttered, vainly examining the man looking at them on the other side of the Aegis.

Memories of meeting Dragomira's identical twin in the cellar at the London home of Orthon McGraw—then her hated maths teacher—rose to the surface. She instinctively caught hold of Tugdual's arm as he stood stiffly beside her. Frightened by how motionless he was, she turned to look at him. Tugdual seemed a million miles away, isolated by his pain. When the Croakettes appeared in a furious whirr of wings to carry off the undesirable interloper, he soared into the soot-black sky and disappeared. Tugdual shivered, blinked and gazed at the Runaways in bewilderment.

"Are you all right, lad?" asked Abakum in a choked voice.

Tugdual nodded. Oksa was trembling all over, as breathless as if she'd just run a race. She glanced at Zoe, whose eyes were as dark as the moonless night.

"It was Orthon, wasn't it?" she asked quietly.

Abakum murmured a mournful "yes". Oksa stifled an angry exclamation and with a sad, puzzled glance at Tugdual, she issued an order, sounding more confident than she would have thought possible:

"Corpusleoxes, Squoracles, Croakettes, thank you so much for your help. Please close the doorway. This is *our* home now!"

27

THE CONFINANTS

ALTHOUGH THERE WERE NO SQUALID CELLS IN THE BOWELS of the Glass Column, there were captives. Ocious had brooked no opposition or dissent and had imprisoned these men and women with the Confinement Spell he'd discovered in the Gracious Archives. He'd added to their torment by gagging them with a Granok that had long ago fallen into disuse: the Sealencer. These poor wretches had been condemned to a living death in some airless underground passages of the Column, locked away from society and suffering an ill-fed existence in miserable silence.

"Those people need your help," declared the Corpusleoxes. "You're the only one who can free them."

The magnificent creatures were walking smoothly beside the Young Gracious.

"We've examined their hearts, and they're all on your side," they continued. "You need have no doubts about their loyalty. Thousandeye City has been cleared of all the Felons who might still be hidden here."

"I have every confidence in you," nodded Oksa. "Let's get a move on! We mustn't let those poor people suffer a moment longer than they have to."

Although she was exhausted and hungry and it was the middle of the night, she hurried towards the Column, which soared into the dense, low-level clouds. Everyone else, supporters and Runaways alike, had been urged to rest. "Tomorrow is another day," Oksa had assured them. Only her father, Abakum, Tugdual and Zoe were still with her, following close behind and escorted by the Ageless Fairies.

A faint light spilled out of the houses bordering the streets, lengthening the shadows and distorting the appearance of shrubs, low walls and bushes. In any other circumstances the atmosphere would have been oppressive, even scary. But there was nothing to fear now—Oksa and her entourage had no misgivings as they walked over the ground with its thin covering of mud. The sweetish smell rising from it induced a strange state of lethargy, as if the freshly watered land were communicating its relief to the humans.

"Young Gracious!" they heard suddenly.

Abakum held up his Polypharus and a girl emerged from the darkness.

"It's Lucy!" exclaimed Oksa.

The young Long-Gulch's face was filled with overwhelming hope.

"My father's in there," she said simply, gesturing to the Column.

Oksa looked at her sympathetically. She knew how hard it was to be separated from the people you love.

"Let's not hang around, then!" she said. "It's about time you were reunited with him."

⁂

As they walked through the corridors with their remarkable crystalline walls they could see no sign of an entrance into or out of any room, apart from the door in the seventh basement, which they knew led to the Cloak Chamber. However, the Corpusleoxes seemed to know exactly where they were going, threading their way through the narrow corridors with impressive ease, despite their size. Oksa and her entourage followed them down to the eighth level, where the Corpusleoxes stopped before a wall no different from the others.

"We're here," these creatures announced.

Looking sceptical, Oksa ran her hand over the opalescent surface which, although uneven, was smooth, as if polished by a thousand caresses.

"I can't see anything," she murmured, frowning as she examined the wall.

"Cover your ears, Young Gracious and the rest of you, we're going to open the door," warned the Corpusleoxes.

Putting their hands over their ears as they were told, they witnessed the unexpected effect on inorganic matter produced by these creatures' extraordinary roar. Rising from deep within, their low, powerful call gradually became louder and louder, like a hurricane sweeping away everything in its path. Oksa staggered, thrown off-balance. Tugdual caught her just in time and made her crouch down to minimize the effect of this ear-splitting roar. Oksa grimaced with alarm and pain: her eardrums felt like they were going to burst. Helplessly she watched Tugdual remove his hands from his own ears to cover hers, doubling her protection, and pulling her tightly against him with her face buried in the crook of his shoulder. She could feel his body straining against the unbearable, unstoppable noise.

The din eventually died down and the air stilled, leaving everyone speechless and dishevelled. Tugdual helped Oksa to her feet to see the miracle they'd worked: there was now a semicircular opening in the wall, wide enough to accommodate several people abreast. The Corpusleoxes were standing on either side and gesturing with their huge paws for Oksa and her entourage to enter. Abakum went first, Granok-Shooter in hand, followed by Oksa and the others.

In the glow of Abakum's Polypharus, the outlines of a long, narrow room appeared at right angles to the hallway. The milky whiteness of the stones made the place seem less squalid than they'd expected, given its use. There were no signs of life.

"More light," urged Abakum.

Oksa and all of the Runaways summoned a Polypharus and advanced, Lucy clinging to Zoe's arm. The Fairyman was right: a very strong light was needed to make out the shadowy human figures behind blocks of crystal so thick that it was almost impossible to see through them

"There are people in *there*!" exclaimed Oksa, her hand over her mouth. "They've been walled in!"

"Dad?" cried Lucy. "Where are you?"

The shadows immediately huddled closer to the walls separating them from the living, moving restlessly like ghostly shapes made of black vapour. Stinging tears blurred Oksa's sight and she turned to Abakum.

"What should I do?"

"Confinement has been the exclusive domain of the Graciouses since time immemorial," replied Abakum. "Despite that, although Confinement and Impicturement are difficult spells to cast, it can be done by others, as Orthon and Ocious have reminded us. However, and this restricts their usefulness, Deconfinement and Disimpicturement require a power possessed only by the Graciouses."

"One final safety measure," murmured Oksa. "Do you think that creep Ocious was aware of that tiny *detail* before he sentenced these poor people to Confinement?"

"Ocious, like Orthon, is the type of person who tends to overestimate his abilities and become blinded by his own power," said Abakum bitterly. "No doubt he thought he could master everything, and he was willing to condemn those poor innocent people to a fate worse than death if he couldn't."

Oksa looked at the shadows pressing against the blocks of crystal. Instinctively she put her hand on the wall and, to her great surprise, felt her fingers sink into it, as if the crystal were soft. She turned to look questioningly at Abakum.

"Is that because of my Werewall abilities?"

165

By way of an answer, Abakum asked Tugdual and Zoe, who were both of Werewall descent, to imitate Oksa. They did, but nothing happened.

"Your Werewall abilities aren't any help here," remarked Abakum with a smile. "I'd say it's more down your Gracious powers."

Itching to begin, Oksa was filled with a dizzying sense of exhilaration. Taking a deep breath, she placed both hands on the crystal, which instantly softened on contact with her skin. She then parted the wall as easily as if she were opening a pair of taffeta curtains. The interior of the stone prison appeared, and a loud groaning could be heard. Oksa recoiled, horrified at the terrible sight before her: a hundred men and women surged forward, eyes bulging and skin livid. They were all muzzled by a large, flat, iridescent blue insect, whose six legs were embedded in the flesh around their lips, sealing them hermetically.

"That's revolting!" stammered Oksa, feeling sick. "Is that what the Sealencer is?"

Abakum nodded, his face white.

"That's a vile Granok!" protested Oksa grimacing. "We have to free those poor people!"

"Listen and repeat," said Abakum to everyone around him.

By the power of the Granoks,
Think outside the box.
Your claws apply the seal
Your wings remove the seal.

The four Runaways aimed their Granok-Shooters and diligently uttered the magic words. The Sealencers broke away with a sucking noise which convinced Oksa once and for all that she'd never be able to stand insects. Rising above their heads, the Sealencers formed a rippling swarm with vibrating wings that gave off a repulsive stench. Then, breaking up into several small groups, they swooped down towards the Runaways'

Granok-Shooters, slipped inside and disappeared. Oksa dropped her blowpipe in disgust and wiped her hands on her trousers. Tugdual bent down to pick up her Granok-Shooter, carefully examined its mouthpiece and handed it back to Oksa with an amused glance.

"Don't laugh at me!" she huffed, pretending to push him away.

Tugdual gently took her hand and laced his fingers through hers.

"Look," he said.

Lucy was clinging to her father, Achilles. All around them, the Edefians who'd rebelled against Ocious's tyranny were joyfully thanking their liberators. The oldest among them began weeping when they recognized Abakum, who couldn't conceal his emotion at seeing a man with long plaited hair and craggy features.

"Sven? Is that really you?" asked Abakum, his lips trembling.

"Abakum, my friend," replied the old man. "I always knew you couldn't be dead."

The two men hugged long and hard.

"And not only have you come back, but you brought us a priceless gift," continued Sven, turning to look at Oksa.

Gazing deferentially at the Young Gracious with radiant faces, no one seemed brave enough to approach her. Oksa squeezed Tugdual's hand even tighter and edged closer to him until their shoulders were touching. Being the centre of attention always made her want to run away and hide at the top of the Glass Column. Finally meeting Lucy's joyful gaze, she ventured to examine the other men and women properly. Tactfully ignoring their filthy, emaciated bodies, she saw them for what they truly were: representatives of an exhausted yet loyal nation standing in solidarity before her. She straightened, took a deep breath and smiled triumphantly at them.

"Long live our Young Gracious!"

The unanimous cry rang out in the basements of the Glass Column as though announcing an end to the Years of Tar. Recovery was long overdue.

PART TWO

RECOVERY AND DISILLUSIONMENT

28

ACCEPTANCE

A SUPERCHARGED ATMOSPHERE OF HYPER-VIGILANCE prevailed in the first days of the reign of Gracious Oksa. The Aegis—that vast transparent, shifting membrane over Thousandeye City—was proving very useful, and its effectiveness was put to the test on several occasions when the Felons tried to break in, either in the air or through the only entrance, or even by tunnelling under it. Accompanied by the Corpusleoxes and supported by the whole nation, the Squoracles thwarted even the cleverest tricks. The tiny hens were infallible, spotting the use of shape-changing powers, Werewall abilities and Muddler or Hypnagogo Granoks.

From her vantage point at the top of the Glass Column, Oksa was watching a group of Long-Gulches who were Vertiflying back and forth along the membrane, checking for breaches. In a few minutes she was going to the large Council Room to name the High Enclave, her new government. She sighed.

"Is anything wrong?"

Oksa turned round and looked at Tugdual without replying. He was stretched out on the bed, his arms behind his head and his legs crossed.

"Make yourself at home, why don't you!" snapped Oksa, her hands on her hips.

"It's so comfortable here," said Tugdual, smiling.

"Isn't sir happy with his own apartment?"

"Perfectly happy. But yours is so luxurious."

"As it should be!" replied Oksa with a shrug.

She tried to tip Tugdual off the bed, but ended up being pulled down beside him. Lying on her stomach, elbows propped up on the silky bedspread, she looking around distractedly and started pulling a thread loose. Since Ocious and the Felons had fled, the Runaways had taken over the top floor, which was traditionally reserved for the use of the Gracious's family, as well as a few levels below. Some of the top-floor apartments and the Memorary had been badly damaged during the Great Chaos, then restored when Ocious came to power. Although a little shabby, their former splendour seemed to have increased over the passing years, as if they'd become more beautiful with time. Oksa loved her apartment, which had many separate levels, dividing the enormous main room into various attractive areas. The crystal columns and translucent glass mosaic tiles on some of the walls were breathtakingly beautiful, even though they showed signs of wear and a few tiles were missing. Oksa's only complaint was the preponderance of inorganic materials and the lack of greenery. But she'd soon remedy that, she promised herself.

For the moment she had more important things to worry about, as Tugdual could see.

"So what's wrong?" he asked.

Oksa hesitated before replying:

"I'm not really sure what to do."

Tugdual glanced reassuringly at her.

"You'll be brilliant, I know you will. And don't forget you're not alone. You can trust everyone here. They just want what's best for you and for Edefia. You have no right to doubt yourself."

Hearing this, Oksa sat up.

"What do you mean, I have no right to doubt myself?" she protested.

"The only person who's allowed to have doubts is me," replied Tugdual in a low voice.

Oksa stared at him, but he avoided her eyes.

"What doubts? About me?"

Her voice broke. That was all she needed. If Tugdual left her it would be the end of the world.

"I've never had any doubts about you," he said. "Never."

Oksa opened her mouth, but nothing came out.

"Come here," murmured Tugdual.

Oksa knew he wouldn't say any more. She let him wrap his arms around her and snuggled up against him. Every day, her need for physical contact grew stronger. There was no comparison between the emotions she'd felt at fourteen and the feelings that tormented her constantly now she was over sixteen. She caressed Tugdual's chest through his black tee-shirt, her heart on fire.

"I'm not normal," she whispered.

Tugdual kissed the corner of her lips.

"You're the Young Gracious, remember. That makes you different, not abnormal."

Oksa pressed even closer against him and finally succumbed to her desire to slip her hand beneath his tee-shirt. His skin was soft. Incredibly soft.

"I'd like to stay like this for the rest of my life."

"You'd get bored."

"I love being with you."

"I'm never far away," murmured Tugdual, before kissing her.

Oksa couldn't think straight. A jumble of confused sensations and images filled her head—Tugdual's chilly gaze which set her heart on fire. The symbolic illustrations on her Cloak. The liberated people of Edefia soaring into the sky and poignant thoughts of her mother stuck in her wheelchair in the middle of the damp living room in Bigtoe Square. Gus's

173

scent and the taste of his lips. Shocked by the turn her thoughts were taking, she opened her eyes and gently extricated herself.

"I'm telling you," she murmured, burying her face in the crook of Tugdual's neck. "I'm definitely not normal."

*

About two hundred men and women were waiting in the large Council Room, which was bathed in the milky glow from the light shaft. All two hundred, wearing Edefia's traditional dress of wide trousers and double-breasted top, enthusiastically rose to their feet as one when Oksa appeared at the top of the amphitheatre, clad in clean jeans and a white blouse set off by her loosely knotted lucky tie. She scanned the assembled throng standing in a semicircle, remembering the last time she was here: a horribly vivid memory that still made her wince. It had been Ocious, surrounded by his vile sons and allies, who'd "welcomed" her in the most dangerous circumstances imaginable. Today, though, there was nothing to fear in this room with its awe-inspiring symbolic magnificence—the mingled respect and belief in all the faces looking at her proved it.

It was quiet enough to hear a pin drop. She walked down the tiered steps, her cheeks flushed but her head held high, and everyone bowed as she passed them. Unable to meet anyone's eyes, she reached the rostrum facing the amphitheatre and turned round to see the Runaways in the front row. Her father, Abakum, Zoe, Tugdual, the creatures... they were all there, their faces glowing with excitement and pride, which boosted her confidence and energy.

This solemn atmosphere was suddenly heightened by the golden halo of about ten Ageless Ones, who flooded out from the shaft descending through the ten upper floors of the Column and filled the huge room with a cone of light. The Ageless Ones floated over to Oksa and she found herself studying them hopefully, even though she knew it was pointless. Not one of the silhouettes swaying in front of her bore any resemblance to the one she wanted to see more than anything: Dragomira, her beloved Baba, wasn't with the Ageless Ones. She missed her so much... it would have been so comforting to have her with her, particularly on such a special day.

"Rest easy, sweetheart," whispered a voice that Oksa recognized as Malorane's. "Dragomira will be nearby for ever."

Oksa glanced fiercely at her. Her words, even if they were true, were small consolation, but life went on and she had to look to the future. In her open palm, Malorane presented Oksa with a tiny multicoloured ball which, when unrolled, proved to be her intricately embroidered Cloak. Oksa let them drape the Cloak over her shoulders, and felt its legendary power spread through her body as it had done in the Chamber in the seventh basement. An admiring murmur ran through the amphitheatre. Someone began clapping, followed by scores of other people, and the room was filled with thunderous applause. Gnawing her lower lip, Oksa eventually found herself infected by the general euphoria. With a dazzling grin, she held out her arms to her father and Abakum. The two men joined her on the rostrum and the applause grew even louder. She looked around the packed amphitheatre, from the first rows to the ceiling dotted with patches of shifting light, noticing the Lunatrix, dressed in his best dungarees, and the Incompetent, whose look of total bewilderment was as amusing as ever. The voice of an Ageless Fairy rang out:

"It is time to appoint your High Enclave, Our Gracious. May your choice be enlightened and your decision respected by all."

Then, one by one, the coronas of light floated towards the shaft and vanished with a golden sparkle.

"I think everyone expects a speech, darling," Pavel whispered in Oksa's ear.

Oksa looked at him in alarm.

"Oh, no, please," she groaned.

"Just a few words..."

He backed away and walked down the steps leading up to the rostrum from the front rows of seats. Oksa cleared her throat, breathed deeply then took the plunge, as if jumping into water—a prospect as tempting as swimming in a freezing lake in the middle of winter.

"Go on, Oksa-san, don't think, just speak from your heart and everything will be fine," she thought encouragingly.

"Well," she declared, "I feel very honoured to have been chosen as your New Gracious. The discovery of my origins and your existence completely changed my life, making it exciting, complicated and dangerous. It also catapulted me into an amazing new dimension—the world of magic—and not everyone gets that opportunity. All the same, it wasn't easy to come here: planning the journey was hard and putting our plans into action even harder. Still, even though my friends and family have sacrificed a great deal to be here, I know how necessary it was and what it has meant to us all. I've also come to realize that my destiny belongs to you as much as it belongs to me and that, behind the magic, there is… us. So I'm more than happy to accept what I am, your New Gracious, and I know that I can. But I don't want to do it alone. I… I need you."

Breathless, she stopped, her eyes blazing, as loud cheers and applause filled the room with its curved walls. She waited for the frenzied clapping to stop, but it showed no sign of abating. Her Lunatrix had to step in to call for attention.

"Our Gracious and the people of Edefia meet with a joy that invades their hearts, eyes and mouths, but they must not neglect the necessity of making the appointment of the new High Enclave!" shouted the little steward perched on the long table situated on the rostrum. "Your voices must proceed to the adoption of a concentration stuffed with muteness."

Silence was eventually restored with the help of the creatures that had a certain amount of authority—namely the Squoracles, Getorixes and Ptitchkins. The Lunatrix climbed down from his perch in satisfaction and stood beside Oksa, his eyes full of reverence. Oksa sat down behind the long embossed metal table in the middle chair, which was upholstered in brown leather and adorned with brass studs.

"It's time to get down to work," she announced clearly. "So, if he accepts, I'd like Abakum to become First Servant of the new High Enclave."

Everyone warmly supported this sound decision, as Abakum stood up to join Oksa on the rostrum. With his hand on his heart he bowed, his bright eyes imbuing his face with unfailing wisdom.

"Oksa, sweetheart, my Gracious, I shall honour your decision until I die."

Oksa couldn't help herself: forgetting the solemnity of the occasion, she threw herself into the arms of the Fairyman who had earned the title of Watcher of the Runaways and the Gracious's family a hundred times over.

29

THE SEVEN MISSIONS

O KSA HADN'T COME TO THE COUNCIL ROOM UNPREPARED: she'd done a great deal of research before taking such a critical step for Edefia's future. She'd had long conversations with elderly—and not so elderly—Edefians about the best way to approach things. Then, with the help of her Lunatrix, she'd spent hours among the dusty shelves of the Memorary, unearthing fascinating archives about the different High Enclaves over the centuries.

"My Gracious is full of exactitude," the little creature had confirmed nasally. "The constitution of the High Enclaves and the attribution of the duties of the Servants experience variation and connection with the needs of the current moment."

"Look!" Oksa had added, bent over the crystal pages of a fat register. "At one time, there was even a Servant for the Division of Wealth!"

"Affirmation fills the mouth of your domestic staff, my Gracious. It was needful to create that Mission in the reign of Gracious Edith, the prior grandmother of my Dear-Departed-and-Much-Beloved Old Gracious, in order to proceed to the prevention of the proliferation of imbalance. Because, as my Gracious possesses the knowledge, the nature of man occasionally propels him towards the inspection of his own navel rather than towards neighbourliness."

※

A few hours later, sitting before the gathered throng in the Council Room, she smiled at this recent memory and winked at her Lunatrix, who flushed an eye-watering purple. On the table sat a new crystal register which would be added to the many others kept in the Memorary: her personal Elzevir, in which she'd have to record all the major events in her reign. A stylus was attached to the Elzevir by a slender chain, whose links formed the letters of her name: Gracious Oksa. Oksa placed her hands on the patinated metal table and suddenly noticed her Curbita-Flatulo. The little living bracelet was peacefully curled around her wrist, clearly unable to detect any anxiety in its young mistress's mind. Pleasantly surprised by the smooth feel of the table under her hands, Oksa gazed for a few seconds at the crowd silently waiting in the auditorium. She met her father's eyes and saw him nod. Then she felt ready to begin.

"Edefia has lived through some difficult years," she announced, "But we must now put all the pain and suffering behind us. Goodwill and determination are vital if we are to make a full recovery. However, you know as well as I do that the circumstances are exceptional and that it will not be easy to restore equilibrium. There are those who will do everything in their power to stop us. Which is why, following the advice of the most experienced citizens among you and learning from the lessons of the past, I think it's crucial to split the High Enclave into seven Missions."

She broke off, flustered by her serious tone and by being the centre of attention. Where was the headstrong schoolgirl now? Zoe and Tugdual had to be thinking the same thing as they watched her admiringly, the former with fierce admiration and the latter with chilly approval.

"I don't know you all, unfortunately," continued Oksa. "But without trust or solidarity we'll achieve nothing. So I'm going to appoint two Servants to lead every Mission: one Runaway and one Insider, which will make it possible to combine the best ideas from our two worlds. These Servants will then choose whomever they want to help them work more efficiently and, above all, motivate the whole nation."

Everyone in the amphitheatre nodded vigorously.

"Now I'll introduce the seven Missions and their Servants, giving you the reasons for my choices," continued Oksa, her voice quivering with excitement. "First is the Reconstruction Mission, with Olof and Emica. Olof is the son of Naftali and Brune Knut. In our world, he was an architect and his experience will come in useful for rebuilding the towns, with the help of Emica who, I've been told, is one of the best carpenters in Edefia."

The Ptitchkins took flight, chirruping joyfully and landed on the shoulders of the people Oksa had just named. The elegant, powerfully built Scandinavian, as imposing as his father, stood up and waited for Emica, a smiling woman with short hair and a sweet, angelic face. They joined Oksa on the rostrum and bowed low. "Oh I do hate it when they do that," Oksa sighed to herself.

"The Water Conservation Mission will be headed up by Brune and Achilles. I think this is a matter dear to your hearts," added Oksa, smiling.

The two new Servants, zealously accompanied by the tiny birds, nodded with unconcealed delight.

"The Essential Goods Mission will be led by Tin, a friend of Abakum's, and Jeanne. This Mission is responsible for the sound management of everything that might be necessary for our survival," explained Oksa.

She hesitated for a second before continuing shakily:

"My parents owned a restaurant on the Outside with Jeanne and Pierre. And Jeanne was an expert forward planner. She made sure that nothing ran out. Ever."

Gus's mother's gentle face lit up with gratitude.

"The fourth Mission combines Granokology, Pharmacopoeia and Protection. Sven and Naftali will be its Servants, Naftali because he's always been so vigilant against our enemies, and Sven for his supreme mastery of plants and minerals. You were trained by Mirandole, like Abakum, weren't you?" asked Oksa, addressing the elderly man with long white braids.

"Abakum was and is the best of us," replied the latter, "and I hope you'll permit me to take advantage of his shrewd advice and long experience on the Outside?"

Oksa smiled at him: the Fairyman was universally loved and revered.

"The Integrity Mission will be well served by Sacha and Bodkin," she continued. "Bodkin is a Runaway of great wisdom and I know that Sacha has devoted her life to fighting injustice and disloyalty at the cost of her own freedom."

Bodkin, the Runaway who was dressed like an English dandy, politely offered his arm to a middle-aged woman with clear, piercing eyes. She wore her hair scraped back in an impeccable bun, which only heightened the intensity of her gaze. Sacha was one of the Sealenced prisoners who'd been freed two days earlier. She was said to be a woman of unshakeable principle and a passionate fighter for justice and fairness. Oksa had been struck by her determination—a stubborn, unwavering resolve which made her as immovable as a mountain.

"Thank you, Gracious Oksa," she said, her voice still hoarse from weeks of Sealencing. "You can count on me."

"I know," said Oksa reassuringly, before continuing. "The sixth Mission is the Wealth and Property Redistribution Mission, which was directly inspired by the Mission set up by my ancestor, Gracious Edith. I think it's important to rebalance things on this level too. Cockerell, as you know, was treasurer to the Gracious family before the Great Chaos. He'll be an excellent Redistributor because he's fair."

She then looked over at a woman with a mass of red curls and freckled skin.

"Mystia, several people have assured me that you'd also be a good Redistributor. I hope you'll be happy to work alongside Cockerell."

The woman gave a dazzling smile and came to sit at the High Enclave's table.

"Last but not least, the seventh Mission will be the Initiation Mission, led by Pierre and Olenka. Olenka has taught the pharmacopoeia to generations of Insiders and is a fine teacher, like Pierre. I'll never forget that he was the one—sorry, Dad!—who taught me to ride a bike!"

The Runaways couldn't help laughing, while the creatures showed their amusement in their own way: the Lunatrixes chuckled hysterically, the Squoracles cackled stridently, the Getorixes guffawed wildly. Only the Incompetents showed some restraint, and that was purely down to their lethargic mental abilities. Most of the Insiders, however, didn't know what a bike was. Those who'd fortunately remembered Malorane's public Camereye sessions explained what it meant to "ride a bike" and everyone soon understood why the Runaways were laughing.

"With regard to the Granok-Shooters," continued Oksa, her cheeks scarlet, "I think it's really important for everyone to get theirs back. After all, an Insider without a Granok-Shooter isn't a true Insider, don't you agree?"

Everyone was struck dumb by this announcement. There was scattered, hesitant applause at first, but when Leomido's Lunatrixes arrived, weighed down by heavy locked chests, everyone erupted into joyful cheers. Oksa stood up and they all fell silent again. Embarrassed at interrupting this enthusiastic reception, she announced:

"In the sixth basement of the Column there's a secret storeroom with two hundred chests like these. They contain the thousands of Granok-Shooters stolen from you during the Great Confiscation ordered by Ocious, as well as massive stocks of Granoks. I intend to task our Servants for Wealth and Property Redistribution with returning everyone's property to them. Then we'll get down to work. Edefia needs us badly!"

Oksa's Getorix and another appeared, each clutching a pot of earth. Jumping up and down with excitement, they kept almost spilling their precious cargo on their way to the Young Gracious. By some miracle, the pots reached their destination intact and Oksa looked at them in surprise. She glanced questioningly at her father, but all became clear when she saw the gesture he made with a smile. She plunged both hands in the earth and the pots began shaking so hard that they made a loud clattering noise on the metal table. Finally, with great wonderment, Oksa saw two small green shoots emerge from the earth. The stems surged upwards and blossomed into a flower she'd seen before, an Inflammatoria with blazing petals. The stems climbed even higher and caressed her wrists and forearms with what seemed like true affection. From the centre of the flowers jumped a few tiny sparks which stung her skin, then the stems reared up, jiggling in their pots, which looked more like amputated stumps and unexpectedly shot towards the ceiling. When they reached a height of ten feet they showed their delight by putting on a scintillating firework display, which flared as brightly as the blaze Oksa had kindled in her people's hearts.

30

THE EPHEMERAL
SECRET

F ROM HER BALCONY SHE'D SPENT OVER AN HOUR WATCHING
the first Granok-Shooters being returned to their rightful owners,
fully loaded with all the existing Granoks. Everyone was deliriously happy
and not one person forgot to look up at the top of the Glass Column,
where their benevolent New Gracious resided. Then tiredness had hit
her as suddenly as a bird of prey swooping on a mouse, and she'd gone
inside, her heart full of emotion.

Back in the peace and quiet of her apartment she relaxed, absent-
mindedly stroking her Lunatrix and thinking over everything that had
happened. It had been a long, intense day. A strange day. And, above all,
a very complicated one.

Earlier, she'd caught sight of her reflection in the tarnished mirror that
covered almost an entire wall. She'd warily gone over—it had been so long
since she'd looked at herself. She was very pale, perhaps paler than she'd
ever been. She'd tossed back her hair and combed her fingers through her
fringe. Her face bore traces of the tension of the past few days, but this
hadn't hardened her features. Although her forehead was creased and
there were deeper bags under her grey eyes, which looked a little darker,
there were no drastic differences between "Oksa before" and "Oksa after".

"What were you thinking, idiot?" she'd muttered. "You don't turn into a different person just because you've made a few important decisions. Get a grip, Oksa-san!"

She gnawed her lip. That last phrase was something Gus would have said if he'd been there.

"Stop it, Oksa," she'd concluded. "You'll only upset yourself."

Then she'd turned sideways to examine her figure. No one could accuse her of being obsessed with her appearance, but her new curves still took some getting used to, although she was gradually feeling more comfortable with them. And the way Tugdual looked at her certainly helped.

⁂

She'd been curled up in the comfy, worn leather chair, which had fast become her favourite, for over an hour. Nearby, on a beautiful Majestic-wood bureau, her Elzevir was glittering in the soft glow cast by the illuminating tentacles of the Polypharuses. She ought to get down to writing up the first steps she'd taken as a Gracious. But was she supposed to record everything?

"My Gracious makes display of great confusion in the recesses of her heart," remarked the Lunatrix, gazing at her with his wide blue eyes.

"It's about the Secret," explained Oksa.

The Lunatrix sighed.

"This Secret does not meet the same composition as the precedent one. It does not dispose of the consequences and constraints similar to the ones possessed by the Secret-Never-To-Be-Told. Do you have knowledge of its name? It is overflowing with meaning."

"No, the Ageless Ones didn't tell me. But if you know the name of the new Secret, then please tell me!"

"The Ephemeral Secret. Such is its appellation."

185

Oksa thought for a few minutes. She looked from the Cloak, carefully draped over a wicker dummy, to the vast bay window which afforded a view of sleeping Thousandeye City, dotted with a myriad of shivering pinpricks of light.

"The Ephemeral Secret," she repeated. "Ephemeral, perhaps. But primarily a secret."

A noise jerked her from her reverie: someone was knocking at the door. The Lunatrix stood up, but the dishevelled Getorix was already hurrying over energetically.

"Who goes there?" it yelled at the door. "Who dares to disturb our Gracious? Speak now or for ever hold your peace!"

Oksa smiled. The Getorix never did anything by halves.

"It's Abakum," said a voice, muffled by the thickness of the door.

"Open the door immediately!" Oksa told the creature.

Abakum came in and gave Oksa a big hug. She snuggled up against him.

"Would the Fairyman and my Gracious feel the attraction of lapping up a drink full of comfort?"

Oksa laughed softly, as Abakum patted the Lunatrix's bald head.

"Thank you, that would be very nice."

The Lunatrix vanished and a clatter of crockery could soon be heard in an adjoining room.

"How are you, sweetheart?" asked Abakum, sitting down beside Oksa on a sofa covered by a dark fur throw.

"I don't think I've ever had such an… odd day," she replied. "I felt like I was in a computer simulation game, you know, when you have to build towns, set up a government and draw up laws… even though I know it's all very real."

"It certainly isn't the sort of thing you do every day," conceded Abakum. "But you did very well indeed. You acquitted yourself admirably! Well done. And, since you went off fairly quickly after the Council Meeting, let me give you a little feedback."

Oksa put her hands over her face in embarrassment.

"You've won over the hearts of our Insider allies, and the Runaways are proud to stand beside you. Everyone was very impressed by your air of confidence. I promised Tugdual that I'd tell you he was blown away and that you did a great job—I'm quoting here."

Oksa pulled a face, so Abakum asked:

"What's bothering you?"

Oksa pretended to be distracted by the Lunatrix, who was returning with a tray. The little steward began serving them, glancing in concern at his young mistress.

"It's my father," Oksa said finally.

Abakum took a deep breath.

"Everyone realized you must have had very good reasons for not putting him in charge of a Mission."

"Maybe, but it was still awful! He must be so upset with me."

Abakum took a sip of tea and looked at her wisely.

"Knowing Pavel, that would surprise me."

"Everyone must think I'm such an ungrateful daughter."

"No one thinks that," said Abakum. "We know you love your father and that he'll never be far from you. Your decisions have our unanimous support, sweetheart. You made some sensible, well-thought-out choices which everyone respected."

"Thank you," murmured Oksa. "You've helped me so much. I'd never have managed without you."

"Don't forget that I was your gran's Watcher and now I'm yours."

"I know, Abakum."

"I'd like to ask you a question though. Just one question, which you don't have to answer if you don't want to."

The Lunatrix couldn't help groaning. His complexion turned translucent and his eyes began spinning like tops in their sockets.

"My Gracious…"

He looked about to faint. Oksa put a hand on his downy arm and avoided Abakum's eyes. He frowned.

"Does the fact that you didn't want to make your father a Servant of the High Enclave have anything to do with the new Secret entrusted to you by the Ageless Ones?" asked the Fairyman.

This was too much for the Lunatrix. The poor creature swayed, then crumpled in a heap on a floor cushion. The Getorix hurried to his side and fanned his face by waving its hands in the air.

"Hey, podge! Stay with us!" it squealed.

Farther off, sitting quietly on a chair, Oksa's Incompetent opened one eye and gazed at the scene with its usual bemusement. Then, with a yawn, it blissfully went back to sleep.

Abakum and Oksa knelt down beside the poor little creature, who was already regaining consciousness. Oksa held his head up and trickled a few mouthfuls of piping-hot tea into his wide mouth.

"Baba always said that a nice cup of tea was the best remedy in the world."

"The Dear-Departed-and-Much-Beloved Old Gracious disposed of colossal truths in her mouth," stammered the Lunatrix.

Abakum carried him to a small made-to-measure bed and laid him down on it, massaging various pressure points on his wrists. Then he came back to Oksa and sat back down in preoccupied silence.

"You don't need to answer my question, sweetheart," he said after long pause. "What just happened told me all I needed to know."

❉

A few hours later Oksa was wide awake, even though it was the middle of the night. It wasn't the steady snoring of the Lunatrix keeping her from sleep, though—she was actually lost in thought as she stared out of the huge bay window. The Aegis protecting the city resembled a milky jellyfish as the lights of Thousandeye City at night reflected off it—an entrancing sight that, in other circumstances, would have been reassuring. Tonight, though, she could find no comfort.

She turned over and heard the clothes she'd carelessly rolled into a ball tumble to the floor. Irritated, she stretched out her arm to pick them up. Her jeans, her tee-shirt, her tie—the feel of the strip of two-coloured fabric was electrifying and her spirit instantly left her body.

31

RUBBING SALT IN
A WOUND

G US WAS SITTING ON A PLANK OF WOOD ON THE FLOOR,
his back against the wall and his elbows on his knees. He ran his
fingertips over the soaked carpet, which reeked of filth and mud. The bed-
rooms had been badly damaged by the last flood, which had hit London
a few days earlier. For the first time since the Spurned had come back the
upstairs rooms had ended up under a foot of water, which had sapped
their morale. Then the water had fallen as suddenly as it had risen, and
the sun had reappeared, but this wasn't enough to lift the spirits of the
Outsiders throughout the world or of the occupants of the small house
on Bigtoe Square, who couldn't imagine ever feeling optimistic again.

✲

Oksa's bedroom was in a terrible shambles, but Gus often took refuge
there. And it was here, transported by her Identego, that the New Gracious
found him, looking serious and lost in thought. Her first reaction was to
run to him, tilt his chin up so she could look him in the face and shout:
"I'm here, Gus! I'm here!" He might not have heard her, but he might
have sensed her presence. However, the Identego forced her to keep

her distance, very much against her will—she had to look, learn and understand—so she merely watched, hovering over the wrecked room.

When Gus brushed away the strand of hair covering part of his face, she could see that the ordeals of the past few months had left their mark. Despite the baggy Aran sweater swamping his body, it was impossible not to notice that Gus had lost a lot of weight. His gaunt cheeks emphasized the angular line of his jaw, making it seem firmer. His hands looked much the worse for wear after nailing down, tearing up, sanding, replacing and repairing everything that had been destroyed by the storms and floods. The pure dark blue of his eyes was muddy and it looked as if an inky curtain had dropped down to hide his deep sadness. It hurt Oksa to see him like that. He put his head in his hands and groaned softly. The Identego relented and she was able to draw closer.

Just as she was about to touch her friend's hand, the bedroom door opened and Kukka came in. Oksa jerked back, although no one would ever know she was there.

"You okay, Gus?" asked Kukka softly.

"Sure, apart from the fact that my head feels like some fiendish machine is drilling into it…"

Oksa was irritated to see Kukka shoot Gus a sympathetic look and sit down beside him. She tossed back her long blond hair and the sweet scent of vanilla wafted in Oksa's direction. Even though she was thinner and looked exhausted, she was still undeniably beautiful.

"Those monster bats really did a number on me," added Gus.

Kukka rested her hand on Gus's forearm. And her head on his shoulder. Six feet away, Oksa was rooted to the spot. Gus wasn't doing anything to shake her off! *How had it come to this?* Oksa's Identego didn't move.

It couldn't move.

Because Oksa wanted to know.

"As soon as things improve, Andrew will take you to see all the best doctors," murmured Kukka.

Gus didn't say a word. He lifted his head and leant it against the wall. His face relaxed gradually as Kukka snuggled closer to him.

"You know as well as I do that no doctor on Earth can help me," he said eventually. "The countdown started the moment I was bitten by that bloody Death's Head Chiropteran. And even the Werewall transfusion can't save me. The only thing that can is a concoction made from the sap of an outlandish plant, a stone that doesn't exist here and the snot of a creature that gets high on human emotion. I don't want to seem pessimistic or anything, otherwise you'll tell me off again, but it's not looking good. I'm not going to break any records for life expectancy, that's for sure."

Oksa stiffened. At any other time the Identego was a brilliant power, but right now it was agony, allowing her to watch when she couldn't do anything to help.

"You'll get through this," continued Kukka. "The alternative is unthinkable. Otherwise, who would I play endless games of chess with?"

The Identego didn't react, even though Oksa's mind was desperately urging it to do something. Kukka's words pierced her like poisoned arrows. Thousands of miles away—in another dimension—she was lying in bed and suffering as badly as if she were really in her bedroom in Bigtoe Square, near Gus and that… girl. Apart from Kukka's pathetic attempt at humour, she'd found out something she never thought she would, something she'd always dreaded: that she had a rival. Her heart pounded. Why didn't her Identego do something? Why didn't it grab hold of that bimbo's gorgeous hair and send her flying to the far end of the Earth with a flawless Knock-Bong? And since when did Gus play chess? That simpering bitch must have taught him.

"As it's your birthday tomorrow," said Gus, "perhaps you'll be magnanimous enough to let me win?"

"That's the kind of thing you have to earn!" replied Kukka.

Oksa saw Gus smile. She clenched her fists.

"You know, it's twelve years ago today that I was adopted by Olof and Lea. It was the day before my fourth birthday."

Oksa cried out in her bed as her Identego lurked in a corner of her bedroom in Bigtoe Square. Kukka had been adopted! Like Gus! That must have brought them closer. But that revelation made Oksa realize how uncharitable and thoughtless she'd been: she'd never even wondered why the daughter of two Insiders hadn't been able to enter Edefia. The only thing she'd been interested in was Kukka's relationship with Tugdual, and then Gus. Nothing else. She'd never tried to find out anything about Kukka's personal life. And now, the fact that she was learning the answer to questions she'd never bothered to ask felt like rubbing salt in a wound.

"Do you remember anything from before, then?" asked Gus.

"Only a few vague memories. Olof and Lea were so wonderful that it was easy to forget what had happened."

"What you went through was awful."

"Yes, it was," said Kukka softly.

She paused as her eyes misted over, then she continued:

"What about you? Do you remember anything?"

"No. I was a baby when my parents came to collect me from the Chinese orphanage. They're the only parents I ever knew."

Neither of them spoke for a while.

"Do you think we'll ever see them again?"

"No," whispered Gus.

Oksa's blood ran cold. Had Gus lost heart? Was he that demoralized? She had to do something. A tear slid down her cheek. She surrendered control and gave free rein to her Identego.

Gus shivered violently, staring wide-eyed. Kukka pulled away and looked at him in surprise.

"What's wrong?" she gasped.

"It's Oksa!" gasped Gus.

Kukka sat up suddenly.

"Gus!" she exclaimed reproachfully. "Stop it! It *can't* be Oksa!"

But the Identego was already surrounding Gus, filling him with an intense sensation of pleasure that felt so real it was almost physical.

"It is Oksa," he insisted, his face transfigured.

Kukka gazed at him wearily. Then she got up and left the room, looking miserable.

"Oksa, if you can hear me, do something!" begged Gus.

Concentrating hard, Oksa tried to make a discernible movement or gesture. It was incredible that Gus sensed her presence, but she had to do better than that. She focused on the tie that Gus, like her, never seemed to take off, and tried to catch hold of the end to yank it upwards. The few ounces of fabric felt heavier than a block of concrete. With her body drenched in sweat and her heart in pieces, she wept with frustration in her bed. Then it occurred to her that maybe she should leave well alone.

Perhaps a hope destined never to be realized was worse than despair?

Yielding sadly to the will of her Identego, Oksa let it embrace her friend one last time, which gave her a melancholy pleasure. Then, after a few seconds, she finally realized her efforts hadn't gone unnoticed when she heard Gus murmur "Thank you".

⁂

After a while, feeling comforted and delighted, Gus decided to leave Oksa's bedroom, unaware that he was being followed by the Identego, which took the Gracious upstairs.

Dragomira's strictly private workroom was in shadow. Only a small oil lamp was burning inside one of the many niches in the walls, shedding a yellowish glow over the room, which had been converted into a dormitory.

Oksa watched Gus lie down with a tired sigh. Her Identego allowed her to caress him lightly one last time, promising to return soon, then she looked around to see which of the seven beds might belong to her mother.

She located her without difficulty: the wheelchair was a dead giveaway. With a silent cry, Oksa felt herself rush over to what she recognized as Dragomira's old bed. Marie Pollock was lying on her side, fast asleep. Oksa rested her head on the pillow a few inches from her mother's face and studied her. Even asleep, she looked exhausted. The dim light made her skin appear waxy, but Oksa was sure it was probably worse in broad daylight. She reached out a hand and stroked her hair. It seemed coarse and much thinner than she remembered. Suddenly Marie shifted in her sleep and her chapped lips parted to let a plaintive murmur escape.

"Oksa…"

"I'm here, Mum," whispered Oksa. "I'm here."

Marie, who was in a deep sleep, sighed and her face relaxed. Oksa stretched out beside her, keeping her eyes fixed on her mother's much-loved features. Then the late hour got the better of her and she fell into a comforting, yet short-lived, doze.

32

A Guided Tour

O KSA WAS EVEN MORE AMBIVALENT ABOUT THE BENEFITS of her visit to Bigtoe Square than the last time. When she awoke it took her a few minutes to realize she was in her apartment in the Glass Column, in the invisible dimension of Edefia, so near and yet so far away. Her heart and mind were still in London, in Dragomira's strictly private workroom, with her mother fast asleep in bed. And it was so very hard to come back.

"The pain of waking performs its inscription on the face of my Gracious."

Still lying down, Oksa turned her head to glance sceptically at her Lunatrix.

"My Gracious must proceed to the repatriation of her entirety," the creature instructed nasally. "Her heart cannot allow disappointment to exert destructive dominion over it. It must feast on the hope that resides in the future because the solution possesses existence within the Ephemeral Secret."

Oksa nodded silently.

"The lumpy throat of my Gracious may be suppressed by the ingurgitation of a morning snack, does she possess the desire to make the attempt?"

When Oksa didn't react, the steward sprang into action. Combating his natural reserve, he grabbed his young mistress's hand and pulled at her, puffing and panting, with all his might.

"Horizontal positioning and melancholy converge on pointlessness," he continued. "The list of tasks for my Gracious experiences proliferation and does not allow forgetfulness of the integration of the healing of her mother and her friend. This list demands the return of the will of my Gracious."

The Getorix made a standing jump onto the bed, trying to pirouette at the same time, which brought a wan smile to Oksa's lips, while the Lunatrix continued to pull on her arm.

"That girl looks very heavy," remarked the Incompetent from the armchair, doing a good imitation of a household object which has been put down and forgotten.

This remark was too much for Oksa, who couldn't help giving a hysterical guffaw which brought tears to her eyes.

"Hey, mush for brains!" exclaimed the Getorix, jumping back onto the bed. "Don't forget that girl is our Gracious!"

The Incompetent looked at it in confused suspicion.

"It doesn't seem to be making her very happy," he said.

Oksa stopped laughing immediately, and the Getorix threw himself at the Incompetent, beating small, angry fists against its wrinkled abdomen. But the laconic observation spoken by the soft-headed creature had struck a nerve. Cut to the quick, Oksa got up from her bed, tidied her hair by combing her fingers through it and went over to the Incompetent. She grabbed the Getorix by the scruff of its neck and held it at arm's length while she gave the lethargic creature a well-deserved kiss.

"Thank you!" she said. "From the bottom of my heart, thank you. You've just hit the nail on the head."

The Incompetent gazed at her blankly before sinking back into its hazy reverie. Oksa dropped the Getorix, which was struggling violently, and turned to her Lunatrix.

"Didn't you say something about a morning snack?"

The Lunatrix nodded, beaming from ear to ear.

"I need to regain my strength," added Oksa, looking fiercely at him. "I've got work to do, you know."

᠅

Although sunshine was still rare, Edefia's temperature had risen by a few degrees and, more tellingly, the daylight was noticeably brighter. Although the sky was still overcast with depressingly grey clouds, as in London, the sun was managing to force its way through in places to cast patches of comforting brilliance.

Guided by Emica and Olof, the two Servants for Reconstruction, and accompanied by her usual entourage—Abakum, Pavel, Tugdual, Zoe and the Lunatrix—Oksa walked down the wide avenues of Thousandeye City, which had been laid out in a semicircle. What she'd seen of the city while imprisoned by Ocious in the Glass Column bore no resemblance to what was before her now—the thick layer of grey dust carpeting the paved streets, the skeletal trees and the dilapidated houses had gone. The rain that had fallen when the Heart of the Two Worlds had been healed, and equilibrium restored, had revived the city, along with all Edefia, even though it still bore the scars of countless wounds. Built in a circle around the Column, the city's surface area had gradually been eroded by desert-ification over the years. The centre, however, was relatively unscathed, although the buildings, which couldn't be maintained in good order, hadn't escaped the depredations of the Years of Tar. These poignant, noble houses, although flaking, cracked and sometimes partially demolished, still retained some of their former splendour. Built on movable bases that allowed the whole building to follow the sun throughout the day, most of them were composed of different-sized cubes stacked in pyramids or less conventional forms. Metal or stone frameworks supported walls made of slabs of opaque glass or blocks of wood covered with all sorts of climbing plants. Vertical farming, which Oksa had seen carried out in

Leafhold, had been adopted here on a grand scale. However, although the buildings had valiantly braved the crippling shortages, the few surviving plants were dying, despite the recent rain.

"What a shame," said Oksa, fingering the dead shoots of a gnarled vine hanging over the entrance to a building.

"It's a disaster, that's what it is!" bawled some Getorixes passing by, their arms full of building stones.

"That's why water conservation will be so important," added Emica, her clear eyes fixed on Oksa. "You were quite right to create a special Mission. Before the Great Chaos, we managed our resources sensibly, but we didn't anticipate what was going to happen. We had no experience of shortages and we didn't know what that meant."

Staring ahead, she concluded:

"It was simply beyond our imagination,"

"But that's only natural!" exclaimed Oksa. "When everything's always gone smoothly, it's hard to imagine anything different. But I think you adapted brilliantly to the situation, you managed…"

She broke off, gazing into space.

"To survive?" suggested Emica.

Oksa looked at her attentively.

"Yes, you managed to survive," she nodded.

"And survival is what it's all about, if it leads to recovery," said Abakum, scratching his short beard. "Come over here, sweetheart, my Gracious," he continued with a smile.

He gestured to her to kneel at the foot of the dead vine. Watched inquisitively by around twenty creatures—stripy-legged Velosos, shape-changing Polyglossipers, hairy Getorixes—the Young Gracious complied with impatient enthusiasm, especially as she knew what would happen. As soon as she plunged her hands in the dark, slippery earth she felt warm life vibrating through her fingers, spreading into the ground and imparting its beneficial effects to every particle of soil. On the surface the vine stem began to tremble, at first imperceptibly, then more vigorously. It inflated and deflated, as if taking deep breaths in and out, while tiny buds emerged along its shoots. Soon these exploded into bloom, liberating green and purple leaves which soon covered the trellis. The first bunches of delicious-looking grapes were forming already. Oksa stood up and, resting her hands on her hips, took a step back in wonderment while the Velosos cheerfully did pull-ups on the revitalized branches.

"My Gracious has possession of the gift of Greenthumb," explained the Lunatrix.

"That's what I thought", said Oksa quietly.

She shot her father a conspiratorial glance, full of nostalgia. They both vividly remembered the French Garden, the restaurant founded jointly by the Pollocks and Bellangers in London. Pavel had employed the incredible power which Oksa had just used to create a unique indoor garden with hawthorn bushes, climbing roses, daisy-strewn lawns and even a magnificent oak tree right in the middle of the restaurant. Pavel winked at his daughter: she was going to enjoy the gift of Greenthumb. Oksa was in her element as she raced from withered flower beds to shrubs with bare branches, busily bringing springtime to Thousandeye City. Citizens and domestic creatures at work on roof terraces or in gardens stopped what they were doing to encourage their New Gracious and applaud the wonders being performed before their eyes. Suddenly Oksa stopped. Her cheeks flushed with excitement and her hands dirty, she asked:

"There's something I don't understand: why didn't the Sylvabuls use this power earlier? I thought they all had it."

"That's not strictly true, darling," replied Pavel. "It's not enough to be a Sylvabul, you also have to possess Gracious blood to have the Greenthumb power. As a result, only a few of us can speed up Edefia's recovery."

Oksa pouted, showing her dimples.

"There's you and me," she said, thinking hard.

"The Fortensky clan," continued Pavel, "my cousins, Cameron and Galina, as well as their children. And, because of his unusual origins, our dear Abakum."

Oksa thought for a moment.

"It that all?" she cried finally.

Pavel pursed his lips in a grimace of resignation.

"That's still quite a lot, don't you think?"

Oksa was still racking her brains.

"Okay, leaving Orthon and his vile sons out of the equation, what about Reminiscens and Zoe? They should have this gift, shouldn't they?"

"Malorane wasn't a Sylvabul," explained Pavel. "She was a Long-Gulch. Greenthumb is only passed down to Sylvabuls who are direct descendants of the Gracious."

"Oh, I didn't know that," sighed Oksa. "What a shame, that would have helped us go a bit faster."

She thought again for a second.

"But Zoe must have it then!"

"Yes, because of her shared ancestry with Leomido."

"Brilliant!" cried Oksa enthusiastically.

"Gracious Oksa, would you like to continue our tour?" broke in Emica.

"Oh yes! Let's go."

The group headed towards some concentric avenues farther away from the Column and the cube-shaped houses. Here the buildings were rounder with softer curves, some shaped like yurts, others similar to demi-spheres, all of them covered in partly broken plates of glass forming hundreds of shimmering facets. Everything was in ruins here—it was a bleak sight.

"This part of Thousandeye City was founded some twenty years after the Great Chaos," explained Emica. "Our land was devastated by storms the like of which we'd never seen before. The wind inflicted enormous damage, particularly on the type of houses you saw in the centre."

"The cubes certainly weren't very aerodynamic," remarked Oksa.

"Most of the dwellings in this area were wrecked by the bad weather," continued Emica. "At that time, no one realized the full extent of the decline we were facing. We knew everything had changed and that nothing would be the same again, but none of us thought things would get so bad so quickly. There were still a lot of us too, the birth rate remained high and there was a terrible shortage of accommodation due to widespread destruction. That's why everyone got down to work rebuilding the houses that had been flattened, adapting to the circumstances as best we could, the way we'd always done. This led to the construction of this belt of rounded houses, which was called the 'Dome District.'"

"What a good idea!" remarked Oksa.

"Like the cube-shaped houses, they pivot on their foundations to harness the rays of the sun."

"That's ingenious. But they're in a terrible state," added Oksa, gazing at the debris strewn over the ground and the general state of disrepair.

"The population dwindled dramatically, people gathered in the centre of the main cities, abandoning certain parts of the territory," explained Emica. "These houses have been uninhabited for over ten years. Until your allies came to live in them again a few days ago. There were so many of them that the inhabitants of Thousandeye City couldn't accommodate them all, so they came here and look, they're already hard at work!"

Oksa narrowed her eyes. A sunny interval allowed her to glimpse inside some of the dome-like houses. Men and women wearing wide blue or khaki kimono trousers were bustling around with tools in their hands and smiles on their lips. Some large hedgehogs and odd-looking blue marmots were climbing over the glazed walls. Intrigued, Oksa walked closer.

"I've seen those creatures before in Leafhold," she said. "But we weren't introduced."

Abakum took her hand and led her towards the first house, a vast residence shaped like a cheese-bell. He gently picked up one of the hedgehogs and one of the marmots, both of which wriggled frantically before they noticed Oksa and froze like statues.

"Oksa, this is a Dirt-Sucker and this is a Lusterer!" he said placing them at her feet.

33

The Safety Zone

"**D**ELIGHTED TO MAKE YOUR ACQUAINTANCE!" SAID OKSA, carefully kneeling down.

The two creatures' eyes grew impossibly wide, then a shrill scream issued from their narrow mouths, which were filled with tiny teeth. Oksa jumped up and took a few steps backwards. The creatures were shaking like leaves.

"They're such cowards!" laughed the Getorix.

Abakum gave it a stern look, which didn't stop the roguish creature from jumping around the others, who were transfixed by fear.

"Don't be afraid," said the Fairyman softly, bending down. "This is our New Gracious."

The creatures immediately stopped trembling at this announcement and Abakum turned to Oksa with a smile.

"Oksa, despite their apparent awe of you, these creatures are a dab hand at household chores."

Oksa couldn't help laughing, which did nothing to ease the anxiety of the two little helpers or lessen their rigidity.

"The Dirt-Sucker derives its name from its main function," continued Abakum. "It sucks up dirt. See those long, soft spines? It uses them to pick up the dirt, which it then swallows and digests. Although it would never say no to a piece of corn or a grape, its staple diet is dirt."

"Excellent!" exclaimed Oksa. "It's a one-stop recycling system! What about this... marmot?"

"The Lusterer? It works alongside the Dirt-Sucker. Its role is to polish and buff things to a high shine; its luxuriant blue fur contains the ideal ingredient for that kind of chore."

Oksa was dying to plunge her hand into the Lusterer's magnificent electric-blue pelt. She ventured a gentle touch and the lustrous marmot immediately rewarded her by arching its back under her fingers.

"Fantastic!" sighed Oksa in delight, her fingers buried in its fur. "I haven't touched anything so soft since the cuddly octopus I had when I was little! Nor anything so greasy since I had to clean up that bottle of oil I broke in the kitchen," she added, withdrawing her glistening hand.

The Lusterer gave a sort of husky chuckle and, from its delighted expression, Oksa surmised that her praise hadn't fallen on deaf ears. This reaction encouraged Tugdual and Zoe to copy her and the three of them began stroking the remarkable cleaner, which lay flat on the newly cleaned paving, offering as much of its body to their caresses as possible. Oksa was laughing heartily when she suddenly noticed Abakum's worried face. The sky instantly darkened and everyone stood up, looking around, as the Dirt-Sucker and Lusterer scurried inside a house. Everyone working in the buildings nearby came out, looking up, on the alert.

❋

Granok-Shooters in hand, Pavel, Abakum and Emica surrounded Oksa while Tugdual, Zoe and Olof rose ten feet above the ground. Oksa surveyed the sky carefully.

The Dome District bordered the outermost zone of Thousandeye City, a belt of barren ground, devastated by the insatiable desert, whose carpet of black dust had turned to a sticky paste in the recent rainfall. The barely visible, opalescent membrane of the Aegis was fastened to the outer edge of this belt. No one would know it was there but for the breeze and the odd sunbeam, and this transparency meant that the Felons outside could see everything that was going on in Thousandeye City—and vice versa. Standing there in terror, everyone soon realized what had darkened this area of the sky: part of the surface of the Aegis in front of Oksa was covered by tens of thousands of Chiropterans and Vigilians, which were beating their wings ominously against the shield, making it quiver.

"How disgusting!" murmured Oksa, her hand over her mouth.

The Gracious squadrons soon converged from all districts of Thousandeye City to position themselves along the transparent membrane, Granok-Shooters at the ready. On the other side the first Felons appeared, clad in leather armour. The two clans couldn't come to blows as they were separated by the almost invisible barrier which, although effective, didn't stop Oksa and her supporters from feeling intimidated by this show of force: despite being perhaps five times less numerous than Oksa's allies, the Felons were terrifyingly battle-hardened. And they had those diabolical insects, which struck fear into even the bravest hearts. Furthermore, despite being muffled by the shield, the strident whistles of the Chiropterans continued to assail their eardrums and disrupt their nervous systems.

Oksa glanced at Abakum.

"There has to be a way of fighting *that*!" exclaimed Oksa.

The Fairyman nodded with the air of someone who's already thought long and hard about the problem. Oksa waited wide-eyed, anxious to hear the details, especially if they could allay her fears, but Abakum had already turned away to focus on the dark swarm. The red-eyed bats and caterpillars with their stinging hairs were pressing against the membrane, stretching it like elastic, trying to bore a hole in it. On every side, Felons were cutting through the scudding clouds yelling war cries at Oksa and her protectors and firing Granoks or Fireballisticos which, although they bounced harmlessly off the shield, were still designed to provoke.

"I hope it's strong enough!" gasped the Young Gracious.

"The Aegis isn't indestructible," replied Abakum, "but don't worry, it's strong enough to withstand this kind of attack. The Felons just want to appear stronger than they really are. For the moment, though, they aren't ready to go further than a display of strength."

This remark took Oksa's breath away.

"You mean one day they will?" she asked. "They might be stronger than us?"

"Of course," replied Abakum gravely, almost inaudibly.

Oksa noticed that Tugdual and Zoe were Vertiflying very close to the hideous creatures and punching them through the stretchy material. She was dying to join them and give vent to the anxiety provoked by those flying monsters and the Felons. She'd just decided to take to the air when a familiar figure appeared among the Chiropterans. Orthon was hovering a few yards away, a nasty smile on his grim face. A cry rang out: as Zoe watched, Tugdual had just been propelled suddenly against Orthon. The two of them stared at each other, the Felon with dangerous resolve and Tugdual with helpless, yet distressing, submissiveness. Then, as violently as he'd been drawn towards Orthon, Tugdual was thrown backwards and, spinning out of control, he crashed to the ground.

Oksa raced over to him. Kneeling at his side, she took his hand, which was as icy and stiff as the rest of his body. He didn't appear to be injured, but the dark mist over his eyes revealed a deep confusion. He was staring at the exact spot where Orthon had appeared. Oksa turned. She could again see the sky and the Peak Ridge Mountains bristling along the horizon. The Felon had disappeared along with the swarms of Chiropterans and Vigilians.

"Are you all right?" asked Oksa, a lump in her throat. "Have you broken anything?"

Tugdual struggled to a sitting position and rested his elbows on his knees.

"No, I think I'm fine," he stammered, still in shock.

Oksa's Lunatrix came to stand in front of him and peered into Tugdual's ashen face.

"The confrontation of Gracious Hearts has consequences stuffed with gravity for the equilibrium of mental faculties."

Oksa cocked her head to one side. She frowned dubiously at her little steward.

"The breakage of bones or the sprainage of limbs do not give cause for any lament," the latter hurriedly continued. "The body of the beloved of my Gracious presents the conservation of an intact constitution."

Oksa couldn't help feeling embarrassed by the Lunatrix's description of Tugdual, even if it was the simple truth. She let her hair fall over her face to hide her crimson cheeks and walked mechanically towards the membrane. She probed it with her fingers, feeling the texture. Although she'd imagined that the substance was similar to plastic or silicone, she found that it was a dense, almost living matter, like flesh made water. And, like any living thing, it was impermeable but could absorb what it needed and defend itself instinctively to stay alive. As a result, while letting in the wind and the rain, it would obstruct anything it deemed undesirable or harmful.

"It's like a giant Nascentia."

A commotion roused her from her observation: the Corpusleoxes were racing towards her, escorted by a score of Squoracles, including her own two, dressed in their multicoloured mohair sweaters. The huge creatures, half-lion, half-woman, skidded to halt before Oksa in a spray of dark mud.

"Our respects, our Gracious!" boomed one of them. "Please be advised that your enemies have just tried to enter Thousandeye City on the south side."

Oksa paled.

"Did they... succeed?" she stammered.

The Corpusleoxes threw their heads back and roared, batting the air with paws bristling with lethal, blood-stained claws. "Stupid question," thought Oksa, gnawing her lip.

"How did they go about it?" asked Abakum.

"They began by firing Fireballisticos which had no effect," replied one of the Squoracles. "The Aegis doesn't react to heat or cold, unlike those of us whose delicate metabolism is extremely sensitive to variations in temperature—not that anyone cares. We could die of hypothermia and no one would notice."

"Oh, I think we would," said the Getorix, cackling. "Things would be a lot quieter round here!"

The little hen shivered and looked up at the sky before continuing:

"Then they started firing Granoks loaded with an acid we've never come across before. The doorway was damaged, but they couldn't breach the reinforcement. The Corpusleoxes dissuaded those impertinent Felons from continuing their attack and, in our view, some of them will probably remember the lesson they were taught for a long time to come! We immediately strengthened the door hinges with the help of the Servants for Granokology and Protection."

"Nicely done!" exclaimed Oksa.

The Squoracle fixed her with tiny eyes like marbles.

"Our Gracious, did you know that Cameron—the son of our late-lamented Leomido—was one of the best locksmiths in that horrible wet, icy city called London?"

"I had heard as much, yes," confirmed Oksa.

"Well, he's now part of the Protection Mission and has joined forces with Sven in Granokology. Their combined talents have worked wonders in reinforcing the door so that it is now stronger than ever! Which is more than can be said for us poor Squoracles. We have to put up with freezing temperatures when we're carrying out our nightly guard duties," the little hen couldn't help adding.

Oksa tried not to laugh. The Squoracles never missed an opportunity to elaborate on their favourite subject.

"I'll bring you some braziers," announced Abakum with a smile.

"You have our eternal gratitude!" squawked the Squoracles in unison.

"Oh, I know," said Abakum, looking amused.

Oksa glanced around for Tugdual, hoping he would be just as tickled as she was by this entertaining interlude, but met Zoe's serious gaze instead. Tugdual was farther away in one of the circular streets of the Dome District, standing with his narrow back to them. Oksa clenched her fists. She was about to call to him when she thought better of it, her heart heavy with a strange sadness.

34

INEVITABLE

OKSA WAS BREATHING IN SHORT, FAST GASPS AS SHE SAT on the edge of her bed with her elbows on her thighs. The nightmare she'd just woken from had really shaken her. She sat there for a few seconds, then stood up and went through the shadowy room to the bathroom. Her Lunatrix sat up in bed.

"Go back to sleep," murmured Oksa before he had time to ask any questions. "Everything's fine."

The little steward looked sceptical, but obeyed without saying a word.

✻

Heated deep underground, the water flowed into the oval bathtub made of bluish crystal. Oksa lit a small candle, took off her pyjamas drenched with sweat and slipped into the water. She poured in a few drops of Nobilis oil, which smelt a little like cardamom and reminded her of those blissful few moments with Tugdual among the roots of the Monumental Tree in Leafhold.

Tugdual had played a starring role in her nightmare during which she'd killed him, guided by Orthon's cold, implacable hand. She'd seen herself, Granok-Shooter in hand, committing this terrible deed, then collapsing beside her victim's body as Orthon looked on, his eyes bright with mingled triumph and sadness.

Lying in her fragrant bath, she shook her head to banish these horrible, meaningless images. She closed her eyes and sank lower in the bathtub, hoping to be soothed by the tranquil quiet of the night, but her mind wouldn't let her relax. She jumped up, splashing water over the Feetinsky-wood floor, and grabbed her dressing gown. Wrapping it around her, she threw herself into her armchair by the bay window.

Tomorrow was another day.

Bring on tomorrow…

❋

The Velosos sped through the corridors of the Glass Column and the streets of Thousandeye City, their long striped legs pumping as if they were clearing hurdles. Their New Gracious had given them a mission— their first—and they were determined not to fail.

The first person to receive a visit from one of these diligent creatures was Abakum.

"A Gracious message for you!" sang out the Veloso. The Fairyman ushered it into his apartment and closed the door behind him.

"I'm listening."

"Our Much-Loved Gracious wishes to call a meeting of the High Enclave," announced the messenger. "Gather in the Round Room on the top floor of the Column in an hour, by Outside time, or in twenty grains of the hourglass, by Edefian time."

Abakum smiled, not at the way the message was conveyed, or at its contents, but in satisfaction.

"You can tell our Beloved Gracious that I wouldn't miss it for the world!" he exclaimed.

In the next few minutes, all the Servants of the High Enclave received a similar visit from a Veloso and were given the Gracious's message. Although not a member of the High Enclave, Pavel was also invited to attend as Special Adviser. He finished his steaming drink in a hurry, pulling a face: he'd forgotten to think of his preferred beverage—a strong cup of coffee—and unflavoured Zestillia tasted disgusting.

Exactly an hour later, everyone met in the room that Oksa had discovered and deemed perfect for uses of this sort. Shaped perfectly like a fishbowl, it was at the centre of the fifty-fifth and top floors, between the Memorary and the Gracious's apartments, which ran around the perimeter of the Column. The honey-coloured glass ceiling softened the light, although traces of the damage caused during the Great Chaos could still be seen. In fact, unlike other parts of the building, this room had been neglected, because Ocious had thought it too plain for a man of his stature. Oksa had immediately fallen in love with its small proportions and intimate feel. The Dirt-Suckers and Lusterers had cleaned the walls from top to bottom, then the Lunatrixes had been given the task of furnishing it with odd, unused pieces of furniture, which gave the Round Room the appearance of a comfy living room rather than an impersonal meeting room.

"There are several questions worrying me," declared Oksa gravely, sitting in a pinkish snakeskin armchair, her arms on the armrests. Although her father and Abakum weren't completely fooled by her outward composure, the concern in their eyes gradually turned to encouragement and admiration. They had to admit she had courage. She studied the Servants of the High Enclave grouped around small tables before her and tensely asked point-blank:

"What are we going to do? What should we do?"

Most of the Servants seemed taken aback by her frankness. Some of them squirmed in their seats, while others froze and a leaden silence fell over the room.

213

"I mean—what do we want to achieve? What do we want?" continued Oksa, her eyes shining.

Abakum cleared his throat, taking his time before replying:

"Sweetheart… my Gracious… what we are able to do depends partly on the Secret entrusted to you in the Cloak Chamber," he said finally.

"Why?" exclaimed Oksa, tense with incomprehension.

"If Edefia has to remain closed, that will affect what… we do," replied Abakum carefully. "As well as what our enemies do too."

No one missed the intense look Oksa gave him.

"Our future depends entirely on the conditions of the Secret."

"I understand," Oksa murmured.

She was aware that Abakum knew the gist of the Secret. And she appreciated both his tact and the fact that he'd left her room to manoeuvre. The Graciouses' Watcher was staying in the background and leaving her in charge of the situation. She took a breath, leant back in the armchair and continued:

"The Ageless Ones couldn't impose a secret identical to the Secret-Never-To-Be-Told because it no longer exists. That's why they confided a new one to me: the Ephemeral Secret."

The Lunatrix, who was standing nearby, hanging on his mistress's every word and attentive to her every need, twitched anxiously. He was clearly flustered by the very mention of the Ephemeral Secret.

"Like the previous Secret, it's bound by the rules that govern any secret: it must not be told to anyone," continued Oksa with an anxious frown. "However, it's very different. You will have realized from its name that, due to the situation we're in and the problems we're facing, it's a temporary measure."

Everyone nodded solemnly.

"I can't tell you everything…"

"Don't put yourself in danger!" Pavel broke in quietly.

Oksa looked reassuringly at him.

"My life isn't in danger from the Secret."

First Pavel, then everyone else, looked immensely relieved.

"Will it be possible to open the Portal again?" he couldn't help asking.

It was inevitable that someone would ask about opening the Portal if Oksa brought up the subject of the Secret, but it still made her heart pound. She looked to the Lunatrix for comfort; but he was translucent, paralysed with anxiety, while Abakum had closed his eyes. Everyone there was listening intently and trembling with impatience so, in a stronger voice than she would have thought possible, she replied:

"Yes."

The tension suddenly dissipated. They looked at each other with tears in their eyes, while Oksa struggled to come to terms with the ramifications of this shock revelation. In her mind's eye she again saw the Spurned on the banks of Lake Gashun-nur. Breathlessly, she shook her head to chase away the flood of painful images, but it was no good, random memories ran through her head. The Russian airport crowded with hysterical passengers, the lemony fragrance of Gus's hair, the mildewed smell of the house on Bigtoe Square. The despair in her mother's eyes, her body ravaged by pain.

Nearby, Pavel looked shaken by this news. He slumped down in his armchair as if, freed from doubt, his last ounce of strength had deserted him. Tears began to flow quietly down his face. The other Runaways who'd left behind family members on the Outside—the Bellangers, the Knuts, Cockerell—were even more deeply affected. Oksa couldn't look at them: the weight of hope she'd rekindled with that simple "yes" was unbearable.

Three little letters—three little letters that would radically change everyone's future.

Prevented from saying more by the Ephemeral Secret, she looked away in horror, feeling panicky. If she couldn't tell them everything, she could at least avoid giving most of them false hope.

"It will be possible to open the Portal and it won't kill me," she confirmed, doing her best to keep a grip on herself. "But it's not that simple, there are constraints."

"You've told us the crux of the matter!" interrupted Abakum.

Despite his mild tone, this contribution by the Fairyman, First Servant of the High Enclave, made everyone anxious. What were these "constraints" that he clearly wanted kept under wraps?

"What you've told us is crucial, Oksa," he continued. "Knowing that it will be possible to open the Portal means that we can plan ahead and answer the questions you asked. What are we going to do? What do we want to achieve?"

Oksa looked gratefully at him.

"For the time being, we're protected by the Aegis and we're rebuilding Thousandeye City, which represents a tiny part of Edefia," he went on. "But, like the new Secret, this is only a temporary situation."

"There are too many of us to live like this for long," said Sven, the old man with long braids. "We'll end up running out of space and supplies. The city is largely an urban area with very little arable land and few basic resources. Even if we use them as wisely as possible, we won't last for long."

"We'll soon need Green Mantle and the whole territory," added Emica. "But we also need to defend ourselves. We're not ready to fight the Felons."

"Why not?" Oksa couldn't help asking.

Nervously, she chewed her nails until her fingers bled.

"We have to prepare as many weapons as possible," replied Abakum, his short beard rustling under his fingers.

"How long will that take?" continued Oksa.

Everyone looked at each other, their expressions ranging from scepticism to total confidence.

"The time it takes for the Felons to decide to attack," Naftali said eventually.

"What?" cried Oksa, sitting up straighter. "You mean we're waiting for the Felons to attack us?"

"That's right," admitted the towering Swede.

"But there are far more of us than them!" protested Oksa. "We could crush them like woodlice today, I just know we could."

Mystia and a few of the other Servants shivered. In Edefia, nothing and no one was ever crushed, not even woodlice. But Oksa was too lost in thought to worry about niceties. She settled back in her armchair and crossed her legs with an annoyed look on her face. Then her slate-grey eyes scanned the small gathering, glowing with new intensity.

"We let them come to us, retaining the advantage of terrain and superior numbers," she said softly, thinking out loud. "Then we hit them with everything we've got and stamp them out once and for all! Sorry about the image."

"You've got it!" said Abakum with a smile.

"It's a good plan."

"Irrespective of the conditions governing the opening of the Portal, a clash with the Felons is inevitable," continued Naftali.

There was a murmur of agreement: everyone seemed impatient to cross swords at last with those who'd kept them down for years.

"Thanks to Abakum's Tumble-Bawler, we know that all kinds of tensions are putting our enemies at loggerheads," added Sven.

"I didn't know you'd sent a spy!" remarked Oksa in surprise.

Sven and the other Servants who weren't Runaways looked down in remorse.

"It was an excellent move, though," continued Oksa, discomfited by their reaction. "And what did your spy see?"

"The relationship between Andreas and Orthon appears to be causing conflict," explained Abakum. "Both of them want to be Ocious's golden boy and he'd rather let them kill each other than take sides."

"What a creep!" exclaimed Oksa. "But that plays into our hands, doesn't it?"

Abakum looked sceptical.

"Yes and no. Any rift between them works to our advantage. However, equilibrium can't be restored while they're in a position to harm us and we can't make any real progress, whether we stay or leave."

Oksa nodded. Everything he'd said seemed very sensible and the tactful way he'd mentioned the Portal filled her with gratitude. The Portal was important, but they had other priorities.

The Young Gracious shivered, her head filled with contradictory yet complementary feelings of fear and impatience. With her blood racing through her veins and her temples pounding, she asked anxiously:

"Do we know what we're going to do? Do we have a tactical approach? A strategy?"

The Servants of the High Enclave looked at her with such fire in their eyes that a long explanation was unnecessary.

"Are we ready?" she asked finally with narrowed eyes.

"We become readier with every passing hour," replied Abakum.

Oksa stood up, her heart thumping, but her head held high. The Felons would soon know whom they were dealing with.

35

HALFTONE

O KSA WAS HARD AT WORK WITH HER HANDS BURIED IN
the soil. This morning, she'd decided to concentrate on replanting
the shopping street, which had been refurbished by the city's inhabitants
with an enthusiasm born of their desire to return to normal. Many shops
now lined the semicircular main road, a clear sign of better days to come,
even though shelves were still quite bare.

However, the black, seething patches which regularly covered the
protective membrane were a continual reminder that this long-desired
return to normality was still a distant dream. And, although the sudden
reduction in light intensity when the sky darkened caused widespread
anxiety, the attacks by night were even more harrowing.

The impact of Fireballisticos and Granoks loaded with acids of different types produced showers of sparks which at night looked like a
lethal attack by hundreds of blowtorches. Military surveillance units,
named the "Hawk Brigades" and the "Owlet Squadrons", had formed of
their own accord to mount guard day and night. Men and women of all
ages, Aeropeller riders or Vertifliers, patrolled the entire Aegis, checking for breaches. When they found an area of weakness they alerted the
Servants for Granokology and Protection, who stepped in immediately to
strengthen the membrane. In this society under reconstruction, everyone,
whatever their status, did what they could without complaint.

Oksa frequently visited the wise Corpusleoxes and overwrought Squoracles to give them moral support. New candidates still occasionally turned up to join the Gracious's camp and it was crucial that the sentries guarding the entrance to Thousandeye City were incorruptible. However, the Young Gracious was careful not to mention her real reasons for visiting the borders of the Dome District so often: she had an urgent, deep-seated need for reassurance. The Felons' frequent attempts to enter the city had put her in a blind panic that she couldn't and wouldn't admit to anyone. She was the Gracious—she had to show everyone she was strong and set an example. Even when she didn't feel like it.

Several times a day, she'd check that the only way into the city was as impregnable as everyone claimed. Moreover, Cameron, the gifted locksmith, had moved into a tent beside the entrance to keep an eye on it during the Felons' attacks. It was clear that Leomido's son, like the rest of the Runaways, had thrown himself into this mission to avoid thinking about the Spurned. His three sons had passed through with him when the Portal had opened, but Virginia, his wife, had been left behind on the banks of Lake Gashun-nur in the middle of the Gobi Desert. And the wound inflicted by this enforced parting was becoming harder to bear with every passing day.

Two days earlier, at the sight of Cameron's grief-stricken face, Oksa had decided to tell him what she'd seen via her Identego: his wife, Virginia, was in London with some of the other Spurned. She was doing well and showing great courage. Cameron's eyes had immediately lit up, then filled with tears. That was when he'd decided to erect a tent near the entrance and devote himself heart and soul to his work, which was the best thing he could do in the present circumstances. Overjoyed at having an audience for their continual grumbling about the weather, the Squoracles had soon grown very fond of this thin, stylishly dressed man, who'd not only inherited Leomido's looks but also his kind nature, and they hadn't hesitated to invade his tent at every opportunity. Cameron hadn't minded since the tiny hens had proved to be entertaining—if extremely voluble—companions.

※

The prudent citizens had taken the precaution of storing vast quantities of seeds, which had become increasingly precious as Edefia declined. "There is nothing more durable than seeds in the world of nature," Abakum had reminded Oksa, opening one of the four giant silos in Thousandeye City.

Carrying a bag full to bursting with priceless seeds, Oksa was recreating the landscape. Every plant and tree that sprang from the earth needed considerable energy, which she drew and replaced from a kind of endless inner loop: the more energy she used, the more she received. There were eleven of them with the gift of Greenthumb, but hers was the strongest. Although Zoe and the Fortensky clan could only produce flower beds and vegetable plots—which was no mean feat—Oksa could cultivate the largest specimens of plant life in Edefia. Her favourites were the Parasol trees. Unfortunately, Abakum and the Sylvabuls had advised her not to "sow" too many: the tangled root system of trees that grow to a height of over fifteen hundred feet could lift several blocks of houses. The Parasol tree wasn't an urban species and Oksa was told to propagate safer trees such as Broad-Leaved Ball trees and Dwarf-Majestics.

From time to time, she couldn't resist taking a few Inflammatoria seeds from her bag and burying them in the earth. These plants were a great favourite of hers and it only took a few seconds for the first flowers to start screaming with joy at being reborn and ejecting tiny spurts of incandescent lava, which gave birth to a new plant as soon as each touched the earth.

"You look like you're having fun!" said Tugdual, clinging like a huge spider to the top of a wall.

"I'm having a whale of a time!" replied Oksa with a grin. "Watch this!"

Brandishing a baby pink seed, she presented it to Tugdual, turning it this way and that with a theatrical flourish, then buried it in the soft earth.

"Pah," sniffed Tugdual with a wicked smile, "you'll have to do better than that if you *really* want to impress me!"

"Just wait."

A new plant shot up from the earth, its stem rapidly putting out countless little shoots covered in thick, hairy foliage. Scores of leaves unfolded as Oksa and Tugdual watched this extravagant speeded-up growth spurt.

"Welcome to Earth, Pulsatilla!" Oksa said quietly. "Would you do me a favour?"

The plant, now sixteen inches tall, shook itself like a wet dog and wrapped a stem around Oksa's wrist with surprising tenderness for a plant. Then, suddenly changing its mind, it stretched out to curl around Tugdual's ankle and pull him towards the ground.

"Hey!" he cried. "That's not fair. You're ganging up on me!"

Hands tightening into claws, he clung to the wall with all his might. The Pulsatilla was stronger than his Alpinismus, though, and he soon had to give in. With unexpected gentleness, the playful plant floated him through the air and set him down beside Oksa, who looked very smug. The Pulsatilla gathered its stems together and rolled them up to form an abundance of tight curls.

"Brilliant!" exclaimed Oksa, applauding. "From now on, I'll call you Curly Pulsatilla."

The plant chuckled with pleasure. Tugdual smiled when Oksa met his eyes and her face brightened.

"Okay, I admit it," conceded Tugdual, stroking Oksa's cheek with his fingertips. "That was a pretty impressive trick."

He studied her, his head tilted to one side, his expression irresistible as always.

"Your Greenthumb power is pretty good," he said casually.

"So's your Alpinismus power," replied Oksa in the same tone.

"Do you want to take a short break?"

Oksa nodded and they sat down on a thick, freshly planted lawn.

"Everything's such a mess," she said looking around.

"Work in progress!" replied Tugdual with a chuckle.

Make do and mend was the motto on everyone's lips, but magic was proving to be a godsend. Everything was happening much faster than anywhere on the Outside and it all seemed so easy: not only did the men and women of Edefia know how to process materials and use their gifts wisely, but they were also more than happy to join forces for a common cause. They were working hard to restore the former glory of the rundown buildings. Materials floated from hand to hand, people Vertiflew from place to place or climbed along walls with an ease that never ceased to amaze Oksa, even though she'd seen it all before. Dirt-Suckers and Lusterers crawled around them, removing all traces of dirt, Getorixes were bustling about trowels in hand, hair covered in plaster dust or splinters of wood. The three Incompetents were doing their bit too. Tireless fetchers and carriers, doubling as workbenches on legs, they followed or tried their best to follow their companions, handing them any tools they might need. More often than not their responses to the requests of the creatures working as makeshift stonemasons, joiners, plumbers or roofers left a lot to be desired: in their lackadaisical minds, hammers became saws and screwdrivers became drills. Nevertheless, they gave their help generously with endless goodwill.

"Everyone's working so hard!" remarked Oksa.

As she said that, she gave a remote helping hand to her Incompetent— which was trying in vain to determine the meaning of the word "bolt"—by depositing the correct object directly in the hands of an impatient Polyglossiper.

"I love doing that," she said quietly.

"And you do it so well," remarked Tugdual. "Like a lot of other things."

"I'm far from perfect," retorted Oksa.

At that moment a group of Felons appeared some hundred and thirty feet up, on the other side of the membrane. The dark figures flew through the pearl-grey sky and disappeared after a loud explosion, accompanied by an enormous burst of flame. A few seconds later, the Hawk Brigades appeared in order to carry out a thorough inspection.

"You see!" growled Oksa, frowning. "Sometimes I think we'll never be left in peace."

Her Incompetent came to sit beside her. Stroking its wrinkled head absent-mindedly, she continued:

"Don't get me wrong, I love it in here. It's absolutely fantastic and there are loads of things to do, but it's a bit like a large, beautiful prison, isn't it? I don't think it would take long for me to go stir-crazy. If only I could visit Leafhold or even the Distant Reaches... or the Peak Ridge Mountains! I'd love to go back to those caves lined with precious stones and see Edefia from Mount Humongous—we can't live under this bubble for ever."

"You know very well we won't," replied Tugdual.

Oksa ducked her head, letting her hair hide her face.

"I'm not talking about the Portal being opened," he said. "I know you have to keep it secret."

"I don't know when it'll open!" she snapped. "It could be tomorrow or in ten years' time. How stupid is that?"

Tugdual looked at her in surprise.

"I'm talking about the battle, Oksa. It's inevitable, you know that. It can only be a matter of days."

Oksa took a deep breath and then lay back on the velvety grass. The Incompetent looked at her incredulously.

"I wonder how they can devote so much energy to doing all that, when they know it could all be destroyed again overnight," she said.

"They need something to hold on to after so many hard years. What would you have them do? Wait patiently, Granok-Shooters in hand, or do endless drills? They proved they can fight not so long ago."

"But they don't know that the worst is still to come!"

"The worst?" asked Tugdual in surprise.

"People aren't stupid, are they? We all know it's going to be terrible."

"Are you frightened?" asked Tugdual.

"Not a bit!" exclaimed Oksa.

He stretched out beside her, his eyes fixed on the sky.

"You're becoming a true warrior," he said, sounding amused.

"You've noticed, have you?"

They laughed softly.

"And a bloody good one," added Tugdual. "Brave and determined."

"Don't you mean formidable?" asked Oksa.

Tugdual looked at her sideways.

"Formidable, sure, why not?" he conceded.

They were quiet for a moment, lulled by the clouds moving above them and by the sounds of people working around them. Despite the Aegis, there was a warm, soothing breeze.

"Everything that's happening is insane, isn't it?" said Oksa softly.

"I'm not sure if that's the word I'd use, but it is pretty surprising."

Oksa punched his arm. Faster than a snake, he grabbed her hand and imprisoned it.

"You went back to London, didn't you?" he asked point-blank in a pained whisper.

"It wasn't me," protested Oksa, almost inaudibly. "It was my Identego."

"You or your Identego, it's the same thing, Lil' Gracious."

"It isn't!" protested Oksa.

Tugdual squeezed her hand harder.

"It is," he insisted. "Your Identego goes where you want to go."

"What are you trying to make me say?"

"Do you think about him a lot?"

Oksa looked at him, aggrieved. She started to sit up, then changed her mind, her cheeks burning and her breath ragged.

"If you *must* know, I do think about him a lot, because I worry about him a lot! And not just about him, about my mother too, and everyone who stayed behind! Gus…"

Her voice trembled and her body was rigid with anger. She tried to pull her hand away from Tugdual, but he wouldn't let her.

"Do I have to remind you that Gus and my mother might die?" she raged. "So, yes, I do go and see what's happening when I can't bear it any more. And yes, it's really exasperating to watch your very beautiful cousin Kukka doing her level best to make Gus fall into her arms, especially as he does nothing to stop her!"

She broke off, surprised and winded, then continued in a strangled voice:

"But I'm far more worried about the condition he and my mother are in."

She glared at Tugdual.

"Okay? Are you happy now? Did you get what you wanted?"

An enormous black cloud was fast forming above them. Tugdual released Oksa's hand and she sat up, burying her face in her knees.

"Can I answer?" murmured Tugdual.

Oksa groaned her approval.

"Firstly, no, it's not okay," began Tugdual tightly. "Secondly, no, I'm not particularly happy. And thirdly, yes, I got what I wanted and more. Is there anything else you'd like to ask?"

Oksa shook her head. Tugdual gently rolled a flyaway strand of Oksa's hair around his index finger. She tried to push him away, but he put an arm firmly around her shoulder. Despite her anger, she couldn't help leaning against him.

"Look what a state you've got yourself into," he murmured in her ear. "Calm down or you're going to start another rainstorm."

"Too late," said Oksa, wiping away the drops of rain spattering her forehead as well as a tear trickling down her cheek.

She put her arms around Tugdual's waist and hugged him as tightly as she could, burying her face in the hollow of his shoulder as if she wanted to disappear into him.

36

FULL-SCALE PREPARATIONS

T HERE WERE TWO BIG ADVANTAGES TO THE TORRENTIAL
rain which had just fallen: it had removed the thick mud tracked
onto the paved streets of Thousandeye City by the constant comings and
goings, and it had dissipated some of Oksa's choking anger by allowing
her to let off steam.

"Would you like me to show you something?" asked Tugdual.

Oksa looked at him gratefully.

"I might be wrong, but it seems like you're one step ahead of me
again!" she said. "You know your way around this land better than I do.
I won't have it! You'd better watch your step or I really will lock you up,
on my word as a Gracious. You can't say you weren't warned!"

Tugdual's teasing smile was infectious.

"Show me what you've discovered then," she sighed, pretending to be
exasperated, even though her eyes were shining.

"Come with me."

He led her through the labyrinth of circular streets in the direction
of the hills bordering the northern part of the city. Oksa was captivated
by the faded magnificence of some of the derelict houses they passed on
their way up to the hilltop.

From the summit, they had a panoramic view of Thousandeye City
spread out below in an intricate maze of interlocking semicircles that

surrounded the Glass Column like small commas and large brackets. On the other side of the city, the perfect oval of a vast lake shimmered in the rare sunshine, its white sandy shores forming a sharp contrast to the dark sheen of its waters.

"Oksa, what you see before you is Brown Lake," announced Tugdual.

"I thought Edefia's lakes had dried up!" said Oksa.

"You've made it rain so much, though," he countered.

"What, that much?"

"Looks like it."

Oksa recognized her father in the distance, putting his Greenthumb power to good use. Around him, Parasol trees were shooting up to tower ten feet above the ground in a matter of minutes.

"Dad!" Oksa couldn't help shouting.

Pavel straightened up and waved, then returned to work.

"It's so peaceful here," said Oksa. "It's gorgeous!"

As if to contradict her, various groups of men and women suddenly Vertiflew at top speed over Brown Lake, followed by others clinging to Aeropellers.

"What are they doing?" asked Oksa, intrigued by their intricate spins and aerobatics.

Tugdual grabbed her arm and made her turn round.

"Hey!" she protested. "What are you hiding?"

"It's a surprise," replied Tugdual. "Come on, let's go."

Oksa pulled away, a smile on her lips.

"A surprise? What surprise? Tell me!"

Tugdual put his finger over his lips to indicate secrecy.

"You're so annoying!"

He raised his eyes to heaven.

"Will somebody here tell me what's going on?" she yelled, cupping her hands around her mouth like a megaphone.

The Vertifliers and their companions on Aeropellers immediately stopped performing aerobatics and shot over her head, greeting her deferentially. No one said anything.

"Great," groused Oksa, running her fingers through her hair. "I have no authority here at all."

"Poor Lil' Gracious," teased Tugdual.

"Couldn't you find it in your heart to give me a clue? Or do I have to throw myself at your feet and beg?"

Tugdual reached out to ruffle her hair. She decided to let him.

"Don't tempt me!" said Tugdual, laughing. "The only thing I'll tell you is that you're going to love it."

Oksa shrugged.

"If you say so..."

And she shot off in a fast Vertiflight.

*

When she reached the Glass Column, her Incompetent was waiting for her with a Ptitchkin on either shoulder.

"I was asked to wait for someone and take them somewhere, but I can't remember who or where," the bewildered creature confided candidly.

Oksa burst out laughing. The Ptitchkins began chirping and flying around the Incompetent.

"You're expected in the third basement of the Column, our Gracious!" they peeped.

"What are we waiting for, then?" said Oksa.

The tiny golden birds pushed the Incompetent with minuscule pointed beaks, as sharp as rose thorns.

"It really hasn't got anything between its ears," remarked one.

Oksa took the Incompetent's hand. He looked at her earnestly and announced:

"I'm a little lost. I wonder if you were the one who was supposed to wait for me and take me somewhere…"

Oksa hugged it.

"That's entirely possible!" she exclaimed.

"That's what I thought," it concluded, looking defiantly at the birds which were warbling with hilarity.

The Young Gracious headed for the transparent lift which took the small group to the first basement. From there, they had to continue on foot down gently sloping, interminable corridors covered with rough stones. The Incompetent walked slowly, the bristling golden crest running the length of its large, flabby body swaying unsteadily from left to right. The Ptitchkins, on the other hand, were flying all over the place, swiftly skimming past the narrowing walls.

From the minute they entered the third basement, Oksa and her companions could see light spilling a hundred feet or so from the farthest room and hear the commotion. As they drew nearer, a Getorix shouted:

"The Gracious is coming!"

Abakum's face appeared in the doorway.

"There you are, sweetheart!"

He ushered her into a huge vaulted room, whose walls were tiled with worn and uneven mosaics which must once have been magnificent. Polypharuses hung by one tentacle from the capitals of the column, shedding an intense light on a singular hive of activity.

"So what's the correct term?" Oksa asked Abakum. "Is it a farm or a plantation of Goranovs?"

The Fairyman gave a chuckle, echoed by three other people and a score of Attendants working alongside them. On long tables, about fifty Goranov plants were swaying in the draught caused by the blades of an enormous fan, over ten feet in diameter, which had been built into the back wall. Getorixes equipped with tiny hoes were going from pot to pot, aerating the earth and removing any moss on the surface. Nonetheless, it seemed that these hypersensitive plants still felt that the attention lavished on them left a lot to be desired.

"Is anyone ever going to milk us?" cried one, extending its branches towards the ceiling. "Or are they waiting for us to explode? Is that really what they want?"

The plants were shaking with agitation. The Attendants hurried over and began milking them, gently squeezing the swollen buds between their hooves.

"Wow!" cried Oksa, marvelling at the magic plants and their no less incredible helpers.

She turned to Abakum and his friends, who were wearing aprons and gloves. She recognized Sven, the ancient old man with braids, and two younger women who'd been liberated from Confinement and Sealencing in the eighth basement a few days earlier.

"Do you realize you're witnessing something of a miracle?" asked Abakum. "We were within inches of losing the last living Goranov plant in the two worlds."

Oksa looked questioningly at him, as a plant more imposing than the rest trembled from top to roots.

"There was only one left in Edefia after Ocious's reckless management of Goranov farming, and that was several years ago," explained the Fairyman. "On the Outside, Dragomira, Leomido and I had shared the three plants we'd managed to take with us in my Boximinus when we were ejected from Edefia. Despite the harsh conditions in Siberia, the Goranovs acclimatized pretty well."

"Unlike the Squoracles!" said Oksa, smiling mischievously.

"Poor chicks!" remarked one Getorix.

"That's right," continued Abakum. "When we emigrated to France, then England, they survived because of our constant care and attention. I even managed to get Leomido's plant to procreate and the one I possessed—"

"My children!" shrieked the large Goranov with a heart-rending wail.

Two Getorixes immediately rushed over to gently massage its broad, shiny leaves. But the poor plant had already fainted with grief at the mention of its offspring.

"As you know, Dragomira's plant was abducted by Mercedica and Orthon's eldest son, Gregor, when we we ictured," continued Abakum. "Imprisonment on the Island of the Felons as well as the fear caused by this ordeal was too much for it and it didn't survive. Then, on our way to the Gobi Desert, the Goranov I'd managed to keep alive all those years couldn't cope with our stressful journey, despite being safe inside my padded Boximinus. The pitching and tossing of the boat, then travel by air, train and bus, had been too much to expect of one of the most sedentary plants in existence. When we got to Edefia I discovered its corpse at the bottom of the Boximinus, with two dead seedlings from Leomido's plant."

"It was terrible!" broke in Oksa's Getorix. "There they lay, stone-dead, grey leaves shrivelled. The Goranov and its three surviving children almost died of shock too."

"Fortunately, the other creatures had the presence of mind to isolate the poor plants while they were temporarily in a coma. The damage had been done, though. The youngest seedlings were too badly traumatized to survive, particularly when faced with the fearsome prospect of extensive farming and the industrial extraction of their sap by the Felons. Only Leomido's Goranov was strong enough to handle the enormous pressure."

The Fairyman had whispered these last words, since the newborn Goranovs were stretching out their leaves to listen. The nearest plants however managed to catch a few scraps of conversation and paid dearly for their curiosity: unable to cope with such horrific details, they screamed with terror and collapsed.

"Watch out! Watch out!" yelled a Getorix. "Mass fainting fit in the front row! Quickly, Incompetent crest balm urgently needed! I repeat: Incompetent crest balm urgently needed!"

There was the sound of hooves clattering over the mosaic floor as the Attendants galloped to the aid of the sick, weaving their way between tables and jostling each other with their gnarled antlers.

"Perhaps they would benefit from a cardiac massage," suggested the Incompetent with unusual presence of mind.

Oksa's Getorix looked at it in exasperation.

"Thanks for that brilliant medical advice, lamebrain! And how exactly do you want us to perform a cardiac massage on plants that don't have a heart?"

"Excuse me, but we do have a heart!" protested the Goranovs, which hadn't fainted, or at least not yet.

Oksa was crying with laughter, despite the gravity of the situation.

"I'm sorry," she gasped, waving her hands in the air to fan herself.

Keeping a straight face with difficulty, she turned to Abakum.

"If I understand you correctly, then, it's a good job you managed to retrieve your Boximinus when you escaped from the Column."

"Indeed," nodded Abakum. "And that's all down to Tugdual. In the general confusion he was the one who had the idea of taking my Boximinus with us. Without him, our creatures and the last surviving Goranov would be in the hands of the Felons."

Oksa looked thoughtful for a second, gazing at the plants as they gradually regained consciousness.

"Does that give us an advantage?" she asked.

"The Goranov represents a huge advantage," replied Abakum. "Its sap has always been the vital ingredient in the manufacture of Granok-Shooters and, of course, Granoks."

"That's brilliant!" cried Oksa exultantly. "It means the Felons can't make Granoks."

"You're right, but we shouldn't count our chickens before they hatch. I have it on good authority that Ocious was very cunning—he divided up the vast stocks produced over the years, as well as those seized from the population. Part of that hoard is here, in the underground passages where we found the confiscated Granok-Shooters, but there are more in the Peak Ridge Mountains, our enemies' stronghold. And from what we've seen, they've succeeded in perfecting some new weapons, such as the acid-bearing Granoks they've been firing against the protective membrane."

Oksa's slate-grey eyes darkened as the Attendants watched her with benevolent curiosity.

"We're working round the clock to counter as many dangers as possible," broke in an apple-cheeked woman. "Would you like to come with me?"

37

THE GHASTLY GRANOK

OKSA FOLLOWED HER TO THE BACK OF THE ROOM, WHERE the blades of the giant fan were turning slowly with a faint grinding noise. To the Young Gracious's surprise, the woman plunged her arms into the stone wall, then smiled confidently at her and disappeared.

"But…" stammered Oksa.

"Try!" urged Abakum.

"I've never managed to do it before," she confessed in annoyance.

The woman's arm popped back through the wall. Oksa put her hand in hers and found herself pressed flat against the stone, which remained impenetrable.

"It won't work," she complained. "I'm a Werewall and I can't even pass through a lousy dividing wall!"

"Some things you can do just like that and others take a bit more effort," remarked Abakum. "This new skill probably needs a little practice, that's all."

"That's top of my list then!" exclaimed Oksa. "I really want to be able to do this."

"Tugdual would make an excellent teacher, given half a chance," added Abakum with a wink.

Oksa looked away, pleased and embarrassed at the same time, as a section of the wall swung open to reveal a concealed door.

"A back-up solution for failures like me," she said, slipping through the half-open door. "Good thinking!"

On the other side, the apple-cheeked woman was waiting for her in a room with an impossibly high, domed ceiling. With a warm smile, she invited Oksa to see for herself how accurate her words had been: everyone watched with bated breath.

"Oh, I see!" breathed Oksa, flabbergasted at the sight before her.

The walls of this secret room were entirely lined with shelves laden with enormous bottles of Granoks and Capacitors, while other even bigger containers stood on the floor, painstakingly labelled by Attendants concentrating hard on their task.

"Hello, Oksa!" came a voice.

"Reminiscens!"

The fragile-looking woman emerged from the shadows, a Polypharus on each shoulder. Although the ordeal of her Impicturement and the injuries inflicted by her twin brother, Orthon, could still be seen in her face, she looked more radiant than ever. Her long, plum-coloured silk tunic rustled as she approached and her pale blue eyes shone with determination.

"How are you?" asked Oksa politely.

From the day Oksa had met her in the Maritime Hills, she'd been impressed by Reminiscens. The daughter of Ocious and Malorane, Orthon's sister, Zoe's gran, and a brave fighter to boot, Reminiscens had been through the mill: subjected to Beloved Detachment by her own father, ejected to the Outside, left to her own devices when pregnant by Leomido—whom she didn't know was her half-brother—deprived of her son by Orthon, who'd ordered him to be killed, then Impictured: she'd suffered so much.

"To tell you the truth, I haven't felt this well for a long time," replied Reminiscens cheerfully.

Oksa could have sworn she was smiling at Abakum. She glanced quickly at the Fairyman. She might only be sixteen, but she knew he'd loved Reminiscens for ever, even though life had seen to it that his love would remain unrequited. Reminiscens had been prevented from feeling anything but friendship for him, at first by her devotion to Leomido, then by Beloved Detachment. Oksa thought it was terribly sad, even though Abakum seemed over the moon about things now.

A crackling noise roused her from her thoughts. A still, ten times bigger than the one that had held pride of place in Dragomira's strictly private workroom, was vibrating steadily some distance away in the vast room. Its tubes intertwined to form a network so complex that it defied comprehension. Sweetish smoke was rising from the highest tube while the lowest one was spitting out hundreds of Granoks, which were being gathered carefully by an Attendant. Watching closely, Oksa was amazed to see that such clumsy-looking creatures could be so deft with their hooves—handling anything had to be a real challenge—but the Attendants were doing their job to perfection.

Oksa walked over to some waist-high jars, full to overflowing with Tornaphyllons, Dermenburns, Dozidents, Memory-Mashes, Colocynthises, Arborescens, Putrefactios, Hypnagogos—each one had to contain thousands of Granoks! On the top of one shelving unit she noticed a black glass bottle, much smaller than the others, whose label and lead seal looked intriguing.

"Crucimaphila," she murmured, deciphering the name written in silvery letters. "The ultimate Black Globus."

She stopped herself from saying out loud what she knew about the effects of this exceptional Granok. The highly dangerous Crucimaphila produced a black hole that sucked up and annihilated any form of life.

Abakum came over and stood behind her with his hands on her shoulders.

"Now you're a Gracious, you're allowed to use this Granok," he explained. "In fact, you're the only person who can."

"You can too!" retorted Oksa earnestly.

She'd never forget the courage it had taken the Fairyman to fire the terrible Granok at Orthon when Dragomira was in danger in the Felon's London cellar. Orthon hadn't died, due to his unusual metabolism, inherited from Temistocles, the first and most powerful Werewall. However, the Crucimaphila had neutralized him for a while.

"You know this can only be used in exceptional circumstances," continued Abakum. "Particularly as I've strengthened it," he added, referring to the tragic episode Oksa had just remembered.

Oksa nodded seriously, her eyes fixed on the dark jar.

"Due to the power and unique nature of the Crucimaphila, your Granok-Shooter can only hold one at any given time. More than one will cancel out the effect of the other Granoks and cause irreparable damage to your Granok-Shooter. Likewise, a certain time-lapse has to be observed between uses."

"How long?" asked Oksa, fascinated.

"One hundred days."

She whistled between her teeth and turned round to look at Abakum.

"The Crucimaphila is deadly," he whispered anxiously. "Using it runs counter to the principle of respect for human life which we hold so dear."

He stopped, his face tense.

"Orthon and his followers left us no choice," he added. "I know it's the worst reason of all, but we were in such great danger—we had to be able to defend ourselves, and we had to have this deadly weapon in our arsenal."

"I understand," whispered Oksa.

He stood before her and gazed at her intently, his eyes full of bitterness and sorrow.

"What I'm going to say to you fills me with horror. I wish things could be different, but unfortunately I have to give you one of these lethal Granoks, because it might be the only way to stop the man who's leading us into far worse danger than anything we've already overcome."

"What do you mean?" stammered Oksa. "Am I going to have to kill Orthon?"

Her blood ran cold at the thought. She'd wanted him dead so many times. Orthon was the sworn enemy of the Runaways and she knew that the two worlds would be much better off without him, but the idea of killing him was both terrifying and inconceivable.

"Orthon is our worst enemy. The only way to stop the type of man he is would be to kill him, which is something I regret more than anyone. But don't forget he isn't acting on his own and that the harm has already been done."

Oksa stood rooted to the spot, eyes wide.

"So if you have to do it, then do it," he whispered.

"Abakum, tell me everything!"

"All you need to know is that I'll always be near you, sweetheart. But fate will show you the way, not me."

He turned towards the set of shelves and his arm lengthened by a foot to seize the black jar. An Attendant immediately galloped over to offer its back as a low table. Its velvety brown eyes gazed at Oksa with boundless admiration as Abakum opened the precious bottle. Reminiscens joined him and handed him a chrome-plated set of tongs. They exchanged a serious look.

"Oksa, let me have your Granok-Shooter, please."

Oksa rummaged around in the little bag she never took off.

"Here," she said, trembling.

Abakum took a soot-black Granok from the jar. It was so big that Oksa feared it wouldn't fit into her Granok-Shooter, but it shrank, flattened and elongated on contact with the mouthpiece and was sucked into the depths of the magical blowpipe. The Granok-Shooter's meerschaum surface grew so hot that Oksa almost dropped it, but the Attendant breathed on it and its temperature returned to normal.

"Abakum," murmured Oksa, "please take one too."

He looked at her sadly, then obeyed.

"Listen carefully," he said finally, his face ashen.

He whispered in her ear the magic words that would let her use the ghastly Granok when the time came, although the Young Gracious hoped fervently she would never have to.

38

A Mysterious Surprise

S TANDING ON HER BALCONY ON THE TOP FLOOR OF THE
Glass Column, Oksa was looking out over Thousandeye City in
bemusement. The city, which was usually bustling with activity, seemed
lifeless, almost dead, as if every single inhabitant had disappeared.

"Are you sure there's nothing you want to tell me, my Lunatrix?"

The pudgy little creature shook his head frantically from left to right.

"The will of the domestic staff of my Gracious encounters no opposition to providing the contribution of informative help," he replied.

"Well then?" exclaimed Oksa, squatting down opposite him. "If you're
willing and able, what's stopping you from telling me what's going on?"

"The domestic staff of my Gracious provided a promise to the Fairyman
and the father of my Gracious to keep muteness in his mouth."

Oksa scratched her head.

"Oh, I see—it's a conspiracy."

She forced herself to look at him sternly, then said cuttingly:

"It's very mean."

The Lunatrix gave a gasp of surprise. His large blue eyes began spinning
in their sockets and his face, round as a pumpkin, turned pale with panic.

"Um, my Gracious encounters an immersion in error," he stammered.
"Conspiration and meanness do not experience existence in the hearts
of the Fairyman and the fatherhood of my Gracious!"

Her hands stuffed in her jeans pockets, Oksa gazed at him, then burst out laughing. She bent over to pick up the poor, crestfallen creature, who flushed even more vividly.

"I'm sorry, my Lunatrix, I was just teasing!"

That was all it took for the Getorix to mock the Lunatrix.

"Hey, servant! Do you know what humour is? H, u, m, o, u, r," it spelt out, cavorting around the Lunatrix.

"Bad Getorix!" scolded Oksa. "We don't make fun of each other, okay? Anyway, look at him, he's all dressed up."

The Getorix inspected the Lunatrix's spotless dungarees, gave a cursory bow and went back to dusting the leaves of a Pulsatilla, which owed its birth and phenomenal growth to Oksa. The astonishingly affectionate plant couldn't now imagine life without Oksa. Farther off, ensconced in its armchair in the corner of the large bay window, the Incompetent was counting on its fingers.

"H, u, m, o, u, r," it repeated, its expression full of uncertainty.

The Getorix raised its eyes to heaven, whistling through its teeth while Oksa put her hand over her mouth to stifle a snort of laughter.

"That word has six letters," concluded the Incompetent, clearly pleased with this discovery.

"Brilliant!" Oksa couldn't help remarking, her eyes shining.

"For pity's sake, don't encourage it, my Gracious," muttered the Getorix.

"The steward of my Gracious must make the attribution of a piece of information stuffed with importance," broke in the Lunatrix.

"What's that?" asked Oksa mischievously, pretending to be surprised. "Doesn't 'Humour' have six letters?"

Proving the Getorix wrong, the Lunatrix gave a smile so broad that it split his lovable face from ear to ear.

"The communication of an imminent, cherished visit is to be announced," he said.

Hearing this, Oksa rushed to the door and threw it open. Her father was a few yards away, in the corridor lined with timeworn colonnades.

"Dad!" she cried, throwing herself in his arms.

Touched by his daughter's enthusiastic reaction, Pavel gave her an affectionate hug.

"To what do I owe this outpouring of affection?" he asked with a laugh.

"Hey, that's not fair, I'm always like this with you!" protested Oksa. "Come in, my Lunatrix has made some crazy good walnut biscuits. You'll go mad for them."

"Aren't I mad enough already?" he retorted, following her into the large main room.

Oksa grinned at him.

"I'm so glad to see you!" she said, dropping into an armchair.

The Pulsatilla stretched out its longest stem to stroke the arm of the person it loved most in the world.

"You look ever so smart," she continued, taking in her father's traditional Edefian outfit of dark grey wool. "It really suits you."

The wide, flat-pleated trousers and double-breasted tunic, fastened at the side with leather cords, made him look like a samurai warrior. His short ash-blond hair peppered with grey emphasized the melancholy grey-blue of his eyes. When he leant forward eagerly to sample one of the biscuits Oksa had recommended, she took the opportunity to say:

"I hear you and Abakum are plotting against me."

The Pulsatilla stiffened and turned the candy-pink petals of its single flower towards Pavel. There was clearly a certain amount of animosity in this reaction, even though the plant had no face or eyes.

"I'm only joking, Pulsatilla," said Oksa, pushing the pot back a few inches, and adding to her father:

"It's very protective of me."

"I can see that!" said Pavel, looking amused. "You're certainly in good hands."

"Except that people are keeping things from me," retorted Oksa. "Like, for instance, why there's been all this activity in Thousandeye City, why people stop talking as soon as I come within earshot, the sly smiles... I'm getting paranoid."

Her father's face lit up as he announced:

"You've probably noticed I look even more elegant than usual. Well, you'd better put on your glad rags too, because today is a special day, my darling Gracious daughter!"

The Lunatrix went over to the Cloak, which was carefully draped over the wicker dummy. When he tried to pick it up, the garment pulled away and rolled into a tight ball, as impenetrable as steel.

"Did you see that? My Cloak has its own security system," explained Oksa. "If anyone except me touches it, it armours itself."

"Ingenious," remarked Pavel.

The Lunatrix carefully handed the textile ball to his young mistress, who shook it out to reveal the magnificent embroidered fabric of the Cloak. Oksa smoothed her white blouse, adjusted the tie which she never took off, dusted down her jeans and draped the Cloak over her shoulders. The woven threads had lost none of their power. When they touched the Young Gracious she felt an incredible surge of energy as strength and warmth flooded through her, filling her with the same wonderment she felt every time she donned the Cloak. She looked around for her father, but he'd vanished.

"The advice is given to my Gracious to divert her gaze towards the balcony," said the Lunatrix.

Oksa turned to look outside and saw what, deep down, she'd expected to see: her father was waiting for her with his Ink Dragon deployed above him, his face glowing with happiness.

❊

Perched on the back of the giant creature, Oksa flew over Thousandeye City, her Cloak billowing in the wind. This bird's-eye view of the city only confirmed her earlier impression from the top of the Column: the place looked deserted, as if all the inhabitants had upped sticks and left. The Ink Dragon hedge-hopped over roof terraces and semicircular streets already partially lined with vegetation, which boded well for the future. From time to time the dragon's wing-beats sounded like a heavy velvet curtain being shaken to remove the creases.

"Where is everyone?" wondered Oksa.

Her creatures, which had climbed on board with her, looked at her without replying. They were under strict orders from the "conspirators" not to break their silence and they intended to obey. The Ink Dragon suddenly veered towards the northern hills where Tugdual had taken Oksa three days earlier. Still flying low over the ground, the dragon skimmed over some magnificent ruined buildings and sparsely paved avenues to reach the treeless hilltops.

Although Oksa might have had some inkling about what was going on, nothing could have prepared her for the scale of what had been planned by the whole nation without her knowledge. When the Ink Dragon rose above the hills and she discovered the truth about the surprise waiting for her—*her* surprise—she almost fell off its scaly back.

Seated on ten grandstands built on stilts around the dark waters of the lake were about five thousand men, women, children and creatures who'd joined forces with the New Gracious. When she appeared, everyone leapt to their feet and a loud clamour rose into the sky, bouncing off the Aegis rippling above them. The Ink Dragon dived towards the expanse of water and flew its entire length before doing a U-turn and cruising slowly along the crowded banks. The commotion grew louder as the dragon flew past, whipping Oksa into a state of exultation. With tears in her eyes, she saw thousands of people smiling at her. And it was not only the nation's extraordinary show of solidarity in rallying to her cause but also their heartfelt joy at paying tribute to their Gracious that moved her more than words could say.

39

LET THE
FESTIVITIES BEGIN!

APPLAUDED ENTHUSIASTICALLY BY THE CROWD, THE INK
Dragon landed on the tiny beach beside the smallest grandstand,
which was covered by a large, gently swaying canopy. Streamers and
banners were also fluttering in the breeze and Oksa was incredibly
touched to see that their navy blue and burgundy stripes picked out the
colours of her tie. Sliding down the dragon's flank, she landed on the
white sand and was soon joined by her three creatures—the Lunatrix,
the Incompetent and the Getorix. The dragon resumed its inky contours
on Pavel's back, amazing the spectators whose cries of astonishment
resounded over the waters.

"Would my Gracious encounter the desire to proceed to the ascen-
sion of these terraces?" asked the Lunatrix. "The Runaway friends
and Gracious relations are filled with waiting for your geographical
proximity."

Oksa looked up at the top of the grandstand and saw some familiar
faces: the Knut and Fortensky clans, the Bellangers, Zoe and Reminiscens,
the Servants of the High Enclave—and Abakum, of course, her Watcher,
who looked more magnificent and happier than ever.

"Come on, darling," murmured Pavel at her side.

He was about to put a fatherly hand on Oksa's shoulder, but then thought better of it. Appreciating his self-control, Oksa touched her father's hand lightly. As she did so, the Cloak brushed Pavel's skin, making him flinch in surprise at the power radiating from the embroidered leaves and birds adorning the sleeve. Oksa turned round, tossed back her hair and flew through the air to the Gracious grandstand, where Abakum greeted her with open arms. Over the Fairyman's shoulder she glimpsed Tugdual, with his incandescent, icy gaze, and behind him, as so often, Zoe, her face shadowed in mystery. They were both wearing symbolic Edefian costumes, as were their family and friends. Oksa's gaze lingered on Tugdual. He'd opted for a double-breasted tunic fastened at the side with leather ties, baggy trousers and soft leather ankle boots, all in black, like his hair. As for Zoe, she was wearing an Asian-influenced quilted silk dress with a high collar worn over wide trousers and flat sandals. Her Venetian blond hair was pinned up in coils framing her solemn, freckled face, and there was no doubt she was very beautiful. Oksa gave both of them a bright glance, which they answered in their own way: Tugdual with a knowing wink and Zoe with a small, reserved smile.

Pavel also landed on the grandstand, with the Incompetent clinging to his back and the Lunatrix and Getorix in his arms. A few seconds later a thundering voice boomed out.

"Ladies and Gentlemen, creatures and plants, may I have your attention, please!"

Oksa tried to locate the source of that incredible voice. Surely it wasn't coming from the tiny bird with lemon yellow wings?

"We're gathered here today to honour our new sovereign—I am, of course, referring to Gracious Oksaaaaa!" continued the megaphone-bird.

All eyes were on Oksa, who had spectacular crimson splotches over her cheeks, forehead and neck. Her devoted Getorix began fanning her with a small Parasol tree leaf.

"I'm going to have to say something, I think," groaned Oksa.

She looked at her father for confirmation, a deep vertical crease between her grey eyes: "There's no getting out of it, is there?" Pavel shook his head, amused.

"Okay, fine," she said, reluctantly.

Her eyes wandered towards the packed grandstands built on stilts, where everyone was quivering with impatience for a sign from her. She stepped up to the railing and, gripping it hard, she said clearly:

"I'm very happy to be with you today—" Naftali interrupted her, holding out his hand towards her. An iridescent white ball sat in his palm.

"Everyone will be able to hear you with this Amplivox Capacitor."

"Really?" asked Oksa enthusiastically.

"Of course!" confirmed Naftali, looking wonderful in his dark grey flannel suit.

Oksa took the Capacitor and placed it in her mouth. It melted instantly, creating a strange sensation at the back of her throat.

"Ahem…"

This simple exclamation carried to the far end of the lake. Oksa gave a small, surprised giggle which, amplified and undistorted, was so infectious that it brought a glow to everyone's faces and a sparkle to their eyes. Before long, everyone had erupted into irresistible, deafening laughter, and the louder Oksa laughed, the greater the general hilarity.

"As I was saying, it's a great pleasure for me to be here with you!" Oksa finally managed to say after struggling to regain a straight face. "I shall do everything in my power to restore our lost harmony, but I need you, we need each other, and we will only succeed if we work together."

Making the most of everyone being in the same place, she was reiterating what she'd already said to a fortunate few when she'd formed her High Enclave. A huge cheer interrupted her, as someone's hand came to rest on her shoulder.

"You'd make an excellent politician, Lil' Gracious!" murmured Tugdual.

Oksa's mouth twitched as she pretended to look reprovingly at him, and continued in her amplified voice:

"We've all been hard at work rebuilding Thousandeye City, even though we're well aware of the danger prowling around our borders, and we're far from finished. But today is a special day, I believe. A day of rest, full of surprises that I'm dying to discover—at last!"

The tiny megaphone-bird landed on the railing beside her hand.

"Then let the festivities begiiiiiiiin!" it declared.

There was an even more deafening clamour. Thousands of navy and burgundy flags fluttered on the grandstands, accompanied by cries of joy and impatience.

"The spectacle you're about to see is one of Edefia's oldest traditions!" announced the bird. "Only the oldest citizens among us might remember it, since it hasn't been revived since 1952, during the reign of Gracious Malorane. Gracious, ladies, gentlemen, creatures and plants, I ask you to give the two teams the welcome they deserve before they compete in a thrilling and spectacular Breakball match!"

Oksa stared open-mouthed at Abakum.

"That's amazing," she whispered to muffle the effects of the Amplivox. "I've read loads about this sport in the Gracious Archives. It sounds like a brilliant game!"

Abakum nodded with a smile and urged her to pay attention to eight people who'd just appeared on Aeropellers. The megaphone-bird introduced them:

"In blue are the Speedy Eels, who'll be facing the Scrappy Scarabs in green. Let's give them a big round of appllllllaaaause!"

The two teams flew past the Gracious grandstand, crossing each other at high speed, then came back to hover in front of Oksa, saluting her and her cohort. Then they shot off towards the lake, performing a great many spectacular aerobatics and stunts along the right and left banks, which provoked wild applause and deafening cries from the delighted audience.

"Will you explain the rules to us?" Oksa asked Abakum. She and the younger Runaways listened carefully, keeping one eye on the two teams which were performing some death-defying passes.

"It's very simple," explained Abakum. "It's not all that different to handball, with some rules and variations which you'll love."

"I'm sure!" exclaimed Oksa.

"There are two teams," continued the Fairyman. "The aim is to throw the ball, called the Stinger, into the goals of the opposing team. You can only score a goal after a minimum of three passes between members of the same team, and the Stinger—you'll see why it's called that—can't be held by a player for more than ten seconds. As for the other variations, I'll let you discover those for yourself."

Ignoring his listeners' protests, Abakum settled comfortably in his armchair and pointed to the lake. Around them, the spectators reached new levels of wild enthusiasm. The young Runaways were soon shocked into silence by the creature which had just appeared in the middle of the dark waters...

40

A Thrilling
Traditional Sport

"WHAT ON EARTH IS THAT?" STAMMERED OKSA, LEANING forward over the railing of the grandstand.

No one replied: everyone was much too busy looking at the enormous dinosaur-like creature, at least thirteen feet high, floating imposingly on the water. Its pale grey, bulbous body was as smooth as a whale's and its skin gleamed in the daylight. Swivelling its small head clad in a leather helmet at the end of an exceptionally long neck, the glistening creature looked at the crowd with gentle eyes and Oksa could have sworn that it bowed to her in greeting.

"It looks like an Elasmosaurus," murmured Zoe.

"Or the Loch Ness monster," suggested Oksa, fascinated. The winged commentator, like the spectators, was beside itself:

"And here is the magnificent, the prodigious, the monumental Nestor!"

"So that's what a Nestor looks like," said Oksa in quiet surprise.

It was one thing reading about this creature in the Memory and quite another seeing it in the flesh.

"To give Ocious his due," broke in Abakum, "despite the water shortages, he managed to keep alive a pair of Nestors deep in an underwater cave in the Peak Ridge Mountains. The cave was almost dry when our allies took us there and the poor Nestors were dying. However, fortunately equilibrium was restored, it began to rain and we're all safe and sound."

Oksa shivered at the thought of this extraordinary creature dying slowly from dehydration at the bottom of a barren cave. A golden box fastened by a strap to the Nestor's back caught her attention, as a flaming circle about thirty feet in diameter formed around the creature. She realized then that Brown Lake was being turned into a giant playing field at least as big as four football pitches—by Outside measurements.

At the same time, various Getorixes and Polyglossipers were erecting goals made of woven creepers at either end of the lake. Floating fifteen feet above the water's surface, each goal was guarded by a Polypharus wearing a helmet in the colours of the team it represented. The octopus-like creatures were belligerently waving their eleven tentacles around in the goalmouths.

"Fantastic!" exclaimed Oksa.

"We'll now ask the Shaftshooter for each team to join the other players," announced the megaphone-bird.

Oksa looked at it in amusement. How could such a tiny creature have such a stentorian voice?

"What a remarkable bird!" she muttered.

"It must have fallen into a box of Amplivox Capacitors when it was a fledgling," remarked Zoe, straight-faced.

"You're not kidding!" replied Oksa.

"Who's been chosen?" continued the bird. "We'll find out in just a second."

Two Gargantuhens appeared in the sky, each bearing a player with a bow and quiver on his back. There was a symbol on each saddle: one had a winged eel and the other had a scarab armed with a shield.

"So the Shaftshooters are Gunnar for the Speedy Eels versus Sigurd for the Scrappy Scarabs!" remarked the commentator.

The two Shaftshooters sat proudly on their Gargantuhens and, joined by their teams, flew around the lake to loud applause from the crowd.

"Cheer your teams on, please! The match is about to start!" yelled the yellow bird.

As dignified as swans, the two Gargantuhens made for the centre of the lake.

"Take your places, Shaftshooters, and may the best team win!"

Men and women spread out around the lake and began to blow into their Granok-Shooters, firing a host of Oscillating Granoks into the sky. Bouncing off the air currents, these Granoks caused a swirling wind which made it difficult for the now dishevelled Gargantuhens to remain in the air. The huge flying birds struggled to stay on an even keel, while the two Shaftshooters, whose balance was threatened by every gust of wind, battled to keep their seats. The Oscillating Granoks were wreaking just as much havoc below, creating high waves and dangerous eddies on the water's surface.

After successfully approaching the bright perimeter, one of the Shaftshooters was about to fire a round-tipped arrow when he suddenly listed to one side: his Gargantuhen had just been hit in the flank by a wave at least twelve feet high, causing it to pitch badly. The crowd held its breath, unlike the commentator:

"Gunnar is in danger! Oh no, a fall will ruin the Speedy Eels' chances of winning the title of Best Shaftshooter of Edefia! Gunnar has just grabbed the feathers of the Gargantuhen to right himself. Now that's a brave move, ladies and gentlemen, a very brave move!"

Everyone knew that the enormous flying birds hated their feathers being pulled, as everyone could hear from the noisy screeches of disapproval uttered by Gunnar's mount. The unfortunate Gargantuhen was bucking furiously. During this time, the player from the opposing team was emptying his quiver at the little box on the Nestor's back. The enormous water dragon was leaping around in the water, adding to the choppy waves caused by the endless volleys of Oscillating Granoks. Gunnar drew nearer to the bright perimeter and fired his first arrow, which bounced off the Nestor's thick skin. A second arrow landed in the water as Sigurd prepared to fire again.

"Who will get the Stinger first? The suspense is killing me, Gracious, ladies and gentlemen, creatures and plants!"

However, the very next shot hit home, as all the spectators seemed to have expected: a spray of light shot from the box on the Nestor's back like a sparkling firework. The crowd leapt to their feet in the terraces, shouting with glee.

"Yes! The Stinger has just been released! And it was Gunnar who scored the first point for the Speedy Eels on his third attempt. Well done, Gunnar!"

The ovation spread rapidly through the terraces. The Nestor turned its head and deftly opened the box on its back with the tip of its snout and took out a large ball that sparkled like a diamond in the sunshine. Everyone could see it, even those sitting in the back rows. Holding it carefully in its teeth, the Nestor extended its immensely long neck to Gunnar and dropped the Stinger into his hands with unexpected finesse for such a massive creature. Having accomplished its mission, it turned and dived into the dark waters of the lake, sending up a spray of glittering droplets. It reappeared a few seconds later, escorted by its mate.

"Ballrushers and Ballwarks, please take your places. Our Gracious is about to start the game!" announced the winged commentator.

"What?" spluttered Oksa. "What do I have to do?"

"You Vertifly to the two Nestors," said Abakum. "Gunnar will hand you the Stinger. Then you have to throw the Stinger as high as you can."

"Is that all? Okay, I think I can do that, be back in a tick!" exclaimed Oksa with a broad grin.

In the meantime the eight players, wearing clothing and helmets in their team colours, were seething with impatience. They took up their starting positions with their Aeropellers upended in front of them, as the Polypharuses waved their tentacles in the goalmouths.

"Our Beloved Gracious, it's your turn!" informed the megaphone-bird.

Oksa Vertiflew to the centre of the lake, where Gunnar bowed to her and held out the sparkling ball. An enormous hourglass emerged from the water and rose as high as the Aegis would allow. Oksa drew her arm back for maximum momentum and hurled the Stinger into the air as hard as she could. The hourglass slowly turned over so that the silvery sand within it could begin trickling through.

The crowd yelled with excitement as Oksa flew back to the Gracious grandstand. The hourglass had almost finished turning—it would only be a few more seconds before the match could start.

At this signal, the players from the two teams raced towards the centre of the lake on their Aeropellers. The Stinger, which was only a few yards from the surface of the water, was immediately knocked into the air by a strong blow from a Nestor's tail. The players set off in pursuit and a player in green was the first to catch it.

"Yeeees, and it's Lucy from the Scrappy Scarabs who gets there first!" shouted the feathered presenter.

"Lucy!" exclaimed Oksa. "Brilliant!"

"Careful!" continued the yellow bird. "Remember that the Stinger has to be passed at least three times between members of the same team before they can score a goal. Second pass to Holger. Ooohhh, Spears has just fallen, hit head-on by a wave. We need a team of Croakettes, now!"

Spears had just plunged headfirst into the lake. The frogs with dragonfly wings immediately flew to the aid of the player in distress and lifted him free of the turbulent waters. On the bank, a barrage of Oscillating Granoks was shot into the air, unleashing a raging storm and churning up high waves in the lake, with the help of the Nestors which were smacking the water with their tails to add to the tumult. The ball was thrown between the players who were speeding past on their Aeropellers, trying to avoid being overturned by gusts of wind and towering waves. They used several tactics: some of them surfed the waves, standing on their Aeropellers; some slalomed between the excitable Nestors; while others went for speed, cutting through the rollers breaking on the surface of the lake. Suddenly the crowd started yelling: the Stinger had puffed up in the Scrappy Scarabs player's hands.

"Four... Three... Two," counted the megaphone-bird in a dramatic voice, while Lucy looked all around for a player in her team.

Everyone held their breath. Just in time, Lucy was able to throw the Stinger to one of her team members.

"Yeees! Lucy escaped the Stinger's merciless spines by the skin of her teeth!"

Oksa frowned.

"What does that mean?"

"After it's been in someone's hands for ten seconds, the Stinger turns into a large spiny sea urchin which, as you can imagine, can be rather painful," explained Abakum.

Oksa pulled a face and concentrated again on the exciting match, particularly as a player in green was about to hurl the fearsome Stinger into her opponent's goal. The Polypharus in blue raised its long tentacles to block the throw, waving them around in all directions. But it was no use—the ball shot into the goal over its head.

"One point for the Scrappy Scarabs! One all!" cheered the commentator enthusiastically.

The two teams immediately resumed play, looking even more determined. Suddenly a member of the Speedy Eels rushed at a Scrappy Scarabs player. Focusing her attention on the ball, which was bouncing all over the place, the player in green didn't see the player in blue heading straight for her. The blue player thumped into her, stunning her and sending her crashing into another member of her team with a loud clatter. Their

Aeropellers broke into a thousand pieces and the players fell into the water. The crowd rose to their feet, booing the player in blue.

"Foul!" yelled the commentator. "Foul committed by the Speedy Eels! That's an illegal move! Junius is suspended from the game for a duration of fifteen silver grains. Bring on new Aeropellers for the Scrappy Scarabs!"

❋

The game continued like this for about forty-five minutes, incorporating all kinds of falls, courageous passes and aerobatic Aeropeller manoeuvres, as well as rougher tactics from time to time, which were clearly against the rules, like the move that had led to Junius's temporary suspension. When the last grain of silvery powder had flowed through the hourglass, the tiny megaphone-bird whistled to mark the end of the match, to the cheering of the excited spectators.

"The Speedy Eels scored three points, as well as qualifying for the prize for Best Shaftshooter of Edefia. Bravo, let's have a round of applause for them, please! As for their opponents, the Scrappy Scarabs scored four points, so they are the winners of today's match. Hurrah! Let's hear it for the winners!"

41

A Party No One
Could Spoil

"**T**HAT WAS FANTASTIC!" SAID OKSA.

She'd shouted herself hoarse. The Breakball match had been memorable for a variety of reasons. As soon as it was over, the players' supporters had rushed to congratulate their favourites. Oksa couldn't decide which of the two teams she'd preferred, though.

She'd been amazed by the Speedy Eels' skill in riding the waves, but the Scrappy Scarabs had been just as impressive, surfing through the sky with inimitable flair. Oksa Vertiflew to the crowd around the players, and was immediately joined by the Gracious clan and the members of the High Enclave. As she headed for the Aeropellers, unable to conceal the desire in her eyes, a sinister shadow fell across the beach. Everyone looked up. In just a few seconds all conversations had stopped and were replaced by shouts of concern.

The Hawk Brigades quickly took off for the protective membrane, which was under attack from exploding fireballs. Sprays of sparks bounced off the transparent Aegis, whose flexible surface muffled their crackling but did nothing to conceal this new onslaught by the Felons. Pavel, who was standing on the beach, was so furious that he rose into the air with his Ink Dragon deployed. However, the dark mass of Felons with their airborne weapons had already vanished, leaving behind their calling card in the form of acrid smoke and black rings where the Aegis had been hit. A heavy silence descended as the Hawk Brigades worked hard to reinforce the shield with the help of the Servants for Protection and the leading Granokologists.

Everyone on the shores of the lake was appalled, even though this fresh attack only confirmed what they already knew: that the Felons were daunted by nothing. As if to show their firm resolve, several hundred determined men and women took to the air in a tight group and flew over Oksa, crying at the top of their voices:

"Strong in life, united in death!"

The crowd around the Young Gracious followed suit, chanting this war cry, their fists raised and their heads held high. Even the creatures joined in the spontaneous outburst, jumping, shrieking and flying.

"If those lowlife Felons wanted to intimidate us, then they failed!" swore Oksa, her lip trembling. "They'll soon find out what we're made of and then they'll be sorry!"

She wanted to make an appeal, but her voice wouldn't carry far enough.

"Where's Naftali?" she asked impatiently.

"The Scandinavian friend of my Gracious operates the reinforcement of the sheath that ensures the keeping of Thousandeye City in safety," replied the Lunatrix. "Does the domestic staff of my Gracious have disposal of the power to procure assistance?"

"I need an Amplivox Capacitor," sighed Oksa.

Nearby, Reminiscens heard her and rummaged in the pocket of her long crêpe de Chine tunic to find her Caskinette. She took out an iridescent ball and handed it to Oksa with a smile. Oksa hurriedly swallowed it.

"My friends, today is *our* public holiday!" she exclaimed.

Her voice echoed around lake, attracting everyone's attention.

"And we're not going to let a pathetic handful of Felons spoil our fun or put a damper on things!" she continued, not even attempting to moderate her tone.

This stirring declaration had the desired effect: supportive cheers rang out from the crowd. The megaphone-bird swiftly flew over and landed on her shoulder.

"My Gracious, may I announce the next part of this special day's entertainment?" it cheeped quietly in her ear.

Oksa was thrilled to consent. The remarkable bird shook itself, fluffed up its feathers, took a deep breath and flew a few yards higher.

"Gracious, ladies and gentlemen, creatures and plants, it's time to continue the festivities!" it announced.

The Hawk Brigades and everyone still in the air landed again on the shores of the lake. However, it didn't escape Oksa's notice that several other military units took off discreetly to patrol the membrane from one end to the other. Safety was still a priority.

The megaphone-bird dropped down towards Oksa, brushed past her face and shot up again like a tiny rocket to issue an instruction that amazed Oksa.

"Carpenters, please begin converting the grandstands!"

Several Sylvabuls, led by Emica, grabbed Aeropellers and flew towards the highest terraces, where they took up what looked like strategic positions. A grating sound was heard as a sophisticated mechanism swung into action. The beams underpinning the grandstands swivelled and rose vertically, fitting together to form the framework of a completely new structure. In a few minutes the platforms had joined together to become a huge marquee.

"Wow!" gasped Oksa.

"You haven't seen everything yet," said Tugdual.

A flock of birds appeared in the sky, carrying a vast canopy in shades of navy and burgundy—the new Gracious's personal colours. The little flying porters positioned themselves above the marquee and skilfully draped the fabric over the frame. Putting the finishing touches to this feat of architecture, the Polypharuses picked up the ends of the massive piece of material that were trailing on the ground and draped them in such a way as to form elegant entrance-ways.

Oksa Vertiflew to the impressive tent, followed by her entourage and hundreds of people. Below her, on the ground, a crowd was hurrying along the shores of the lake, heading for the same spot like a multitude of sleek pedigree cats.

Oksa finally arrived at the base of the tent, which was so huge that its top seemed to touch the sky. Numerous people and all kinds of creatures were bustling around the tent and inside, working in pairs or threes to bring in massive platters laden with food. A Gargantuhen appeared, as heavily laden as a mule, led by a zealous Getorix which was taking its job very seriously.

"Come on, hen! We'll have to go faster than this if we don't want our Gracious to die of starvation!"

Without its usual squawking, the Gargantuhen hurried into the sumptuous tent.

"How does it feel to be universally loved?" asked Tugdual, standing as close as possible to Oksa.

Again she felt as if she were burning up.

"You're getting on my nerves with your *one dollar* questions," she replied, eyes bright.

"*Dollars* aren't legal currency in Edefia," replied Tugdual, with his usual mocking smile.

"Ha ha!"

"That's not much of a reply, if I may say so, my Lil' Gracious."

"You realize you're playing with fire?" said Oksa, pretending to be angry and doing her best to keep a straight face. "I've already warned you about the dismal dungeons in the basements of the Column, haven't I?"

"Stop, I'm quaking in my boots!"

"You can laugh all you like, but—"

"Thank you, Your Admirable Highness, for permitting me to enjoy myself on this day of lavish celebrations in honour of Her Immense Highness."

Oksa gave an amused growl.

"Come on, let's see what's going on inside."

She grabbed his arm and pulled him inside the marquee.

The first thing Oksa noticed was the huge crystal chandelier in the centre of the palatial tent. Its countless pendants cast splashes of light over the heavy purple hangings of watered satin which reminded her of the extravagant décor in Dragomira's apartment. Plush turquoise woollen rugs on the floor formed a striking contrast with the hangings and created an atmosphere of stately comfort. Oksa looked enquiringly at Tugdual.

"This is insane," she remarked quietly. "How could they have prepared all this so quickly without attracting attention?"

"Don't forget you're the ruler of a nation of magicians," replied Tugdual.

"I hadn't forgotten. But it still blows me away."

She walked into the midst of the crowds and everyone parted to let her through with radiant smiles and shining eyes. Tugdual, the Runaways and the Servants of the High Enclave followed her at a respectful distance and, despite the press of people in the marquee, their footsteps and voices were deadened by the exceptionally thick rugs and decorative draperies. Even the shrill tones of the excited Getorixes seemed muffled, which was truly remarkable. The docile Gargantuhen stood at the back like a giant feathered figure on a carnival float and seemed to be keeping a stern eye on everyone—including a thousand or so plants in pots hanging from beams running the length of the marquee.

"Does my Gracious encounter the desire to proceed to sustenance?" asked the Lunatrix suddenly, crimson with pleasure.

"I can't think of anything better!" replied Oksa.

42

A LAVISH BANQUET

THE LITTLE STEWARD POINTED OUT THE TABLES ARRANGED in a semicircle and draped with raspberry-coloured linen tablecloths. Countless dishes were covered in domed metal covers which didn't stop mouth-watering smells from filling the air, a foretaste of all the gastronomic delights to come.

An excited group of Getorixes and Velosos approached, followed by the three Incompetents, looking vague and bewildered. Gesticulating wildly, the creatures grabbed the dish covers and tossed them into the air with no apparent concern for the bystanders. Instinctively Oksa and the Runaways adopted a defensive stance, ready to use their Magnetus power to stop the tableware from crashing down onto their heads. However, the Polyglossipers, who were keeping watch, turned their shape-changing limbs into countless arms and caught the dish covers with reassuring skill. The unsurprised inhabitants of Edefia clapped and whistled enthusiastically. Oksa also applauded as the Inflammatorias put on a sensational firework display and the affectionate Pulsatillas rolled their tendrils around the wrists of anyone within reach.

"Sweetheart, they won't want to take any credit for it, but you should know that your Lunatrix and Leomido's Lunatrixes were responsible for organizing this incredible banquet," said Abakum.

Oksa looked at the Fairyman in delight, then rushed over to the four

Lunatrixes. To their huge embarrassment she bent down and kissed them all, murmuring sincere thanks. The Lunatrixa—who'd been in Oksa's great-uncle's service for many years—turned crimson and tottered on her spindly legs.

"Ooohhh, my Gracious!" she stammered, her bright yellow tuft quivering on her head. "Your domestic staff has only proceeded to the fulfilment of her duty by making intense use of her brain and the culinary recollections of the gerontocrats of Edefia."

"But this is superb," insisted Oksa, gesturing to the tables laden with dishes. "You've worked miracles! I know we don't have a lot of things, and Edefia's former abundance is still a thing of the past—so how on earth did you manage?"

Like the Goranovs, but for very different reasons, the Lunatrixa looked about to faint and, eventually, the inevitable happened. While the Getorixes rushed over to ventilate the plants unable to stand the "unbearable" emotion of this scene, the two Lunatrixes held up the over-emotional Lunatrixa. Her toddler wailed at her side and a ripple of concern ran through the room. No one who knew how sensitive the Lunatrixes and Goranovs could be was surprised: strong emotions always caused them to faint. But the younger generations, who'd never come across them before, watched open-mouthed as legend became reality.

Mortified, Oksa picked up the baby Lunatrix. He hadn't grown much and was still as adorable.

"Don't worry, sweetie-pie," she crooned, "there's nothing wrong."

His entire body was covered in translucent down, which tickled her nose—there was nothing better than cuddling such a sweet-natured, irresistible baby.

"Waah, the Lunatrixa experiences weakness full of regrets!" wailed the poor steward as soon as she'd regained consciousness. "She has brought about the spoiling of the celebration and offers the suggestion to my Gracious to commence a procedure of removal."

Assisted by her two companions, she stood up and smoothed down the huge apron she'd wrapped around her.

"Out of the question!" exclaimed Oksa cheerfully. "You'll stay here with us. We're all very touched—and we're dying to polish off this feast."

Without putting down the little Lunatrix, which was now snoring on her shoulder, she headed towards one of the tables.

"If our Gracious encounters any gastronomic questioning, her domestic staff has the ability to procure culinary explanations," explained the chief steward.

"Okay!" said Oksa.

She picked up a tiny sandwich which she'd been eyeing hungrily for a while.

"Green tomato and Gargantuhen egg morsel," announced the Lunatrix ceremoniously.

Oksa looked at the huge hen, which had proudly fluffed up its feathers, hesitated for a second, imagining the size of the egg, and finally bit into the sandwich.

"Yum, delicious!" she exclaimed in delight.

Immediately the megaphone-bird flew onto the crystal chandelier and declared in its resounding voice:

"Our Gracious said: 'Yum, delicious!'"

This public announcement brought a flush to Oksa's cheeks.

"If I'd known, I'd have said something a bit more intelligent," she groused.

"What you said was perfect," said Pavel reassuringly. "Look, you've begun the feast!"

Oksa's supporters were gathered in their thousands at the tables, enjoying the astonishingly tasty dishes prepared by the Lunatrixes: multi-layered cakes with aromatic herbs from Green Mantle, brioches with candied blueberries, soufflés made from giant carrots and Broad-Leaved Ball nuts, salads made from "Nestor-neck" squash, cheeses made from the milk of Lusterers—Oksa was astonished to discover that not only were they wonderful cleaners, but also prolific milk-producing mammals.

The Lunatrixes followed Oksa closely, telling her about every dish. Although some of these Edefian recipes sounded a little odd, Oksa was won over by their unusual flavours and their originality. She loved the Squoracle egg omelette—another big surprise—filled with blood-red mushrooms, but her absolute favourite were the cubes of Zestillia jelly, which tasted of whatever you wanted them to taste. It was such a simple idea and Oksa couldn't get enough of them.

Suddenly Oksa heard some chords, faint at first, then more insistent. She and the Runaways tried to work out where the sound was coming from. None of them had heard a note of music since they'd been in Edefia, and Oksa had found that harder than anyone. In her life before, on the Outside, she'd listened to music every day and, when she heard the sound of instruments tuning up, she realized how much she'd missed it.

A platform rose and floated above the tables, revealing about ten musicians. Oksa stared in amazement to see Tugdual up there with a kind of guitar made of dark wood slung across his chest. A murmur ran through the marquee as the Ptitchkins and a flock of tiny indigo birds urged the assembled crowds to stop talking. Everyone fell silent, burning with impatience.

The music, when it began, filled everyone's hearts. Tears brimmed in their eyes and prickled their nostrils. No one could remain unmoved by this melody, which was both intense and cheerful. The main theme was carried by the stringed instruments, which looked like a lute, mandolin and violin, made of shiny wood with a beautiful grain. But the percussion section wasn't to be outdone. Tall casks with canvas stretched over their tops were being played deftly by four girls. People started to pair up and began dancing everywhere in the tent. Pavel took Oksa's arm.

"But, Dad, I don't know the steps!" she protested.

"I'll show you," replied Pavel gently.

She couldn't help glancing at Tugdual, who winked at her, then she let her father lead her onto the makeshift dance floor.

"Since when do you know the dances of Edefia?" she asked, struck by the ease with which he was dancing.

"Since your gran taught me, a very long time ago," he replied, spinning her around. "There were some gifted musicians in the Siberian village where I grew up. As soon as Dragomira hummed the melodies, they could play them by ear. That's what we're hearing now. The instruments are a little different, but the music sounds remarkably similar," he added, his voice trembling slightly.

Captivated by the rhythmic harmonies, Oksa danced for a while with her father, then with Abakum, who was still very sprightly, and then with the naturally graceful Brune. The musicians took turns on the platform and, when she saw Tugdual jump the eighteen or so feet down to come over to her, she smiled. Brune gave up her place to her grandson and made herself scarce.

"I didn't know you could play the guitar," said the Young Gracious.

She'd remembered the piece Tugdual had played on the grand piano a few hours before they'd left Leomido's house for the Island of the Felons. The melancholy notes were engraved on her memory. She rested her head on his shoulder and couldn't help sighing.

"There are so many things you don't know about me, my Lil' Gracious," murmured Tugdual.

Oksa gently pulled away to study him. His face was as pale as usual with two deep creases between his brows. Although he looked imperturbable, there was a strange expression lurking behind the seeming coldness of his eyes, depths of passion that Oksa couldn't fathom. Her breathing quickened as she tried to penetrate below his strange blue gaze.

"Don't try to find out everything," he whispered. "Please don't."

He closed her eyelids with his fingertips. Around them hundreds of couples were dancing merrily, but Oksa's happiness was marred by a tinge of sadness.

43

A Disturbing Meeting

THE PERCUSSIONISTS WERE POUNDING ON THEIR INSTRU-
ments and the party was in full swing. It was so stuffy and hot in
the marquee that the hangings had been lifted to let in a cool breeze and
Abakum's enormous Centaury had been dragged into the centre of the
tent to regulate the temperature and purify the air.

Creatures and humans alike were enjoying this chance to let their hair
down. The plants, too, were letting off steam and, despite being naturally
grounded, were moving as much as they could. A Nobilis had been rock-
ing back and forth so wildly that it had managed to uproot itself from its
pot! The Goranovs were in a terrible state at the sight of the plant, roots
in the air, still swaying to the irresistible beat of the music. Fortunately,
disaster was averted: the over-enthusiastic Nobilis was quickly repotted
and the Goranovs were given a massage which soon calmed them down.

Oksa had been trying to find Tugdual for a while. The last time she'd
seen him he'd been dancing with Zoe. Oksa had watched them surreptitiously. Listening hard with her Volumiplus gift, she'd attempted to
overhear what they were saying but had failed miserably. The party noise
was drowning everything out.

Oksa was still perplexed by Zoe. She was even harder to read than
Tugdual. Watching them whispering seriously in the middle of the
crowded dance floor, she realized she still had no idea what her second

cousin really thought about things. However hard Oksa tried, she couldn't get Zoe to give anything away. It was impossible to find out whom she'd made the sacrifice for when she'd offered to be subjected to Beloved Detachment. She'd obviously done it to save Oksa—and the Young Gracious didn't doubt that for a second—but she also knew that either Gus or Tugdual had unwittingly driven Zoe to the brink of despair and had forced her to renounce love for ever. But which of them was it? Oksa could make an argument for either of the boys and there was no way of being sure. When she'd told Zoe about her brief visit to the Outside a cloud of emotion had passed over her cousin's darkly ringed hazel eyes, but that was all. Oksa had taken care not to mention Kukka. The beautiful Scandinavian girl had already got under her skin—there was no point in tormenting Zoe too.

"Aren't you dancing any more?"

Oksa jumped. Zoe was right there, watching her. Even though her face bore the marks of hardship, she looked very pretty.

"I love your hair like that," said Oksa. "It makes you look like Princess Leia in *Star Wars*."

"Thank you," said Zoe, amused.

They stood side by side for a few seconds, watching the dancers and remarking on people's outfits, until Oksa finally spotted Tugdual's dark silhouette weaving its way through the crowd.

"Sorry, Zoe, I'll be back in a mo."

As was often the case, Zoe didn't miss a trick. Her eyes hardened almost imperceptibly and she stiffened. Before Oksa could say anything more, Zoe had already turned away and disappeared among the partygoers, like a fish slipping between her fingers. Feeling irritated, Oksa stood on tiptoe for a better view and tried to find Tugdual again. In desperation she rose about a foot into the air, which was just as well, since she spotted Tugdual heading for one of the exits. She landed on the ground again and set off in the same direction.

The waters of Brown Lake and the distant Peak Ridge Mountains looked blacker than ink in the twilight. A single, more persistent, ray from the setting sun cut through the dense, purplish-red clouds like a golden sword. Farther away, the towering Parasol trees looked like outsize ebony umbrellas. Instinctively, Oksa scanned the Aegis. The Hawk Brigades had been replaced by the Owlet Squadrons equipped with Polypharuses and, even though night was falling, she could still see small groups of Vertiflying Felons shooting back and forth on the other side like lethal rockets. Oksa shivered. She waited until her eyes had adjusted to the dim light bathing the white sandy shores and finally saw Tugdual making for a copse of Majestics, accompanied by a Veloso. Unhindered by the darkness, he was striding ahead as confidently as if it were broad daylight. Intrigued, Oksa followed him.

The dark shadows cast by the trees made it virtually impossible to see anything clearly. With effort, she managed to distinguish two silhouettes: Tugdual and another person, who looked like a man.

She crept nearer, careful not to give herself away by stepping on a twig or kicking a stone. "If I were a Firmhand, I'd be able to see better," she grumbled to herself. It was cool now that night had fallen. Oksa tightened her Cloak around her and paid close attention. Tugdual was chatting to someone in a low voice. Their whispers were swallowed up by the lapping of the lake and the light breeze rustling the leaves. However, from the angry gestures made by Tugdual and the other man, she could see that the conversation wasn't entirely amicable.

Suddenly an Owlet Squadron passed over the treetops and the light from their Polypharuses gave Oksa an unexpected, and alarming, glimpse of the mysterious person Tugdual was talking to.

She leant against a tree, reeling with shock. Silently, her lips formed the name of the person she'd recognized instantly.

Mortimer.

Mortimer McGraw.

The son of her worst enemy.

Deep in conversation with Tugdual.

She pulled herself together as best she could. She had to think clearly and try to work out what was going on. Her mind was buzzing with questions. Firstly, how had Mortimer managed to enter Thousandeye City? It had been proved that no one could trick their way in, so what was he doing here? And why had he got in contact with Tugdual? Why not Zoe, with whom he'd been so close? And what did he want? There were far too many unanswered questions... Trembling with incomprehension and frustration, Oksa felt as though her head were about to explode. Her Curbita-Flatulo started undulating frantically around her wrist to slow down her racing heart.

After twenty minutes that seemed to last hours, the Squadrons flew over again, illuminating the scene, which gave Oksa just enough time to see that the situation had changed. There was no longer any trace of animosity between the two boys, but what she saw didn't make her feel any better: Tugdual was sitting against a tree, his elbows on his knees, holding his head in his hands. Mortimer was squatting in front of him. What was the meaning of all this?

The dull thud of explosions could be heard as the moon rose in the sky. The chilly moonlight filtered through the leaves of the trees, illuminating Tugdual and Mortimer in the undergrowth. Their long, eerie shadows crept along the ground. Although still concealed in relative darkness, Oksa dived behind a bush and pressed herself flat, her chin in the damp earth.

She soon realized it hadn't been a good idea. Venturing to glance through the sparse foliage, she was alarmed to see both boys looking over in her direction, like wild beasts on the alert for possible prey. What was more, she realized they were much nearer than she'd thought—barely twenty yards away! So when Mortimer stood up and began walking in her direction, she hardly had time to curse. This was no time for caution—she had to think and act fast. With lightning speed she took off vertically and landed on the Parasol tree branch above. Perched like an owl, she saw Mortimer examining the bush she'd just left. "Phew, that was close," she breathed. Tugdual came over too and Mortimer stopped searching without thinking to look up, much to Oksa's relief.

"You can count on me," Mortimer told Tugdual. "I know this isn't easy for you, but I'll do everything I can to help."

Tugdual nodded.

"Don't forget to give me what you promised," he said hollowly.

Mortimer took a small packet from his pocket and handed it to him.

"What are you going to do now?" asked Tugdual, slipping the packet into the back pocket of his trousers.

"I'm going back."

"You could stay here…"

"I'd soon be unmasked," retorted Mortimer.

Oksa's blood ran cold when she heard this. Tugdual must have been hypnotized, that was the only explanation. Breathlessly she stared at them, fighting not to shower the Felon's son with Granoks. "Tugdual, what the hell are you doing?" she screamed in her head. Mortimer turned and looked around.

"I have to go now," he said. "We'll stay in touch, okay?"

Tugdual gave a nod, his hands stuffed in his pockets.

Mortimer studied him for a second, then ran as swiftly as a cheetah through the undergrowth and disappeared.

A howl ripped through the night, so loud and surprising that Oksa almost fell off her branch. She leant forward, holding her breath, her nails digging into the bark. Tugdual was lying on the ground, his arms and legs stretched out in an X on the spot where she'd been earlier. The moonlight illuminated his body, his deathly pale face and his intense eyes burning with madness.

44

SECRET DISCUSSIONS

"NEVER!" SQUAWKED THE MOST AUTOCRATIC SQUORACLE. "We've never been wrong!"

"Apart from that time we believed our Gracious, the Dear Departed Dragomira, when she promised that the weather in London would be better than it was in Paris," added another tiny hen just as emphatically.

"I believe you," said Oksa, wringing her hands, "I believe you."

She collapsed into an armchair and leant back, looking up at the seams striping the canvas of Cameron's comfortable tent. When Leomido's son had seen her arrive at dawn, looking upset, he'd immediately realized that something other than the previous day's festivities was bothering her. Oksa had been grateful for his tactful offer of help, but had refused nonetheless. The matter was too serious and discretion was essential.

"We repeat," said the head Squoracle, its feathers fluffed with excitement. "If that boy entered Thousandeye City, it's because none of us could find any ill will in his heart. And if none of us could find any ill will in his heart, then that's because there was none."

"He's Orthon's son!" protested Oksa.

Taking this remark as an objection—or, worse, as a clear sign that she didn't trust them—the Squoracles overreacted as usual and began cackling with agitation. It wasn't long before the tent resembled a psychotic farmyard.

"Calm down!" cried Oksa, her hands over her ears, "I was just reminding you that Mortimer is the son of our greatest enemy and it's…"

She picked her words carefully.

"… entirely within the bounds of probability that he's a Felon."

The Squoracles glared at her with tiny neurotic eyes and the head Squoracle snapped irritably:

"Permit me to correct you: it is not within the bounds of probability, it is entirely outside the bounds of probability! We're adamant that he entered Thousandeye City with honest intentions, so let that be an end to it. Now, if there isn't anything else, we'd like to get back to work as soon as possible."

"You make proclamation of insolent words!" said the Lunatrix indignantly. "The person you are speaking to is the Gracious, forgetfulness should not be perpetrated."

Oksa sighed and nodded to the Squoracles, making them promise to keep silent about their conversation. Then she sat there without a word for some time, lost in thought. She was finding it hard to believe the tiny truth detectors, despite their insistence and their impeccable track record.

She sat up in her armchair, feeling vexed, and called to her faithful companion.

"My Lunatrix, what's your take on this?" she asked the chubby-cheeked steward at her side. "Whether I like it or not, Mortimer has a Gracious Heart."

She mechanically ran her hands through her hair to push it off her face.

"And no one with a Gracious Heart can keep anything secret from you, can they?" she asked.

The Lunatrix sniffed noisily, eyes wide as saucers, and agreed.

"My Gracious makes communication of a fact stuffed with exactitude: her domestic staff possesses this ability, the reading of Gracious Hearts does not encounter any impediment."

He fell silent, standing perfectly still, and waited. As did Oksa, who didn't react for a few seconds: the Lunatrix only answered the questions he was asked—which is just what he'd done, no more and no less.

"What is Mortimer doing in Thousandeye City? Tell me that, please, my Lunatrix."

The little creature squirmed, shifting from one foot to another, which put Oksa on tenterhooks.

"My Gracious encounters the need to receive the assurance that the Squoracles possess the correct words in their beaks: the son of the hated Felon hides no ugly intentions in his heart. Has my Gracious performed the conservation of the memory of the execrable Island of the Felons and the Great Council Meeting of the abhorrent Ocious when the Runaways arrived in Edefia?"

"Of course I remember!"

"Has she proceeded to the safeguarding of her impression with regard to the son of the hated Felon?"

Oksa narrowed her eyes and tapped the armrests with her fingertips.

"Mortimer looked extremely ill at ease during the first Council Meeting," she acknowledged, thinking back. "I didn't think he agreed with what his father and grandfather were saying and doing. He looked miserable too. I even thought to myself that he must be missing his mother badly, like me," she added, her voice breaking.

"Veracity fills the words of my Gracious," agreed the Lunatrix solemnly. "Since Reminiscens attacked him on the island in the Sea of the Hebrides, the son of the hated Felon has endured possession of the knowledge of paternal sentiment towards him."

"I never had a great relationship with Mortimer, to say the least," admitted Oksa. "But Orthon has treated him so badly. He preferred to battle it out with Reminiscens instead of saving his own son. All he was interested in was beating his sister! He didn't care what happened to Mortimer."

"The judgement of my Gracious encounters hypertrophy."

Oksa's face dimpled with amusement as she looked quizzically at him.

"My judgement is hypertrophic?" she asked. "Do you mean I'm exaggerating?"

"That is the significance of the words of your domestic staff."

Gently Oksa stroked the large head of the Lunatrix, whose skin had gone an incredible crimson.

"Exaggerate? Me? How could you think such a thing?" she asked playfully.

"My Gracious has doubtless preserved in her memory the emotion of the hated Felon when his sister made known the utterance of threats: the death of Mortimer in exchange for the death of Jan, the son of Reminiscens and Leomido despatched because of Orthon. The evocation of this retaliation caused colossal emotion in the hated Felon."

"Colossal emotion that he took great care not to show!" retorted Oksa. "He certainly didn't do very much to save Mortimer. It seemed to me that he was making it a point of honour not to give anything away."

The Lunatrix looked disconcerted.

"You know better than me, though," admitted Oksa. "In any case, I can understand Mortimer that might feel a bit… confused. Realizing that his father will always put his personal ambitions above his own family is bound to wreak havoc with the way he thinks."

She sighed, feeling genuinely sorry for Mortimer.

"Do you think he wants to join us?"

"It is the most immense wish in his heart," nodded the Lunatrix.

Oksa slumped back in her armchair. This totally unexpected situation was complicated, but everything was pointing towards that conclusion. Although, deep down, she couldn't help feeling wary.

"Why did he sneak in, then?" she exclaimed suddenly. "He could have come to us openly, instead of confiding in Tugdual."

The Lunatrix fiddled with the straps of his dungarees.

"Courage made the encounter of a deficit in his heart," he replied. "His identity and his family connections overwhelm the son of the hated Felon with a burden that prevented the publication of his visit. Only the Beloved of my Gracious possessed the ability to take delivery of trust."

"Where is he now?"

"The son of the hated Felon has performed his repatriation with his ancestors and the Felon army in the Peak Ridge Mountains, inside the troglodytic caves filled with precious stones. His absence knew brevity, and the perception of a suspicion experiences nonexistence."

"So much the better," murmured Oksa.

Around her, the thick canvas of the tent swelled with the morning breeze like a human body gently breathing. For a moment Oksa fixed her slate-grey eyes on the swaying coloured-glass lanterns as they cast haloes of light in all directions. She gnawed at a nail, unable to break her lifelong habit. Her Lunatrix came over and lightly stroked her arm.

"My Gracious has possession of an idea behind her brain," he announced confidently.

Oksa jumped, roused from her thoughts by her small steward's shrill voice.

"Exactly, my Lunatrix!" she said, jumping to her feet.

Hurriedly, she pushed aside the heavy curtain over the entrance to the tent and resolutely strode out.

45

INTERROGATIONS

"WHAT ON EARTH ARE YOU DOING THERE, INCOMPETENT?" The lethargic creature was ambling around in the ground-floor lobby of the Glass Column, absorbed in contemplation of a small brioche stuffed with pink berries.

"I think I'm a little lost," it replied, gazing at its cake as if it were a priceless jewel.

"You're not supposed to leave my apartment!" said Oksa.

There was an edge of concern in her voice and eyes. The Lunatrix positioned himself in front of the Incompetent, which had started to nibble its pastry.

"Your presence down here requires justification," he said sternly.

"A charming young man kindly told me to go down to the forty-seventh floor for this brioche," explained the Incompetent. "Wasn't that nice of him?"

Taken aback, Oksa stooped down to the creature's level. She put her hands on its sloping shoulders and, trying not to shake it, fired a volley of worried questions at it.

"A young man, you say? What young man? What did he look like? Do you know him? Who was it?"

Her mind was working overtime and one name popped into her head: Mortimer. Which, indirectly, meant Orthon... Unfortunately, the slow-witted Incompetent was far from able to match her mental prowess, as she could see from its vacant stare, although it did manage to come up with a faltering answer of sorts:

"I think I've seen him before, yes. His hair was black and so were his clothes... unless they were grey... or blue..

Delighted to give such "decisive" help, it beamed at Oksa with astounding optimism. Oksa was gripped with worry.

"What then?" she whispered. "What happened next?"

"I went there."

"You went where?"

"To the forty-seventh floor, of course!" replied the Incompetent. "You don't seem very quick on the uptake."

In other circumstances, Oksa would have burst out laughing.

"When I came out of the lift, I saw a brioche in a pretty little dish on the floor. I thought how lucky I was—it's not every day you find delicious cakes like this on the floor."

The Lunatrix lifted his eyes heavenwards.

"But I thought the young man told you where the brioche was!" cried Oksa in astonishment.

The Incompetent stopped eating for a moment, and said offhandedly:

"Oh yes, you're right... then, as I didn't know where I'd come from, I couldn't find my way back."

"What about the young man in black?"

"Oh, he stayed in your apartment."

Oksa groaned with annoyance.

"What! He stayed in my apartment? No one is allowed to be there without my permission. Don't tell me you opened the door for him?"

"I opened the door when he knocked, of course I did."

"I don't believe it," wailed Oksa.

"I did, I assure you!"

"And you didn't close it again behind you when you went out, did you?"

The Incompetent searched its hazy memory, but couldn't find an answer.

"Was this long ago?" continued Oksa.

"Perhaps…"

"Brilliant!" she groaned, with a grimace.

"Do you think so?" replied the Incompetent guilelessly. "Well, that's all right then."

Oksa grabbed its free limb and pulled it towards the glass lift with the Lunatrix trotting behind.

When they reached the fifty-fifth floor of the Column, she shot out of the lift into the corridor, Granok-Shooter in hand, then screeched to a halt in surprise.

"Tugdual?"

He spun round, his eyes cold and tortured, then, a fraction of a second later, he was smiling, even more enigmatically than ever.

"Are you going to attack me, Lil' Gracious?" he asked when he spotted Oksa's Granok-Shooter.

Awkwardly, she returned the magical blowpipe to the bag strung across her shoulder.

"What are you doing here?" she asked.

"Yes, what are you doing here?" repeated the Incompetent.

Oksa looked at it in dismay, while the Lunatrix tugged it towards the Gracious's apartment.

"I was waiting for you," replied Tugdual, coming nearer. "I miss you."

He could see how agitated Oksa was.

"Aren't you going to let me in?"

Oksa pressed her hand against the door to activate the digital control mechanism, reminding her, as it did every time she used it, of her amazement at the double-bass case that had led to Dragomira's strictly private workroom.

"Have you seen anyone hanging around up here?" she asked, walking into her apartment.

"Up here? You mean, on the top floor?"

With a lump in her throat, Oksa nodded "yes" as she let Tugdual inside.

"No," he replied. "But I've only just got here."

He wrapped his arms tightly around her and she didn't resist, her mind in a whirl, although she couldn't help inspecting the apartment, scanning the room like a radar. The Ptitchkins, which had just woken up, were stretching in the tiny nest they'd built in a cavity of the mosaic wall.

Farther away, with its hair standing on end, the Getorix was puffing and panting as it did its daily press-ups. Nothing unusual there. Over Tugdual's shoulder, her eyes suddenly alighted on her desk. The Pulsatilla was asleep and snoring gently beside the shimmering crystal Elzevir and her heart missed a beat.

"What an idiot I am!" she growled to herself. "I forgot to put it back in the Memorary. I'm such a moron."

"What's wrong, my Lil' Gracious?" asked Tugdual, stroking her hair.

Oksa pulled away from his embrace and went over to the bay window overlooking Thousandeye City. On the way, she glanced at her desk and the Gracious register. The chair was as she'd left it, the stylus lying diagonally on the Elzevir, the saucer half filled with pistachios... everything looked in order, although this didn't entirely put her mind at rest.

She stood there for a moment with her back to the room without saying a word, while Tugdual sat down silently in an armchair. Then she turned round to face him, her eyes bright.

"What did Mortimer want?" she asked, her voice surprisingly steady.

Tugdual flinched. He leant his head back, avoiding her penetrating gaze.

"How did you know?" he asked quietly.

"Don't forget I'm the Gracious," retorted Oksa. "The problem isn't how I know, but why I wasn't told in the first place."

The slight trembling of her hands and lips was nothing compared to the storm raging inside her.

Tugdual sat up and, with his elbows on his knees, looked deep into Oksa's eyes. Only the resentment and doubt she was feeling allowed her to endure the intensity of his gaze.

"Mortimer wants to join us," he said steadily.

"How can we be sure he's sincere?" Oksa asked in reply.

"You know he is—after all, he managed to gain entrance to Thousand-eye City."

Oksa took a deep breath. Everyone, including her Squoracles and her Lunatrix, kept harping on about this fact, but it didn't help her shake the nagging feeling of uncertainty at the back of her mind.

"Why didn't he stay, then?" she asked.

"Would we have happily accepted him as one of us?" replied Tugdual.

Oksa glared at him. When would he stop answering her questions with more questions?

"We accepted Reminiscens and Zoe," she said, "and, more recently, Annikki."

"You know very well it's not the same. Anyway, Mortimer is more useful to us where he is, believe me."

"Can I?" Oksa couldn't help asking.

Tugdual's face tensed.

"Can you what?" he replied.

"Believe you."

Those two words began a battle of wills—which of them would look away first? For several long seconds Tugdual seemed to have the upper hand, but Oksa stood firm. She had to know, and it was now or never.

Without taking his eyes off her, Tugdual stood up and, despite the feline fluidity of his movements, Oksa shivered.

"You want proof?" asked Tugdual.

Oksa nodded.

"Wait here, I'll be back."

Two minutes later he was knocking at the door. Oksa opened it with undeniable impatience.

"This will put an end to your doubts," he said.

He knelt down in front of a coffee table and set down a wooden tube the size of a bottle sealed both ends with a cork. He removed one of the corks.

"What is it?" asked Oksa, kneeling beside him.

Tugdual picked up the tube and poured the contents on the table, as carefully as if he were handling something breakable. But it was just blades of grass. Dark green, shiny, fleshy blades of grass which resembled chives.

"I... I don't understand," faltered Oksa.

Tugdual picked up one of the stalks fanned out on the table and offered it to her. She looked at him enquiringly.

"Mortimer has given us this as proof of his integrity."

Oksa gasped with surprise and incomprehension.

"Grass? As proof of his integrity? You've got to be kidding!"

"It's Lasonillia, Oksa," broke in Tugdual. "The plant that will prevent your mother from dying."

Wide-eyed, Oksa took the sprig Tugdual was holding out to her.

And plunged into a spinning black hole.

46

ABANDONED

THE SMELL OF DAMP MINGLED WITH FRESHLY PREPARED coffee immediately filled her nostrils when her Identego deposited her on the first-floor landing of the house in Bigtoe Square, while her head and heart were filled with a familiar melancholy song, 'Summer's Gone' by Placebo.

> *You try to break the mould*
> *Before you get too old*
> *You try to break the mould*
> *Before you die.*
>
> *Cue to your face so forsaken*
> *Crushed by the way that you cry*
> *Cue to your face so forsaken*
> *Saying goodbye.*

Drawn like iron to a magnet, Oksa headed for the room which had been—and still was—her bedroom. Having no physical substance, she was able to pass through walls and quickly found herself beside Gus, whom she wasn't surprised to find there.

It looked like things had improved since her last visit. The house was more comfortable, the electricity was back on, the kitsch wallpaper had been stripped and replaced by white paint, and the floors had been cleaned of the layers of mud left behind by the numerous floods.

Gus, on the other hand, didn't look great. His tee-shirt did nothing to hide his thinness—he was even scrawnier than the last time Oksa had seen him. His face was emaciated, his cheeks hollow and his eyes darkened by intense physical pain and the fear of certain death.

"Gus... God... what's happened to you?" murmured Oksa, standing beside the bed on which he was lying.

His hair, just as black, fell to his shoulders and this detail sent Oksa into a panic. How much time had gone by? *How many months?* She glanced out of the window and almost fainted. The trees in the square were covered with leaves, the sun was shining and, if she thought about it, the temperature was quite mild—warm, even.

It was the middle of summer.

At least eight months had gone by since they'd passed through the Portal.

She shook her head. The weeks in Edefia had been months on the Outside. And time was not on Gus's side... Oksa jumped onto the bed and folded her legs under her. She leant towards him, nearer than she would ever have dared if she'd really been at his side.

"You have to hang in there. That's an order!" she shouted, hoping with all her might that he'd hear her message.

The room was filled with the sound of sad guitar music.

> *You try to break the mould*
> *Before you get too old*
> *You try to break the mould*
> *Before you die.*
>
> *Cue to your face so forsaken*
> *Crushed by the way that you cry*
> *Cue to your face so forsaken*
> *Saying goodbye.*

287

Oksa knew this song so well. She used to listen to it often, before, when everything was... normal. A wave of nostalgia washed over her, bringing no comfort, as Gus closed his eyes. It was terrible to hear those words again now that things were so different and so much worse.

She edged closer still and studied her friend's face. The abnormally bulging veins in his neck and temples throbbed as if transporting powerful, uncontrollable torrents of blood. From time to time, sharp pains wracked his body and caused his face to tighten, bringing Oksa close to tears.

"You're not going to die, Gus," she whispered. "We'll be back together again soon, and I'll save you, I promise."

The door opened slightly, its hinges creaking, and Kukka slipped inside. "What a surprise—I only have to be on my own with Gus for a minute and she shows up!" thought Oksa irritably. Yelling at her wouldn't help though. Her antagonism had about as much effect as an air bubble. Even a ghost would be more effective right now. Kukka unintentionally made Oksa even crosser by throwing herself down on the bed and passing through the Gracious's intangible body. Gus smiled at Kukka, who was still just as gorgeous, and whose dazzling skin and glossy hair did nothing to improve Oksa's mood. Lying on one side, her head resting on her hand, Kukka smiled back at Gus.

"What are you reading?" she asked, gesturing to the object Gus had just put down beside him.

Instinctively, Oksa glanced over. It wasn't so much a paperback as a school exercise book stitched down the spine to make it stronger. The pages inside were worn so thin that they looked about to disintegrate. In astonishment, Oksa recognized Dragomira's bold, flowing handwriting. Did the notebook contain her gran's memoirs? Her secrets from her years as an apothecary or her Gracious spells?

"Andrew found it in a chest in Dragomira's strictly private workroom," said Gus, turning the pages carefully.

"Did she write all this?" asked Kukka.

"Yes. They're short stories about the creatures of Edefia which she wrote for Pavel when he was little. Reading them, anyone would think that Dragomira had an incredibly fertile imagination to invent things like that. It's a bit different when you know all these creatures are real!"

"Just a bit," agreed Kukka, laughing.

"They're all there: Lunatrixes, Getorixes, hysterical Squoracles... plus a few I'd never heard of, like the Nestor and the Lusterer."

"Amazing!"

"It really is—except I'll never see them. Even if, by some miracle, there was a microscopic, freakish chance I could, I'd be dead before it happened."

"Gus!" exclaimed Kukka. "How can you say that?"

An expression of deep despair appeared on Gus's face and his deep blue eyes darkened. Oksa understood his pain. In agonies, she battled against her powerlessness. She clenched her fists, crushing the blade of Lasonillia, and her Identego swept her out of the room.

※

She searched the whole house in vain: her mother wasn't there. On the brink of despair, she stood at the bottom of the staircase and screamed for her at the top of her lungs, hoping against hope that Marie would appear. But her wish wasn't granted, despite her passionate entreaty, so she made herself comfortable on the first step and waited watchfully like a frightened animal.

The front door slammed and everyone clustered around Virginia. They were all there: Andrew, Akina, Barbara—everyone except Marie. Cameron's reserved wife barely had time to take off her straw hat before they bombarded her with questions.

"The doctors are still confident, despite the severity of her last attack," she announced. "They assured me she'd make a good recovery anyway."

Hunched on the step, Oksa froze. Virginia had to be talking about Marie.

"She even told me to tell you to eat properly, because she thinks we're all getting alarmingly thin and she hopes we'll have put some weight on by the time she gets back!" she continued with a chuckle.

The Spurned gave a collective sigh of relief.

"That's Marie all over!" exclaimed Andrew.

"So her face isn't paralysed any more?" asked Barbara happily.

"Fortunately not," confirmed Virginia. "It's still a little swollen, but she can speak and blink again. However, she seems to be taking a bit longer to regain the movement in her right arm."

"When is she coming home?" asked Gus.

"At the end of the week."

There was a long silence, broken by Virginia's final words.

"If all goes well."

Gus cursed and stomped heavily up the stairs.

"Until the next time!" he thundered. "This is already the tenth time since the beginning of the year."

"Gus!" Andrew shouted reprovingly.

Gus spun round on the first-floor landing.

"Marie gets worse with every attack," he cried. "We're both going to die and no one can do anything to stop it. Stop burying your heads in the sand and trying to make us think we're going to get better, okay?"

He disappeared. A door slammed so hard that the walls shook. The Spurned hung their heads, looking stricken.

47

THE FORBIDDEN MISSION

THE LOYAL LUNATRIX DIDN'T HAVE A CHOICE: WHEREVER his young mistress decided to go and whatever the nature of her decisions, it was his duty to stay by her side. When he'd realized what Oksa intended to do, he'd voiced his disapproval of her foolishness in no uncertain terms, but she was determined. And, most importantly, she was the Gracious.

As soon as she'd returned from her distressing expedition to the Outside, she'd sunk into a deep depression. Tugdual had tried to find out more, but Oksa had glared at him with angry eyes and had retreated behind a wall of silence. She'd spent the entire day lost in thought and had only opened up once, when she'd revealed her insane plan to her Lunatrix during the course of a private conversation.

"I'm telling you that the bottle of elixir was at least half-full when I gave it back to Ocious! I saw it when he stoppered it and put it back in the huge metal cupboard at the back of the room, where we all were. I'll be able to find it again easily, I'm sure."

"My Gracious has proceeded to the shattering of her promise," remarked the Lunatrix.

"What promise?"

"The promise afforded to her parenthood and the Fairyman to perform the evasion of danger," replied the Lunatrix knowledgeably. "My Gracious encounters the blindness of despair. The planned enterprise is clothed in exorbitant risk."

"Nothing ventured, nothing gained," replied Oksa, her cheeks flushed. "The Portal will soon open, as you know, and our battle with the Felons is imminent. There are some difficult times ahead. Very difficult. What if the bottle is destroyed and the Diaphan dies? It's the only survivor of its tribe, the last one left, don't forget. If that happened, there would be no chance of saving Gus. Surely you don't want him to die?"

Her voice cracked as she remembered Gus's last words: "We're both going to die and no one can do anything to stop it." But Gus was wrong: Oksa could do something. And, what's more, she was going to!

"We don't have a choice anyway," she'd concluded, taking her Tumble-Bawler from her small bag. "Let's go."

White as a sheet, the Lunatrix had let her lead him onto the balcony where he perched on his young mistress's back, with his arms around her neck. Overcoming her hatred of insects—even totally harmless, magical ones—Oksa had uttered the special words in a low voice:

> By the power of the Granoks,
> Think outside the box
> And summon the Invisibuls
> Which make my form ethereal.

Paradoxically, the first obstacle Oksa had to overcome was her staunchest, and most predictable, allies. Standing in front of the only opening in the Aegis, Oksa had to wait for the verdict from the enthusiastic and discerning Squoracles. She'd promised herself never to use Granoks to force people or creatures in her clan to do anything against their will, but the prevarications of the tiny lie detectors almost made her break this pledge. Even under a thick layer of Invisibuls, Oksa's heart was still beating and, like any other heart, it had to be examined.

"They can be so annoying sometimes!" groaned Oksa. "I'm leaving Thousandeye City, not coming in, so what does it matter if my intentions are good or bad?"

"My Gracious must not encounter the temptation to disregard orders," said the Lunatrix, trying to reason with her.

"You're right, as always," she sighed. "Everyone must be inspected, on the way in and on the way out. That's the rule. I just hope they won't give me away to my father or Abakum. If they tell on me, I think I'll have my knuckles well and truly rapped."

"Keep that fear aside from your mind, my Gracious. The Squoracles accomplish the examination of hearts, not the verification of identities. Anyway, they devote obedience to the silence of specialists."

"You mean they respect professional confidentiality?"

"Exactitude adorns the words of my Gracious," agreed the Lunatrix. "The Squoracles achieve the development of eccentricity, but their obedience to the rules encounters no gaps in their brain. My Gracious should absorb the certainty of their discretion, no information will suffer divulgation because she alone possesses the capacity to break the silence of specialists."

"If you say so," conceded Oksa.

The Squoracles soon let them pass. Chattering non-stop, they opened the doorway and Oksa flew out, intoxicated by the heady feeling of freedom she'd been denied for far too long.

*

She'd flown through the Peak Ridge Mountains for the first time a few weeks ago on the back of her father's Ink Dragon, escorted by Ocious and his vile son. She'd been feeling physically and emotionally drained. Zoe had chosen to sacrifice herself, Tugdual had disappeared and she'd been wracked by doubt. She didn't have so many doubts now, although they still gave her food for thought.

When she saw the first peaks in front, an intense shiver ran down her spine, sending a jolt of adrenaline and fear coursing through her. Magnificent and intimidating, the huge rocky outcrops loomed like teeth in a monster's maw, gaping open to devour her. The stone, washed clean by the rain, had been restored to its former glory and was sparkling in the slanting rays of the setting sun. It was so bright, in fact, that Oksa had to put on her sunglasses to avoid being blinded by the bright flashes of coloured light. This didn't stop her from spotting clusters of antagonistic Chiropterans lurking in the pockets of shadow on either side of the cleft which marked the entrance to Firmhand territory. Oksa stiffened.

"Oh, no!" she cried, feeling nauseous. "There's no way I'm flying through a swarm of those hideous creatures."

"You can avoid them, my Gracious," said the Tumble-Bawler perched on her shoulder. "In order to do so, you must veer from your current route by thirty degrees. There's a crevice that leads into a deserted canyon."

"A deserted canyon? Anything's better than *that*!" exclaimed Oksa with one last glance at the seething multitude of tiny bats.

She suddenly slowed down, looking bewildered.

"But I have no idea what you mean by 'veer from my current route by thirty degrees'," she said. "Geometry's never really been my forte."

Fluttering its bumble-bee wings, the Tumble-Bawler covered itself with a layer of Invisibuls and positioned itself in front of Oksa.

"Put yourself directly behind me and follow me," it whispered.

Oksa had to concentrate very hard to do exactly what the little guide was telling her. However, the invisible crew eventually headed straight for two massive outcrops standing side by side like enormous shining molars.

"Are you sure about this?" Oksa couldn't help asking, since she couldn't see any opening at all.

The Tumble stopped in mid-air and turned round, its wings beating the empty air. It was about to say something when Oksa hurriedly corrected herself:

"Sorry, sorry—of course you know what you're doing! Let's go."

It was only when they were right in front of the rock that she could appreciate her Tumble-Bawler's expertise. There was an almost invisible vertical crack, no more than a couple of feet wide, between the two rocky outcrops. However, what made it so hard to see was not its size but the waterfall in front of it. Only the Tumble-Bawler, who missed nothing, had been aware of its existence. Proud of its invaluable contribution to the mission, the creature led Oksa and her Lunatrix to the wall of thundering water, which could be heard for miles around. Only once they'd passed through the cataract did Oksa realize what the Tumble-Bawler had meant by a "deserted canyon". She flew through the narrow opening and gazed in terror at the hundreds of yards of empty air above and below her. She felt as if she was in a gaping abyss or a bottomless well.

It was as dark as an oven. The fading daylight was a tiny, barely visible patch of orange a long way up. Hovering in the air, Oksa swapped her sunglasses for a Polypharus, which allowed her to examine the overwhelmingly dense black transparent rocks.

"We're not going to get stuck in here, are we?" whispered the Young Gracious, her voice trembling.

"The width of the canyon is twenty-two inches and my Gracious is only twenty inches across at shoulder level," said the Tumble-Bawler. "There's more than enough room."

Despite her severe reservations about her guide's estimate of the available space, Oksa didn't reply.

"My Gracious is very slim," said the creature reassuringly. "Anyone of average build would run the risk of getting stuck in here. But my Gracious is not likely to have that trouble."

"Okay," agreed Oksa.

"We must fly straight ahead for two hundred and seventy-five yards, then the canyon will widen."

"I won't be sorry," admitted Oksa, scanning the rocks around her. "I feel like I'm being walled up alive."

She flew through the narrow passage with the utmost care. The Invisibuls protected her from the sight of others as well as from Granoks and spells, but not from scrapes and grazes if she strayed even slightly from her path. The transparency of the black rocks didn't help; Oksa felt as though she were travelling through a dark jewel gleaming with deceptive shimmers. However, after banging into the walls on numerous occasions, she worked out the right technique and flew straight ahead, yard after yard, with her elbows pressed against her sides, her hands stretched out and her head up.

※

Just as the Tumble-Bawler had promised, the walls of the canyon eventually widened out into a valley lined by sheer cliffs which seemed to go on for ever, both above and below. Looking up, Oksa glimpsed the full moon so high that she felt as though she'd plunged into the bowels of the Earth without realizing. The deep gorge was filled with the milky glow of moonlight and the light shed by the Polypharus. The rocks weren't uniformly dark any more—there were patches of colour which cast glimmers of blue, red, green and even an incredible amber colour which reminded her of gold glass. Below them a thin, winding watercourse resembled a silver garland. Shoals of flying fish suddenly appeared, their scales glinting like a myriad of tiny sparks. It was such a breathtaking sight that Oksa almost forgot her mission and the dangers it involved, until the sudden appearance of a Felon patrol at the intersection with another valley brought her back to reality with a start.

48

IN THE MIDST OF DANGER

THE TUMBLE-BAWLER CAME TO A SCREAMING HALT, BUT Oksa was a fraction of a second too late in stopping. Vertiflying at speed with her Lunatrix on her back, Oksa ploughed into her little scout with a curse, sending them all plunging into the group of Felons, who seemed to feel nothing except a slight vibration, no stronger than a puff of air. Fortunately for the three intruders, the collision was as silent as it was devoid of consequences and they got away with a bad fright.

"All we have to do is follow them!" said Oksa, wiping the perspiration from her forehead.

"My Gracious is right," said the Tumble-Bawler. "They're heading for the central section of the Peak Ridge Mountains."

"Where Ocious and his henchman are holed up in their troglodytic cave," added Oksa, suddenly feeling jittery for a quite another reason. "I have to have that Werewall elixir."

The Lunatrix tightened his arms around her without saying a word. Oksa pressed his chubby hand affectionately. She turned slightly and her cheek grazed the soft down on her lovable companion's arm.

"Everything will be fine," she murmured.

"The words of my Gracious are stuffed with positivity."

The Lunatrix's remarks were swallowed up by the air. Oksa was already flying in pursuit of the Felons, her hair streaming in the wind and her heart racing. The soldiers, who had no idea that anyone was following them, were Vertiflying with a skill she couldn't help admiring—a skill combining strength with an impression of invincibility that marked out the most battle-hardened warriors. "Only the strongest stayed with Ocious and his sons," thought Oksa, "the most aggressive and determined Edefians." For a second this thought dismayed her, however much she tried not to let it. Then she pictured her father, Abakum, the Runaways and all those men and women whose courage, determination and, above all, loyalty knew no bounds, and felt much better.

Loyalty was probably not a quality Ocious could depend on.

✳

When the immense cave suddenly appeared, Oksa's blood ran cold. The shifting light spilling out from the interior bathed the rocky slopes of Mount Humongous, and the cave mouth stood out against the darkness like a blazing archway into Hell. About ten smaller caves were dotted about the mountainside. A fierce fire seemed to be burning in their depths, projecting the silhouettes of the guards standing before each one onto the nearby cliffs. With their distorted, elongated shadows these men looked like monstrous colossuses, ready to crush anyone who came within reach. Swarms of Chiropterans were listlessly flying around—the clicking noise made by their wings in the darkness sounded like laundry being shaken out.

The presence of the guards and their aerial escorts was a strong incentive to turn round and flee for dear life.

Which is what the Lunatrix desperately wanted to do.

And which is exactly what Oksa chose not to do.

✳

She felt very small in front of the vaulted cave mouth, which was almost thirteen feet high. Two men, radiating an aura of unfeigned ferocity, stood on either side of the entrance with one hand behind their backs and the other gripping a Granok-Shooter. When Oksa noticed that their noses and mouths were covered by a blue insect, she couldn't hide her bewilderment.

"Why are they wearing a Sealencer? That's terrible!"

At the same time she felt a strange drowsiness creeping over her, overwhelming her senses. Languidly she noticed the torches crackling as they burned, giving off a heady fragrance of sandalwood, which made her feel dizzy and sluggish.

"My Gracious must not proceed to fall into somnolence," said the Lunatrix, his nose buried in Oksa's hair. "The combustion of the oil from Sleepy Nightshade provides propulsion towards a category of trance."

"Let's get going, my Gracious!" added the Tumble-Bawler, its three-fingered hand covering the lower part of its face. "Otherwise you'll be put to sleep by the emanations of Sleepy Nightshade, or Belladonna, if you prefer."

"Oh, I don't prefer anything," said Oksa groggily.

"Come on, quickly!"

Fighting tiredness with all her strength, Oksa followed her winged guide. Once inside the cave, she slumped against a wall covered in a bluish mosaic. Her Lunatrix clambered down from her back to face her.

"Phew, that was strong!" she whispered, her mind clearing. "The Felons have definitely come up with an effective weapon there."

She opened her bag and took out her Caskinette. She had to have something to wake her up. She swallowed an Excelsior Capacitor with its indescribable taste of wet earth and pulled a disgusted face. The bracing blast of the Capacitor dissipated the fog caused by the Sleepy Nightshade and Oksa stood up, feeling her strength return.

"I'm sure there are all kinds of traps like that, so we'll have to stay alert," she said, helping her Lunatrix onto her back again.

"My eyes will perform the conservation of their peeling," agreed the little steward.

"Yes, let's keep our eyes peeled," agreed Oksa, spurring herself on.

Although she'd been left with a vague feeling of dread after her previous visit to this unique place, she hadn't forgotten how breathtakingly beautiful it was. She still vividly remembered the corridor paved with cobbles of diamond: that was the route they'd taken, she was sure of it. Following that trail would help them find their way through this maze of tunnels lined with emeralds, topazes and other precious stones that would be worth a king's ransom anywhere else than in these mountains.

"On the Outside, men would kill to get their hands on a place like this," murmured Oksa, running her fingertips over a wall covered in blood-red rubies.

She kept walking, wide-eyed at such magnificence. The stones looked even more lustrous in the light of the torches—the flames reflected endlessly off their myriad facets, creating a glare so bright it almost hurt her eyes.

She didn't pass many people, just a man and a woman deep in conversation, followed by a youth accompanied by two Abominaris. Fortunately, the shriek Oksa gave was deadened by her protective covering of tiny worms.

"I'd forgotten those things existed," she grumbled, flattening herself against the wall. "They're just as revolting as ever."

The slimy bodies of the Abominaris brushed past her, giving off a stink of sweat and mould. One scraped a gnarled nail along the wall of precious stones, unaware of the terror it was inflicting on Oksa and her companions. The Lunatrix's down bristled and he wrapped his arms so tightly around Oksa's neck that he almost suffocated her.

"There are five Vigilians at the next junction, my Gracious," the Tumble-Bawler warned suddenly. "Exactly eighty feet and nine inches away as soon as you put your right foot on the ground."

Oksa stopped immediately. Perspiration beaded her forehead and her whole body stiffened. She'd faced some terrible, fearsome creatures, such as Abominaris and Leozards, not to mention the Airborne Sirens—those vile fairies spawned by a fallen Ageless One—but the Vigilians filled her with real dread.

"You're invisible, Oksa," she reminded herself quietly. "You're invisible and those revolting creatures can't see you."

She crept forward, even though the covering of Invisibuls muted her words and masked her movements. The end of the tunnel of rubies appeared. She could already see the next fabulous diamond-lined tunnel—the last one before she reached the heart of Mount Humongous and Ocious's lair. The Vigilians were slyly lurking at the junction of the two tunnels. If she listened hard, she could hear them buzzing. She took a deep breath.

"You can do it, Oksa-san!" she told herself. "Come on, get a move on."

Without looking right or left, she strode across the intersection more steadily than she'd have thought possible. Two Vigilians, more sensitive than the others, fluttered nearer, their antennae erect on their hideous heads. They snooped around the apparently empty corridor, then rejoined the group. Oksa rubbed her hands together.

"That fooled you!" she rejoiced, as she stepped into the tunnel of diamonds.

※

The light grew brighter and brighter as she walked deeper into the bowels of the mountain—which suggested that the Diaphan was still alive. The members of the fifth tribe had become dependent on intense light as a result of the Confinement Spell cast by the Ageless Ones several centuries ago, and they couldn't have survived until the Great Chaos without it. The upheavals of the last few decades, and the waning light, had wiped out nearly all the Diaphans. The last member of that foul tribe only owed its salvation to Ocious's stubborn determination and his ancestral affection for them.

And the survivor was there, a stone's throw from Oksa. She could sense its nauseating presence. She entered the large chamber where Zoe had been subjected to Beloved Detachment, which had prevented her from experiencing romantic love ever again—a fate worse than anything except perhaps death. As Oksa thought about her second cousin's sacrifice, her outraged heart lurched. She blinked, dazzled by the unreal light whose source was still a mystery. She took out her sunglasses and helped the Lunatrix down from her back. The small steward clung to her, terrified.

"Hold on to the belt loop of my jeans and don't let go under any circumstances, okay?" whispered Oksa.

The Lunatrix nodded and obeyed. Whatever happened, they had to avoid breaching the layer of Invisibuls. The thought of this eventuality made the poor creature tremble all over.

"The domestic staff of my Gracious does not possess the texture of an adventurer," he wailed.

"You're doing brilliantly, honestly!"

※

The chamber was as vast as the hall in the seventh basement of the Glass Column and its distinctive sound-absorbing acoustics were due to its location deep beneath thousands of cubic feet of rock. Oksa scanned the walls, tiled with beautiful lapis lazuli mosaics on top of which tiny interlocking silver squares formed animal figures or depicted the solar system in all its immensity. Apart from the doorway through which Oksa had entered, there was no other way in or out.

"It's a dead end," she muttered, looking around nervously.

Despite its size, the chamber was virtually empty, except for four massive columns and, in the centre of the room, a circular sofa—the largest Oksa had ever seen—which could easily accommodate forty people. She looked for the large metal cupboard, but it wasn't there any more—panic began churning in the pit of her stomach and tears welled in her eyes. Surely she hadn't gone through all this for nothing? She walked round the room, knowing full well she wouldn't find anything. The cupboard must have been moved. But where to? It could be anywhere...

She received an answer of sorts when a door concealed in the mosaic wall suddenly swung open, revealing another entrance as about ten people entered.

"I'm in charge here!" thundered Ocious. "The decision isn't yours to make. Not today and certainly not tomorrow."

A few yards from Oksa, Orthon was glaring daggers at his father. He took a few paces forward and stopped in the middle of the room with his sons, Gregor and Mortimer, behind him. Ocious, followed by Andreas, sat down on the sofa with deliberate slowness. Then he leant back, crossed his legs and looked challengingly at the son he'd always despised.

49

ACIDS

OKSA SPONTANEOUSLY DRAGGED HER LUNATRIX BEHIND one of the columns. She hadn't forgotten the enormous advantage afforded by the Invisibuls, but finding herself face to face with a group of her worst enemies made her a bundle of nerves. Two Felons brushed past without suspecting she was there—a woman with thick brown hair and an authoritarian air, and a man Oksa recognized: Agafon, the former Memorarian. She flattened herself against the cold stone of the column. Given the particular location of the giant troglodytic cave, being this close to the Felons made her heart race and her breath come in short gasps, but it did nothing to shake her resolve. Gus's life was at stake! The Lunatrix looked up at her with large, frightened eyes.

"My Gracious must take delivery of the information that her domestic staff knows the experiencing of a situation laden with terror," he murmured, his voice shaking badly. "Her steward presents the suggestion of immediate flight."

Oksa stroked his downy head as the Tumble-Bawler landed on her shoulder, like a lookout.

"Not yet," she whispered. "We're bound to learn a lot if we stay."

With her hands pressed against the column, she tilted her head to observe the scene unfolding a few yards away.

Ocious still looked superior, his head held high and his gaze fixed on Orthon. He had all the arrogance and strength of an old lion, even though the last few weeks had left their mark on his face, now furrowed by two deep creases between his eyes. Despite his father's disdainful expression, Orthon looked just as haughty as he'd always done, his eyes burning with unhinged hostility. "Nothing gets to him," thought Oksa, "absolutely nothing."

His hair shone with the strange aluminium sheen that had been the colour of his eyes, until they'd turned inky black. He certainly cut a fine figure, having lost none of the stark, impeccable elegance that had become his trademark. Even in battle he was stylish. Oksa couldn't help thinking of Tugdual, who also shared this characteristic. His resemblance to the Felon stopped there, though, she thought, immediately ashamed of making such a comparison.

"Father's right!"

Oksa had no trouble recognizing Andreas's dangerous, hypnotic voice. Despite their differences of opinion and deep animosity, Ocious's two sons had many similarities—the same air of refinement, the same lean build and the same merciless, chilly demeanour. Watching them face off, Oksa was more aware than ever of Orthon's eagle-like incisiveness and Andreas's snake-like cunning.

"No, Father isn't always right!" Orthon retorted, giving his hated half-brother a look of insufferable exasperation. "It would be foolish to attack Thousandeye City now."

"Spare us your strategy lessons, please," broke in Ocious. "You're the last person in this room who can teach us anything about strategy."

Oksa shivered, which made her covering of Invisibuls tremble. There was complete silence for the next few moments and she took this opportunity to examine the people attending this extraordinary meeting.

Agafon and the woman with the grim face were standing slightly to one side. They were staring straight ahead with a neutral expression, motivated, Oksa assumed, by extreme caution. At the back of the room Lukas, the famous mineralogist, was standing beside two perfectly identical women. The twins, who had the same long, delicate nose and a crown of grey hair, clicked their tongues, although it wasn't clear whom this sign of disapproval was aimed at.

Stiff as a poker, Orthon looked immovable with his hands behind his back. His son, Gregor, was standing resolutely by his side, showing his unequivocal solidarity. Although thin, his whole body radiated an impression of ruthless strength, from the nasty smile playing over his thin lips to the palms of his hands, which seemed poised to unleash lightning bolts.

Mortimer didn't look so aggressive. His attempt to put some distance between himself and his father and Gregor had failed miserably when Orthon had unceremoniously pulled him close. Mortimer was deathly pale. His eyes were darting back and forth, unable to focus on anything. Unintentionally his gaze met Oksa's, betraying the deep desolation and overwhelming panic he was doing his best to hide. "Mortimer wants to join us," Tugdual had said. The confidence he had in the Felon's son had been convincing, but it was Mortimer's visible unhappiness that really swayed her. He clearly no longer belonged with his family.

And Oksa would never—never!—forget that Mortimer had braved the dangerous and hostile territory of the Distant Reaches to bring her some Lasonillia.

That couldn't be a trick.

That couldn't be a trap.

"I trusted you," continued Ocious, "I gave you a free hand and the unprecedented opportunity to show me—to show us all—that your theories were better than mine."

Orthon's composure was exceptional. He didn't bat an eyelid and the expression in his eyes was unfathomable.

"We put so much faith in you," added Andreas, ramming the point home.

"And your mistakes caused me to suffer a stinging defeat," continued Ocious curtly. "A bitter failure."

Orthon took a long breath.

"I'm sorry, Father," he began, then stopped. Everyone looked at him in surprise. Orthon wasn't the kind of man to ask forgiveness from anyone.

"I'm sorry," he continued, "but I don't think you needed me to suffer defeat and failure."

This time no one was surprised by Orthon's insolent, and somewhat predictable, retort. They all held their breath. This skirmish was only just beginning.

"You said Green Mantle would be easy," counter-attacked the ageing leader.

"It was a fiasco," remarked Andreas.

Orthon greeted his half-brother's remark with a dismissive wave.

"Your strategy was faulty," continued Ocious.

"My strategy was flawless," retorted Orthon. "But when men are commanded by leaders with so little talent for waging war or governing a country, it's hardly surprising that even the simplest mission would end in fiasco, as my dear half-brother put it."

Everyone heard Andreas's gasp of indignation.

"May I remind you that you were in command of the entire operation?" roared Ocious.

"True," admitted Orthon, "with a second-in-command who was always getting in my way and blocking my decisions," he added, glaring scornfully at Andreas.

Ocious sighed. The two creases between his eyes deepened further. The elderly ruler raised his head, but his face and body were sagging with weariness.

"Anyway, one thing's for certain: we're now paying for mistakes made by everyone," he announced. "This has to stop and we have to regain control."

"We haven't lost control," remarked Orthon.

Andreas raised his eyes to heaven.

"Then I don't understand why you're trying to put off the moment of truth," continued Ocious. "Do we have the wherewithal to breach the Aegis, Lukas? Yes or no?"

The venerable mineralogist nodded.

"We've stabilized the composition of the acid bombs," he said solemnly.

Oksa felt a surge of panic beneath her layer of Invisibuls. Her allies were ready to fight the Felons, but would they be proof against their powerful weapons?

"Can the bombs destroy that blasted protective membrane and allow us to enter Thousandeye City?" asked Ocious.

"We've tested them," replied Lukas. "The result was conclusive. The acid burned a hole and one of our number even managed to get into Thousandeye City."

Oksa's heart dropped. She immediately glanced at Mortimer. What if Lukas was talking about him? What if he was really working for his father? Mortimer kept looking at the floor with a tormented expression, his back bowed, weighed down by treachery—towards his family or those who wouldn't hesitate to welcome him among them?

"We closed the hole to avoid attracting suspicion, so that we wouldn't lose the element of surprise," explained Lukas. "But I'm positive that the acid works and we now have enough to melt the Aegis in its entirety."

Oksa groaned and her Lunatrix staggered.

"So we're ready!" cried Ocious. "We'll attack tomorrow."

His triumphant expression gave Oksa the impression of being face to face with a barbaric and predatory monster.

"It's too soon," objected Orthon.

At these words Ocious bounded from his seat and, in a flash, was standing in front of the man who'd just questioned his decision again.

"Believe me, Father," insisted Orthon.

His dilated pupils lent him an even greater air of inscrutability than ever.

"Why is it too soon?" bellowed Ocious. "What remarkable strategy are you going to extract from your exceptional brain this time?"

Andreas gave a nasty snigger. Orthon paid no attention, his eyes fixed on his father.

"The opening of the Portal is imminent, it will only be a few days at most. Entering Thousandeye City too soon would be a foolish risk."

Looking perplexed, the elderly leader smoothed his hand over his bald head.

"When the Portal opens, we'll need to take advantage of the general confusion if we're going to pass through as well. If we attack tomorrow as you suggest, we could ruin everything."

"How do you know this?" hissed Andreas.

"As a leading strategist from the Outside once said: 'An army without spies is like a man without ears and eyes.'"

The Felons looked at each other in silence. As for Oksa, she was besieged by a flurry of new questions which felt like a volley of poisoned arrows. Who was Orthon's spy? Someone close enough to her to know about the imminent opening of the Portal—one of the members of the High Enclave? They'd all been screened by the Squoracles: none of them had evil intentions. Had one of them leaked information? It was highly unlikely, but not impossible.

Tormented by her questions, she gradually turned her thoughts back to Mortimer. No. He'd entered through the doorway in the Aegis, not through a hole created by the Felons. And if he'd managed to enter Thousandeye City, it was because he didn't have the heart of a Felon. Otherwise the Squoracles would have spotted it.

What about Annikki, Agafon's daughter? Pavel had never been able to trust her completely. Perhaps he was right, despite the Squoracles' opinion?

Or Tugdual? She couldn't help picturing him again in the top-floor corridor of the Column. Oksa shook her head, as if to prevent herself from recalling the brief look she'd glimpsed, which had upset her more than she cared to admit. Although it had only lasted for a fraction of a second, she remembered perfectly the intense suffering she'd seen in his eyes. As if it had been very painful for Tugdual to be there then. "Stop imagining things, Oksa," she scolded herself with a shake of her head. "You're becoming completely paranoid!"

"You have a spy, do you?" continued Ocious, torn between amusement and irritation. "Who is it?"

Orthon smiled sarcastically.

"We all have our little secrets... what's important is that our loyal friend—let's call him or her that—will alert us as soon as there's no doubt that the Portal is about to open. Then we can act."

Facing him, a few paces away, Ocious didn't look overly enthusiastic about this decisive information.

"Andreas will lead the attack on Thousandeye City when I decide, which is, as I said, tomorrow at dawn!" he declared, his head held high and his chest puffed out.

"You're making a big mistake," retorted Orthon with a grimace.

Suddenly, looking very serious, he said quietly:

"Trust me, Father. Let me take you to the Portal. I'm the only one who can."

Ocious studied him searchingly. Then his face hardened, his eyes narrowed and his mouth twisted into a nasty sneer as he snapped:

"What have you ever done to make you think you deserve my trust?"

50

FATAL CONFESSIONS

E VERYONE FELT AS THOUGH THE TEMPERATURE HAD
dropped by several degrees.

"The fact that I'm here today should be the only answer you need,"
replied Orthon.

For the first time since this tense conversation had started, the Felon
appeared seriously upset. So upset, in fact, that Oksa almost felt sorry for
the man who'd caused her family and friends so much pain and heartache.
His jaw was set, his temples were throbbing with suppressed anger and
his breath was coming in fast, ragged gasps. No one in the room said a
word. Lukas, tight-lipped, shook his head slowly from left to right, looking
disgusted by Ocious's attitude. Farther away, Agafon covered the lower part
of his face with his hands, his expression more despairing than saddened.

"You're my grandfather and you're a great man," broke in Gregor, his
fists balled. "But you have no right to talk to my father like that!"

"I can talk to your father any way I like," snapped Ocious scornfully.
"I'd put all my hope in my descendants. My child should have been truly
superior with the combined bloodlines of our ancestor Temistocles
and Gracious Malorane. Fate saw fit to give me twins, so I was doubly
blessed. But what did they do with the huge opportunity I offered them?
My daughter sacrificed everything for a cheap love affair, and my son…"

His eyes drifted towards Orthon, before coming back to Gregor:

"… my dear son Orthon preferred music, poetry, daydreaming and wasting time. I struggled to make him see that his choices weren't worthy of the man he should be. Orthon had enormous potential and he's spent his whole life frittering it away."

"My father is a powerful man!" interrupted Gregor.

"Powerful? A powerful man wouldn't have diluted our family's lineage by having children with an Outsider!"

Gregor gave a cry of rage. He was about to launch himself at his heartless grandfather when Orthon grabbed his arm to stop him. His expressionless mask dropped for a second, revealing a gleam of sheer hatred in his eyes. Then the icy mask reappeared.

"Orthon isn't up to the task," declared Ocious. "He's never measured up and never will."

His cutting tone was sharp enough to pierce the hardest rocks. Or the hardest hearts.

"I've never measured up to whom, Father?" asked Orthon finally, his tone admirably controlled. "Up to a man whose whole life has been a failure? You didn't even manage to leave Edefia while I, your pathetic son, did, and will do so again. But perhaps your contempt is actually a way of hiding your intense jealousy and wounded pride. Am I right, Father?"

He glared at him challengingly.

"And let me remind you that without the help of our beloved Oksa Pollock, Edefia would have died, and so would the Outside. And who caused all that damage? You did, I'd say. You did, all by yourself."

His dispassionate voice made him more frightening than ever. All hell tended to break loose after these periods of deceptive calm. Oksa had learnt that to her cost on several occasions. Still waters always run deep and dangerous.

Ocious was just as cool and collected. Instead of replying, he stiffened and studied his son for a long time, his face blank of any feeling or emotion. Only his mouth twisted into a nasty grimace.

"It took a little girl," hissed Orthon ominously, "to correct your mistakes. Fancy that! And you'd have me believe that I'm the one who doesn't measure up?"

He gave a mirthless laugh full of deep bitterness.

"You failed, Father. From the start, you've done nothing but fail."

"My biggest failure was you," declared Ocious.

These words resounded like a gunshot aimed to kill and, although they didn't strike Orthon down, they shattered the final taboo, eradicating the last vestiges of Orthon's humanity.

※

The unstoppable lightning bolt flashed from Orthon's hand and hit the elderly ruler in the middle of the chest.

No one reacted.

The impact sent him flying to the other side of the room like a cannon ball. He smashed into the mosaic wall, crushing the little blue and silver squares that had been firmly attached for centuries. A large charred circle appeared in his tunic, revealing the mangled flesh, while a trickle of blood from his head looked even redder in comparison to his chalky-white face. Eyes wide with incomprehension, he stared at his despised son, who was keeping him suspended in mid-air from a distance. Orthon's black pupils expanded until his eyes were almost entirely covered with a dark liquid rage. Stretching out his arm, stiff and gnarled as a tree trunk, he was venting years of pent-up bitterness, and it seemed that destruction was the only possible outlet for this extraordinary surge of energy.

A death rattle escaped from Ocious's bluish lips: Orthon had just tightened his grip around his father's neck. Everyone looked in horror at the Felon's fingers, which had clenched into eagle-like talons, and it was easy, and horrifying, to imagine their effect on the elderly ruler.

Realizing what was happening, Andreas threw himself at his half-brother with a cry of rage. But nothing and no one could stop Orthon—his insatiable hunger for revenge made him invincible. With his free arm he hurled a Knock-Bong at the brother he hated. Andreas was catapulted against the column behind which Oksa was hiding. She clapped her hand over her mouth and moaned, tears stinging her eyes.

"He's going to kill everyone," she murmured, trembling.

"Not the totality of personages, my Gracious," corrected the Lunatrix, on the verge of fainting. "Strictly the execrable fatherhood."

Oksa was breathing faster and her heart was beating so hard and so loudly that it hurt her chest. Her whole body was reacting to the violence she was witnessing unseen. Andreas was semi-conscious on the ground in front of her. His hair, which was usually so tidy, lay across part of his white face. With his eyes half closed he looked dazed, although he had to be in severe pain from his left arm, which was twisted at an odd angle.

No one dared to move. Gregor and Mortimer stared at their father, the former with real respect, the latter terrified. The oldest Felons there—the twins, Lukas, Agafon and the hard-faced woman—were watching Ocious. Coldly. Without pity. Immobilized against the wall, the suffocating Docent looked pleadingly at them. His bloodshot eyes were gradually clouding over and death was fast approaching.

None of them moved except Orthon, who stepped forward. The others backed away.

"You do know that you brought this on yourself, don't you, Father?" he asked, his head tilted back to gaze deep into Ocious's eyes.

He spread the fingers of his hand, relaxing the hold that was suffocating the old man. Still conscious, although bruised and battered, Ocious collapsed onto the shards of broken mosaics.

"Look at me," murmured Orthon, kneeling down to get as near as he could to his dying father's face.

Oksa was closer than anyone. She heard every single word of the conversation, unlike the others who remained silent spectators.

"Why... did you come back?" groaned Ocious, between two rattling breaths. "You could have... become... the ruler of... the Outside."

Orthon's eyes widened and he looked visibly shaken by these words.

"Is that why you're annoyed with me?" he breathed. Too weak to reply, Ocious closed his eyes, then opened them again, looking even more exhausted.

"Your return... was my worst failure," he managed to murmur with huge effort.

Orthon no longer tried to hide his feelings of hurt or rage during this painful conversation.

"I just wanted to show you that you could be proud of me! I wanted you to know that I wasn't the weak, timid boy you thought! But you always find fault with what I do and the decisions I make, and you always will—always."

His face tensed and his hands began to shake.

"Why did you always run me down?" he continued, almost inaudibly. "Why don't you love me?"

"It was better... if I didn't love you," replied Ocious.

"Why?"

This time Orthon's voice had been loud enough to break the heavy silence, making everyone jump.

"You should be... grateful to me..."

"Grateful?" hissed Orthon through clenched teeth. "You want me to be grateful to you for despising me, belittling me and humiliating me, ever since I was a child?"

"You were... so sensitive... if I'd shown you... that I loved you... you'd never have been..."

He closed his eyes. Blood trickled from them.

"I'd never have been what?" roared Orthon, shaking him by the shoulders.

315

Ocious didn't resist. He reopened his eyes and stared at Orthon, before whispering in resignation:

"The mightiest of us all…"

His head slumped to one side. His body had given up the fight. The aged ruler was dead.

51

A High-risk Operation

INSTINCTIVELY OKSA RECOILED, WHILE EVERYONE ELSE remained rooted to the spot, staring at the blood-stained corpse of the man who'd ruled Edefia for nearly sixty years. No one was quite sure how to react to a tragedy that they'd all known deep down was inevitable.

Orthon closed his father's eyes. After a final glance at the man who'd made him the person he was, he stood up and turned to face the Felons, who seemed to be in a horrified daze. He raised his head and tidied his clothes. His face had regained its customary harsh, arrogant expression, as if what had just happened had already ceased to matter.

"I think everyone will have realized that I'm now in command of the Felon army," he said in an implacable voice. "Does anyone here dispute that... fact?"

They all hung their heads. No one spoke. Out of allegiance? Fear? Oksa wondered what these men and women really felt.

Orthon glanced at Andreas, who had fully regained consciousness.

"My dear brother, I have a job for you," Orthon continued, his eyes gleaming with intense delight.

Andreas struggled to his feet, his broken arm hanging limply by his side, as if it were about to drop off. He grimaced and avoided his half-brother's sharp gaze.

"Deal with him!" the latter ordered, pointing at their father's corpse.

Andreas walked over without a word, looking devastated. He kissed Ocious's forehead and lifted the lifeless body onto his back with his undamaged arm. The woman with the thick mane of hair made as if to help him.

"No!" ordered Orthon, in a tone that brooked no opposition. "He has to do it by himself."

Showing no reaction, Andreas walked past Oksa, who was amazed at the phenomenal strength he showed, despite being injured, humiliated and grief-stricken. These people were something else.

"Now get out!" thundered Orthon. "All of you!"

His sons and the Felons immediately obeyed. In choked silence they headed towards the little concealed door and disappeared. Oksa slipped through behind them, accompanied by her tottering Lunatrix and her Tumble-Bawler, before the door swung shut again. A cry rang out from the vast, four-columned chamber, spreading like a dark, powerful shock wave through the cave at the heart of Mount Humongous. The lights trembled and dimmed sharply as a shower of precious-stone dust fell from the walls in countless tunnels.

What was the meaning of that cry? Deliverance or grief? Victory or failure? It was impossible to guess.

❋

Orthon's sons and the Felons went their separate ways without a word to each other, some of them hurrying down the corridors, others going to help Andreas, who looked about to faint. Shocked and terrified by this parricide, Oksa felt the adrenaline pumping around her body. Brutally dismissing images from the scene she'd just witnessed, she forced herself to focus on what really mattered: her pressing need to find what she'd come for.

"Tumble, I need your help," she murmured. The winged scout hovered in front of her.

"At your service, my Gracious!"

"We have to find the large black metal cupboard that contains the last bottle of Werewall elixir. If I remember rightly, this was no ordinary cupboard. It was at least six feet high and had about thirty compartments."

"Hmmm," said the Tumble-Bawler. "A piece of furniture like that shouldn't be hard to find."

"I hope you're right!" agreed Oksa.

The creature raised its head and swivelled it slowly from left to right, sniffing enthusiastically at the stuffy air.

"I'm picking up a strong smell of metal over there, thirty-five degrees to the north-east," it announced after a few seconds.

It flew down a tunnel of purple stones so fast that Oksa had difficulty keeping up, especially with her Lunatrix laboriously trotting by her side. Eventually she put him on her back and raced after the Tumble-Bawler. There were more Felons in this part of the cave than in the previous area and she passed a large number of men and women talking about Ocious's death. The news had travelled quickly and opinions seemed divided.

"It's nothing to you, Oksa-san," she told herself, "keep going!"

At the end of the purple tunnel, and after passing numerous crossroads, the three intruders reached a wall formed of an enormous faceted clear black stone.

"Are you sure the cupboard is in there?" she asked the Tumble-Bawler hovering before her.

"I'm certain, my Gracious," it declared. "It's seven feet and ten inches away, twenty-seven degrees to your left."

"With or without the wall?"

Oksa's sarcastic tone didn't hide her concern as her slate-grey eyes darkened. Taking her question seriously, the Tumble-Bawler inspected the wall and lost no time in communicating the results of its analysis:

"The wall is thirteen inches thick, which is included in the seven feet and ten inches between you and the metal cupboard."

"Thirteen inches thick," sighed Oksa. "Is that all? And I suppose there's no door so I'll have to pass through that very, very thick stone to reach the room behind it."

"My Gracious encounters the imperious requirement of proceeding to the application of her Werewall constitution," added the Lunatrix, still perched on Oksa's back.

"That's what I thought," she acknowledged, tossing back her hair. "Well, I'll have to manage. Failure just isn't an option!"

She put her Lunatrix on the ground. He looked so distraught that she felt sorry for him and stroked him briefly.

"This is what we'll do: I'll have to remove the Invisibuls to pass through the wall and get hold of the bottle. I won't be able to do that without a physical presence. I'll have to keep them with me because you never know what might happen, so I'll only leave you with the bare minimum. You have to be protected, because there seems to be a lot of toing and froing out here. Wait here for me patiently. Okay?"

The two creatures nodded vigorously.

"Tumble, can you detect anyone on the other side of that wall?"

"Not a soul," guaranteed the Tumble-Bawler.

"See you soon then," she said, removing her protective layer.

❄

Wedged between the Invisibuls which were squirming around on the creatures and the wall, which looked impassable, Oksa concentrated harder than she ever had before.

"Think of Gus," she kept repeating. "Think of Gus: if you don't get that bottle, he'll die. Come on! Make an effort, Oksa-san!"

When her body sank halfway into the stone, she almost screamed with joy. Behind her the Lunatrix seemed to be pushing her, not only to hide her from the sight of any Felons who might be tempted to walk down this tunnel—which seemed unlikely, fortunately—but also to encourage her. A timely phrase uttered by the strange head-root she'd met when Gus was Impictured sprang to mind: "Your footsteps will lead wherever you want to go." Those words were particularly appropriate today. Physical strength counted for nothing, and there was no point flexing her muscles. The solution was in her head and heart. "Your footsteps will lead wherever you want to go." Once Oksa had perfectly assimilated this principle, the solidity of the stone was no more than a temporary barrier. As if turning to gas, the enormous crystal ceased its resistance and Oksa sank into the material, dripping with sweat but feeling triumphantly determined.

The claustrophobic, low-ceilinged room was so small that a torch was enough to illuminate it. And, as the Tumble-Bawler had said, the cupboard was in there. Oksa recognized it immediately with its five rows of six compartments, each with a little handle in the form of a ring. She gave a relieved smile, congratulating herself on the beneficial effects on her memory of the Excelsior Capacitor. She had just made a dive for the middle compartments, which is where she remembered seeing Ocious put the bottle, when the sound of voices stopped her.

She just had time to think the magic words summoning the Invisibuls when a door opened in a blind spot opposite the black rock. Illuminated by the dazzling light of a powerful Polypharus, Mortimer entered the room, followed by the last of the Diaphans.

52

UNEXPECTED HELP

A S SOON AS THE REVOLTING CREATURE CAME IN, IT
froze and the room was filled with the appalling stench of garlic,
rotten eggs and dust that Oksa associated with it. Beneath its translucent, greasy skin, Oksa could see the black blood coursing through its
veins and outsized heart. She was also aware that its heartbeats had
suddenly quickened and that its melted nostrils were quivering. She
flattened herself against the wall as the alerted Diaphan frantically sniffed
around.

"What's wrong with you?" grumbled Mortimer as he tried to open
one of the cupboard's compartments.

"I can smell love," replied the Diaphan in its horrible scratchy voice.

Oksa froze. The vile Sniffler had an extraordinary sense of smell if
it knew she was there! Neither the Vigilians nor the most experienced
Firmhands could sense her presence when she was protected by her
Invisibuls. Only Orthon had almost succeeded.

"You're repulsive," said Mortimer, looking deeply disgusted. "I
loathe you."

"Mmmm, it's so delicious!" continued the Diaphan, without paying
the slightest heed to Mortimer's remarks. "There's someone here.
Someone who's passionately in love. I can smell that rich, smooth,
mouth-watering perfume."

It shuffled over to where Oksa stood and sniffed greedily at the covering of Invisibuls. Horrified, she held her breath.

"Someone who's passionately in love? Hardly likely to be me then," retorted Mortimer, trying another compartment. "Why don't you stop babbling and tell me exactly where the bottle is!"

"My Master Ocious ordered me to keep the bottle safe at all times," said the Diaphan, its nostrils still quivering. "As I said, you're not authorized to have it."

Mortimer turned to glare imperiously at it.

"You know Ocious is dead," he said firmly.

Although his voice deepened, he showed no sign of weakness. Given the circumstances and what had happened only a few minutes earlier, his self-assurance surprised, and worried, Oksa. His eyes, black as his crew cut hair, gleamed with unmistakable authority.

"My father is now the Master of the Felons," he insisted, "and yours. He was the one who ordered me to come and get the bottle. You know what he's like and you wouldn't want to annoy him, much less disobey him, would you?"

The Diaphan groaned and shook its head, looking uncertain. Every movement it made filled the room with whiffs of stinking odour, turning Oksa's stomach.

"The bottle is there," it said finally, stretching out its emaciated arm towards the bottom of the cupboard. "You need to turn the ring halfway to the left, a quarter of the way to the right, then three-eighths to the left and two-fifths to the right."

Mortimer bent down and touched the ring of the compartment in question, then did what the creature had told him to do, and the small door opened. A bluish vapour floated out, revealing the infamous bottle.

It was despair that made Oksa show herself, not courage. Mind-numbing despair at seeing Mortimer take hold of the flask that represented Gus's last chance of survival.

By the power of the Granoks,
Think outside the box
And retract the Invisibuls
Which make my form ethereal.

The mimetic worms disappeared inside the Granok-Shooter in a fraction of a second.

"Oksa?"

Mortimer gaped at her in amazement.

"What are you doing here?" he asked in a panic. "You have no idea how dangerous it is!"

"Give me the bottle, Mortimer!"

Granok-Shooter in hand, Oksa had adopted an attacking position, her body crouched forward and trembling with tension. She was about to open fire when, to her great surprise, Mortimer handed her the object.

"I was getting it for you anyway," he said.

Oksa grabbed it and stuffed it into her bag, glowering at Mortimer with a severity that was probably unfair, but she didn't know if she could really trust him. The boy she'd nicknamed "the Neanderthal" for so long had been one of her worst enemies at St Proximus, and she wasn't about to forget how willingly he'd participated in Orthon's attacks on her.

"I'll help you get out of here," he said hurriedly.

"I can manage on my own, thanks."

"Oksa, I'm not the person you think I am. I... I'm not like them."

His eyes were filled with deep suffering. He'd changed so much—he looked so tortured.

"You saw what your father did, didn't you?" murmured Oksa, confused. Mortimer's face froze and his breathing quickened.

"How do you think I can bear it?" he whispered.

Oksa gnawed the inside of her cheek.

"I've made my decision," he continued. "I don't belong here any more."

Oksa was about to tell him what she knew about his desire to join the Gracious supporters when there was a commotion in the tunnels. They both jumped.

"Come on!" exclaimed Mortimer, pointing to the door.

"Hold on! My Lunatrix and Tumble-Bawler are waiting for me on the other side! I can't leave them behind."

"And I can't let you leave without sampling your intoxicating perfume," said the Diaphan, sidling dangerously close to Oksa.

Its enormous eyes, covered in an opaque film, had already begun to immobilize her. Unwillingly, Oksa found herself gazing into their bottomless depths, feeling helpless to resist. The Diaphan was now so close to her that she could hear—as well as see—its blood pulsing through the veins of its vile body.

"Leave her alone!" ordered Mortimer.

His fist smacked into the Diaphan's head with a dull thunk. The surprised and angry creature turned round, spitting out a nasty growl, which didn't faze Mortimer. He summoned his Polypharus back into his Granok-Shooter, plunging the room into darkness, which was agony for the Diaphan. Then he grabbed Oksa by the arm and pulled her towards the black stone.

"Quick, hurry!"

He sank into the stone as if the wall were made of cotton wool.

"Mortimer!"

Half his body had already disappeared. He turned to see a white-faced, panic-stricken Oksa, her other arm held in a vice-like grip by the Diaphan. Her Granok-Shooter had fallen to the ground, leaving her disarmed and defenceless.

"Give me your feelings of love and I'll let you live," rasped the monster. "Give them to me! I need them."

Mortimer pulled on one side and the Diaphan on the other. However, the creature's determination and ferocious appetite made it the stronger of the two. It dug its clawed fingers into Oksa's flesh, not caring if it broke the skin, and the more she tried to free herself, the harder its nails bit into her arm. Blood began dripping onto the flat paving stones. The Diaphan was dribbling with ecstasy. It ran its black, pointed tongue around its mouth, and its nostrils flared inordinately wide at the prospect of drinking in such a large dose of romantic love.

"Let me go, Mortimer, so that I can put an end to this once and for all!" exclaimed Oksa, terrified.

Mortimer hesitated briefly, then obeyed. With her free hand, Oksa swiftly picked up her Granok-Shooter and brought it to her lips.

She whispered into it, eyes wild.

She'd never have thought this would happen so soon.

She'd never have thought she'd be capable of it.

A spiral formed above the Diaphan, dark as a moonless night. It began spinning, at first slowly, then faster and faster. The Diaphan looked up and fear filled its opaque eyes. It released Oksa's arm in a bid to escape its fate, but the Crucimaphila was implacable. Wherever the Diaphan ran, the grim spiral followed.

Without an ounce of remorse, Oksa watched in fascination as the black hole positioned itself above the Diaphan, then dropped lower until it lightly touched its head, sending it into a blind panic. Time seemed to stand still.

The black hole expanded.

And the Diaphan exploded.

Hands on her thighs, Oksa stared shakily at the small black cloud that had just sucked up the vile creature.

"How horrible," she whispered, with a shudder.

Mortimer glanced at her surreptitiously. The Crucimaphila had stirred up bad memories: his father had fallen victim to it a few months earlier, in the cellar of their London house. He hadn't died, but the event had been so traumatic that Mortimer was hardly likely to view what had just happened with indifference. He shivered, but this time it was because he was remembering a more recent tragedy. Zoe, the cousin he loved like a kid sister, who'd had her future ruined by the Diaphan.

"Foul creature," he said bitterly.

"It was the last one," faltered Oksa. "I've killed the last of the Diaphans."

Mortimer took her hands in both of his.

"You did the right thing," he said, gazing at the cloud that was gradually dissipating. "That monster got what it deserved."

"I killed it," repeated Oksa.

"And you should be proud of yourself! But you have to go now. After all that's just happened, things are going to get complicated. It's not a good idea to hang around here."

He pulled her towards the stone inset into the wall and they both disappeared into its myriad dark facets. However, before Oksa covered herself in Invisibuls again, she called to Mortimer.

"What?" he said.

"Thank you," Oksa said simply. "For this," she added, patting her bag, "and for the Lasonillia."

With a faraway look in his eyes, Mortimer said:

"Don't mention it."

"Good luck, Mortimer."

"And to you, Oksa."

❈

Finding her way back through this maze of corridors felt like braving an obstacle course, even though the Tumble-Bawler and Mortimer were excellent guides. Their biggest problem was the commotion in the main cave of Mount Humongous, as well as those surrounding it. Ocious's death—and particularly the circumstances surrounding it—had created a stir, and the former Docent's most faithful followers—the vast majority of the few hundred Felons sheltering in the Peak Ridge Mountains—had been thrown into a panic. They were not as convinced of the legitimacy of Orthon's immediate seizure of power as the Felon would have liked. Only the radicals and supporters of extreme force were in favour of such a decisive style of leadership. However, whatever their opinion, they all understood one thing: Orthon was a formidable man who deserved to be feared. If not loved...

Zigzagging between the hordes of Felons and Abominaris, Mortimer finally led Oksa and her companions to the mouth of the cave. The two guards, protected by their Sealencers, bowed to the son of the man who'd become their leader.

The Young Gracious cautiously pinched her nose shut so that the hypnotic fumes from the torches didn't send her to sleep. She walked to the tip of the rocky outcrop and looked down into the canyon filled with Felons Vertiflying in all directions, entering and leaving the numerous caves in the cliff. A swarm of buzzing Vigilians flew past very close to her, almost causing her to lose her balance.

Mortimer had a brief chat with the guards and joined Oksa, endeavouring to look as natural as possible.

"My father appears to have increased the number of guards on all routes to the caves," he murmured with his hand over his mouth, pretending to watch the coming and goings of the Vertifliers. "I know that isn't a problem for you, but be careful all the same."

Oksa took off into the eerie, torch-lit darkness. Before leaving the canyon she turned round to cry out a message to Mortimer, standing at the entrance of the main cave, lost in misery. He wouldn't be able to hear or see her, but she hoped her words would somehow find their way to his heart.

"You're not alone! Hang in there!"

53

TAKING STOCK

O KSA HAD NEVER VERTIFLOWN SO QUICKLY. SQUEEZING her bag tightly against her, she shot through the narrow valley, then over the plains separating the Peak Ridge Mountains from Thousandeye City. The Lunatrix kept uttering little cries of exhilaration or fright—she had no way of knowing which—while the Tumble-Bawler struggled to keep up with its hot-headed mistress, despite its unfailing enthusiasm. In the end, an attack of cramp in its wing put paid to its efforts and it travelled home sheepishly on Oksa's shoulder.

✺

It was still dark when the three adventurers arrived at the entrance to Thousandeye City. Two Squoracles welcomed them, complaining about the cool night air, and Oksa was finally able to remove her layer of Invisibuls.

"The risk faced by my Gracious was colossal," sighed the Lunatrix, clambering down from Oksa's back. "But the challenge was worthy of the candle!"

Oksa couldn't help bursting out laughing. The Lunatrix's use of vocabulary never ceased to surprise her.

"You're right!" she said, patting her eccentric steward's head. "The challenge was worthy of the candle... mission accomplished, right?"

The Lunatrix shook his head from left to right, looking vexed.

"My Gracious provided the demonstration of her immense courage while her domestic staff presented his considerable cowardice and the completion of his uselessness," he wailed.

"You are joking, aren't you?" protested Oksa. "I can't do without you, you're simply in-dis-pen-sa-ble!"

The Lunatrix snivelled.

"My Gracious applies a restorative balm over the heart of her domestic staff. Her indulgence towards her steward knows no limits."

Oksa looked at him affectionately.

"Right, it's time to tell everyone about all *this*," she said, suddenly solemn. "And I need you by my side even more than ever."

※

Was it a father's instinct, or had Oksa's creatures alerted Pavel? Oksa had no time to find out the answer: her father was waiting outside the door to her apartment, sitting against the wall with his forearms on his knees. He looked at Oksa, his sad eyes full of anxiety.

"Dad? What on earth are you doing here?"

"What am I doing here?" he repeated, with barely suppressed rage. "What about you, Oksa? What are you doing here?"

Oksa turned away. Her father was going to give her such a telling-off when she told him where she'd been. He made things easier for her, though. In a way.

"Don't tell me you went to the Peak Ridge Mountains. You didn't, did you?"

When she didn't say anything, he put his head in his hands.

"What have I done to deserve this?" he sighed. "How can someone as sensible and cautious as me have a daughter like you? Why couldn't I have had a well-behaved teenager interested only in painting her nails, shopping or going to synchronized swimming? Instead I've ended up with an impulsive, stubborn child whose sole aim in life is to worry her poor father to death!"

Oksa hesitated, then ventured in a small voice:

"I'll start synchronized swimming, if you want, as soon as things get better—I promise! But will you let me think about painting my nails?"

Pavel glared at her, still furious, then his face relaxed. He opened his arms and Oksa knelt down beside him to give him a hug.

"Oh, Dad! I've got thousands of things to tell you!"

"Only a thousand?" grumbled Pavel, grinning broadly.

"We're going to be able to save Mum and Gus!"

At these words Pavel sat up straight. He put his hands on Oksa's shoulders and looked her in the eye. Suddenly, he didn't look so old, as his heart swelled with new, if fragile, hope.

*

The Runaways and all members of the High Enclave were roused from their sleep for an extraordinary meeting in the Round Room. Watched by her appalled, yet very proud, father, Oksa gave them a detailed report about her visit to the cave in Mount Humongous. Emotions were running high when she described Ocious's death, fatally wounded by his own demented son. There was a stunned silence, which Oksa respected, followed by an outcry as everyone reacted violently to the news, although they all came to the same conclusion: Orthon was by far the worst Felon, far more dangerous and uncontrollable than Ocious. A man sent insane by a hunger for revenge that he could never satisfy. Now his father was dead, who knew where his madness might lead him and, above all, who or what would be its target?

The mention of a spy also caused concern. The Runaways and the Servants of the different Missions looked at each other in amazement.

"We must find him or her!" exclaimed Sven.

"But how?" asked Oksa. "We don't know which clan they belong to. It could be one of us or an infiltrated Felon. The best thing to do would be to find the hole. Lukas said it had been resealed, but the spy will have to go back through it to tell the Felons about the opening of the Portal. It would be terrible for the Outside if Orthon manages to pass through the Portal—we must do everything in our power to stop him."

They all considered this for a while. Ashamed of her thoughts when Orthon had talked about the spy, Oksa didn't dare look at Tugdual, as if the things she refused to let herself imagine might be written all over her face. She also carefully avoided looking at him when she told everyone about Mortimer. Nor did she mention the secret meeting she'd watched in the undergrowth by the lakeside. Still, Tugdual obviously had no intention of hiding what had happened. He stood up and with exemplary calm told the packed room about Mortimer's desire to join Oksa.

"Don't forget he has a Gracious Heart," he reminded those who appeared more sceptical than the others. "He, like Reminiscens and Zoe, doesn't believe blood is thicker than water. And, from what Oksa has told us, watching his father murder his grandfather has given him the impetus to sever the family ties that might once have given him pause for thought."

"How do we know this isn't one of Orthon's tricks?" said Jeanne. "He might be the spy!"

"Using the tactic of the maggot in the fruit!" added Emica.

"A Trojan horse!" cried Olof.

This time Oksa came to Tugdual's help by telling everyone about the reaction of the Squoracles. However, it was the tube containing sprigs of Lasonillia that really laid any remaining doubts to rest.

"You mean Mortimer went to the territory of the Distant Reaches to find some Lasonillia for you, when your families are such bitter enemies?" asked Mystia in amazement.

"Not for me," corrected Oksa. "For my mother."

"Do you realize the risk he took?" continued Sven. "In the past few years, the Distant Reaches has become the wildest and most dangerous area in Edefia. The creatures living there have always been very hostile and the climate changes over the past few years have only made matters worse. None of us has managed to enter that territory for at least ten years."

"Do you really believe his story?" interrupted Emica "What if those sprigs are poisonous?"

Pavel made a gesture of irritation. Oksa frowned. She tried to catch Tugdual's eye, but he looked away. He was so pale that she thought he might be sick. He gripped the back of the seat in front and closed his eyes, his face as expressionless as a statue. It hadn't escaped Oksa that certain details were missing from his story, which made her anxious. Why had he left certain things out? She stared at the tube holding the precious sprigs.

"Abakum, you'll be able to tell us exactly what this is, won't you?" she exclaimed, feeling out of sorts.

The Fairyman hadn't said a word until now. He'd listened to Oksa's account, then Tugdual's story, with a solemnity that made his handsome face look haggard. The drastic action taken by Orthon against his father must have upset him deeply, thought Oksa. He walked heavily over to her and picked up the sprigs. He studied them, smelt them, held them up to the light, tasted a tiny piece, then finally gave his verdict:

"It's definitely Lasonillia. Purer and healthier than we could have hoped!"

Oksa sighed with relief and Pavel immediately relaxed.

"Will you let me take it with me, Oksa, my Gracious?" asked the Fairyman. "I'm going to prepare the remedy for Marie."

"Do you know the formula?" she couldn't help asking, then immediately bit her lip.

She could be so tactless sometimes.

"I know it," confirmed Abakum, giving a bow.

"So we have everything we need now!" Oksa concluded.

"We just have to wait for the Portal to open," added her father.

"And for Orthon to attack," added Abakum, a strange sadness misting his eyes. "But before everyone takes up their positions, as agreed, I suggest we make a few decisions regarding our imminent future. Starting with the appointment of the person who will stand in for you while you're on the Outside, Oksa, my Gracious."

54

Everything Has To Go Without a Hitch

ELZEVIR OF GRACIOUS OKSA, PAGE TWELVE

PLACE: *Gracious apartment, Glass Column in Thousandeye City.*
DATE: *Unknown. Equivalent to the fifty-sixth night after my Sovereign Hourglass was turned over.*

I received an unusual visit today. My Phoenix came to see me. It brought me a message from Dragomira. I miss her so badly…

It was an extremely important message.

It contained the information we've all been waiting for.

At the moment, I'm the only one who knows it.

And the only one who is worrying about what will happen. Will I be able to bear it?

It is now three days and three nights since I came back from the Peak Ridge Mountains. Three endless, difficult and depressing days and nights for my family and friends.

But it will be worse when they know what I know.

I know all the details.

But it isn't that simple. Nothing ever is and nothing ever will be. "That's the Pollocks for you," as Gus would say.

I'm going to be able to open the Portal in exactly nine hours, in other words when one hundred and eighty grains have flowed through the Hourglass in front of me. I'd like to turn it over, stop time, go back and start again. Do things differently.

I'm the one who has the key.

The keys. Because there are two.

The Portal will only open twice. After that, it will remain closed for ever. So everyone will have to choose.

The Outside or Edefia.

The Ageless Ones didn't tell me everything before—there is more to the Ephemeral Secret now.

More than just the opening.

Everything can be told, because the keys are the Secret. Only the keys.

They're in my head. That's the safest place for them. But even though they're only words, they weigh heavily on me. Very heavily.

My mother and Gus will be cured. The thing I want most in the world is to find them and save them.

If everything goes without a hitch, they'll be able to come back with me to Edefia, Abakum has promised me that. If I had to give up my powers in exchange for the Integrator Capacitors he's just created, I'd do it willingly. No doubt at all!

Abakum is a genius. He is extraordinary. In every sense of the word. What would I do without him?

Integrator Capacitors—what a brainwave! We just have to wait thirty-three days for the substance to become deeply rooted in the bodies of the Spurned and the Portal will no longer be an insurmountable barrier for them!

They'll be able to pass through as easily as any Insider.

If everything goes without a hitch.

Everything has to go without a hitch.

What I've said isn't strictly true, which is why I have such mixed feelings on a day when I should be so happy.

I don't know whether to laugh or cry. I'm torn in two and it's impossible to reconcile the two halves.

What did I think would happen? What did I hope for?

Not just any Insider will be able to pass back through the Portal. Only my Watcher Abakum and those with Gracious Hearts.

Jeanne and Pierre…

Naftali and Brune…

Tugdual…

They'll have to stay behind.

Why do we always have to be parted?

Will we see each other again?

Will we be happy one day?

I shall use one of the two keys in a few hours. My mother and Gus can't wait any longer.

But before I do, I shall start the rumour that the Portal is about to be opened.

That's the best way to draw Orthon. Acting on information from his spy, he'll lose no time in attacking Thousandeye City so that he can access the Portal.

We have to thwart him and I won't open the Portal until we have. We can't run the risk of him passing through to the Outside. He's too dangerous.

Everything has to go without a hitch.

55

THE WAIT

TELLING EVERYONE THAT ONLY ABAKUM AND THOSE WITH Gracious Hearts could leave Edefia was hard for Oksa. Jeanne and Pierre were devastated, the members of the Knut clan put a brave face on things, but they were obviously disappointed. All of them, including Bodkin, Cockerell and Feng Li, would have to stay behind and wait.

"Tugdual! Don't go!"

Oksa ran after Tugdual, who'd just left the Round Room and was disappearing down the corridor. He passed through a wall and Oksa followed him, not even noticing that she'd managed it easily. She found him on the terrace of the fifty-fifth floor, staring at the soft dawn light, his face expressionless. Like him, she leant her elbows on the railing and their shoulders touched. Tugdual shifted away, putting some distance between them.

"Hey!" said Oksa, stung. "What have I done to upset you?"

Tugdual didn't say a word, and turned his head away.

"Maybe you think I wanted things to turn out like this?" cried Oksa hoarsely. "This is hardly my fault, is it?"

Her nostrils prickled and she gripped the parapet, her arms tense. She felt a terrible desire to scream, then take flight and disappear. A growl of frustration and anger rose in her throat, twisting her face into a grimace.

"Don't you think things are complicated enough already?" she continued, tears brimming. "But no, you have to make things worse and blame me."

Tugdual whirled round to stare at her. His expression shook Oksa. Hot, black, corrosive ink seemed to be spreading over his eyes. Oksa thought she'd never seen such a tormented expression in her life.

"I'll come back quickly, I promise!" she said. "You won't have to wait long."

Her tone had softened. Tugdual started to say something, but couldn't.

"Speak to me, please," begged Oksa. "Don't leave me like this."

The words refused to come.

"Is it because of Gus?" persevered Oksa.

Tugdual tensed.

"I love you, Tugdual."

This murmured declaration surprised even her. She'd never said that to anyone. Never. Did Tugdual realize what it meant?

Looking devastated, Tugdual caressed her cheek lightly with his fingertips, then silently took off into the sky, which was veined with purple streaks.

❉

The news spread like wildfire: the Portal had just started to open! Pavel and Abakum were the only ones who knew it wasn't true—only Oksa could begin the process. However, spreading this rumour ensured that Orthon was bound to be informed about it by his spy.

The guard had been strengthened around the entrance to Thousandeye City: no one was allowed to leave under any pretext, and the Corpusleoxes were keeping close watch with one of the trusty brigades. Endless searching hadn't located the breach made by the Felons, though, and Oksa was almost relieved. It didn't really matter. The quicker Orthon was informed, the quicker he'd attack and the sooner this unbearable wait would be over.

From her balcony, with Abakum and Pavel at her side, Oksa watched the silent city through a Reticulata as big as a pillow. For the past three days Naftali and Sven, the Servants for Granokology and Protection, had been working flat out to perfect a strategy based essentially on mobility and the use of unconventional weapons that were likely to take their enemies by surprise. Vantage points had been cleared of rubble, priority targets had been identified, Granok-Shooters had been filled to overflowing and everyone was on the alert, trembling with impatience and fear.

❋

It began with a soft noise, like a flag floating in the wind.

This noise swelled to resemble the beating of thousands of hands on thousands of drums, drawing closer and closer and becoming louder and louder.

Finally, it appeared.

A vast, buzzing swarm darkened the sky and the horizon. Above the Vertifliers surrounded by Vigilians in the front line were thousands of Chiropterans. Their wings clicked frantically and from between their pointy teeth erupted a shrill whistling noise which was agony on the ears.

Powerful creatures, each more frightening than the last, pounded over the ground: slimy, nauseating Abominaris; blue rhinoceroses with improbably long horns; enormous tigers with silver fur and canines as long as swords; thick, gleaming zebra-snakes.

"They've managed to tame them," murmured Abakum, lowering his Reticulata.

"And we'll make mincemeat of them!" exclaimed Oksa, keeping her eyes on the throng heading for Thousandeye City. "We managed to beat the Leozards, didn't we?"

"There weren't nearly as many Leozards," objected Pavel.

Oksa looked at him in exasperation.

"Dad! Surely we're not going to let a few beasts scare us?"

Pavel anxiously raised his hands in surrender and turned his attention back to the advancing enemy. When the humans and creatures reached the edge of the Aegis, they fanned out to surround the transparent membrane. The monsters on the ground pawed the earth impatiently around the bottom while the Vertifliers and Chiropterans positioned themselves so that they covered as vast a surface area as possible. In a few minutes, the Aegis had turned completely black, as if attacked by a lethal gangrene.

At the top of the Column, Oksa held her breath.

"It's time you made your way down to the seventh basement," said her father hotly.

"But Dad..." she groaned.

"Oksa, would you please do what I tell you for once?"

"Orthon will be focusing on you," said Abakum. "He needs you to lead him to the Portal. He won't endanger your life, but things are bound to get rough, so you should stay somewhere safe."

"Whereas with me acting as bait, you could get at him much more easily!" snapped Oksa.

"We've already discussed this," snapped Pavel. "It's out of the—"

It wasn't Oksa who prevented him from finishing his sentence. Granok-Shooters in hand, a hundred Felons were gathering on the west side of Thousandeye City to lead an attack that threatened to exceed even the gloomiest expectations. Pavel looked at his daughter one last time then took flight, his Ink Dragon deployed above him. A tongue of fire split the gloom, accompanied by a long roar. Abakum grabbed Oksa's arm and pulled her out of her apartment. Without a word, they took the lift down to the Column's first basement.

"Take shelter, Oksa. One of us will come and get you when this is over."

341

He studied her intently, then turned and went back up to the lobby and left the Column. As soon as Oksa was left alone, however, she retraced her steps instead of going down to the underground passages.

"As if I could hide underground while they're all risking their lives!" she declared passionately. "Orthon and his cronies are going to find out what a real Gracious is like."

56

RENEWED CHAOS

OKSA HAD BARELY CROSSED THE SQUARE IN FRONT OF THE Column when a huge explosion shook the ground so violently that fragments of stone and glass broke away from the tall building and crashed at her feet. Oksa flattened herself against the wall and hugged her Cloak around her for courage and energy. In horrified fascination she looked at the Aegis, which had been hit simultaneously by hundreds of acid bombs. A gaping hole formed in the thin, yet strong, protective membrane as other smaller, and equally destructive, bombs made holes here and there. In a few minutes, the Aegis shrivelled like incense paper and disintegrated, showering the area with charred fragments.

Thousandeye City had lost its protection.

A heavy silence descended while pieces of ash, light as grey feathers, floated in the humid air. Time seemed to stand still, and everyone stood rooted to the spot, well aware that this was only a temporary respite. Then a fearsome, belligerent shout arose and the ring of Felons gradually closed in like a shrinking circle. From their positions on the terraces of houses, the Gracious's supporters began firing volleys of Granoks at their enemies, who were wearing armour and helmets of dark leather. From where she stood, Oksa saw the first bodies falling from the sky, but also swarms of Chiropterans swooping down on the districts farthest from the centre of Thousandeye City.

"Oh no!" she cried.

She shot into the air, a burning rage in the pit of her stomach.

⁕

It was a clever move to surround the city, but applying the strategy simultaneously on two levels, both on the ground and in the air, was a masterstroke. As Oksa flew over the Dome District she had good cause to lament the destruction being wreaked. Felons sitting astride rhinoceroses flattened everything in their path, trampling people and knocking down houses. It was sheer carnage. Then swarms of Chiropterans attacked, crawling through the holes made in the walls by the long horns of the blue-skinned monsters to bite the poor wretches trapped inside their own homes.

And yet the Gracious's supporters showed great courage in defending themselves. Men appeared suddenly above the houses, dragging a gigantic hoop net behind them. As the net floated past, Oksa immediately realized its distinctive origins: it had been woven by Spinollias. The men Vertiflew towards the swarm of approaching Chiropterans, hovered in front of them and then shot forward and cast the hoop net over them, trapping them inside. The strident noise of the whistling Chiropterans was soon cut off when the net soaked in Inflammatoria sap caught fire, incinerating all its prisoners.

The Felons were making inexorable progress, though, and the violence escalated as they advanced.

Distraught, Oksa Vertiflew above the streets farthest from the centre of Thousandeye City. Everywhere, people who had once lived together were pitted against each other in terrible hand-to-hand combat.

"What a waste," murmured Oksa, with tears in her eyes.

⁕

Seen from the sky, the city had become a vast morass of men and women fighting with Granoks. Oksa recognized the Fortensky clan, grouped around Galina—Leomido's daughter—attacking a rhinoceros with Putrefactios. Confronted by this unexpectedly aggressive woman with untidy braids, the animal was writhing in pain as its body putrefied by the second. In any other circumstances these fighters would have felt deep pity for the creature. But neither pity, kindness or mercy had any place in this slaughter. Only the strongest had any chance of survival.

Sven, Sacha and Bodkin were unfortunately not among them. They were some of the first victims of this chaos, lying spreadeagled in the mud.

Farther away, Naftali, Brune and their children were bombarding a group of rebellious Felons with Stuffaraxes. The men fell one by one, suffocated as the insects filled their throats. Tugdual wasn't with his family and Oksa's heart lurched when she thought he might be in danger. Or worse...

Oksa's creatures also did their bit, fighting with all the powers they possessed. The Incompetents spat their corrosive saliva, the Corpusleoxes disarmed the Felons with violent swipes of their claws, and the Attendants charged at the Abominaris, tossing their slimy, mangled bodies into the air. All humans and creatures had abandoned their long-standing pacifist principles to become fierce and courageous warriors.

Both clans seemed surprised at the violence of the raging battle. Neither Felons nor Gracious supporters had thought they might have to face such ferocious adversaries. Lifeless bodies lay everywhere, some dressed in leather, but many in simple double-breasted jackets.

❈

At the other end of the city the Felon vanguard, aided by vicious zebra-snakes and Vigilians, was just as savage in its attack. The Young Gracious glimpsed Tin and Olof fighting one of those enormous reptiles with striped scales. A powerful axe blow severed the monster in two but didn't kill it. Half its body reared up, towering above the men. It turned a glassy stare on its attackers, its forked tongue darting in and out evilly, then it spat at them. Tin was spattered by its venom and collapsed with a terrible scream.

In an attempt to protect Lucy, who was firing a large number of Granoks at the snake without being able to hit it, Olof was also struck by the venom. Oksa couldn't bear it: her phenomenal Knock-Bong hurled the two halves of the snake against a wall. The horrible creature finally died in an explosion of flesh and venom. Shocked to see their ruler in their midst, the Gracious's supporters looked gratefully at her, while the Felons advanced with ominous determination, their fists clenched and their faces hard.

"No one lays a finger on her!" yelled a voice she would have recognized anywhere.

Oksa looked up to see Orthon, floating a few yards above the ground, Granok-Shooter in hand. Everyone scattered.

"No harm must come to her," he hissed fiercely, without taking his eyes off Oksa.

He landed on the ground in front of Oksa, whom he hated with a vengeance, even though she was his key to success. His fawn-coloured leather breastplate made him look even stiffer than usual, but his face was just as lacking in humanity. Muscles taut with tension, Oksa glared at him defiantly.

"I can imagine how hard that must be for you to say!" she said sarcastically. "Having to spare my life when you're longing to kill me."

Amused surprise gleamed in Orthon's unfathomable eyes.

"Kill you?" he asked. "Tut-tut, not before you've done me one last service!"

Several Arborescens Granoks spurted with lightning speed from the group of Felons, immediately countered by the Fireballisticos fired by Oksa's supporters. The fireballs intercepted the Granoks, reducing them instantly to ash, before being extinguished in their turn to form small orange plumes in the air, thick with dust. Orthon raised his hand and the attack stopped immediately.

"Do you really think I'll lead you to the Portal?" sneered Oksa. "In your dreams!"

Saying this, she fired a volley of the worst Granoks she possessed at him, regretting that she'd wasted a Crucimaphila on the Diaphan—she'd have to wait a hundred days before using the supreme Granok again. Battle-hardened and skilful, Orthon easily parried the tiny balls laden with spells, deflecting them with fine electric currents from his fingertips. Suddenly they both stopped, unsure who had the upper hand. Orthon gazed at Oksa, his eyes narrowed and cold as a dagger blade. She had to stay unharmed and that was her greatest weapon. Orthon took off and disappeared into the sky with a long, triumphant laugh, leaving Oksa furious.

She was about to take flight in pursuit of her enemy when she was stopped by her supporters.

"Gracious Oksa, you shouldn't be here!" said a woman, midway through dealing with an Abominari.

"Oh, here comes Lady Muck!" grated the vile creature. "You know that I puke on your family and loathe your ancestors, don't you?"

"No one talks like that to our Gracious!" said the woman, delivering a fatal blow to its head, which exploded like an over-ripe watermelon.

"Watch out, Oksa! Behind you!"

Mortimer jumped down from the terrace of a burning house to join her. Oksa just had time to turn round to see a silver tiger leaping straight for her. She held out her hand and her quick reaction floored the big cat, as a fireball shot straight into its gaping maw. The animal roared, writhed and snapped its fearsome teeth in an attempt to put out the flames consuming it, but it was no good—the tiger collapsed at Oksa's feet as she gazed in wonder at its terrible beauty.

"Mortimer? You okay?" she asked.

He nodded, then turned to face an Abominari that was rushing at him with all its claws out. Oksa noticed that Mortimer had taken off the distinctive leather armour and helmet which marked out the Felons. It looked like he had chosen his side.

"What are you doing here?" shouted Zoe suddenly. "You're supposed to be safe in the Column."

"I was looking for Orthon," admitted Oksa.

Zoe gave her a sidelong glance, while firing Colocynthises at a group of Vigilians. They fell to the ground, turned to glass and were reduced to a small pile of shards by some Attendants, which trampled them underfoot.

"Have you lost your mind?" exclaimed Zoe. "It's too dangerous!"

"This won't stop until he's beaten!" cried Oksa, firing a Putrefactio at a Felon who was bearing down on her.

Then she took off again, on the lookout for the man responsible for this chaos.

❀

The two clans battled for hours. The Gracious supporters had the advantage of greater numbers, but the Felons had brute force on their side. Although the latter initially had supremacy, Oksa's army finally gained the upper hand, after heavy losses on both sides.

Most of the Felons were dead or had been taken prisoner. Only a few diehards still opposed Oksa's forces around the Column, and Oksa had no doubt that Orthon would be among them.

A crowd had formed near the Gracious's gardens. She approached cautiously, although she was relieved to recognize some of her entourage: Abakum, Cameron, Naftali, Jeanne and Pierre...

Tugdual.

A great weight lifted from her heart.

But when she heard their sobs, she feared the worst. She felt as though her blood had drained from her body. Who was it? Who were they weeping for? Who was missing? Zoe? Reminiscens?

Her father?

57

THE END OF AN ERA

S HE THOUGHT SHE WAS GOING TO FAINT. HER WHOLE BODY
went weak as a sharp pang of grief more intense than any physical
pain shot through her. A shadow passed overhead. She looked up: Pavel
and his Ink Dragon were hovering above the small group, accompanied
by her fiery-winged Phoenix. Her relief felt like a true liberation. Her
father was alive! He landed nearby and ran to her.

"You're here," he said, hugging her.

"Surely you didn't think I'd wait for you all on my own in that basement?" she murmured, her face buried in the crook of his shoulder.

Pavel gave a long sigh. A little farther away, a shout interrupted their
reunion.

"No, Cameron! Wait!"

It was Naftali's voice. A choked voice full of sorrow. Pavel and Oksa
anxiously hurried over. The Runaways who were there parted to let them
through. Eyes wide, Oksa covered her mouth with her hand.

The lifeless body of Helena Knut was lying on the beaten earth.

Kneeling by her side, Abakum had taken ten or so vials from his bag
and was doing everything he could to revive her. She looked almost
serene, as though she were sleeping. Abakum's back suddenly slumped.
With his slender wrinkled hand, he closed Helena's faded blue eyes,
which were staring vacantly at the smoky sky. Numbly, Oksa looked at

Tugdual, while Brune ran into Naftali's embrace. Tugdual seemed to be in shock, his arms hanging at his sides and a long strand of hair hiding half of his expressionless face.

His mother had just died before his eyes.

He'd lost both his parents.

What was he thinking? What was he feeling? He must have fought hard because his clothes and skin were covered in dust, burns and blood. His grandparents attempted to put their arms around him. He did nothing to stop them as tears like drops of ice filled his eyes. Then he pushed them away to join Cameron, who was beside himself with anger and brandishing his Granok-Shooter at the man they all hated: Orthon.

"It was him!" cried Cameron. "He killed Helena!"

Sitting with his back against the foot of a tree, the leader of the Felons was injured. He had a nasty purple mark around his throat, as if someone had tried to strangle him. He tried to speak but, instead of words, a trickle of blood emerged from his mouth, which was contorted with pain. Only his eyes revealed his true feelings as he glared venomously at Cameron.

"He killed Helena," repeated Oksa's cousin. "I saw him, he showed her no mercy!"

Orthon shook his head, which only worsened the bleeding. He stretched out his hand and fired a weak, derisory bolt of lightning, then patted his jacket.

"It this what you're looking for?" asked Cameron, showing him a Granok-Shooter.

Oksa recognized it. It was Orthon's, made of dark horn adorned with slender silver threads. The Felon's eyes widened and turned black as ink. He tried to stand up by awkwardly pushing his fists into the ground, but his arms buckled as his last strength deserted him.

Cameron drew nearer, surprising everyone with his severity.

"It's over, Orthon."

And, before anyone could intervene, he hit him with a Colocynthis Granok. In a fraction of a second, the leader of the Felons had been turned into a glass statue which Cameron shattered into a thousand fragments with a lethal punch.

The Runaways were dumbstruck.

Orthon was dead.

It was both momentous and very simple.

Cameron turned to face his family and friends. His customary mild expression had returned, although there was still a trace of cruelty in the depths of his bright eyes. No one knew what to say. None of them could have predicted the way things had turned out. This day had been one of the worst they'd ever experienced, and Orthon's death, despite hundreds of other regrettable deaths, felt as if it marked the end of a tragic era.

As if to point up this impression, a fragile yet resolute ray of sunshine pierced the thick layer of cloud and smoke and swept across Thousandeye City. The sound of wing-beats roused Oksa from her dazed state. She looked up to see her Phoenix and held out her arm in welcome. It landed gently, its talons barely touching the Young Gracious's skin, and from its beak came words that only Oksa could hear.

When the Phoenix had taken to the air again, she looked at each of her entourage one by one. Breathing raggedly, her lips trembling slightly, she hugged her Cloak more tightly around her body and announced:

"The time has come... to open the Portal."

❊

The long lines of Felon prisoners, solemnly flanked by Gracious support-ers, watched Oksa and the Runaways pass by. Their faces were serious as they crossed the devastated city. The sound of cheering soon filled the air: the people of Edefia were paying homage to the girl who'd saved the Heart of the Two Worlds and those who'd fought with them against

Ocious and tyranny. When they reached the outer limits of Thousandeye City, they took flight for the shores of Brown Lake.

The Portal was there, beneath its dark waters.

Abakum was waiting for her with Reminiscens by his side. Bent double under the weight of his Boximinus, the Fairyman looked as though he'd aged twenty years.

"We'll see each other again soon, my friend," Reminiscens told him, pressing his hands between hers.

Abakum nodded mutely. Oksa walked over to the woman who was to govern in her absence.

"Thank you for agreeing to do this, Reminiscens," she said to the elegant woman. "We'll be back in thirty-three days."

"I hope so, my dear Oksa."

Oksa looked away, not wanting to show how moved she was. She was surrounded by people she loved, the Gracious Hearts who were going with her, and those who were staying behind in the lost land they'd found again, but hadn't always chosen.

"I'll bring Gus back, I promise!" she cried, hugging Jeanne and Pierre.

Pierre "the Viking" cupped her chin with his enormous fingers.

"We're depending on you," he managed to say.

Oksa wiped her eyes with the back of her hand. Yet again her heart was being torn in two equal halves—leaving behind those she loved to be reunited with those she loved. Was life always this strange? And this unfair?

"Thirty-three days, Oksa," whispered her father in her ear.

She pressed her small bag against her. The knowledge that she was carrying the two vials that were going to save Gus and her mother was a huge comfort—it felt almost miraculous. She felt a chubby hand slip into hers.

"My Gracious must take delivery of my gratitude."

"My Lunatrix, here you are at last!" she cried.

"The domestic staff of my Gracious encounters the intoxication of gratefulness for adding his participation to the excursion bound for the Outside," said the creature.

"Wherever I go, you go," said Oksa. "That's the way it is."

The Lunatrix blushed with pleasure.

"Oksa?" called her father.

She jumped. It was time to go. Time to save her loved ones and embrace her destiny. Silently she hugged all those who'd become Spurned in their turn, lingering beside Tugdual, who seemed strangely cold.

"Don't forget what I told you," she said simply.

Over her shoulder she noticed Mortimer standing at the edge of the forest. She glanced one last time at Tugdual and was scalded by his icy gaze.

"Mortimer!"

The Runaways turned round. Mortimer didn't dare come any nearer.

"Come on!" cried Oksa.

He hesitated, then approached, hanging his head. They parted to let him through, silently supporting Oksa's decision.

❊

Oksa finally came to the edge of the water after Abakum had given all the Gracious Hearts an Aquagill Capacitor, which would allow them to reach the Portal without drowning. Oksa had such a big lump in her throat that it was hard to swallow the pill. Nevertheless, she was still first into the water.

"Oksa!"

She turned round, recognizing Tugdual's voice.

"Wait!" he said. "I'll go with you to the Portal."

Oksa's heart leapt. She kept walking until the water was too deep to stand; then, with Tugdual beside her, she dived in.

The Aquagill Capacitor was fantastic. When swallowed, it released numerous cells filled with oxygen into the lungs of the swimmers, allowing them to swim for about half an hour without needing to breathe. Relieved of this problem, they cut through the water, parting long grasses that floated like underwater banners. The dense, disquieting darkness was pierced only by a few pallid rays of sunshine which didn't penetrate much deeper than the lake's surface. Oksa was tempted to use a Polypharus and was just wondering how dangerous it would be for the octopus with illuminating tentacles, when a shoal of phosphorescent fish swam past the Gracious Hearts to take the lead. Guided by this unexpected escort of tiny sparks, Oksa and Tugdual swam rapidly through the dark waters, followed by Pavel, the Fortensky clan, Zoe and the Lunatrix, Abakum and Mortimer. Cameron brought up the rear, slowed down by an enormous bag strapped around his chest.

Finally, the Portal appeared.

❋

Although Oksa had expected something elaborate and imposing, the Portal turned out to be a much more modest affair—a simple flat stone arch standing in the mud at the bottom of the lake, with an ancient-looking wrought-iron gate. Oksa reached it in a few strokes. She wanted to speak to Tugdual, but only bubbles of air emerged from her mouth. Tugdual swam over to her, touched her lips with his fingertips and forced her to turn towards the Portal, so that she could no longer see him. "Thirty-three days," Pavel had reminded her.

All the Gracious Hearts were now clustered around her. Unbelievably, the time had come at last. She concentrated, summoned the words of one of the two keys in her head, and repeated them carefully, barely moving her lips. She looked at her father and friends anxiously: the Portal had just vibrated in the depths of the water, raising a cloud of silt. Fascinated, they all edged closer to watch the ray of light growing brighter and broader with every second.

Then the Portal was wide open.

Without further ado, Oksa took a standing jump inside and disappeared into the light. Immediately, the hinges grated dully: the gate was already starting to close. There was no time to lose! They all rushed through one after the other.

When it was his turn, Cameron paused. The Portal would be closed in just a few seconds. He scrutinized the depths of the lake, grinned and jumped through.

Two silhouettes laden with bags slipped through behind him.

A second later, the Portal closed and disappeared in the dark vegetation.

58

THERE ARE SO MANY THINGS YOU DON'T KNOW ABOUT ME...

T HE PROCESS WAS THE SAME AS THE ONE THAT HAD TRANS-
ported the Runaways from the Outside to Edefia and the feelings
it aroused were identical, except for the blinding light. The Gracious
Hearts were sucked inside by an extraordinary force and swept through
dimensions they barely noticed. The speed of this journey was beyond
all human perception. They knew only that a tremendous energy was at
work which they were powerless to control.

Oksa tried to look back to check that everyone was there. When she
turned her head, her hair whipped so violently into her face that she gave
up trying. From inside her bag, her Tumble-Bawler provided information
about the speed they were going, the direction, the air penetration rate,
the temperature, the humidity... She couldn't help smiling. Then she
closed her eyes and, like everyone with her, let herself be carried along,
impatient to reach their destination.

It didn't take very long, a few minutes at most. And when she saw where
fate had decided to eject her, she thought to herself that the journey had
been extremely short.

She'd immediately known where they were when she'd arrived. Anyone
who lived in London would have recognized the fountain in Trafalgar

Square. Oksa had passed it hundreds of times on her way to St James's Park. The problem was that the fountain was hardly the most secluded destination for their arrival from another world... When Pavel emerged in his turn, sending up plumes of water, various passers-by looked surprised, even disapproving. Fortunately it was dark, there were few people about and the Gracious Hearts who kept suddenly appearing were deemed to be drunkards with little respect for public places rather than who they really were.

Abakum, Mortimer, then Galina climbed out of the clear waters of the fountain, stunned but relieved to find themselves in London—an incalculable advantage on two counts.

"Just think how awful it would have been if we'd all been ejected to the four corners of the world?" said Oksa, cuddling up to her father.

"You're telling me," said Pavel quietly.

The Lunatrix appeared too, ashen-faced and soaking wet. He ran to Oksa.

"Ooohhh, my Gracious! Your domestic staff makes the contribution of a message stuffed with alarm!"

Feeling suddenly worried, Oksa bent down to his level. His bulging, panic-stricken eyes were spinning in their sockets. It didn't appear to be the cold night air that was making him shiver like a leaf.

"What's going on?" whispered Oksa.

A few yards away, the Gracious Hearts continued to emerge one by one from the fountain. Zoe, Cameron's twins, Galina's daughters...

"Supplementary Gracious Hearts have experienced the crossing of the Portal, my Gracious."

Oksa frowned.

"Reminiscens?"

She knew that old lady could sometimes be impulsive. Perhaps, at the last moment, she'd decided to go with Abakum? The Lunatrix wailed.

"Two Gracious Hearts have made the addition of their presence beside the man who has accomplished the appearance of the cousin of my Gracious."

Oksa looked at her father and Abakum, her heart in her mouth. As she straightened, Cameron appeared in the fountain, his enormous bag on his back. All twelve of them were there. They'd succeeded! Cameron climbed out of the water, helped by his sister, Galina, and, standing on the stone steps, he adjusted his soaking clothes and smoothed back his hair. These gestures made Oksa feel uneasy, although she didn't know why. Pavel and Abakum looked equally worried, which did nothing to reassure her.

"Okay, Cameron?" asked the Fairyman, his hand in his jacket pocket.

"I couldn't be better!" replied Cameron exultantly.

Oksa stiffened. Something wasn't right. Zoe and Mortimer came over, their arms by their sides and their Granok-Shooters in hand, looking wary. Behind Cameron, the waters of the fountain were seething furiously. A couple of passers-by turned away, unsettled by the way these drenched men and women were glaring at each other. Oksa just had enough time to push her Lunatrix behind her. They were going to end up attracting attention... It looked as if the policemen on the beat in the distance might also be heading their way.

As the fountain bubbled even more frantically, two dark shapes appeared in the water. The Lunatrix was right. Dismayed, Oksa continued listing the Gracious Hearts in her head. She had her answer before she could finish: a man leapt out of the water and stood next to Cameron.

Gregor. Gregor McGraw.

Everyone took up defensive positions. Intrigued, the policemen quickened their pace.

"Cameron? What's the meaning of this?" stammered Galina, seeing her brother put his hand on Gregor's forearm.

"Cameron didn't come through the Portal, Galina," murmured Abakum, sounding choked.

Tragically illustrating these words, Cameron's features began to melt like a wax mask to reveal the man who'd fooled them all: Orthon.

"You're right! Cameron didn't pass through the Portal!" he said triumphantly.

Cameron's three sons cried out in despair. If Orthon had changed into Cameron, then who had been turned to a pile of shattered glass?

"I'll never be able to thank dear Cameron enough for giving up his place!" sneered the Felon.

"I'm going to kill you," said Galina, grief-stricken.

"Hey! You there!" called one of the policemen. "What are you doing? Stop that immediately!"

The water was now bubbling so violently that the fountain was overflowing.

At long last, the final Gracious Heart appeared. He stepped over the stone parapet and directed an intensely despairing look at Oksa. Then, instead of joining her, he let Orthon and Gregor embrace him, before all three disappeared into the London sky.

❋

The policemen went off juggling merrily with their helmets, diverted from reality by the Hypnagogos fired in extremis by Abakum. Standing on the steps of the fountain in Trafalgar Square, Oksa and her entourage were in shock and the Young Gracious was by far the worst affected.

Tugdual.

Tugdual was a Gracious Heart.

And he'd left with Orthon.

Her whole world had come tumbling down in a few seconds.

She couldn't even cry. She needed to be able to understand before she could do that. Her father put his arm around her shoulder and hugged her to him. On the steps in front of her, Zoe and Mortimer were sitting side by side, their backs bowed. Everyone was locked in their own pain.

The Lunatrix walked slowly over to Oksa and put his podgy hand on her forearm.

"What did you try to tell me that I wasn't able to understand?" she whispered.

The Lunatrix shook his large head and sniffed noisily. Searching for an explanation, Oksa's mind was full of jumbled thoughts and memories, as certain words took on a new meaning.

"There are so many things you don't know about me, my Lil' Gracious…"

"Don't try to find out everything…"

She recalled one scene in particular. Orthon and Tugdual, on either side of the Aegis, hurled towards each other, then violently repelled. What had the Lunatrix said at the time? "The confrontation of Gracious Hearts has consequences stuffed with gravity for the equilibrium of mental faculties." Oksa grimaced. She'd thought he was talking about Orthon and her. She'd got it so wrong—he'd been talking about Orthon, certainly, but the other Gracious Heart had been Tugdual, not her!

"The domestic staff of my Gracious has been incapable of affording answers to questions which have not been posed," said the little steward.

Oksa flinched and put her head in her hands. She knew her Lunatrix only answered questions he was asked. She'd never asked him what she should have asked.

"My Gracious must not enshroud her heart in blame," continued the creature. "No clue had the power to cause awakening of a serious suspicion about the grandson of the Knuts and the beloved of my Gracious"

Oksa slumped against her father.

"The domestic staff of my Gracious gives confirmation of what has been uttered in the past: the grandson of the Knuts and the beloved of my Gracious, has in his possession a black heart, but filled with purity."

"Is that what you really believe?" asked Oksa bitterly. "Well, I'm not so sure."

"It is an assurance, my Gracious. The heart of your beloved has taken delivery of a revelation which has achieved the pollution of his entire being."

The Lunatrix broke off, looking uncertain. With tears in her eyes, Oksa motioned to him encouragingly.

"Will my Gracious accept delivery of the truth?"

She nodded sadly, with a resigned expression.

"The beloved of my Gracious is in possession of a clandestine lineage. Seventeen years and a few months before today, Orthon, the hated Felon, utilized metamorphosis with Helena Knut. He committed the theft of the appearance of Tyko Knut, the husband of Helena Knut, and produced a birth with Helena, who had no knowledge of this stealing of appearance."

"You mean Orthon shifted his shape to pass himself off as Helena's husband?" broke in Oksa.

She couldn't bear to think about the consequences, however predictable they were.

"Helena Knut has always been ignorant of this deception," continued the Lunatrix. "Nine months later, she became the mother of the beloved of my Gracious."

This catastrophic confirmation was like a dagger blow to Oksa's heart. Not only was Orthon still alive, which was terrible, but Tugdual was his son. Nothing could be worse.

"A warning should be provided to my Gracious: her beloved made the acquisition of the revelation of his origins only a few days ago. His heart has endured colossal torment and encountered a dive into compelling darkness."

"Why didn't he talk about it?" stammered Oksa, her face wet with tears.

"The Felon Orthon produces an absolute hold on the mind of the beloved of my Gracious. The beloved of my Gracious does not possess any Felony. Only his kinship produces an effect on his personal will."

"Orthon is manipulating him."

"In totality, my Gracious," assured the Lunatrix.

Oksa stood up, her shoulders hunched and her heart in pieces. She walked away from the fountain, aiming an angry kick at an empty can in her way and sending it flying for several hundred yards. She looked back at her entourage, then shot into the air in the direction of Bigtoe Square.

She'd thought the worst was over.

But it had only just begun.

THE ANNOUNCEMENT OF GRATITUDE

Thanking encounters the choice of numerous targets, highly esteemed by the novel-writing duo:

The members of the High Enclave of XO, resident in the top floors of the Glass Column in Paris under the aegis of Gracious Bernard.

Every person, male and female, provides colossal labour at every level and must imperiously gather gratitude devoid of boundaries.

All the links in the bookish chain, shops, librarians, archivists, teachers and journalists, whose involvement stuffed with enthusiasm provides a contribution to the growth of Oksa.

The Pollockmaniacs of widely varied ages, origins, sensibilities and temperaments, whose enthusiasm forms the fabrication of a compost full of nutrients and durability.

The foreign publishers and translators in numerous countries, with the accompaniment of their website administrators and Facebook pages, to whom Oksa owes polyglot expansion and the multiplication of friends.

The cinematographic producers, SND and Jim Lemley, who operate the preparation of the metamorphosis of words into images.

Last, and not at all least, the men and women who have afforded the lending of their ears, their presence and their complicity for digressions of priceless value.

May they have the will to recognize themselves.

INDISPENSABLE ACCOMPANIMENTS

Lunatrixa Anne usually produces the writing of the adventures led by Oksa with warmth from the presence of her cat, and a musical escort.

The writing of *Tainted Bonds* has thus connected with the rhythmic and melodious cadences from these sources:

Massive Attack – *Heligoland*

Depeche Mode – *Remixes 2: 81–11*

Dave Gahan – *Hourglass*

Lisa Gerrard – *The Black Opal*

Morrissey – *Vauxhall and I*

Hans Zimmer – *Inception* (*original film soundtrack*)

Coming soon

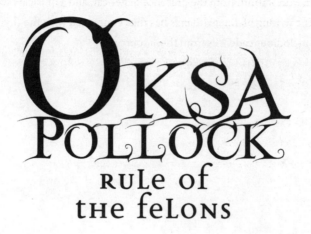

OKSA
POLLOCK

RULe of
THe feLoNs

PROLOGUE

WITH A CLATTER OF WINGS, THE PIGEONS GAVE UP THEIR place to the three men who'd just landed on the cornice around the dome of Saint Paul's Cathedral, and swiftly disappeared into the night sky above a silent, sleeping London.

"We did it, Father!" said one of the strange visitors after a few minutes' silence.

"Yes, we succeeded beyond my wildest dreams," agreed the eldest.

He raised his head proudly, then unexpectedly took off like a rocket through the fluffy strips of mist. He zoomed along the Thames, over Westminster and Buckingham Palace, then rejoined the two younger men still perched on top of Saint Paul's. He stretched, raising his arms towards the sky, and exclaimed:

"Well, we're back! What a turn-up for the books, eh?"

"I never doubted you for a minute, Father."

"I know, Gregor."

"The look on Oksa Pollock's face when she and those self-righteous Runaways saw us coming out of the fountain was priceless," continued Gregor with a mocking snigger, echoed by Orthon. "You've always known how to make an entrance, Father."

Orthon nodded without false modesty and turned to the other member of their party, who hadn't said a word.

"What about you, Tugdual? Aren't you happy to be back on the Outside?"

Tugdual's icy gaze swept over the vast city spread out below them.

"Of course I am, very happy," he muttered.

"Especially as you've gained a new family," pressed Orthon. "A real family who accept you as you are and who have always believed in you."

Tugdual remained expressionless. Only a tiny vein pulsed at his temple. Orthon put his hand on his shoulder and made him turn to face him. He stared long and hard at Tugdual, then folded him into a tight embrace.

"Mortimer has chosen sides and betrayed me without a moment's hesitation," he whispered in Tugdual's ear. "I may have lost a son, but I've gained another, and one who's much more valuable. Welcome to the fold, my son. You're free at last to become who you truly are."

Tugdual's eyelids lowered and his breathing slowed. For a second, he looked almost dead. Then he reopened his eyes.

"Yes, Father…" he said at last.

1

BITTERSWEET HAPPINESS

LONDONERS MAY HAVE GROWN ACCUSTOMED TO THE power cuts after the disasters that had rocked the world, but Oksa and the Runaways had never seen the city so dark. Visibility was so bad that Pavel Pollock had to ask Oksa's Tumble-Bawler to help them find their way through the night skies, which were blacker than a bottomless pit.

And down a bottomless pit was exactly where Oksa felt she'd been dropped since they'd come back to the Outside. Numb with the pain of watching Tugdual, whom she loved, abandon her so suddenly, she was Vertiflying like a zombie, her eyes fixed on her father. When he began his descent towards a block of houses lining a park, she realized as she followed him that all her heartfelt hopes and dreams of the past few months were finally coming true: the Runaways were on their way back to Bigtoe Square! Not all of them, unfortunately, because only Abakum and the Gracious Hearts had been able to pass through Edefia's Portal—eleven Runaways had set off and fourteen of them had arrived, due to the three stowaways who'd tagged along for the ride.

Although everyone had believed him dead, Orthon—who else?—had shocked everyone by emerging from the fountain in Trafalgar Square a few minutes after the Runaways. He'd made good use of his shape-changing abilities to assume the appearance of Cameron, one of their own, fooling them all. And that hadn't been the only surprise the Felon had kept up his sleeve for his sworn enemies.

Until then, everyone had believed Orthon had only two sons, Gregor and Mortimer. The latter had made a strong case for joining the Runaways and, despite some scepticism, had finally been accepted among them— Gracious Oksa and Abakum, the First Servant of the High Enclave, had vouched for Mortimer's loyalty. However, none of them had known that Orthon had a third son, born seventeen years earlier as a result of one of the Felon's most despicable tricks.

And that son was Tugdual.

He wasn't happy about it, according to Oksa's Lunatrix, but it was still a bitter pill to swallow: Tugdual had left the Runaways to join his real father, leaving Oksa and her entourage devastated.

✸

"There he is!" cried Zoe, pointing to a large figure heading towards them at incredible speed.

Abakum, who didn't have the gift of Vertiflying, had raced through the dark streets to Bigtoe Square with the Lunatrix hidden beneath his capacious coat. He joined his friends in the middle of the square and looked anxiously at them, particularly Oksa, whose face was set with misery.

"Explanations and convalescence will encounter the heart of my Young Gracious at a later period," the Lunatrix whispered to Oksa, his large, kind eyes fixed on his mistress. "Now is the time for a reunion with the Spurned when rejoicing and relief will experience an overflowing, are you in agreement?"

Oksa shivered then nodded, on the verge of tears. Once again, her little steward was proving to be the soul of good sense and wisdom.

"Let's go," said Pavel.

He put his arm round his daughter's shoulders and led her towards the Pollocks' house, which looked almost unreal after their long months of absence. It was smaller than Oksa remembered, but that could have been because of the intense darkness. Although it was in a terrace of ten other identical houses, they could tell it apart by the candle on the window sill of what had been Oksa's bedroom. The weak, flickering flame looked as bright as a beacon to the Runaways. The Spurned had clearly been waiting for them day and night.

⁂

Battered by the violent storms that had hit London, the wrought-iron gate squealed as Pavel pushed against it. A few seconds later, a window opened on the top floor and they heard a stifled shout:

"It can't be!"

Lights came on in several windows and they could see moving shadows. Numerous bolts were unlocked from the inside and the front door finally swung open to reveal some of the inhabitants.

The Runaways and the Spurned stood rooted to the spot, frozen in disbelief. The flight of stairs leading up to the door seemed like an insurmountable barrier and no one dared to step forward in case this all turned out to be a dream. They wanted to believe it was really happening for just one more minute, before everything vanished into thin air again.

But this was no dream.

Mortimer was the first to run up the steps and throw himself into the arms of his mother, Barbara. Galina and her two daughters rushed to greet Andrew, who disappeared under the joyful embraces of his long-lost family. Akina and Virginia soon appeared too. Torn between happiness at being reunited with their dear friends and disappointment at the absence of their much-missed children and husband—who were still in Edefia—the two women dissolved into tears as they hugged the Runaways.

"Let's not stay out here!" said Andrew, looking around. "Let's go inside, quickly."

As soon as she'd set foot on the first step leading up to the house, Oksa had desperately looked for her mother, Marie, and her beloved friend, Gus. There was no sign of either and panic began to set in. Once inside the hall, she almost fainted when she saw a dishevelled Gus stumbling from the room opposite the staircase on the first-floor landing—her old bedroom.

His face set and his movements stiff, Gus had changed even more since the last time Oksa's Identego had brought her to this house on the Outside, which had become a place of refuge for some of the Spurned. Gus and Marie hadn't understood exactly what was going on, but they'd sensed Oksa's presence, and the Young Gracious had relished this strangely intangible, and rather frustrating, form of contact. Now Gus was here in the flesh. He looked so different that she wondered how much time had gone by. It couldn't be more than a few weeks, judging by the autumnal foliage of the trees in the square and the chilly night air.

"Oksa? Is that you?" he said, looking as if he'd seen a ghost.

Scanning everyone who was hugging and kissing in the hall, his face dropped. His parents weren't among the "returned". He slowly made his way downstairs and came to stand before Oksa. His dark blue eyes studied her at length, examining her from head to toe in great detail. Embarrassed by this scrutiny, Oksa wondered if she'd changed a lot too. She probably had, from the way Gus was looking at her.

"I don't believe it," he murmured, his hand over his mouth. "You came back—I never thought you would."

Speechless with indignation, Oksa had to stop herself from yelling at him. Gus didn't seem to realize that her return wasn't a matter of choice—from the moment she'd been separated from him and her mother on the banks of Lake Gashun-nur, she'd been obsessed with the idea of returning. Did he think he was the only one who'd suffered? Her annoyance was clear from the indignant, disappointed look she gave him. Still, she of all people knew what Gus was hiding by his reaction—in that way, at least, he hadn't changed at all. He was still just as grumpy and exasperating. The hard set to his face softened gradually until he looked much more like the Gus she knew and loved. Overjoyed, Oksa gave him a tentative smile and went to hug him, or at least to show him how glad she was to see him again.

At that moment she saw what, deep down, she'd feared more than anything else.

Her heart stopped and her blood froze. Kukka had just appeared at the top of the stairs.

Blonde, frosty Kukka. The Ice Princess, looking gorgeous even in baggy pyjamas, stunning even when she'd just climbed out of bed. And, what was worse, Kukka was coming out of her old bedroom, the one that Gus now occupied.

2

ON THE EDGE

"WHERE ARE MY PARENTS?" KUKKA DEMANDED ABRUPTLY from the landing.

"They're fine, don't worry," replied Abakum, beckoning her down to join them.

"Where are they?" she asked again, shaking with nerves.

There was a shrill edge to her voice and she clung to the banister as she descended unsteadily.

"Gus?" she asked, looking around for him.

He turned to face her.

"Mine aren't here either," he replied miserably.

"Like many others, your parents weren't able to pass through the Portal with us," declared Abakum, putting his hand on the two teenagers' shoulders. "But they're in good health, and everything's fine, I promise."

"Everything's fine?" repeated Kukka on the verge of hysteria. "I'd say it's anything but fine!"

"Kukka, please…" groaned Gus.

Was Oksa imagining it or did Gus sound irritated? Kukka was so upset that she didn't even seem to notice that Oksa was standing right in front of her. Oksa felt almost sorry for Kukka. She knew just how disorienting these kinds of situations could be. Her compassion soon evaporated, though, when Kukka flung her arms around Gus's neck and

376

her ponytail came undone. Long, silky hair tumbled over her shoulders, grazing Gus's shoulders in the process. The sight felt like a slap in the face—Oksa would much rather have died a thousand deaths than have to watch that.

※

How could she survive two colossal emotional blows in one evening? How could she stop herself sinking into despair, when this reunion was nothing short of a miracle?

How could she hold on to her dignity when all she wanted to do was fly at that bimbo who'd ruined everything and scratch her eyes out? Even though her chewed nails were far too short to do any real damage, and she was much too proud to let that girl, who'd been her enemy from day one, see how rattled she was.

※

"Why?" sobbed Kukka, clinging to Gus. "Why aren't my parents here?"

"Abakum just told you they're fine. Isn't that all that matters?" retorted Gus, extricating himself. "Would you rather find out they were dead?"

Oksa felt dizzy, dismayed by the turn her thoughts had taken and her skewed priorities. She'd been torturing herself because Gus had his arms around another girl when she'd braved all kinds of dangers to get here and she hadn't seen her mother, whom she missed dreadfully, for months.

"Mum?" she murmured weakly.

Marie Pollock wasn't there.

Like Kukka's and Gus's parents, Cameron, Tugdual and so many others, she was conspicuous by her absence.

No one said anything. A door slammed in a draught. The wind was getting up outside, mirroring the Young Gracious's rising panic as her inner defences crumbled. She stood there, pale and motionless as a marble statue about to implode. Their return to the Outside was turning into a disaster of epic proportions. What else could go wrong? Could things get any worse? A clap of thunder split the night, rousing Oksa from her waking nightmare. Wide-eyed, she shook her head, as if suddenly realizing where she was. The sob constricting her chest dissipated, bringing little or no relief as waves of misery spread through her body.

"Where's Mum?" she whispered.

Kukka harrumphed scornfully and turned her back on her with clenched fists.

"Oksa! I'm in here!"

When Oksa heard her mother's dearly loved voice, she stifled a cry and rushed into the living room with Pavel hard on her heels.

※

There are few things harder than hiding your shock at something unimaginably painful. Although Oksa was young, life had already dealt her some hard blows—the death of her beloved grandmother, Dragomira; the Diaphan's theft of her cousin Zoe's romantic feelings; Orthon's murder of Ocious and Helena Knut; Tugdual's departure with the Felon... but seeing her mother in that state was almost more than Oksa could bear.

Were it not for the deep well of kindness in her eyes and the affection in her voice despite her exhaustion, Marie Pollock would have been unrecognizable. If she hadn't spoken, Oksa might have thought it wasn't her. Oh, how she wished it wasn't...

An old woman on her deathbed was the first thing that came to mind when she looked at Marie. The waxy skin clinging to her frame was so tightly stretched over her cheekbones, ribs and fingers that it seemed ready to tear at the slightest movement. Her hair, once so smooth and shiny, was like a handful of rough, fraying grey twine.

Making what seemed to be a superhuman effort, Marie held out her arms to Oksa, grimacing as the needle of the drip pulled against the papery skin in the crook of her arm. Nothing was going to stop her, though. She struggled to sit up and Barbara McGraw rushed over to help her prop herself up against her pillows.

Pavel and Oksa stared at her in horror.

"Do I look that dreadful?" asked Marie in an exhausted whisper.

Oksa didn't know how she was supposed to react as she took the few steps separating her from her mother. How could she revel in the warmth of her gaze, which was so alive, while ignoring her emaciated body, which was so near to death? However, once Oksa was snuggled up against her mother, she forgot the protruding bones, the medicinal smell and the dark rings around her eyes.

They were soon joined by a grief-stricken Pavel.

"It's about time you came back," murmured Marie.

Oksa looked up, trying not to show how panicked she was. Were these her mother's last few minutes? Had the Runaways arrived just in time to watch her die? As if to give credence to this awful thought, Marie shut her eyes and her head lolled to one side.

"Marie—no!" groaned Pavel, cradling his wife's head in his hands. "You can't go! Not now!"

He kissed her with a strength born of despair. Beside him, Oksa was wringing her hands in torment.

"You have to give her the remedy—Abakum, quickly, save her!" she cried.

Standing motionless at the foot of the bed, the Fairyman was watching Marie with obvious concern. He shuddered violently and hurriedly rummaged in the bag he was still holding. Grabbing his Caskinette, he took out a small pellet the size of a marble.

"Stay with us, Mum!" said Oksa, while Abakum unhooked the drip. "This is Lasonillia, you're going to get better!"

"You managed to find some, then?" croaked Marie.

"Mortimer did," Oksa couldn't help replying with her customary spontaneity.

The sudden apprehension in Marie's eyes escaped no one. She swept her hand through the air, yanking out the needle of the drip. Blood stained the sheets as she slumped back against her pillows.

"No, Abakum,"

"Don't worry, Mortimer's one of us now!" Pavel hastened to add.

"He took a huge risk going to the Distant Reaches to find some Lasonillia," added Oksa, furious with herself.

Why on earth hadn't she kept quiet? Her mother was in this state because she'd used the poisoned soap that Zoe had reluctantly given them on Orthon's orders. In view of that, her fear that the Felon might be using his son for some new stratagem was hardly unjustified.

"I made this medication myself," broke in Abakum. "I promise it's safe."

Despite their reassurances, Marie wouldn't let anyone give her the remedy. There was no arguing with her until, suddenly, with one final convulsion, she collapsed, her eyes half closed and glassy.

"She's dying!" screamed Oksa. "Quick, Abakum!"

"Help me, Pavel!"

The two men busied themselves around the IV. Abakum dropped the pellet of Lasonillia into the drip bag and the substances blended, boiling furiously at first, then fizzing. Acrid red fumes escaped, irritating everyone's throats. They held their breath, looking at each other.

Abakum lifted Marie's arm and reinserted the needle that had been pulled out earlier. The blood-red liquid flowed from the bag into the transparent plastic tube and disappeared beneath the skin. The patient's eyes closed gently, as her body sank into a slumber they all feared might be permanent.

PUSHKIN CHILDREN'S BOOKS

Just as we all are, children are fascinated by stories. From the earliest age, we love to hear about monsters and heroes, romance and death, disaster and rescue, from every place and time.

We created Pushkin Children's Books to share these tales from different languages and cultures with younger readers, and to open the door to the wide, colourful worlds these stories offer.

From picture books and adventure stories to fairy tales and classics, and from fifty-year-old bestsellers to current huge successes abroad, the books on the Pushkin Children's list reflect the very best stories from around the world, for our most discerning readers of all: children.